His thumb dropped over the detonator

The resulting series of explosions destroyed the guardhouse and ripped the gates from their moorings. Flames from the incendiaries kicked in and dropped a lake of fire over the surroundings. Waves of concussive force shivered through the length of the limousine as it hurtled down the highway toward the point where they would leave it behind and link up with Levin once more. By the time the security guards got organized, they'd be long gone.

Bolan settled back, checking on his newest prisoner. Weizman huddled defensively in the center of the wide floor, his arms crossed over his chest. He was bleeding from the mouth.

"Who are you?" Ruben Weizman demanded, struggling to get up.

Dropping the shotgun in line to cover the man, Bolan said, "Believe it or not, but I'm the guy you're going to tell your deepest and darkest secrets to. And damned quick, because I don't think we have much time."

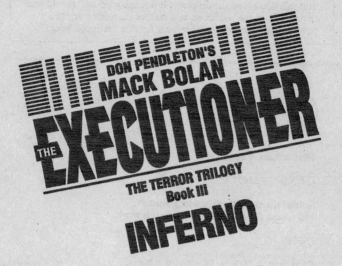

DON PENDLETON'S
MACK BOLAN
THE EXECUTIONER

THE TERROR TRILOGY
Book III

INFERNO

A GOLD EAGLE BOOK FROM
WORLDWIDE®

TORONTO • NEW YORK • LONDON
AMSTERDAM • PARIS • SYDNEY • HAMBURG
STOCKHOLM • ATHENS • TOKYO • MILAN
MADRID • WARSAW • BUDAPEST • AUCKLAND

If you purchased this book without a cover you should be aware that this book is stolen property. It was reported as "unsold and destroyed" to the publisher, and neither the author nor the publisher has received any payment for this "stripped book."

First edition August 1994

ISBN 0-373-61437-3

Special thanks and acknowledgment to
Mel Odom for his contribution to this work.

INFERNO

Copyright © 1994 by Worldwide Library.

All rights reserved. Except for use in any review, the reproduction or utilization of this work in whole or in part in any form by any electronic, mechanical or other means, now known or hereafter invented, including xerography, photocopying and recording, or in any information storage or retrieval system, is forbidden without the written permission of the publisher, Worldwide Library, 225 Duncan Mill Road, Don Mills, Ontario, Canada M3B 3K9.

All characters in this book have no existence outside the imagination of the author and have no relation whatsoever to anyone bearing the same name or names. They are not even distantly inspired by any individual known or unknown to the author, and all incidents are pure invention.

® and TM are trademarks of the publisher. Trademarks indicated with ® are registered in the United States Patent and Trademark Office, the Canadian Trade Marks Office and in other countries.

Printed in U.S.A.

This is the one best omen, to fight in defence of one's country.

—Homer

No matter where the fight for my country will take me, I will follow the path of blood left by the destroyers and bring their own war home to them.

—Mack Bolan

CHAPTER ONE

Keeping to the long shadows, draped with military hardware, Mack Bolan moved through the darkness shrouding the back streets of Oruro, Bolivia. The silenced Beretta 93-R was hard and sure in his hand.

He stopped across the street from his target. A red neon light burned in the latticed window of the tavern, blurred in places by the strips of strapping tape holding the broken panes together. The interior of Lucheno's Laughing Blue Parrot Tavern was paneled with dark wood that dimly reflected the soft golden glow of oil lanterns hanging from the ceiling. Three men carried on an animated conversation at the long bar, all of them sharing a uniform appearance of sleeveless flannel shirts or olive green military blouses and bandannas holding their long hair out of their faces.

Reaching up to the side of his head, Bolan tagged the transmit button of the ear-throat radio headset he wore. "Jack?" he said softly.

"Here, buddy," Jack Grimaldi's calm voice echoed back. "Back door's secure. Nobody gets a free pass unless we okay it."

"Roger. Ernie?"

"In place, amigo. I've got you covered." Ernie Gallardo had a history with the DEA and was relatively new to the Executioner's style of hands-on dealing with the criminals the DEA usually only tried to out-finesse or intercept. The DEA agent had shown a lot of promise.

Provided they made it out of the country without getting killed by the men they hunted or the police squads out beating the bushes for them all the way from Sucre, he had a good career ahead of him.

"Okay, then," the warrior said. "Let's do it." He shoved the 9 mm pistol into the shoulder rig under the loose, midthigh jacket, then checked the Whip-it sling of the 12-gauge Ithaca Stakeout on his shoulder. Extra magazines for the pistol and the shotgun were shoved into the pockets of his jacket. The rest of his gear had been cached with the stolen jeep they'd liberated outside Sucre after kicking down the walls of Bernardo Gomez's house almost twelve hours ago. After tucking the headset away with the transmit button locked on, he pulled on the cord around his neck and clapped the straw peasant's hat onto his head to further shadow his features.

A gentle breeze filtered through the alley, carrying with it the scent of rotting vegetables, urine and cleaning chemicals. He was damp with perspiration from the humidity, and the wind felt cool when it touched the warrior's body.

To the north, toward the more civilized sections of the city, the sounds of a fiesta in progress punctured the heavy silence around the tavern. Excited voices rang out, interspersed with the din of Latin music and occasional fireworks that left colored streaks and sparks hanging in the black sky amid the hard, bright stars.

Lucheno's Laughing Blue Parrot was in the heart of one of the poverty-stricken neighborhoods of Oruro where the Indios tried to maintain their cultural heritage despite the mining companies and the centuries-long Spanish influence. Anyone who had hope in his heart would be at the fiesta, leaving the shadows here for the predators to stalk.

Bolan was stalking some of those predators. Last night had shown the culmination of his two-week-old attack against the Aryan Resistance Movement. The white supremacists had been linked by Phoenix Force to a Jordanian conduit spiriting cash and valuables out of Iraq despite the trade embargoes against that country as a result of unsatisfactory arms talks and the war. While the Executioner had worked on shutting them down inside the United States, Phoenix Force had been working toward the same end in Germany, following the trail on into Zurich.

The ARM people had fallen before the warrior's guns, but had revealed the rat's nest they'd been attached to as they went down. Bolan's own efforts to track down ARM leaders had brought him into Bolivia. Modern-day Nazis in La Paz had been working with the ARM, helping fuel and equip the terrorist strikes against Israeli businessmen and military leaders two weeks ago. Their power base had been cocaine trafficking, turning narco-dollars that had fed an army silently gathering strength. The Executioner had razed most of that organization to the ground. What he hadn't destroyed would be broken up at least temporarily as a result of the portfolios and ledgers he'd turned up and given to the press and DEA regarding the Nazi operations in Bolivia.

Even so, the final tumblers of the overall design hadn't fallen into place. There was much that had been left out, and the Arab connection to the neo-Nazis had yet to be explained.

Bolan stepped out of the alley and walked across the one-lane road. His boot heels clicked against the worn, dusty cobblestones. He kept his head tilted down, but at an angle that let him keep watch over the patrons of the bar. The two-and three-story buildings on either side of the street were lightless and silent. A battered Ford station wagon and an old but serviceable orange Land Rover were parked in front of the tavern.

One of the targets had escaped the assault on Gomez's ranch. Colonel Hector Rivera y Mendez, La Paz's minister of the interior, had made the jump out of the hellzone a heartbeat ahead of the Executioner's lethal reach by military helicopter. The man had wasted no time making his way out of the country. Aaron Kurtzman and Barbara Price were tracking Rivera's escape route as well as they could by computer and educated guesswork from Stony Man Farm, but Rivera's final destination remained a mystery.

There were no doubts that Rivera's destination—if they were able to follow—would turn up further pieces to the puzzle.

And the Executioner was beginning to feel as if they were looking at a puzzle. Everything seemed to fit, but none of it really made any sense. The Stony Man campaigns had been hurriedly set up and put into action, and had been staggeringly successful, but there was no sense of closure. On the surface the strikes against the Israelis had been retaliatory rather than preemptive. The logic was tangled and confusing, but it was there. A few more stones would have to be turned over before any definite conclusions could be reached.

Bolan cleared his mind of the thoughts and focused on the job at hand as he stepped through the tavern door.

Conversation between the three men at the bar stopped immediately as their heads swiveled to the mirror behind the bartender to inspect the new arrival. The man nearest Bolan was heavyset, his stomach rolling out from between the unbuttoned tails of his shirt. The oily black

finish of a .357 Magnum was revealed in a paddle holster at his side.

"Something I can get for you?" the bartender asked.
He was short and lean, his face showing fifty-plus years
of sharing stories of shattered dreams. In his practiced
hands, the stained bar towel made its way quickly around
the shot glass he'd just washed.

"A beer." Bolan took his place at the bar only a few
feet from the three men. He dropped coins on the scarred
surface.

Moving unhurriedly, the bartender took a mug from
the stack behind him, filled it from the tap and set it in
front of Bolan while scooping up the coins with his free
hand. They went into a leather pouch tied at the man's
waist.

"Hey."

Bolan sipped the beer, then checked the mirror to make
sure the barrel-shaped man was talking to him. In his reflection, he saw that the greasepaint smudges on his face
could easily be passed off as dirt.

"Hey, I'm talking to you."

Bolan turned and looked at the man. "What?"

"Why aren't you at the party?"

"My wife and her mother are there."

The other two men chuckled.

A tentative smile touched the big man's lips but didn't
reach his eyes. "It's a big party. Probably half the town
turned out for it."

"I know. My wife and her mother probably still think
I'm there."

The men laughed again, and this time the bartender
joined them.

Bolan scanned the rest of the bar quickly. The structure was no more than thirty feet long, laid out in rail-

road-car fashion. The bar counter took up a third of the room up front, leaving the back two-thirds open for the tables and chairs clustered there. At the very back, next to a door that undoubtedly opened up to the alley beyond, was a small stage that might hold a three-piece band if they were careful. Moth-eaten maroon curtains with beaded designs hung from a semicircular track mounted on the ceiling. The smell of stale cigars was thick in the room, overpowering the odor of fresh pine. One section of the wall gleamed whitely, showing where new boards had been nailed into place, bullet holes visible around the patched-up area.

The Laughing Blue Parrot had been listed in the ledgers he'd discovered in La Paz. Felix Eusebio ran the actual moneymaking end of the business, trafficking coca paste through the region and paying off the local constabulary to look the other way. When the money hadn't turned the trick, Eusebio had used the gun and the knife. According to Bolivian police records that Price had turned up through Interpol, and scuttlebutt Ernie Gallardo had been aware of, several bodies that had been found floating in Lake Poopo and the Desaguadero River had been put there by Eusebio. Many of them—including thieves, two DEA agents and nearly a dozen Bolivian undercover Intelligence people—had been there as a result of Eusebio's own appetite for destruction.

"Do I know you?" The big man's eyes narrowed as he pushed himself off his stool and swaggered toward Bolan.

"I don't know you." Bolan acted as if he was concentrating on his beer and simply wishing to be left alone. He watched the man in the mirror.

"Hey, Jose," another of the men called out. "Leave the poor guy alone. All he wants is a night out from the hens."

Ignoring the unwanted advice, Jose said, "Where are you from?"

"Outside the city."

"Where do you work."

"In the mines. Is there any other work for an honest man?"

"Not for an honest man," another of the men agreed.

The distant percussion of fireworks rattled the loose panes in the bay window overlooking the street.

"You don't look Indio," Jose commented, closing the distance till he stood next to the Executioner. His breath stank of beer and peppers.

"No." Bolan kept subtle watch in the mirror.

The bartender finished with a final glass, stacked it neatly and worked his way to the other end of the bar.

"I have a nose," Jose said.

"I don't think there are many who could miss it. And from the looks of it, most people haven't missed it when you offended them."

Jose's companions laughed out loud.

Jose's eyes turned dark and hard. "But this nose of mine, she is a most wondrous nose, able to smell out many things." He sniffed loudly. "And right now she tells me she smells a policeman."

"You're wrong," Bolan said quietly.

"I don't think so."

Whirling, Bolan brought the heavy glass mug around in a swift arc and smashed it against the big man's temple. Glass fragmented and splinters flew and flashed in the mellow lantern light.

Jose went down slowly like a bag of wet cement.

The two men were frozen for a moment, as if doubting what they'd just witnessed.

Still on the move, Bolan came off the stool onto his feet, shoved the jacket out of the way and brought the Ithaca Stakeout up by the pistol grip. He squeezed the trigger, aiming between the two men.

The double-aught spread created a small pattern that caught both of the men and added speed to their efforts to clear their stools.

Riding out the powerful recoil of the short 12-gauge, Bolan gripped the slide and racked a fresh shell into the chamber.

The man nearest Bolan heaved both hands forward over his stool as he gripped a 9 mm pistol and fired blindly, screaming with incoherent rage. His right shoulder was bloody. The stool provided little cover.

Dropping the barrel of the Ithaca Stakeout, Bolan fired from the point. The double-aught charge caught the man in the chest and blew him backward. He racked the slide again and searched for the remaining targets.

The bartender had dropped out of sight on the other side of the bar while the remaining gunman sprinted for the back door.

Jose squirmed at Bolan's feet and came up with the .357.

Bolan lashed out with a boot and caught the big man's gun wrist. Bone snapped. The Magnum went flying, then skated across the hardwood floor till it smacked up against the wall on the other side of the room. Another kick sent the big man down again, but he tried to crawl away.

The gunner at the back of the tavern was having trouble with the door. His hand slipped off it twice as he attempted to yank it open. He fired his pistol rapidly in

Bolan's direction. A lantern, shorn by a stray round from the chain that held it to the ceiling, dropped to the floor with a loud clang, a pool of fire blossomed outward, following dozens of curling fingers of oil.

A bullet plucked at Bolan's jacket collar as he spun to face the gunner. The shotgun belched another charge. He racked the slide and fired again. Both loads smashed into the gunner and pummeled his body against the wall beside the door.

The Executioner took four shells from his pocket and thumbed them into the shotgun's loading gate as he approached the bar, bringing the Ithaca back up to its maximum capacity of five rounds. Letting the 12-gauge lead, he peered over the bar.

The bartender was on his hands and knees, a stubby .38 Chief's Special clutched in his fist as he crawled for the far end of the counter. His eyes locked with Bolan's, and the warrior could see desperation flare in the man's eyes.

The bartender's hand holding the .38 quivered in anticipation.

"Don't," Bolan said in a graveyard voice, taking deliberate aim with the shotgun, "you'll never make it."

"You might shoot me anyway."

"And I might not. You keep the gun, it's a sure bet."

The bartender's eyes closed. "Okay."

"Slide the pistol out, toward the front."

The .38 went scooting away.

A quick glimpse in the big mirror was all the warning the Executioner got as Jose flung himself into Bolan's back. Edged steel glinted in the man's uninjured hand. Jose's face was a mask of blood.

Staggered by the sudden weight that slammed into him, Bolan bounced off the bar with enough impact to break his ribs and remained standing only with great effort.

The knife arced up in Jose's beefy hand, then came stabbing back down toward Bolan's throat. "Die, you son of a bitch!" Jose screamed.

Levering the Ithaca Stakeout up, Bolan blocked the knife thrust. The sharp blade slid along the blued barrel with a metallic hiss and left bright scratches to trace its passage. The knife came to a stop at the pump action. Before the big man could free the blade, Bolan launched three quick elbows to Jose's impressive stomach and felt the man's hot breath burn along the side of his face with each blow. As Jose stumbled back, Bolan took a step forward and swung the shotgun around. The barrel caught Jose at the side of the jaw and dropped him like a poleaxed steer.

Breathing deeply to test his ribs, Bolan slid the ear-throat headset from his pocket and slipped it on. "Jack?"

"That's me at the back door." At the other end of the tavern, Grimaldi stepped through with an Uzi held confidently in his hands. He was dressed in peasant's clothing, as well, his face streaked with black camo paint. "It's clear that way, but those gunshots made a lot of noise."

Bolan nodded and took another deep breath. His ribs hurt like hell, but they felt more bruised then broken. He keyed the transmit button again. "Ernie?"

"I'm holding," the DEA agent responded. "How're things in there?"

"Under control. Maintain your position. If there's another way out of here that we don't know about, Eusebio or his people might try for it."

"Roger."

Bolan pointed the bartender out for Grimaldi. "Keep him covered."

The pilot nodded and moved forward.

The Executioner tossed his battered hat away, walked behind the bar, knelt and pulled the long rubber mat lining the floor behind the counter. Underneath was a steel door with a sophisticated keypad locking device.

"Everybody's high-tech these days," Grimaldi grumbled.

Bolan thunked the steel plating with a fingernail. It sounded sure and solid. He glanced up at the bartender. "Soundproofed?"

"Yes."

It meant they still had a chance at surprising Eusebio or whoever might be below. For the moment he discarded any plans for using the explosive charges contained in the gym bag Grimaldi carried. The doomsday numbers on the operation were still viable. Chances were that the fireworks set off during the fiesta had masked some of the noise made by the gunplay, but those chances were slim and he didn't want to rely on them. "Is Eusebio in there?"

The bartender nodded.

"Do you have the combination?"

"No."

"Who?"

"Jose."

Rising, Bolan fisted a bottle of whiskey from the racks lining the wall around the big mirror, pulled the cork from it and walked back to the unconscious man. He poured the contents across the man's face and let the Ithaca Stakeout hang from its Whip-it sling on his shoulder.

Jose coughed and moaned, struggling to right himself.

Bolan palmed the Beretta 93-R and waited.

The big man's eyes took a moment to focus, flickering in and out of sight and occasionally becoming only empty pools of white.

The headset tweaked in Bolan's ear and he answered it.

"We're made," Gallardo said. "Police frequency just broadcasted a possible armed robbery in progress at the tavern. Some solid citizen just called it in."

They'd picked up a forty-channel radio along the way to monitor the Bolivian military task force trying to close in on them after the hit on Bernardo Gomez.

"Make your way back to the wheels," Bolan ordered.

"What about you guys?"

"Give us fifteen minutes. If we aren't able to make the rendezvous, you're on your own. If you make the meet at the U.S. Embassy in La Paz, you should have a way out."

"Fifteen minutes," Gallardo echoed.

"Move out. You're wasting time." Bolan broke the connection.

With a final groan, Jose locked eyes with the Executioner.

"I want to go downstairs," Bolan said. "Help me or you can die right here."

"You're a dead man," Jose said. He brushed at the blood running down his face with the back of his hand.

"I'm counting to three, then I don't need you anymore. One."

Jose gave the number quickly.

Bolan made the man repeat it more slowly, then removed a pair of disposable plastic restraints from his pocket, ordered Jose to lie facedown and cuffed the big man's hands behind his back.

Grimaldi cuffed the bartender and pulled him out of the line of fire.

The keypad felt cold and stiff as Bolan punched the number sequence. The electronic tumblers fell through themselves in a series of rapid clicks, then the light beside the handle switched from red to green. Gripping the handle, the 9 mm Beretta tight in his other fist, Bolan pulled upward.

The door rose noiselessly on well-oiled hinges, gull winging toward the tavern ceiling. A soft light illuminated the narrow corridor below, trickling down the metal steps of the ladder mounted on the wall.

The Executioner went first, placing his boots on the outside edges of the ladder and sliding effortlessly to the concrete floor seven feet below with a *shush* of rubber soles against steel.

A shadow moved to the left, closing, hard lines coming up in its fists. The muzzle-flash from the pistol gripped in the man's hands rippled across his sharp profile, and the detonation sounded like a cannon shot in the enclosed space.

Bolan squeezed the trigger twice, and both 9 mm rounds caught the man in the face, shoving the body backward. The warrior moved out, his free hand trailing along the poured-concrete wall. A naked bulb hung from a short cord overhead, and he had to duck as he went past it. His shadow suddenly stretched in front of him. His ears continued to ring with the gunshot.

Twenty feet farther on, the narrow corridor opened onto a small room with Spartan furnishings. A thin young man sat at a table in front of a laptop computer with a telephone cradled in the modem seat. He turned to look over his shoulder. When his eyes locked with Bolan's, he reached for the pistol beside the laptop.

Without hesitation, the Executioner fired the 93-R and put two rounds through the laptop's monitor. The computer went whirling away.

The young man halted his reach for his weapon.

"Hands behind your head," Bolan ordered as he came into the room.

The guy complied at once. "Don't shoot, man. I don't have anything here I'm ready to die for."

"Down on the floor." Bolan reached out and helped him to the floor, grabbing his collar and keeping him off balance while shoving him down. The warrior swept the room with his gaze.

An old floor model Mosler safe sat in the far corner. It had been repainted black but showed the gray scuff marks and scratches of feet that had been propped on it. A wood-burning stove sat across from it, littered with greasy sacks that held remnants of tacos and burritos. A flue trailed up the wall like a straight black worm and eased through the floor above. Metal shelves along the wall contained armament, chemicals and the familiar football-shaped packages of cocaine marked with different colors and symbols denoting the growers. Four folding metal chairs sat in disarray around the table.

A man stepped through the room's only other door. He was at least six and a half feet tall and lean, almost cadaverous, with his black hair cropped close to the skull. A dangling gold earring hung along the left side of his face. He wore a faded black T-shirt, jeans and a fatigue jacket with a single bullet hole through the left lapel. He carried a machete and a leather strop, and the blade gleamed wickedly.

Bolan turned to confront the man, recognizing him as Felix Eusebio at once. The Beretta tracked on target in unconscious reflex. Before he could squeeze the trigger, the machete came whistling at him, aimed at his wrist with enough force to sever flesh and bone. Bolan moved his arm out of the way, and the blade missed by bare inches, biting solidly into the stone floor and sending sparks flying.

Eusebio trailed his weapon with a wild yell, moving faster than most men had any right to.

Unable to bring his pistol back into play, Bolan grabbed the man's machete arm and blocked the next blow.

The man's strength was much more than would have been expected from someone with his lean build. It felt as though he'd been put together with whipcord and leather. A glance at the dark pits of Eusebio's pupils told the Executioner the reason why. The drug trafficker obviously sampled the product that filtered through the transportation routes he managed.

"You made a mistake coming here, you stupid bastard!" Eusebio yelled. "I've never been taken down! Not by the locals and not by the goddamned DEA!"

Breaking the deadlock, knowing Grimaldi was blocked from taking part in the action by the computer operator, who'd sprung to his feet and gone for a gun of his own, Bolan let the Bolivian come to him. The warrior lifted a vicious knee and caught the drug trafficker in his unprotected groin.

Eusebio screamed.

Still on the offensive, Bolan butted the Bolivian in the face with the top of his head when the man automatically started to bend forward. Flesh pulped under the impact. Bracing the back of the man's head with his right forearm, the Beretta still locked in his fist while maintaining his hold on the machete arm, Bolan dragged Eusebio's head down and met the guy's face with a knee coming up.

Eusebio's head popped up with a sharp crack. Growling incoherently, the man pulled away, tearing free of Bolan's grip. The Executioner let his opponent go and brought up the 9 mm pistol, knowing Eusebio would immediately launch himself into an attack again.

Rivulets of blood ran down the drug trafficker's face. He came around in a whirl, the machete following his movements in a flashing crescent of light that cut horizontally from shoulder height.

Stepping inside the blow, Bolan blocked it with his left forearm, thrust the Beretta into Eusebio's throat and pulled the trigger twice.

The dead man fell away from him, weaving drunkenly for a moment while the last signals from the brain trickled through the spinal cord, then collapsed.

Grimaldi already had the other situation under control. The computer operator was lying flat on his back, hands touching his ears, and staring at the muzzle of the Uzi that almost pressed into his forehead. The pilot had a knee in the middle of the Bolivian's chest, and the pistol was under the table.

Bolan crossed the room, letting his silence and impassive features be more intimidating than the 93-R in his hand. He locked eyes with the computer operator. "Do you have the combination to the safe?"

There was a hesitation, then the man shook his head. "No. Eusebio was the only one who had it."

"Fine." Bolan glanced at Grimaldi. "Kill him and blow the safe."

Grimaldi nodded and leaned harder onto the man's chest as he took more deliberate aim, and Bolan started to turn away.

"Wait," their prisoner said.

Bolan looked at him.

"I know the combination."

"Get it open."

Grimaldi helped the man to his feet and hustled him over to the Mosler.

The Executioner stepped across the corpse lying in front of the second doorway and went into the next room. It was a small dormitory that would easily sleep eight men in bunk beds. Apparently the only other guards at the site had been the men upstairs. A quick search through the quarters revealed nothing more than a collection of skin magazines, porno videos for the TV and VCR, clothing, extra weapons and ammo and personal effects that really said nothing about the men who owned them.

The headset tweaked in Bolan's ear.

"Go," he said softly.

"More bad news," Ernie Gallardo said. "The military army captain who's been on our heels since the strike at Gomez's has just reached the outskirts of the city. He's joining up with the Oruro PD."

Bolan reflected on that. "Can you get clear?"

"I'm with our wheels, man, but I'm not leaving you guys. If it hadn't been for you, I wouldn't be here now." At the beginning of the Bolivian campaign, the Executioner had rescued the DEA agent from assassination.

"It would be a shame to throw that second chance away." Bolan glanced at the metal rungs set into the wall to his right.

"I don't see it as throwing it away. At this point, it's become an investment."

Building a mental image of the underground rooms in his mind, superimposing the surface structures he'd memorized while staking out the hard probe, Bolan guessed that the second route led into the boat warehouse two buildings down from the tavern. The question was whether or not anyone outside of Eusebio's organization knew about it. He tapped the transmit button on the headset. "Are you mobile?"

"I'm not leaving," Gallardo replied stubbornly.

"That's not the question. Can you get to the north side of the city?"

"Where?"

They'd scouted the city earlier, too, and had acquainted themselves with the layout.

"The bicycle shop two blocks from the marketplace."

"You'll be there?"

"That's where we'll be headed. It's six blocks from here, and if the military police and the Oruro PD congregate on the tavern, we can put the fiesta between ourselves and them. After that we've got a chance at losing ourselves in the jungle before they can regroup."

"Give me ten minutes. I'll be there." Gallardo cleared the frequency.

Bolan returned to the storeroom and found Grimaldi shoving stacks of American and Bolivian currency into the gym bag. The computer operator was on his face on the floor, secured with disposable cuffs that held his hands behind his back. "You heard Gallardo?"

"Yeah. We're going to be cutting this one kind of close."

"We knew that when we decided to stop here." Bolan reached into the gym bag, shoved the money aside and

removed the ordnance he wanted. At the other end of the
tunnel he could hear the staccato voices of the police
squad invading the tavern above. He climbed the ladder
and ignored the rattling trapdoor. The iron bar set in
hooks across its surface would hold the police out for a
short time.

Working quickly, he rigged a trip wire that would set
off a smoke grenade and a small shaped charge that
would exhaust most of its concussive force toward the
floor and away from anyone coming down the ladder. It
wasn't meant to hurt anyone, but it would buy more time
with confusion and fear while they tried to make their
escape. In the years of his war everlasting, one of the
Executioner's foremost rules had been to never fire on a
man wearing a badge. Even in the riskiest of circumstances, he'd held true to that.

He jogged back down the tunnel just as the twin teeth
of a crowbar edged under the trapdoor and started to pry.
Wood splintered, but the iron bar held. A gap of light
showed through, and hurried voices cursed and encour-
aged in loud Spanish.

The Executioner glanced down the rack of weapons in
the small armory and selected a Mini-14 Ranch Rifle with
open sights. He checked the action and the magazine. It
was chambered in 7.62 mm rounds, and the clip was full.
He slung the rifle over his shoulder and moved on. Grimaldi had been waiting and quickly dropped onto his
backtrail.

As Bolan clambered up the steel rungs set into the wall
leading up to the boathouse, he was grimly aware that the
numbers on the operation were falling faster than ever.

Holding the Beretta in his fist, the Ithaca Stakeout
under his arm, Bolan unfastened the retaining bar from
its mounts and shoved the door upward. He followed it,

letting the Beretta move into position ahead of him. He stepped out into blackness as the double explosions of the smoke grenade and shaped charge mushroomed out behind him.

He found the floor by feel, then stepped up onto it. A quick search with his free hand determined that they were in a closet space of some sort. By the time he found the latches on the hidden exit, the frantic voices of the Bolivian militia hot on their heels were audible from below.

The boathouse was silent and dark when the warrior stepped through the door. Moonlight dappled the sleek shapes of powerboats and personal fishing craft. The odor of the sea clung to the building, as well as the vessels. A rickety wooden stairway climbed the wall to Bolan's left, leading up to a circular second floor that left the center open for the block-and-tackle gear necessary to lift and move the boats and their engines as they were worked on.

He paused to set off a CS grenade inside the hidden room, then jammed a thick-bladed combat knife under the door to prevent it from moving easily. He led the way up the stairs and felt them creaking underfoot as he and Grimaldi ran.

A dirty window smudged by dust and black stains of diesel exhaust overlooked the street in front of the boathouse and the tavern. Nearly a dozen official vehicles, the military-marked ones outnumbering the police cruisers, were parked in the street. The whirling red-and-white cherries threw off long, garish shadows that streaked the dark buildings of the neighborhood. Hard, angular forms took cover behind the open doors of the four-wheel-drive trucks and the more economical sedans of the local PD.

A military officer waved his cap, and a team of four men in standard two-by-two deployment surged forward toward the boathouse.

"They made us," Grimaldi said. "Now what?"

"The rooftop," Bolan replied. "It adjoins the next building. It'll give us running room. They've got the ground covered." He surged forward, staring through the gloom at the wooden maintenance ladder bolted into the wall. The Beretta slid into shoulder leather.

Glass shattered and came spinning loose from the windows they passed. The hum of flying bullets was familiar inside the quietness of the boathouse, followed a heartbeat later by the flat cracks of bolt-action sniper weapons.

Bolan was halfway up the wooden rungs when the hidden door below erupted outward and released a half-dozen men into the work space. They moved two by two, maintaining cover over each team as they progressed.

Pushing through the hatch at the top of the ladder, Bolan shrugged through, coming out in a shoulder roll onto the rooftop. The wind felt cool and clean as it swept by him. At the rear of the boathouse, the encroaching jungle was alive with animal noises. He ignored it. That route would only delay the inevitable. Attempting to hide out was no answer. They needed the speed of the waiting vehicle. He unslung the Mini-14.

Grimaldi threw himself up and out of the hatch, skating across the rock-and-tar surface of the roof as bullets kicked through the wooden door slamming shut behind him. The pilot reached into his gym bag, and his hand emerged with a grenade. The bullets had stopped ripping through the hatch. He pulled the pin and slipped the spoon, counted down, then raised the hatch and dropped the sphere through. A repressed *bamf* sounded just after he released it.

The bullets started a fresh assault on the hatch.

"Smoker," Grimaldi said as he got to his feet and came to join Bolan at the side of the building. "Give them something to think about and keep them honest."

Five spotlights mounted on the military vehicles below suddenly flooded the top of the boathouse and leached the color from the night. Sporadic gunfire chewed through the eaves for a brief instant before the commander could regain control of his troops.

"You know," Grimaldi said into the quiet that followed the silencing of the assault weapons as he hunkered down behind the low wall running around the rooftop, "I'm beginning to understand how Butch and Sundance must have felt after they got down south of the border."

Bolan ignored him. The last handful of doomsday numbers were in free-fall now. He spun and got to his feet.

"Get ready," he said, and raised the rifle to his shoulder.

CHAPTER TWO

"As far as this agency is concerned, Ernie Gallardo is a rogue agent." The voice at the other end of the phone connection sounded final and unforgiving.

"That's a costly misconception on your part," Barbara Price said. The Stony Man mission controller leaned forward over the neatly organized stacks of paperwork covering her desk in the small office she maintained off Aaron Kurtzman's computer lab. "Gallardo has helped orchestrate the end of a large cocaine network set up and fueled by neo-Nazis in South America and the United States. The producers were Bolivian cartel members your administration has been unable to touch after years of investigation."

"We know about Gomez and the others."

"Yes, but you were hamstrung by international diplomatic ties and the sieve they'd turned your Intelligence network into."

"And you people weren't."

"I didn't say that."

"So far, you haven't appeared to have said much of anything."

Price shook two tablets from the half-empty bottle on the desk beside the vase of flowers she'd taken from the Farm's flower bed during a brief break from the ongoing negotiations to cover Striker and Phoenix Force. Unlike her, the flowers still appeared fresh, unaware that the sun had gone down hours ago. "I can give you Ernie

Gallardo.'' She let the words hang, waiting like a good poker player.

"So?"

"You've got people out beating the bushes in Bolivia looking for him." Price put the tablets into her mouth, and washed them down with orange juice that had sweated up to room temperature during the past hour.

"You've got him in protective custody?"

"No." Price had known when she made the call to the special agent in charge of the Bolivian sector that she was dealing with a lawman more interested in good politics than in good police work. Gallardo's confirmed involvement with Striker and Grimaldi had to be a nightmare to the man.

"Then what do you have?"

"Like I said, I can give him to you."

The man paused, obviously thinking things over. Monte Hardell had come up from the streets by being a hell of a cop at one time, but he'd learned to curry political favor along the way. He'd never failed to go the distance after the people he was pursuing, but he never used anyone else's misfortune for his own gain. That attitude had gotten him several quick promotions over the years. Still, Hardell had become addicted to seeing his name in the papers, associated with a successful foray by agents under his command. At present, the last big bust was months in the past. The drug trade in Bolivia had been tightly controlled by the latest regime.

Price had been counting on the man's hunger when she placed the call.

"Why would I want him?" Hardell asked.

"Because he—and I—are in a position to give you more than just the top brass of the neo-Nazi connection, both in Bolivia and stateside."

"Why would you do that?"

"I've taken what I wanted out of it."

"So you leave us with the rest of it?"

"Yes."

"You make it sound like we're a couple of vultures discussing roadkill."

"Sometimes," Price said, "it feels that way, too."

"I don't even know who you are or how you got the passwords to get to me."

"That should tell you something."

"It tells me I should watch my ass. Believe it, I am."

Price waited the other man out to see if Hardell was willing to ante up. She was certain the answer was going to be yes. She'd learned a long time ago to never sit down at the table with anyone who was a total cipher.

"I need a name," Hardell said.

"Seth Watkins."

"You've already given me that one."

Watkins was an interagency go-between who often negotiated between agencies that had problems working out overlapping jurisdiction. In this case Brognola had asked Watkins to represent his office at Justice regarding conflicting fields of interest. Watkins had referred him to Hardell, which was where Price had banked on the man turning, while cutting her more or less out of the loop.

"I want to know who I'm dealing with," Hardell said.

"You can call me Cassandra."

"Cassandra."

"Right."

"Cassandra what?"

Price rubbed her temple. The headache seemed to be abating a bit. "We're wasting time here. In another few hours you may not be able to provide the help I want."

She made sure to emphasize the word "want" so Hardell realized she hadn't said "need."

"I know most of the women who head up top agency jobs here on the Hill," Hardell said. "You're not one of them."

"No, I'm not." As mission controller for the Farm, Price was relatively unknown to more than a handful, including the President. In her former capacity as mission controller for another agency, she'd also been buried behind layers of secrecy. The people who knew her before did not know whom she was associated with now. Stony Man Farm was top secret, responsible only to the chief executive.

"Despite your Yale background," she continued, "I take it you're not familiar with classical Greek mythology."

"Should I be?"

"If you were, you'd understand the reference to Cassandra."

"Maybe you can explain it to me in small words."

"Cassandra was a woman who was in love with the sun god, Apollo. As a token of his love, he gave her the ability to foretell the future. She betrayed him, and as a result—since he was unable to take away his previous gift—he added the curse that although she could predict coming events, no one would listen to her."

"Sounds like a real drag."

"Actually," Price said sarcastically, "it sounds like petty bureaucracy. You know the kind—where a guy gets more interested in covering his own ass than in making sure he's busting that ass doing the best job he knows how. Ernie Gallardo put his ass on the line to do a job that needed doing, and I for one don't intend to see him lose everything because he found the balls to do it."

"Maybe you don't understand the complexity of this administration's position."

"Let's cut to the chase. The potential for word of Gallardo's freestyle solutions to the Bolivian drug problem could give you and your agency a black eye if it hits the press. Cooperate with me, and that never happens. If I have to get Gallardo and my people out of that country on my own, I'll guarantee there'll be an investigation into your handling of the Bolivian sector that will reveal how inept and timid your operations have been. By the time everything gets sorted through, there won't be anything left of your political career but ashes."

"You're making a lot of threats."

"I look at them as promises."

"I'm taping this conversation."

"Great. Afterward you can play it back and make sure you got it all straight."

"Jesus Christ, lady, you really think you can back all of this up?"

"Try me."

"If you're so all-powerful, why do you need me?"

"I don't. But you've got teams floating through the back country in Bolivia with TOS orders that could complicate what I'm doing." Price had found out about the TOS—or terminate on sight—orders against Gallardo barely forty-five minutes ago. They were to be executed only if Gallardo didn't willingly come with the agents. With Bolan and Grimaldi in the mix, that wasn't going to happen easily. "And your cooperation could cut four hours off my present timetable. Frankly I could use the four hours."

"In return, what do I get?"

"Agent Gallardo healthy and well, and telling the major news media that he owes it all to the DEA, especially the efforts of SAC Monte Hardell. And you get a copy of the hidden books regarding the trafficking connections between the Bolivian producers, South American neo-Nazis and the Aryan Resistance Movement along the West Coast. I can also tell you that political thinking will be open to the DEA taking offensive action against the network still in existence down there. A few months from now you could be looking at another promotion."

"Or being responsible for an international incident."

"Depends on your choice of perspective. Is a glass of water half-full or half-empty?"

Hardell appeared to be considering. "You're willing to turn loose that much of the operation?"

"I've got other things to do."

"What?"

"I'm not at liberty to say."

"Horseshit."

"Not at all. My people have gotten what they needed out of the Bolivian end of things. At present the drug network in Bolivia is a headless corpse with Gomez and the others out of the way. But that corpse has the ability to resurrect itself in a matter of weeks, then it will be business as usual. We have a chance between us to stop it for a lot longer than a couple of months."

"Agreed. What do I have to do in return?"

"I need DEA jackets for my people. Something that will stand up long enough to Bolivian police interests to get them out of the country."

"I figured something like that would be easy for you to do."

"The best I can arrange will take me four hours longer than you could do with a phone call." Price paused. "Of course, that could change."

"For good or worse," Hardell pointed out.

"Not worse," Price said. "One way or the other, my people are coming out."

"What about Gallardo?"

"He's coming out, too."

"When do I take control of him?"

"After I talk to him and let him know he's going to be okay."

"Where?"

"On the plane is fine."

Hardell chuckled. "Do I ever get to meet you?"

"No."

"That's a shame because I'd love to buy you dinner and try to figure out what your real interest in this is."

"It would never happen."

"I'm better at face-to-face confrontations."

"So am I. Do we have a deal, Mr. Hardell?"

"Yeah. Just give me the specifics on when and where."

Price did, said thanks and broke the connection. She glanced at her watch. Negotiations with Hardell had taken almost fifteen minutes longer than she'd estimated.

She checked the memo lists she had stuck across the surface of her desk and the piles of paperwork she'd already read or needed to read soon, jotted another note on the one she'd started regarding Striker's agenda, then pushed herself out of the office chair.

She was dressed in a gray-on-white Confederate-styled blouse and charcoal gray jeans tucked into round-toed, alabaster-colored cowboy boots. With her blond hair, blue eyes and delicate features, she could have still graced the magazine covers she'd modeled for while putting herself through college. A cellular phone clipped to her belt completed the attire and kept her in touch with any last-minute events that Kurtzman's teams might not be aware of. And on this operation there seemed to be more than a few.

She opened the door and stepped out into the computer lab. The cooler temperature surrounded her at once and made her skin prickle despite the long sleeves.

Aaron Kurtzman, the Farm's resident cybernetics specialist, loomed big and blocky in his wheelchair behind the horseshoe-shaped desk where he carried on his portion of the fight. The orange-and-yellow tennis ball in his hands was juggled back and forth as he worked on his forearms and his frustrations.

At the other end of the room, just below the raised dais Kurtzman's workstation sat on, were the three people whom the big man most heavily relied on. Carmen Delahunt was old-line FBI, wooed away from Quantico by Brognola. She was a fiery redhead who'd managed to raise her three children on her own and manage a challenging career at the same time. When Price thought of patience and persistence, she thought of Delahunt.

Kurtzman's prodigy in cybernetics circles was Akira Tokaido, the young man holding down the center workstation of the three scattered around that end of the room. Barely into his twenties, Tokaido had never attended college. Instead, he'd gotten his education by hacking his way into different systems, private and government. Cocky and borderline arrogant at times, Tokaido worked efficiently and never gave less than a hundred percent.

Dr. Huntington Wethers still dressed like the university professor he'd been at Berkeley. Tall, black and distinguished, his unlit pipe clamped between his teeth, Wethers punched relentlessly at the keyboard in front of him, pausing occasionally to make notes.

Iced bins at the rear wall behind Kurtzman held a selection of drinks and foodstuffs. With the irregular hours the staff was putting in on the operation, the menu included breakfast, as well as lunch. A five-gallon coffee container was beside them.

Price chose a container of apple juice and a blueberry muffin, warmed the muffin in the microwave, then went to join Kurtzman.

The big man looked up as she approached, and she knew he'd seen her reflected in the depths of the computer monitor in front of him.

"How'd it go with Hardell?" he asked.

"He rolled over," Price answered as she came to a halt beside him.

"Good. I've got the backup covers ready to drop into place if we need to."

"Keep them. Striker and Grimaldi aren't out of the jungle yet. Any word from them?"

Kurtzman shook his head. "Akira monitored some of the police bands around Oruro. It sounds like maybe the military attaché that's been on Striker's heels since Sucre may have him treed. They've got somebody in a bad way."

"Have him stay with it and let me know."

"Done."

Price knew that people were often lost on covert operations. She'd lost some of them herself over the years. With the private demons that lived within her own mind, there were days she felt as if she was one of the lost ones. But she pushed that thought away and focused on the job she had before her. There was no other way to live this kind of life and get the missions accomplished. Still, she shivered slightly thinking that the men she was ultimately responsible for were somewhere she could no longer offer aid. She tried to cover the response, but Kurtzman knew her too well.

He also knew her well enough not to comment on the slip in control.

"Where's Rivera?" Price asked.

Kurtzman stroked the keyboard, and the monitor before him pulsed, then changed images. A map of the world spread out, orange landmasses over sapphire blue of oceans. An emerald line jetted out from a small Caribbean island and streaked out across the ocean. "Transatlantic. Three hours out from Nassau."

"London?"

"Hunt confirmed it. Rivera dumped his military title and identity while he was cleaning his bank accounts out. He's now Miguel Saura, a gynecologist on holiday from Brazil."

"A gynecologist?"

"Maybe he's always had dreams of somebody asking if there was a doctor in the house." Kurtzman grinned. "Sorry. Couldn't resist. Carmen backtracked the alias. It's solid. There really is a Dr. Miguel Saura listed in Rio de Janeiro, and he's maintained a low profile. We could have him checked out locally."

"That would be a waste of time," Price said. "Whether the identity is one that Rivera fabricated or borrowed, the result is the same—our pigeon is airborne."

"He's got a hell of a lead on Striker and Jack."

"That doesn't matter. Once we get them to a military base, they can practically turn the clock back on Rivera's escape. And I've got a feeling I know where he's running."

"Switzerland?"

Price nodded. "That's where a lot of the monies on this thing are headed back to. The Jordanian front men brokering the Iraqi sales for Saddam Hussein's carpetbaggers have a number of accounts listed there. We've only uncovered a partial list of them."

"That neck of the woods is about to become crowded. Katz and Phoenix Force are still operational there."

"I know. But it can't be helped."

Kurtzman leaned back in his wheelchair and regarded Price's image in his monitor. "Do you know where all of this is headed?"

"Maybe." Price didn't comment any further. She wasn't prone to idle speculation, and Kurtzman knew that.

If he was offended by her reticence, Kurtzman didn't show it. His eyes swept the wall-screen monitors in front of each of his team, taking in the information automatically.

"Did we identify the Arabs Phoenix chased out of the woodwork in Zurich?"

"Yeah. Uri Dan tagged Shiraz al Najaf out of the gate." Kurtzman brought the man's picture up on the computer monitor. The man was a hawk-featured Arab in his forties with hooded eyes. "He's attached to the Iraqi government. We sorted through the other Intel Phoenix was able to gather, including the dead Jordanian gunmen on-site at their latest blitz and came up with Tarim Sudair as the other main player."

The computer screen flickered and cleared again, revealing another face. This one was at least ten years older, and each of those years seemed etched into the features.

"Sudair represents the Jordanian end of the money-washing operation between Iraq and Jordan, and a liaison of sorts with the neo-Nazi factions linked to the strikes against Israel.''

Price studied the face. It was a familiar one. ''Has Hal been briefed?''

''Hours ago.''

Glancing at her watch and realizing the information was almost thirteen hours old, Price knew she'd been operating on her own internal clock too long. That was the problem with having too many agendas running at one time. ''What's Phoenix working on?''

''They spread out from the original hot zone after encountering the Arab link and have turned up what looks like an Iraqi terrorist support cell in Zurich.''

''Any signs of Sudair or al Najaf?''

''Not yet. They've only had the group under observation for little more than an hour. They've got a tactical probe set up for just before dawn. They'll know more then.''

''Okay, make sure I get the relay as soon as it comes in. We'll try to dovetail Striker and Rivera in there to shut this thing down all in one fell swoop.''

''Ms. Price.''

Price looked up and saw Delahunt waving at her. She picked up the interroom headset and held it to her ear, the curved mouthpiece only inches from her lips. ''Yes.''

''Carl Lyons is on line three, waiting for you.''

''Where is he?''

''Boston. Logan Airport.''

''I'll take it in my office.'' Price headed that way, knowing she was leaving Kurtzman's mind whirling behind her.

She slid behind the desk and clicked the phone over to Lyons.

The big ex-LAPD cop was the leader of Able Team, the domestic arm of Stony Man. During the period that Striker and Phoenix Force had first taken up the fight against the neo-Nazi–Arab terrorist faction setting up to begin a series of strikes against Israel, Able Team hadn't been in a position to take part in the campaign. Now they were fresh from past battles and ready to take up the slack on this one.

In quick, terse sentences, she outlined what she had in mind for Able to do, then gave them the cover IDs and tickets that Kurtzman had arranged for them at Logan Airport. A Stony Man blacksuit—one of the Farm hands borrowed from other agencies for extra training or limited covert operations—was waiting there with everything they needed in a rental locker.

Once Lyons had all the information he needed for the preemptive foray his team would initiate once in California, he cleared the phone.

Then, guts churning with mixed emotions, Price reached for the phone again and started the first of a series of calls to Israel. The thought that lives were perhaps hanging in the balance and she had her thumb on the scale like a greedy butcher wouldn't leave her. The first connection was made, and she started talking to the person at the other end.

"HOW CLOSE ARE WE getting on this thing?"

"Basically we're still setting up the foundation," Hal Brognola answered. He looked at the President of the United States and saw the weight of the past days marring the man's boyish good looks.

They were in the Oval Office. Night stained the grounds on the other side of the bulletproof glass. The

TV-VCR combo across the room was set on CNN and depicted debates in Tel Aviv that had raged all night.

"How much can we prove?" the Man asked.

"That the Nazis were linked with Bolivian cocaine producers in South America and were helping move monies from Iraq despite the trade embargoes placed on that country by the United Nations."

"And that's not enough?"

"No, sir. We've uncovered one of the biggest terrorist alliances this world has ever seen, but we still don't know what their goals are."

"On the surface it seems pretty obvious that they intended to do as much harm to Israel as they could."

"On the surface," Brognola agreed. "But I find it amazing that the Mossad apparently didn't know to what depth negotiations between the neo-Nazis and Arab terrorist groups had reached."

The President glanced at the Stony Man liaison sharply. "It was my understanding that we gained our initial information about those groups primarily from Mossad sources."

"True. But we 'borrowed' the information."

"I know your people hacked their way into the Mossad cybernetic network and picked this up. That means that agency was already involved."

"To a degree. We still don't know how deeply. They appear to have been as ill prepared for this as we were."

"I wouldn't think that the events that have happened in California, Germany, Bolivia and Switzerland would count as ill prepared."

Brognola nodded. "That's partly because of the quality of people we've fielded on this play. You've seen them in action. Once they've identified a potential threat, they neutralize it as quickly as possible. But they've been wading in blind. Everything we've picked up along the way has resembled the trail of bread crumbs Hansel and Gretel tried to leave behind to mark their passage. And those crumbs can disappear at any time now."

"Yet they haven't."

"No, they haven't." Brognola fumbled in his pocket for the roll of antacid tablets he habitually carried there. These days the head Fed spent more time reaching for those than he had for the cigars he used to enjoy. "And frankly, sir, that is something that has been bothering Price and me."

"In the proper perspective," the Man mused, "that line of thinking is troubling."

"Yeah."

"Would you say that Jordan and Iraq are aware of our knowledge of Tarim Sudair and Shariz al Najaf?"

"Yes. It's no secret that the Mossad have friendlies located within our Intelligence spheres."

"So it stands to reason that the people controlling those agents would pull them in rather than risk further exposure."

"Maybe. You've also got to factor in that the Nazis might not willingly change the faces of the people they've been dealing with. Their faith in the arrangements that had been made can't be exactly stable now."

"No." The President paused. "How much trouble can the Nazi contingents continue to give us?"

"Not much. Price has made arrangements to close out the factions we uncovered in Bolivia and California. There still remain a few hands to be played out with those people, though."

"So we're left with the Arabs."

"Basically."

"And it looks like the only thing they're guilty of is helping a brother nation out of a tough financial situation."

"Yeah."

"Doesn't exactly leave us in a favorable light if our involvement in this mess comes out, does it?"

"No," Brognola sighed, "but that's why we're softening up on the surface and buying time to sort out all the pieces. There's something missing here. We have enough of it to figure that out, but not enough to guess at what it is that's missing."

"What if your people are compromised?"

"They won't be."

The President pinned him with a glance.

Brognola had spent a considerable amount of time with the new President. He'd liked the man's down-home approach to things, and his soft humor. But the Man hadn't had a chance to see how committed the Stony warriors were to their cause. "Those men knew when they took this mission on that it wasn't completely sanctioned. If they fall, they'll fall alone and there won't be any concrete evidence to point to this office."

"Dammit." The Man rubbed his face tiredly. "I worry about this country being implicated in eradicating terrorist cells within our borders and in breaking up a cocaine supply route from Bolivia—both of which are perfectly legal operations and within our guidelines—and I see Israel on the point of reopening the Gulf War all by themselves, without any help on our part."

"It would be better if they would stay out of it."

"I know, but try telling them that. For the last six hours, they haven't been returning my calls."

Brognola sipped his coffee. Israel had been a wild card from the beginning. The country had slipped from favor in the minds of most Americans since the Gulf War because their hawkish tendencies had come to the forefront during the conflict and threatened to embroil all of the Middle East in a lasting conflagration.

But if Israel entered the operation at this point, there would be no way to contain the blood that would be shed on all sides. The truths that were still missing could be years away, then, if they were ever found at all.

The President sat up, giving more attention to the events taking place on the television. "Look at this."

Brognola focused on the news broadcast as the Man turned up the volume by remote control.

A riot was taking place outside the Knesset in Jerusalem. The city and the place were identified by headers running across the top of the screen. The reporter's name—Desiree St. Cyr—trailed across the bottom.

The elegant parliament building was surrounded by military vehicles, soldiers and protesters. The cameraman was back in the crowd and was jostled quite often as the people surged around him, baiting the black-clad Israeli soldiers carrying riot shields and wearing Plexiglas face masks. A troop carrier rocked forward into a more protective position in front of the rioters. The soldiers manning the two machine guns fired warning bursts over the heads of the people.

St. Cyr, brunette and athletically trim, went quickly to ground with the rest of the protest group. For a moment the cameraman lost her as the video camera swung out of control, then the perspective locked on target again.

"Hostilities here continue," St. Cyr said in a voice that was tight with undisguised emotions, but her words were clear. "For the last several days, parliament members have met to discuss what actions Israel will take against terrorist activities that have claimed the lives of several countrymen."

The rioters got to their feet again and moved forward once more when they realized none of them had actually been shot, which had actually happened several times in the past. Most of them appeared to be Arabic, representing the Muslim faction in the divided city.

"As always," St. Cyr continued, "the country is torn. The Arab community is against any national efforts regarding suspected attacks stemming from Iraq and possibly Jordan, while the Jewish citizens are demanding protection from further attacks."

Brognola was impressed by the newscaster's poise. A lot of seasoned reporters wouldn't have been standing in the thick of things that way. He made a mental note to have Price further research the woman in case other options came up later.

"So far," St. Cyr said, "no blame has been issued regarding the deaths of Asher Blum and his fellow countrymen both here and abroad. The flags continue to be flown at half-mast in their honor."

A metal shopping cart, filled with automobile tires and wreathed in smoke and flames, was shoved at the front ranks of Israeli soldiers. A young soldier jumped from the troop carrier with a red fire extinguisher in his hand and directed a stream of white foam that quickly smothered the flames. Before he could safely withdraw, a thrown brick smashed into the side of his head.

"One proponent suggesting immediate reprisal against those responsible for the terrorist actions in Israel and Germany is Dr. Enoch Harel. He's flown from Tel Aviv today to speak before the government and should be arriving soon. We'll be bringing you back for that telecast."

Abruptly the CNN viewpoint changed, pulling the audience back into the studio newsroom.

The President hit the Mute button. "We haven't got much time to get a handle on this thing."

"I know."

On the television there was a flurry of scene cuts showing Jordanian tanks advancing on the shared border with Israel and of Israeli F-16s thundering through the skies near the same border.

"Who's Harel?" the Man asked. "I haven't heard his name before."

"He's a big gun in Israeli political thinking and in economic circles." Brognola crossed the room to his armored briefcase and carefully set the coded locks so the contents wouldn't be vaporized when he lifted the lid. With everything disarmed, he reached inside and pulled out a manila file folder thick with sheets and photos. He put the file on the Man's desk. "Dr. Harel has the potential to be a big player in the scheme of things. He's been active in financial circles inside Israel and the U.S. for almost fifteen years and has been responsible for renewed interest in economic diversification in European and Japanese holdings. He's good at what he does."

"And that is?"

"Making money. He's also heavily invested in AIPAC, the Jewish lobbying group here on the Hill."

Opening the file, the President took out the top photo and studied it.

Brognola glanced over the Man's shoulder.

Dr. Enoch Harel was a man who appeared to have a capacity for enormous appetites. The picture, a head-and-shoulders shot, didn't really do justice to the man in Brognola's opinion. Harel was almost six feet six in his stockings and tipped the scales at almost three hundred pounds, filling out a frame that was hard and broad and not really fat at all. His head was large, made to look smaller because of the enormous width of his shoulders. Dark skinned from exposure to the sun, Harel wore his dark hair slicked back from his face and temples. A thick and fierce goatee stood out prominently on his chin. Pince-nez glasses gave his light blue eyes a scholarly look that was carried out in the pressed lines of the pin-striped suit he had on.

"You've already researched him?" the President asked.

"Price did. She believed from the beginning that Harel would involve himself in this if it lasted more than a few days."

"And what will his stance be regarding the terrorist attacks?"

Brognola didn't pull any punches. "Harel's a hawk. He's aggressive and sure of himself. You see that from his business portfolio over the last few years. He took his father's business—a pharmaceuticals company in Tel Aviv—and turned it into a multimillion-dollar-a-year business by the time he opened outlets in the U.S. and Europe. At present he's developing the Eastern European market and could be making a move into what were once the most steadfast countries of the East Bloc."

"So I would guess his word carries a lot of weight in Israel these days."

"Yeah. He's also opened his coffers to military funding over the years. He's got significant influence in those circles, too."

"What's his stance on the current crisis?"

"He's all for armed response."

The President continued flipping through the contents of the folder. "I'm surprised Harel wasn't assassinated," he said after a time.

"They tried." Brognola held up three fingers. "Three attempts. All of them failed. Bombs and snipers."

"You'd think he'd keep a low profile."

"He's not if he's planning to address a media conference later this morning there."

"That poses the possibility of another international incident."

"I'm sure Harel's probably counting on it."

"And gambling with his life in the process."

"It's a calculated risk. His security people are among the best in the world."

"No man is safe from someone who wants him badly enough. That was one of the first things the Secret Service told me when they started guarding me."

Brognola knew it was a motto the Executioner lived by, as well, only from the other end of the gun.

The Man closed the file and put it away. "If this terrorist organization was so threatening, why haven't they done more damage than they have? Granted, they've killed some people around the globe, but why haven't their strikes escalated? Most of their retaliation has been in response to attacks by our people, GSG-9 and the Mossad. I have a hard time believing we simply caught them that off guard."

Brognola had a hard time believing that, too. It was the fly in the ointment. He chewed another couple of antacid tablets before answering. "It's possible that we were suckered into this whole scenario."

"Would you care to explain that?"

"I don't know that I can," the head Fed replied honestly. "It's a gut feeling. Price and I have discussed the possibility and are investigating it."

"You might have mentioned that before now."

"I didn't have anything to offer that could back it up. I still don't. Studying the overall scheme of things, we've done everything we could have done. Negotiations between the U.S. and Jordan and Iraq have broken down regarding the trade embargoes. While researching Mossad files, we discovered that caravans were being routinely routed through Jordan from Iraq, with the monies turning up in Swiss bank accounts. It was puzzling that the Israelis hadn't done something about it, but maybe we just beat them to the punch. They're operating under severe restriction in the Middle East these days. If they'd been discovered themselves, we'd still be facing war in that part of the world."

"However," the President said, "if the U.S. intervened on a special search and turned up the terrorist organization, they would be in a better position to draw world sympathy before involving themselves."

"Yeah. Only we didn't send in conventional special forces. We sent in Phoenix Force and Striker to disassemble the terrorist network, and we kept the information to ourselves."

"And they can prove nothing about where the terrorist teams originated."

"Right," Brognola confirmed.

"How did we get the initial information?"

"It was passed off to a double agent code-named Canary."

"I don't recall seeing or hearing that name in your reports."

"No, sir. It was deliberately left out."

The President fixed Brognola with his eyes. "You have my attention."

The head Fed took a final sip of his coffee and began the explanation. He knew the antacid tablets weren't going to be much help.

CHAPTER THREE

His first shot lined up, Mack Bolan squeezed the trigger of the Mini-14. The rifle butt recoiled against his shoulder. Out in the street the right front tire of one of the police vehicles suddenly went flat as the soldiers and policemen went to ground. He worked mechanically, spacing some of the shots to disable his selected targets among the cars and trucks, and placing others to keep aggressive moves on the part of their pursuers to a minimum.

Thunder rolled over the street as he ran through the clip. With the 7.62 mm rounds instead of the 5.56 mm slugs, there was less chance of deflection. The heavy bullets cored into their targets and spent their energy instead of skewing off in all direction. Besides tires, his chosen targets also included the five klieg lights spotlighting the rooftop. The big lights went out in quick succession, followed almost immediately by the glass explosions of the spinning cherries atop the police car.

Sporadic fire still pelted the rooftop as the policemen and soldiers tried to dig in. The basso chatter of a .50-caliber machine gun mounted on the deck of a truck ripped into the silence following Bolan's last shot.

Grimaldi swung over the lip of the building and raked autofire from his Uzi across the front of the truck. The hood stuttered under the impacts, and the windshield was punched out in fist-sized hunks of flying glass.

The two men manning the gun jumped over the sides.

Sliding back behind cover, Bolan dropped the empty clip from the Mini-14 and slammed a fresh one home. "Let's go," he said. He pushed himself into a run, drumming his feet hard against the tar-and-pebble-covered rooftop. Grimaldi was on his heels a moment later.

From his peripheral vision, the warrior could see the roof hatch opening again as a rifle snout was pushed through.

Without pause he leapt up onto the low rampart running around the top of the building, pushed off hard with his foot and threw himself across the intervening distance to the next building. For a wild moment he thought he'd misjudged his own ability and that the gap of the alley was wider than he'd at first guessed in the darkness. His equipment had slowed his momentum more than he'd thought. He tensed, then flailed out with his free arm, maintaining his grip on the Ranch Rifle.

His forward foot made contact with the building's eave as his back foot skated down the side of the building. He threw himself forward into a roll and worked momentum and gravity to his advantage. The sharp white rock covering the rooftop bit into his shoulder. Continuing the roll, he came up on his feet, then turned back to check on Grimaldi.

The pilot might have been the king of the sky, but he lacked something when it came to unassisted flight. Falling short of his mark, Grimaldi lunged forward and grabbed at the rooftop, managing a grip with one hand.

Leaning over the rooftop, Bolan reached down and grabbed a fistful of Grimaldi's jacket, then hauled him up.

A sudden burst of gunfire from the other building indicated that the soldiers had gained the rooftop. Bolan reached into Grimaldi's gym bag and found a smoke grenade while they hunkered down in the shelter of the rampart. He pulled the pin and tossed it only a few feet away. The fuse lit.

"Are you ready?" the Executioner asked.

"Yeah," Grimaldi said as he redistributed his load.

Bolan nodded and glanced back at the smoker as it spewed a dark cloud that looked foggy and gray in the moonlight.

Bullets continued slamming into the building or whizzing by over their position.

Satisfied that the smoker had laid out enough of a cover to make any attempts by their pursuers at following the same course they'd laid out to be foolhardy, Bolan checked the street.

A few of the vehicles were in motion. Headlights flashed in the confusion and sparked reflections off building windows. No one had been hurt in the exchange of gunfire, but none of them seemed to be sure of that at the moment. They also hadn't realized the disabled vehicles were blocking their path. Commanders screamed orders that further confused the situation, urging their people to move the vehicles blocking the street out of the way, by hand if necessary.

"Now," Bolan said.

Grimaldi got to his feet.

The smoke layer was thick enough to provide a good cover for a while. Bolan took the point, staying low and moving from memory as much as visual inspection. He used his free hand to make contact with the HVAC units on the building.

Finding the other side of the building, Bolan ran his hand along the edge until he located the fire escape trailing down the side of the structure. He threw a leg over, and metal clanged when he dropped onto it.

He ran down the steps till he got to the second-story landing, then threw himself over. He landed heavily but remained on his feet. The alley was narrow, lined with trash containers filled to overflowing and populated by long-tailed sewer rats.

Bolan surged into motion when Grimaldi landed beside him. Together they ran for the opposite end of the alley and made it just as the first wave of soldiers and policemen entered from the street.

"Break left," Bolan said as they ran out onto the other thoroughfare.

"Right behind you," Grimaldi answered.

The warrior tossed the Mini-14 into a thin strip of grass fronting the building at his side. The rifle was too long to hide under his jacket and would only attract unwanted attention. Grimaldi tucked the Uzi out of sight under his jacket.

They ran on under a loose green-and-white canopy fronting a small café that had been closed hours ago. The street rose slightly over the next fifty yards. At the end of that the fiesta began, flowing down over the next incline.

A number of vehicles, most of them decrepit looking, lined the street. Flatbed trucks seemed to be the favorite. Here and there pockets of celebrants sat on the backs of the trucks or on cars with brown bottles of native beer in their hands. Woven baskets contained paper-wrapped tacos and burritos.

Bolan never broke stride as he ran past them. He hated involving the civilian sector of the city, but all other choices had been eliminated. If he'd been chased by the neo-Nazis or their Bolivian compatriots, that list of options would have been different. He wouldn't have involved noncombatants because his enemy wouldn't hesitate to fire anyway.

The warrior ran hard, the adrenaline kicking his reflexes into full fight-or-flight mode that enabled him to sprint at full speed despite the hours spent in the jungle dodging the military attaché. Perspiration ran in trickles down his back underneath his shirt and followed the planes of his face. He blinked the salty sting out of his eyes as the breeze cooled him.

Deep-throated thumps that sounded like mortar fire erupted somewhere ahead of them. Then a colorful spray of reds, greens and whites scattered across the sky in an elaborate design.

They were close enough to the crowd now to hear the appreciative murmurs that followed.

Behind, an authoritative voice rang out harshly. "Stop those men!"

Bolan risked a glance over his shoulder and saw a handful of soldiers mixed with policemen spill out into the street.

"Stop those men, damn you!"

The men sitting on the parked vehicles looked uncertain. A couple of the younger ones started to move forward.

Bolan reached under his jacket and freed the Beretta, carrying it pointed up at shoulder level in obvious warning.

The opposition ahead of them quickly and quietly withdrew. A few bottles of beer were thrown at them and smashed on the sidewalk, but no one tried to block their way.

"Get to the other side of the street!" the man bellowed behind them. "Hurry! Try to pick them off before they reach the crowds!"

Knowing they could be caught in a cross fire, Bolan changed directions and ran toward the row of cars on his side of the street. A few stray rounds scraped sparks from the sidewalk and punched holes in plate-glass windows from surrounding stores. The warrior threw himself in a baseball slide across a Cadillac. At least two rounds smashed into the right fin and knocked pieces of the ruby taillights to the ground.

"Stop firing!" the man shouted as he raced into the center of the street himself.

The gunfire died away as Grimaldi came scooting across the big sedan. He stumbled and would have fallen if Bolan hadn't grabbed his arm and hustled him toward the crowd of partiers. They ran full tilt toward the festivities.

When they hit the outer ring of pedestrians crowding the street, their pursuers were less than thirty yards behind them. They jostled through the packed thoroughfare, losing precious yardage in heartbeats.

The street was filled to overflowing. Inside the loose ring of spectators, clowns, jugglers and costumed demons performed, backlit by the fireworks display that continued to assault the night sky. Children and adults clapped to show their appreciation. Musicians played at different posts on impromptu stages. Revelers sang, and beautifully garbed women danced to folk songs. Colorful piñatas in the form of mystical beasts and farm animals hung from cords tied to long poles held by men who kept them just out of reach of the children gamboling below with sticks ready to smash them and release the surprises and candies inside.

"Trouble," Grimaldi said.

Not breaking stride, Bolan glanced back over his shoulder and saw the three army jeeps roaring up the street. The transmissions' whines cut through the sounds of the party, and the whirling cherries mounted on the back roll bars attracted immediate attention. The crowd started to part to allow passage.

Bolan halted inside a shadowed doorway. At the other end of the street, he saw Gallardo waiting in the jeep they'd liberated for their escape.

The passenger in the front army jeep stood up holding a bullhorn and gripped the windshield to steady himself. "Out of the way! Those men are foreign spies! Out of the way!"

Parents worked quickly to gather their children and pull them from the street. The clowns and jugglers gathered their props and dodged for the sidewalks. The path continued to widen as more and more of the fiesta goers realized what was happening.

Bolan knew they wouldn't have a chance of escaping without pursuit if the jeeps were allowed through. He gripped the Beretta and moved out again as spotlights on the jeeps tried to pick Grimaldi and him out of the crowd. He set himself near a utility pole that provided cover from any would-be sharpshooters and raised the Beretta into target acquisition. He fired from the point, moving from target to target deftly. With the fire selector on 3-round burst, the silenced 93-R cycled brass out onto the sidewalk.

The rounds took direct hits on four of the suspended piñatas still hanging over the street. Since there was no sound of gunfire, no one knew shots had been fired. The piñatas exploded and spilled treats over the street. The children immediately surged after them, scrambling to avoid each other and the concerned parents who trailed after them.

"Go," Bolan told Grimaldi.

The pilot gave him a quick, affirmative nod and ran for Gallardo and the waiting jeep.

Bolan trailed after him, watching as the jeeps ground to a stop despite the shouted orders through the bullhorn. Immediately the men in the jeeps bailed out from the vehicles and launched themselves through the crowd. The Executioner scored on two more piñatas before he cleared the party area. The fireworks grew uncertain, and only sporadic bursts colored the night.

Out of the crowd, Bolan moved his pace back up to a sprint. Grimaldi was heaving himself onto the rear deck. "Move out!" the warrior ordered.

Leaving the lights off, Gallardo eased the jeep into motion, aiming it for the other end of town.

Bolan came abreast of the vehicle, then grabbed the windshield and swung himself aboard.

The DEA man floored the accelerator, and the jeep's engine wound tight, shoving them toward the waiting jungle.

When Bolan looked back, he saw the military jeeps still mired in the fiesta, their whirling cherries looking like something that fit the party's mood. The soldiers on foot quickly fell behind, and the shots they fired were well off the mark. Bolan settled into the passenger seat, then took out his war book and a penlight.

Gallardo kept running dark till the jungle had swallowed them.

The warrior's mind was busy turning over the options facing them, trying to figure out how the commander of the military attaché would handle the search after their disappearance. Raiding the Bolivian cartel drop station had provided them funds to effect another leg of their escape attempt. Part of the plan relied on Price being able to leverage some kind of support in La Paz. He charted their course, going over it again in his mind like a pilot gearing up for a final approach. He closed the book and put it away.

Gallardo drove hard, almost exceeding the vehicle's maximum safe speed in the night. The road they followed was little more than a trail, bumpy and treacherous, filled with potholes and gnarled roots. Some kind of big cat crossed ahead of them, then spit out a snarling challenge.

"Hey, Sarge," Grimaldi said. He passed up a packet of trail mix and a canteen of water.

Bolan accepted it and kept watch over their backtrail with Grimaldi. Nothing appeared to be following, but he knew it wouldn't be long.

The trail snaked up the mountainous terrain. The warrior's mind took as many vicious twists as the road. Rivera had escaped and had a place to run to. That was obvious. What was also obvious, though, was that neither the neo-Nazis nor their Arab counterparts had been prepared to move in any unified direction. They had been a threat, yes, but a threat in the making. His instincts told him the Stony Man teams had only managed to uncover the tip of the iceberg.

Ten minutes later they abandoned the jeep while heading in an easterly direction toward the Pan-American Highway, then looped around back to the east to their real goal: the Desaguadero River and the chance at escape Gallardo had brought up. The warrior settled his gear firmly around his body, then stepped into a forced-march routine that had been part of his training for years. Gallardo and Grimaldi fell in behind him. They'd gone only a quarter-mile when they heard the first of the pursuit jeeps close in on their partially hidden vehicle.

Bolan held steady to his pace. The play had already been set into motion; all that remained was riding it out.

THEIR DESTINATION WAS almost a mile upriver from where Gallardo had thought it would be, which cost them an extra twenty minutes doubling back to find it.

Bolan hunkered down behind the cover of brush and tall trees, using the infrared binoculars to scan the area.

A small house built on stilts and constructed of poles under a thatched roof sat off a finger leading to the Desaguadero River on the east side. The water ran smooth and ripple free, capturing the image of the moon in its surface. A dock was erected on thick boles sunk into the river mud. It was small and uneven but led to a pontoon-equipped Cessna covered by a brown-and-green camo tarp. The airplane drifted lazily against the dock and created rhythmic bumping noises.

Refocusing on the small house, the warrior took in the postage-stamp-sized garden growing a few feet away from the house, the chicken pen built low to the ground a short distance away from that and the goat staked under a tree just outside the clearing for the garden.

The house had been placed to take advantage of the natural cover, and the leafy boughs of the trees stretched shielding branches out over the plane. The place wouldn't be noticed on casual inspection, and the only visitors would be people who already knew about it or happened to see it while traveling the river.

Both the house and the plane were owned by Miguel Retana, a free-lance pilot who'd learned his trade in the Bolivian army. Gallardo vouched for the man. After his military career, Retana had briefly done some work for the cartel people, though never flying drugs. It had been to the cartel members' advantage not to press him into flying narcotics, because it provided them with a pilot who had a reputation for staying clean and wouldn't be yanked away by Bolivian officials. Six years ago the cartel that had been his employer had fallen to a combined DEA-Bolivian army raid. He'd escaped arrest, taken his money and lain low for a while. When he reentered the public world three years ago, he'd bought the Cessna, built a house on the river and gone into the air-charter business for himself.

The money that had been liberated from the cartel underground in Oruro was for Retana. They didn't need his services, but the plane was something else again. Ground transport was a poor choice. The military unit had gained on them, and Rivera already had several hours' head-start.

Ernie Gallardo joined Bolan, leaving Grimaldi as rearguard to secure the flank. The DEA agent's shirt was damp with sweat. "Anything?"

"No," Bolan replied.

"Good." Gallardo peered toward the house. "Retana's a stand-up guy. I've used him myself during the time I've been here. I don't want to see him hurt."

"He won't be." Bolan put the night glasses away. "I give you my word."

The DEA man nodded.

A single light burned in one of the windows and threw shadows over an alabaster-colored window shade.

"He's going to know we're coming," Gallardo said.

"I saw the dog," Bolan said.

"Most people don't."

Bolan understood that. The canine hadn't stirred from under the house. It was a huge mastiff mongrel the color of wet ashes striped with curving black lines.

"The dog doesn't bark," Gallardo warned. "And if he can, he'll come up on you from behind. A couple of agents I know still carry scars from times they tried approaching the house without letting Retana know they were coming. Kind of like what we're doing here tonight."

"I'll keep that in mind." Bolan stood up and slung his equipment pack over his shoulder. A hundred yards away the mastiff tracked the movement instantly, and its big head swiveled in their direction. Instinctively it moved into position behind one of the support struts of the house and made itself into a small target.

"The dog's been shot before," Gallardo said. "The only people he cares about are Retana and his family."

Bolan thumbed the transmit button on the headset. "Jack."

"Go."

"We're moving in."

"I'll be here."

Bolan stepped through the brush and moved toward the house at normal speed. The mastiff had disappeared into the shadows. Thirty yards from the house Bolan halted with Gallardo at his side. In their cages the chickens had started a frightened bout of cackling that woke the goat and added to the din. Although he couldn't see the mastiff, the warrior could sense the big animal moving around them to the right.

"Hello the house," Gallardo called out in Spanish between his cupped hands. "Miguel, drag your ass out of bed, man, before the wolf gets us."

The lantern on the outer side of the window flickered, but no shadow touched the shade.

"Miguel," Gallardo called again.

"Who's there?" a man's voice demanded.

"Ernie Gallardo."

"What the hell are you doing out here, Ernie? I heard you'd gone rogue. Of course, that was after I heard you were supposed to be dead."

"We can talk later. Call the dog off."

Bolan sensed the mastiff waiting in the brush fifteen feet away. He emptied his hands and shrugged his shoulders, getting the equipment pack ready to use as a defense if it became necessary.

"Who's that with you?"

"A friend."

"Do I know him?"

"No."

There was a brief pause. "Step away from him."

Gallardo glanced at Bolan.

"Do it," the warrior said.

The DEA man moved forward.

"That's okay," Retana said. "I just wanted to make sure he wasn't holding a gun on you." He raised his voice. "Diablo! Heel!"

The presence in the brush faded.

"Come ahead," Retana said.

Gallardo took the lead. "We've got another man out in the brush. We left people looking for us in Oruro."

"Bring him in, too. Have you eaten?"

"Yeah, but we're still hollow."

"Come. There are beans and tortillas, a little meat and some coffee."

Bolan relayed the message to Grimaldi as he walked to the stilt house. The mastiff was back under the structure before they reached the steps.

Miguel Retana moved out onto the small porch, a short, compact man dressed only in faded Levi's, his arms and upper body scarred. He had unruly hair, and a pencil-thin mustache shadowed his upper lip. A silver crucifix hung from a chain around his throat. He kept a pump-action shotgun canted off his hip, and there was a Government Model .45 stuck in the waistband of his pants. He shook Gallardo's hand, then looked past his shoulder.

Grimaldi was emerging from the jungle.

"Your man?" Retana asked.

"Yes," Bolan answered.

Retana called to the dog again and commanded it to heel.

After Grimaldi joined them, Gallardo made brief introductions, giving Bolan's name as Mike Belasko and also stating honestly that he didn't know which government agency the two men were affiliated with.

Despite the dim light, Retana's gaze was penetrating. He made no move to shake Bolan's hand, nor did he put away his weapons, making it obvious that they were there only because of his trust in Gallardo. "You people have a lot of trouble following you around. I want none of it to enter my home."

"I think we lost the Bolivian militia," Bolan said.

"You have," Retana said. "For the moment. But the commanding officer is hardheaded and very good at his job. As long as you are within the borders of this country, he will hunt you."

"We won't be here much longer."

"You are here about the plane?"

Bolan met the steady gaze evenly. "Yes."

Retana shook his head. "I won't fly you out of here. I refuse to jeopardize my family. You can remain for an hour or two to catch your breath, but then you are out of here."

"We don't need you to fly us out of here," Bolan said. "All we need is the plane."

"The plane feeds my family."

"I know," Bolan said. "I wouldn't do anything to take it away from you without paying you for it." He took the gym bag from Grimaldi, reached inside and removed the money. The thick stacks of currency made an impressive sight even in the dark. "That's just under two hundred thousand dollars."

"Gomez's?"

"Once."

"It's more than enough for the plane." Retana didn't reach for the money.

"Yeah."

"You can buy a bigger plane," Gallardo said. "You've been talking about that since I've known you."

"Gomez might find out about the bush-league pilot who suddenly came into a small fortune."

"If you spend it all at once, maybe," Bolan agreed. "It's possible that you can reclaim your plane without any problems."

"Where?"

"In La Paz. After a few days have passed. All anyone needs to know tonight is that three men threatened you at gunpoint and stole your plane. If we don't make it, you have enough money to replace it. If we do and you're able to regain the plane, you've got a hunk of change set toward your retirement."

A white grin split Retana's dark features. "I like your way of thinking. Come inside and let's eat." He headed through the door. "Luisa, make the table ready. We've hungry men to feed."

The house was neat and organized, taking advantage of the simple floor space. One corner of the front room held a typist's desk, and maps of the surrounding terrain hung on the wall above it.

The living-room furniture was handcrafted from solid wood and looked comfortable. The bedroom was off to one side with no adjoining wall, just drapes that provided privacy. The kitchen was at the rear of the house. A wood-burning stove was built into the back wall. Lanterns hanging on the walls provided a golden glow that looked like early-morning sunshine.

A woman dressed in a long gown and obviously heavy with child was putting plates and silverware on the table. Her face was calm and fine featured, and her raven's-wing hair was braided and ran down both shoulders. A little girl of five or six clung to her mother's leg and watched the new arrivals with a mixture of wonderment and fear.

"Luisa," Gallardo said. An honest smile touched the DEA man's face as he stepped forward and took the hands of the woman when she offered them.

"Ernie," she said. "It has been so long."

"I've been busy." Still smiling, Gallardo touched the woman's stomach with both palms. "And it appears that you have been, as well."

Luisa slapped Gallardo playfully on the side of the head. "Men," she snorted disdainfully. "Give you a few rainy days when you can do no work, and this is all you can think of."

"Tell Miguel to buy a television and VCR, then talk him into buying some of those American movies from the black market. Or a Nintendo."

"Then he would never do any work. Sit. There is plenty to eat."

Conversation fell to a minimum as the three men ate. Luisa kept hot coffee coming, as well as an ample supply of cooked chicken, tortillas and beans. Another bowl held grated goat cheese. The meal finished up with fried cinnamon strips and sopaipillas.

"Everyone," Retana said as his wife poured him another cup of coffee, "is talking about you and your friends these days, Ernie."

"That's the price of fame," Gallardo replied with a grin.

"That's not the only price. The Bolivian cartel and the Nazis have bounties out on your heads. And the last I heard, the DEA had TOS orders on you, as well, if they couldn't get you out of the country."

"Terrific. You really know how to ruin a good meal."

"The cartel and the neo-Nazi organization are walking corpses. But someone will ease into a position of power and they will be operating again soon."

"Not this time," Bolan said quietly. "Information will be placed through channels to excise the entire operation."

"Difficult."

"But possible. Ernie mentioned that you had a shortwave radio here."

"Of course. Luisa."

Bolan followed the woman back into the living room and watched as she removed a wall panel to reveal the radio set. He thanked her, then keyed it to life and set it to one of the frequencies he knew Kurtzman and his team would be monitoring. "Stony Base, this is Stony One. Over." He made two more attempts before he was answered.

"Go, Stony One, you have Stony Base. It's been a long damned time, buddy. Over." Kurtzman sounded relieved.

Quickly Bolan outlined their plan to use the Cessna to get to La Paz, using code-word terminology that would leave a potential listener out of the communications loop.

"You have a green light for La Paz, Stony One. The fix is in. Over."

"What about the alphabet squads? Over."

"They're running the backup. If you can get there at the time you say you can, they'll be able to shave hours off your schedule. Over."

"What about our pigeon? Over."

"Still winging away. He'll arrive a few hours before you do, but the word is that you're a quick study. Over."

"Any idea of his agenda? Over."

"Negative. And the crystal ball is still cloudy. Over."

"Where's the lady? Over." Usually Price monitored communications more closely, involving herself in most transmissions. With this being the first communication in several hours, he'd assumed he would be talking to her.

"Busy," Kurtzman answered. "She's got a lot of irons in the fire on this one. Should I interrupt her? Over."

"No. I don't have anything she could use yet. Over."

"Roger. I'll tell her you asked about her. Over."

"Do that. I'll be in touch again soon. Stony One out."

"Stay frosty out there, Stony One. We're here if you need us." Kurtzman cleared the channel.

When Bolan returned to the kitchen, he found Gallardo staring moodily into his half-empty cup of coffee.

"What do you know about an Israeli double agent code-named Canary?" the DEA man asked.

CHAPTER FOUR

Kurtzman stared thoughtfully at his screen. Phoenix Force had reported action at a terrorist outpost in the Jura foothills in Switzerland, and the loss of Rudolf Wetzel, the GSG-9 operative who had swung his way into their mission. He'd managed to download the terrorists' files and was still mulling over information Katz had passed on about a double agent code-named Canary who was apparently responsible for uniting Arab terrorists and their German counterparts into a single front. Because Canary had some information on Phoenix, the question arose if he was Mossad, and Kurtzman was requested to search Stony Man data for any reference to the double agent.

He glanced around the computer lab and saw that his team was still busy with their assignments. Barbara Price was in her office and appeared to be heavily engaged in her phone conversation. This was the latest in a long string of them, which had prevented her from talking with Katzenelenbogen when he'd called in with Phoenix's report.

Her preoccupation bothered him somewhat, but he couldn't put his finger on why. Price had always been secretive in some respects. However, she usually let him in on whatever she had up in the air. He felt as if that was missing now.

Forcing the issue from his mind, he returned his attention to the files he'd raided from the terrorist cell

Phoenix had put out of business. Already it was beginning to take shape as some kind of money-transfer scheme. Taking into account the Iraqi wealth being shipped out by caravan through Jordan, it made sense that those monies had to turn up somewhere sooner or later.

"Aaron."

Looking up, Kurtzman found Hunt Wethers leaning back in his seat with an aggravated expression on his face. "Yeah."

"That Canary code name Phoenix turned up..."

"Yeah."

"I'm having trouble accessing it."

"Let me see it." Kurtzman saved the file he was working on, then opened a window in the center of his monitor to run the program Wethers had initiated on the code name.

"According to what I've seen," Wethers said, "there isn't any agent listed as Canary."

"Can't be somebody new," Kurtzman mused out loud. "Somebody new wouldn't have access to the Intel Katz said the Arab files contained."

"That's what I was thinking."

Kurtzman stroked the keyboard, coming at the name a half-dozen ways he'd learned over the years, generally resulting in answers of some kind. Nothing showed up. The CIA didn't have any records of an agent named Canary. Neither did Russian military Intelligence, British MI6, German GSG-9 or the French Sûreté. And despite the best taps Kurtzman had rigged into the Mossad's cybernetic network, the Israelis showed no existence of the agent, either.

"Anything?" Wethers asked.

"No," Kurtzman replied in disgust. He hadn't experienced that kind of information lock-out before, except for a few times when the Stony Man systems had inadvertently picked up viruses that his antivirus programming hadn't spotted. Hackers were constantly developing new techniques, so it wasn't really surprising. Being on the cutting edge of technology meant being on the cutting edge of new problems, as well. He'd learned to compensate. "Look, why don't you take over the files I was digging through and let me take a crack at this for a little while. If I can't break through somewhere, we'll let Akira take a shot at it."

"Done." Wethers turned back to his console.

Tokaido was one of the best wild-card hackers Kurtzman had ever seen in action.

Grimly the big man turned back to the keyboard. Thirty-seven minutes later, with a film of perspiration covering his forehead and a sick twisting in his stomach, he found the source of the lock-out. If he'd been looking for it like this, he'd have found out the reason immediately.

Beside the "Canary" enquiry was printed "Stony: Classified."

He leaned back in the wheelchair, stymied. Lifting the lock-out would be easy, but it would trigger a system-wide shutdown that would close out the Farm's computers. He knew because he'd designed the lock-out himself.

He stared at the name on the computer screen. "Who the hell are you? And who's protecting you?"

There had been other times when such lock-outs were used. The basic ones covered Stony Man personnel records. Only he and Price had access to the passwords that would bypass the security programming. Other times he'd been assigned projects from DARPA—Defense

Advanced Research Projects Agency—and the other scientific or Intelligence organizations requiring his input. At those times he'd operated under eyes-only, need-to-know, and no one at the Farm had known what it was he worked on. Price had been aware of those instances, of course. There wasn't much the lady wasn't aware of. But she hadn't known the particulars unless the covert teams had been needed.

As an exploratory move, he entered all the passwords he and Price normally used.

None of them worked.

Given that it wasn't Price or himself, it meant someone else had figured out a way into the Stony computers. And it had to be someone close to the inside of the whole operation. Someone who was gifted enough with technical ability to break into the security program and alter it.

He didn't like the way his thoughts were headed. All of his people were handpicked. Not necessarily by him, but anyone Price or Brognola had brought on board he'd always considered above reproach. Now that necessitated rethinking.

Leaving the cursor flashing after the results of his search, he rolled the wheelchair across the room and got a fresh cup of coffee. He was wondering how best to present his discovery to Price when he saw her leave her office and walk toward him.

"Problem?" she asked as she reached for a container of orange juice.

"A big one."

"What?"

"Look at this." He pushed his way back to the computer monitor and showed her the results.

Something cold and hard flashed in Price's eyes.

Kurtzman figured most people would have missed the change, but he didn't. He'd worked with her too closely for too long not to know her well.

Her voice when she spoke sounded like business as usual. "Where did you get that name?"

"Katz called it in. They turned it up at their last strike."

"What else did they find at the hardsite?"

"Computer files. It looks like we may have a key to some of the banking done by the Iraqis."

"Concentrate on that," Price advised.

"What about this?"

"Leave it."

"Leave it?" Kurtzman twisted in his chair to look at the mission controller. "This means that somebody's broken into our computer systems. Unless I attempt to break through the lock-out, we won't know how much this operation has been compromised."

"I know that. I also know that if you attack the lock-out, we lose the cybernetic systems here."

"Maybe not for long."

She returned his gaze full-measure. "But maybe too long. We can't take the chance. This operation has been spread out across the globe from the beginning. Things are coming to a head, and we need the capabilities this system provides."

"There's no telling how much leaving that lock-out alone could cost us."

"It's a calculated risk."

Kurtzman let out a deep breath. Deciding risks was Price's job as mission controller, and this one—despite involving his computer systems—fell under her jurisdiction.

"With that lock-out in place," Price said in a softer voice, "it also means whoever put it there can't do anything further without shutting the system down."

"They can shut the system down at a time that's critical to us."

"Maybe. That's part of the risk we're taking. Until then, rerun your security programs and make sure our integrity is preserved here as much as possible."

Kurtzman nodded. "There's something else you have to think about."

"What?"

"The person who put the lock-out into the system could be one of us."

Price didn't bat an eye. "All we can do at this moment is hope that isn't true."

"Yeah."

"I need something."

"What?"

"Don't we have access to a satellite somewhere over Bolivia?"

Kurtzman punched up the request on the keyboard and received a confirmation. "I've got an Oscar on-line."

Price shook her head. "That's for shortwave radio operators. Isn't there something with video capabilities?"

"There's a German military satellite in orbit there that will give us—" Kurtzman stroked the keyboard "—about fifteen minutes' worth of viewing time. What did you want to look at?"

"The airport in La Paz. Striker should be arriving soon."

"Do you want radio communications, too?"

"After they're in the air. Have you got an update on their transport links and Rivera's progress?"

"Yeah."

"I'll need that, too."

Kurtzman passed over hard copy on both subjects, then turned back to the keyboard. He didn't say anything further, and he noticed that Price didn't bother to break the uncomfortable silence that had sprung up between them. In all the years of their association, he'd never had reason to doubt her judgment. Now he was to the point of questioning his blind faith in her. As a mission controller, she'd been exemplary. Price had put together some tough operations and had the iron nerve to stick them out without backing off.

He made the connection with the Stony Man Farm satellite in geosynchronous orbit over Virginia, then bounced a signal off the satellite relay system he had access to till he found the German military satellite. The programming blended easily as he tapped into the flow of information. "It's coming up on the center wall screen." He glanced toward the far end of the room.

The world map that had been depicted there vanished like fog lifting from a lake surface. The picture that replaced it was grainy and distorted, with static ripples skating across it like tidal waves. Most of the color was washed out of the scene. Although the satellite was thousands of miles out in space, the view appeared to be from a distance of less than a mile. Runways and hangars were scattered about the La Paz airport in organized blocks.

"Can't we enhance the reception?" Price asked.

"Not without letting the owners of the satellite know we've accessed some of their channels. This is the best you're going to get and remain anonymous. And if we tip our hand, they may suspend transmissions and cut us entirely out of the loop till they figure out what's going on."

"Okay. Can you get in closer? Southeastern sector. Striker's being accompanied by a DEA task force till he's on the plane."

Kurtzman stroked the keyboard and started bringing the focus in more sharply. "Was the escort your idea?"

"Theirs. I bought some goodwill, but I had to force the issue. The section chief thought it was in his best interests to make sure Striker made his flight."

"The phrase 'ridden out of town on a rail' comes to mind."

A ghost of a smile touched Price's lips, but the tension remained evident.

On the wall screen the image lost another degree of sharpness as it zoomed in for a closer scan. The entrance gates in the southeast sector were guarded by military personnel.

Kurtzman checked the digital readout at the bottom of the monitor in front of him. Eleven minutes and forty-three seconds remained of the satellite window they had access to. "You're sure about Striker's arrival time?"

"Yes."

He looked at her. Though they'd been through some incredibly tense moments together in the computer room, he couldn't help feeling this was somehow different. She didn't look back at him despite his certainty that she was aware of his interest. She sipped the orange juice and kept focused on the wall screen.

"There," she said.

Back on the wall screen a dark blue limousine with diplomatic flags on both fenders cruised to a stop at the gates. A rifle-toting soldier marched up to the driver's side of the vehicle.

Kurtzman hit the keys and tightened the view still further, leaving a generous radius around the limousine. Papers were shown to the guard, studied, then handed back. The guard stepped away from the limo and waved it through. The gates jerked mechanically and rolled to the sides out of the way. The limo moved forward smoothly.

The digital readout showed eight minutes and twelve seconds remaining.

"Where's the plane?" Kurtzman asked.

"Runway twenty-two."

Kurtzman looked. A sleek Lear waited there with a flight crew tricked out in orange jumpsuits. He felt the tension radiating through the mission controller, and it fed his own feelings of unease.

Before the limo was halfway to its destination, a paneled green station wagon surged into motion and streaked for the embassy vehicle. The hard snouts of automatic weapons jutted through the windows. Even though there was no audio on the satellite linkup, Kurtzman could tell from the way the weapons jumped and jerked that the gunners had just opened fire.

"FLOOR IT!" Mack Bolan ordered as spiderweb fractures appeared in the bulletproof glass of the limousine.

The driver reacted immediately and pressed his foot hard on the accelerator. The supercharged engine responded immediately, and the vehicle's occupants were thrown back against their seats.

Autofire drummed like heavy thunder against the reinforced body, but nothing penetrated.

Bolan reached under his bomber jacket for the Desert Eagle .44 Magnum. He had taken the passenger seat to avoid the DEA SAC who had been ordered by the Bolivian section chief to accompany them to the airport. Special Agent in Charge Rick Means was a by-the-book operative who made no secret of the way he felt about the people he was escorting out of the country. But he was cunning, as well. During the thinly disguised abuse he was heaping on Gallardo, Bolan and Grimaldi regarding flagrant misuse of American authority on foreign shores, he was constantly sifting through whatever information turned up in the conversations. Grimaldi and Bolan had caught on quickly and stopped speaking. Gallardo hadn't been far behind.

"What the hell?" Means shouted.

"Jack," Bolan called out. "Two o'clock."

"I see them, Sarge."

Bolan watched as the paneled station wagon fell behind and locked on to their backtrail as the limo driver took evasive action. A quick head count revealed at least six men in the station wagon.

"What the hell do they think they're doing?" Means asked as he turned around in the back seat. "This is an embassy vehicle. They can't fire on us."

A bullet clipped one of the miniature American flags from the rear fenders. The flag disappeared in a peppermint flash.

"Take evasive action," Bolan told the driver. "Let's see if we can gain some breathing room."

The man nodded and abruptly cut the wheel. He was good with the car. The limo skidded when he lightly touched the brake then applied the accelerator again. Obediently the vehicle skewed around an idling Cessna twin prop, then lunged forward again, speeding through a pedestrians-only crossing area.

Grimaldi had unleathered one of the MAC-10s they'd brought with them. The flight plan was for them to pick up a military plane arranged through a Brazilian naval station in Belem and make the jump to Europe from there. They'd be parting company with Gallardo there. Price had a team of Stony Man blacksuits waiting to debrief him and turn him over to the DEA.

Bolan rested his off hand on the electric window button but didn't press it. The bulletproof glass that was protecting them also kept them from offering return fire. For the moment preserving the integrity of the limo seemed to be the optimum choice. He pulled the ear-throat headset from his pocket, slipped it into place and switched it on. "Falcon, this is Stony One."

"Go, Stony One. Falcon copies."

"We're coming in hot."

"Roger. I spotted you guys at the gate. So far, I'm clear."

"The takeoff's going to be immediate. With or without clearance."

"Roger."

Bolan cleared the frequency, watching over his shoulder as the pursuit vehicle came into view.

The driver of the station wagon wasn't as skilled as the limo chauffeur. The long car skidded around the abrupt corner awkwardly, like a duck trying to land on a frozen pond, and slid under the starboard prop. The whirling propeller slammed into the roof of the station wagon and shattered. Dozens of deadly bits of metal sailed in all directions as the blades fragmented. Scars appeared along the roof of the station wagon, and in a couple places it looked as if the blades had sliced through.

"Shit," the limo driver said through clenched teeth. "They've got another vehicle on us."

Bolan turned around as the chauffeur jerked the wheel to the right. He kept his balance by grabbing for the overhead roof support.

A white van with courier service markings in English and Spanish came to a sliding, sideways stop in front of them, blocking the corridor they'd been traveling.

The limo driver put his foot lightly on the brake and began slowing.

Bolan kicked his leg over and tromped down hard on the accelerator. "Go through them. If they get us boxed in, they'll cut us to pieces with cross fire."

The driver nodded.

Forty feet away and closing, the first of the passengers in the van disembarked.

Bolan noted the dark features, burned bronze by a desert sun rather than a tropical one.

"Arabs," Grimaldi said.

"Yeah." Bolan shelved the thoughts the Arabs' presence brought to mind and concentrated on strategies for survival.

"I guess this means Miguel's information about Canary was pretty much dead-on," Gallardo said dryly.

According to the free-lance pilot's sources, Canary was an Israeli double agent working for the terrorist groups out of Iraq and Jordan. Despite the surface strikes against the Nazis and the Bolivian drug cartels, Canary had remained enough out of the limelight to assure secrecy. But the agent had tapped into Intelligence sources used by the black-market information brokers. No mention had been made about who the agent was, but the money had flowed freely as information concerning the strikes made by the Executioner and the Nazi and Bolivian responses was gathered.

Three Arabs were on the tarmac now. Automatic weapons chopped fresh streamers of bullets across the limousine from two of them. The third man held a long tube and was settling it over his shoulder.

"That's a LAW!" Means shouted, pointed at the third Arab.

"Hit the rear of the van," Bolan ordered. "There's less weight. It'll give."

"Right," the driver replied. He took a fresh grip on the steering wheel.

Bolan pressed the window button and rolled it down in a smooth electric glide. Settling the butt of the big Israeli pistol in his empty palm, he slipped into sniper mode. He aimed for the center of his target, visualizing the 10-ring in his mind and overlaying it on the LAW-equipped terrorist. He managed two shots before the limousine slammed into the van. There was a brief impression of the man spinning away before the first collisions of the wreck claimed the warrior's full attention.

The limo plowed into the van and shouldered it aside. The luxury car shuddered from the initial impact and tilted back in the same manner as a sailboat cresting an approaching wave. Metal sheared away, and the screeches echoed between the rows of parked planes, audible even through the limo's soundproofing. The windshield glazed over to the point of becoming opaque. Figures on the other side of the glass were blurred and indistinct.

Held in place by the seat belt, Bolan glanced through the back glass.

The van rocked unsteadily on its wheels and was slammed again as the smaller station wagon surged around it in pursuit.

The limo driver touched the brake and started to drift around a sharp corner.

At the front of the van, Bolan saw the LAW settle onto the terrorist's shoulder again. The man moved with a limp, and two ragged tears showed on his chest, giving proof of the Executioner's marksmanship, as well as the Kevlar vest underneath.

"They've got body armor on," Bolan said.

Grimaldi gave him a tight nod. "I'll keep that in mind."

The LAW jerked. An instant later a whirling fireball enveloped the limo's right rear tire. Adding to the centrifugal force already generated by the turn, the explosion flipped the limousine over through the air in a barrel roll.

Bolan was battered and bruised as the limo flipped. The heavy car made one and a half revolutions, flattened a green-and-white Piper Cub and came to an awkward rest on its top. Already in motion, knowing the terrorists wouldn't relax their efforts, the warrior hit the seat-belt release and clambered through the open window. It was difficult. The impact had lowered the roof almost six inches despite the structural reinforcements. He didn't have time to check on the others.

The station wagon screamed to a tire-shredding stop almost thirty feet away, partially blocked by the remains of the Piper Cub and the two twin props on either side. Five men stepped out at once, leaving the driver at the wheel.

Warning Klaxons shrilled through the air, mixing with the sound of roaring jet engines idling up to takeoff speed. Halfway across the airport, two military jeeps were in motion, closing in on the battle zone with flashing yellow lights.

Bolan threw himself in a rolling dive toward the landing gear of the nearest twin prop, bullets chopping the tarmac behind him. He came to a halt in a crouch behind one of the airplane's tires. The Desert Eagle came up in a full extension with the elbow relaxed.

A terrorist carrying a AK-47 scrambled up over the wreckage of the Piper Cub, screaming invective in Arabic.

Tracking the man, Bolan squeezed off a single round.

The 240-grain boattail caught the man in the chin and halted his forward movement at once. His legs went out before him as if he'd been clotheslined. The assault rifle spilled down the wrecked plane and skittered across the tarmac.

Another terrorist came around to the right with an Uzi stuttering fire.

The tire in front of Bolan came apart, and sparks jumped from the metal rim. The airplane sagged on its side, suddenly providing a lower ceiling and a little more protective shelter. The Executioner fired as the terrorist gunner set himself and inserted a fresh clip. The .44 round punched through the Arab's forehead and knocked the man down.

Breaking cover, Bolan ran for the dropped AK-47. A sweeping glance showed him that Grimaldi was scrambling free of the wrecked limo, and that a third terrorist had cleared the other side of the Piper Cub and was taking notice of him.

The assault rifle in the Arab's hands came around blazing.

The Executioner dived toward the loose AK-47, sliding forward on his stomach. The rough tarmac abraded his skin. Firing from the prone position and rolling sideways toward the assault rifle, Bolan emptied the remaining four rounds from the Desert Eagle's clip. All of them struck the terrorist in the chest. Although the bullets didn't penetrate the bulletproof vest, they knocked the man from his feet. By the time the Arab shoved himself back into an offensive position, the Executioner was bringing the AK-47 to his shoulder. He aimed through the open sights and squeezed the trigger.

The 7.62 mm round slammed into the Arab's face just beneath his nose. The nearly decapitated corpse jerked backward and tumbled to the ground.

Bolan scanned the area for the remaining two men but didn't find them. After feeding a fresh clip into the .44, he removed two spare magazines for the Russian assault rifle from the dead man beside him. The magazine in the AK only had three rounds left. He ditched it and shoved in one of the full ones.

Grimaldi was jockeying for position behind other planes, swinging out wide to give them a potential crossfire area.

Bolan thumbed the headset transmitter. "Jack."

"Go."

"How are the others?"

"Mobile. That's the best I can answer."

Sirens screamed as they neared the combat zone, and the sound of shrieking rubber echoed out over the tarmac.

Pushing himself to his feet, Bolan ran toward a grounded de Havilland amphibious plane. Staccato bursts of gunfire rattled over the immediate area as the terrorists turned to engage the arriving military forces. The warrior leapt to the high wing and leaned across the fuselage. The AK-47 settled comfortably in his hands as he switched it from fully automatic to semiautomatic.

The Bolivian army personnel set up a perimeter around the fire zone and exchanged shots with the surviving terrorists from the station wagon. Six more Arabs had disembarked from the parked van sixty yards away. One of them set himself with another LAW, then fired at the nearest military jeep.

The 94 mm warhead struck the front of the jeep and turned it into a spitting fireball that yawed wide, then slammed back down onto the tarmac at least two yards from where it had been. The Bolivian soldiers had scattered and seemed to have escaped the brunt of the blast.

From his position on the de Havilland, Bolan had a full sweep of the entrenched terrorists. He brought the assault rifle to his shoulder, marked the chosen succession of shots in his mind, then started in on his left, letting the recoil drag him back naturally to his right. The first 7.62 mm round caught the rocket-launcher operator in the back of the head as he was shouldering another deadly tube. The second terrorist went down with a bullet through the temple, a half inch above the buttstock of his weapon. Moving with the recoil, the Executioner found the third man turning to yell at his comrades, pointing wildly at the amphibious plane. The warrior stroked the trigger and put a bullet through the man's open mouth, ripping the spinal cord out through the back of the dead man's neck.

Number four came whirling around with his Uzi blazing fire. Bolan squeezed the trigger, checking his progression for only a heartbeat to ensure the hit. The round took the man in the eye and spilled him backward. The fifth man went down unexpectedly, dropped by one of the military sharpshooters. The sixth man's AK-47 was chewing holes in the de Havilland's fuselage when Bolan terminated him.

Evidently choosing discretion over valor, the seventh man attempted to hurl himself over the station wagon to relative safety.

Reacting on the fly, Bolan shot the man between the shoulder blades. He knew the round wouldn't penetrate the Kevlar armor underneath, but it threw the man off balance and past his intended destination into the open. Before the terrorist could regroup, the Executioner hammered home a following round into the man's skull.

The two remaining men on the ground were finished before he could make a move against them. The Bolivian militia hadn't wasted time taking the initiative once it was presented. Jeeps streaked free of the line and blocked the van and the station wagon.

Knowing he'd done all he'd set out to do to prevent any more bloodshed, Bolan slid down the de Havilland and dropped to the ground. Scattered small-arms fire rang out behind him, and he knew the terrorists wouldn't survive to make a jury trial. He tapped the transmit button on the headset. "Jack. Ernie."

"Go," Grimaldi replied.

"Go." Gallardo sounded shaky.

"Strategic withdrawal. Do it now."

"Roger."

"On my way."

A bullhorn cut through the din of the blaring sirens of the rescue vehicles arriving on the scene. "Means!" an authoritative voice commanded in Spanish. "You and your people are to remain here! You do not have clearance to leave!"

Bolan found Means struggling free of the limo's wreckage. The DEA man was bleeding profusely from a cut over his left eye. The chauffeur was at the front of the vehicle with a government-issue .45 in both fists.

Means put a handkerchief to his forehead and noticed Bolan. "Get the hell out of here. I'll take care of the locals. They can't stop you anyway with diplomatic coverage, but they can detain you." He swabbed at his face again. "Stupid bastards should have had better security today. They aren't getting shit from me in the way of cooperation after this."

Bolan went. He streaked through the maze of planes till he found the Lear they'd been assigned. Grimaldi was already scrambling aboard, and Gallardo was limping along close behind. The orders spouting from the bullhorn were urging the Bolivian soldiers to seize the Americans before they could leave.

Running up the steps behind the DEA agent, Bolan grabbed the door and slammed it home. As he dogged the locks, he yelled to the pilot, "Get us airborne!"

The Lear surged forward.

Gallardo stumbled against the seats and dropped heavily into place.

Bolan went forward against the g-forces trying to drive him backward. Grimaldi was buckling himself into the copilot seat when the warrior reached the cabin. The pilot was a young blond guy with a military crew cut. He handled the controls efficiently.

The private jet sped along the tarmac. On the port side two jeeps with military markings took up pursuit. Autofire crackled but nothing touched the Lear.

"They're not shooting at us," Bolan said.

The pilot gave a tight nod. "They're shutting down the airport."

"Find a runway," Grimaldi said. "If you can't do that, then make one."

"Yes, sir." He worked the controls, and the Lear heeled sharply to the right.

The runways were covered with stalled planes.

"There," Grimaldi said, pointing.

The pilot didn't hesitate. The jet thrust increased dramatically as it kicked in the afterburners, reminding Bolan of the times he'd scrambled with Grimaldi from the decks of aircraft carriers on a catapult launch. An army jeep swerved out in front of the jet.

"You've got the lift," Grimaldi said calmly. "Just ease back and get us up."

"The Lear climbed into the air reluctantly, missing the jeep by only a few feet. The soldiers seated in it ducked or dived from the vehicle.

"Life around you guys always seems to be one big party," Gallardo said.

Bolan looked over his shoulder and saw the DEA agent weaving unsteadily. Blood leaked from between Gallardo's fingers as he held his side.

"You okay?" Bolan asked.

"In and out," Gallardo said with a faint smile, "but I won't be able to wear a bikini-cut bathing suit to the beach anymore."

Grimaldi passed a first-aid kit back to Bolan.

"We were set up," Gallardo said as he sat down in one of the chairs in the back. "That double agent Miguel was telling us about must really be a sharp operator."

Bolan remained silent, turning the thought over in his mind as he worked on bandaging the man with experienced fingers. Sergeant Mercy had logged plenty of time tending to the wounded he'd encountered in Vietnam. If Canary had been the one to tip the Arabs off about the airport raid, it meant the double agent had access to American espionage agencies. How far that access went was impossible to guess at now.

"Jack," Bolan called out.

"Yo."

"As soon as you're able, get me a comlink to Stony Base."

"Minutes away, buddy."

"Good."

"THEY MADE IT." Kurtzman breathed a sigh of relief.

At the opposite end of the room, the wall screen blanked out for a moment and was replaced by a radar view of the area. A yellow blip pulsed brightly as it took a northeasterly bearing.

"Find out how things turned out with the Bolivian military personnel," Price said, "then give me a report on their casualties."

"Okay."

"And contact Means to see if we can arrange any interview time with the surviving terrorists."

Kurtzman nodded. Broken glass grated behind him. When he turned to look, he saw the orange-juice container in the mission controller's hand had shattered. "Are you all right?"

She took out a wastepaper basket tucked under his desk and let the debris tumble from her hand. Chunks of broken glass held together by the paper label and drops of juice spattered the papers already in the container. "Yeah. I'm fine."

Her composure was just as calm and cool as ever. Kurtzman let it pass, deciding questioning her assessment of her own feelings would be unwise. There was no blood on her hand.

She crossed the room and washed her hands in the small sink by the coffeepot.

"Ms. Price," Wethers called out.

"Yes."

"There's an incoming communication from Stony One."

"I'll take it. Switch him over." Price took one of the headsets on Kurtzman's desk and plugged into the radio. "Stony One, you have Stony Base. Over."

Kurtzman busied himself with assessing the communications bands used by the Bolivian army, then turned the monitoring assignment over to Akira Tokaido. The young man knew enough of the language to manage.

"We were set up at the airport," Bolan said.

"Acknowledged. Stony Base was monitoring your activities. How may we help you at this point? Over."

If Bolan was surprised, his voice didn't register it. "Information we've gathered at this point suggests that an Israeli double agent code-named Canary was the one who set us up. Over."

"Understood. Where did you get that information? Over."

Bolan outlined the Intel he'd received from the pilot Gallardo had set them up with near Oruro.

"Acknowledged, Stony One. We'll do the necessary footwork here and get you a dossier as soon as we can. Are you clear on the next steps of your present mission? Over."

"We'll be rendezvousing with Phoenix at a site TBA later. Over."

"Roger. Your transport has been arranged. You'll be arriving in-country only a few hours after your quarry. Is there anything else Stony Base can do for you? Over."

"No. Over."

"Then Godspeed, gentlemen, and use the downtime to rest up. I don't know for sure what you'll be facing once you touch down. Stony Base out."

Bolan cleared the frequency, too.

"Barbara," Tokaido called.

"Yes."

"I've got the information on Bolivian military casualties."

"And?"

"Zero. Two men were lightly wounded during a rocket attack."

"What about the terrorists?"

"They're all dead. No prisoners were taken, and none were presumed to have escaped."

Price nodded.

Kurtzman turned his chair around to face Price. "Barb, what are we going to do with the Canary investigation?"

"There's nothing we can do," she replied. "I need you and your team operational. Let it lie for now." She flexed her hand, staring at the palm. "Lucky."

"Yeah," Kurtzman growled.

If she noticed any of the displeasure in his voice, she didn't respond to it. She took a moment to get another orange-juice bottle from the iced bins, then returned to her office.

Kurtzman pulled up the Canary file again and stared at the code that blocked his access to it. There were options to his investigations, and Price knew it. He could call in a favor from a fellow hacker who had a high security clearance and get him to run the chase on Canary. The problem was, no one had security clearance for the Stony Man Farm operation, and most of the people he knew in the hacking field were curious about systems. Using that option could result in a lot more problems they couldn't put a lid on.

He glanced at Price, who had already lifted one of the phones in her office. He ran a diagnostic to trace the phone communication but got bounced out of the communications web. Evidently Price had erected her own barriers on what she was doing. He didn't know if that was new SOP or not. He'd never tried tracing one of her calls before. But then he hadn't had to. Usually he was part of every move she made.

Price was a games player. He knew that. She was one of the best, which was why Brognola had recruited her. But sometimes a gamer had to decide which pieces to forfeit to achieve a necessary win.

It was a dark thought, and one he couldn't entirely shove from his mind as he turned back to the tasks left at hand.

CHAPTER FIVE

"How many dead warriors must Israel suffer before the Americans acknowledge that our country is under attack?" Dr. Enoch Harel roared at the crowd gathered at the Yad Vashem shrine in Jerusalem. "We could lay their corpses out in this hot sun, and still the state diplomats would deny that we are at war!"

Desiree St. Cyr watched the man as he spoke from the flatbed of a large truck parked to face his audience. A yellow-pine stage, striped with black banners and ribbons, had been built on the truck. Israeli flags flew from the corner posts.

Harel was a huge man, standing at least six and a half feet tall, with shoulders almost as broad as an ax handle. St. Cyr was used to thinking in visual terms. Before she'd landed the television career, she'd worked in radio advertising and newscasting, which had given her a strong voice and a long list of similes and hyperboles.

The Israeli entrepreneur's carefully coiffed hair took into account his receding hairline and defined it enough to give him a bold, distinguished look and deny his forty-plus years. His face was hard and lined and—St. Cyr had discovered—was loved by cameras. Harel looked, St. Cyr thought, primeval and explosive, like a man who'd get the things done that he believed in even if he had to do them himself.

Despite her attempt at objectivity, she found herself passionately drawn toward her subject.

"Or maybe," Harel continued, "we should stack the bodies of the slain like cordwood. At least that way, in time we might build a wall to slow down the forces who have been lying like starving wolves outside our borders since 1948. But that would do nothing about the vultures who are already camped within those borders."

A thunderous cheer rolled through the audience, and more than a few weapons were openly brandished despite the presence of uniformed Israeli soldiers standing guard along the perimeters.

St. Cyr had realized some time ago that if this had been a Muslim demonstration, the Israeli military would have already waded in and broken it up. She leaned in close to Andy Marshak, her cameraman. "Don't stay strictly with close-ups of Harel. Pan the camera around over the audience. What he says here today isn't going to be nearly as important as how the people react to it."

"You got it."

St. Cyr fished a miniature walkie-talkie from her handbag and pressed the Talk button. "Buddy."

"Yeah."

"How's the audio pickup?"

"Fine."

"The audience response isn't interfering with it?"

"Some. But I can wash it out later. Trust me."

St. Cyr put the radio back in her handbag. Running dual coverage, the second being an audio backup only, was her idea. Cameras were expensive, and her producer hadn't managed to get more crew or equipment into the area yet. And if Marshak's camera was broken, she didn't want to turn in a story without at least sound bites to back up stock footage.

"We're at war!" Harel shouted. "And the American government would deny us the right to bear arms to defend ourselves. They tell us everything is being taken care of, that no further harm will befall the Jewish people living here on this sacred soil.'' He paused as the audience hung on his words. ''They lie. They act like the changes that are sweeping across this world of ours aren't threatening this country's existence. With a Communist Russia out of the picture, the Americans are more lenient about what other nations of the Middle East do to us. Before, we were a necessary base of operations in the Cold War. We were cared for. And we were supported. Now it appears that we have been discarded.''

The crowd reacted with wild cheers and thunderous clapping.

St. Cyr knew Harel was something of a showman. Politics didn't work without a sense of the theatrical these days. And the Israeli entrepreneur had chosen his location wisely. Although off the main drag of Jerusalem, Yad Vashem was a shrine commemorating the millions of Jews who had died during the Holocaust in German concentration camps.

''The Iraqi viper remains in place,'' Harel said. ''We were promised peace if we stayed out of the Gulf War. Instead, all the Americans and their vaunted allies did was blunt the bully's toys. And they never bothered to recognize the Jordanian threat at all. We live—as we always have—in the shadow of sheathed aggressions and naked jealousies. If we are to grow and take our rightful place among successful nations, we must deal with our enemies once and for all. We won't bend or cower before our enemies. We never have.'' Harel raised his arms triumphantly. ''Masada shall not fall again!''

Yelled cheers swelled into a crescendo that filled the area in front of the museum and library in front of the shrine.

"You know who this guy reminds me of?" Marshak asked.

"No," St. Cyr replied.

"JFK." Marshak grinned ruefully as he panned the camera over the enthusiastic crowd. "Don't ask me why, but he does."

"It's the charisma. And the fact that he is obviously setting himself up as a target."

"Oh, yeah. Harel's an accident waiting to happen."

Without warning, the sputtering pop of a small engine wound too tightly filled the street. Heads turned to track the noise.

A yellow Volkswagen bug made the corner at the end of the street. Red rust areas and dark age spots marred the faded paint. The passenger side of the windshield was cracked and scarred over, but it didn't mask the two people inside. An Uzi appeared in the open side window and opened fire on full-auto.

After years of living in a war-torn environment, the native Israelis scattered quickly, leaving a passage to the flatbed truck like the parting of the Red Sea. A few of the people went down as bullets found them, but relatives and friends pulled them to safety.

The journalists and newspeople were the slowest to react. One of the ABC cameramen was caught almost flat-footed by the speeding car. The sound of the impact was a dull, flat thump, then the man's body arced up, smashed onto the roof of the Volkswagen and rolled off.

St. Cyr was nearly buried by the sudden onslaught of people shoving their way past her. She fought to stand her ground, out of the way of the racing car. "Andy!"

"Yeah."

She saw the cameraman to her right with the camera held to his shoulder. "Tell me you're getting this!"

"I am! I am!"

Security men dressed in plainclothes deployed instantly to intercept the Volkswagen. Several of them were brandishing machine pistols but had a hard time using them because of the crowd.

A woman grabbed St. Cyr by the hair in her struggle to get by the reporter. St. Cyr brushed the woman's hands from her, ignoring the pain and focusing on the car instead.

The Uzi had run dry, and the passenger was in the process of shoving a fresh clip into the machine gun when the car blew by St. Cyr's position.

Two men had leapt on top of the flatbed and were hustling Harel toward the side.

Because of her compact size and lack of body mass, St. Cyr had trouble working her way to the street side of the crowd despite everyone else's attempts to flee the other way. For a moment she was carried along by the human tide, then she broke free and found Marshak standing straight and tall at her side, filming automatically.

The Volkswagen careered madly against the curbing for an instant, then swooped toward the flatbed. The explosion came immediately. Swirling flames wrapped themselves over the small car and the flatbed. The truck buckled a moment later as the fire reached the saddle-mounted gasoline tanks and they erupted.

A heat wave rolled over St. Cyr with real physical presence. She put up an arm to shield her face and tried to blink the blinding spots from her eyes. Flaming debris came down in scattered chunks across the street and the crowd. She touched Marshak's arm and shouted to be heard. "Harel?"

"Christ, I don't know. I think they got him off in time."

A quick backward glance let St. Cyr know the other reporters were regrouping and going for the story. Another ABC man was helping the cameraman to his feet with the aid of some concerned citizens. She took the walkie-talkie out of her purse. "Buddy."

"Yeah."

"Did you see if Harel made it?"

"Yeah."

She couldn't spot the audio man.

"A couple of his people got him out of there."

"He was okay?"

"He appeared to be."

St. Cyr closed in on the scene. A wall of fire ran across the street. Perspiration covered her features and exposed skin from the residual heat. Then something was moving in the flames.

A vehicle took shape in the fire, looking dark in the twisting flames, growing darker and bigger as it slid on through them. St. Cyr recognized it as Harel's personal limousine. The dark burgundy color was coated with soot as it rolled through the blaze, and pools of fire clung to it while the driver pulled out onto the street. No one was visible through the polarized glass.

"Jesus," Marshak said as he continued filming the limo's passage, "what a shot. That's one of those scenes the whole world's going to be viewing for the next few days."

"I know," St. Cyr replied, "and we got our copy of it." She glanced at the burning wreckage and saw security people working on the flames with fire extinguishers. The white, powdery smoke hissed out with a sound like asthmatic snakes. The driver's body was visible through the window, already charred and black, with flames still clinging to it. She took in all the sensory input and began turning it into words, wondering if there was any way to get an interview with Harel.

SEATED IN THE BACK of the limousine as it sped back toward the house he'd bought months ago in Jerusalem, Dr. Enoch Harel wiped at the soot staining his features. "God, but that was close."

"I warned you against this," Benjamin Wellsberg said in thinly disguised reproach. "Even knowing the Jordanians were going to make the attempt, even with the transmitter on their bumper and our people tracking their every move, you could have had your ass blown off back there." The security chief was something under six feet, with a compact shortstop's build and dark eyes that never stopped moving. He looked like a businessman, and the extensive bald spot on his skull gave people the impression he was capable of long periods of intense concentration. Years ago, while still working with the Mossad, he'd learned to take advantage of every misconception other people made of him.

"But that didn't happen," Harel said. Looking at the dour scowl on Wellsberg's face, he couldn't keep a broad smile from twisting his lips. "You worry too much."

"And you don't worry enough."

"Worrying is relative. If things weren't being accomplished, then I'd be worried."

"And if you were dead?"

"Then there'd be nothing to worry about, now, would there?"

"Dammit, Enoch. This isn't just your little campaign. There are several others of us who have invested our time and our wealth into this effort. We knew we had to have a figurehead for this, and no one was better suited for the job."

"Except that you think I'm being careless."

Wellsberg met his glance evenly. "Yes."

Harel felt the brief spark of anger ignite within him but repressed it. "You think I'm taking these chances to satisfy some lust within myself."

"You're an adrenaline junkie."

"You think so."

"I've seen you in action over the years. Money means nothing to you except as a means of getting in to play some of the more dangerous games."

"That's not true."

"It is."

Harel contained himself and reached into the wet bar mounted along the back of the seat before him. He poured himself a glass of chilled Chablis from the small refrigerator and raised an inquisitive eyebrow at his companion.

Wellsberg shook his head.

"We are brokering for incredible stakes against long odds," Harel said as he settled himself back into the seat. He sipped the wine and found it dry and delicious. His appetites and tastes had always been sharper and more demanding than those of most people he'd met.

"I know."

"Yes," Harel agreed, "you do know. So do the other people you represent. However, you're all getting to be like old mother hens. If you're expecting a big jackpot, you can't just start pensioning off your investments."

Wellsberg suddenly looked tired.

The limousine continued rolling smoothly through the city. Three vehicles Harel identified as rentals assigned to visiting press crews were trying to keep up with the luxury car.

"We're only wanting to be prudent."

"Prudent men don't often walk away winners. Not big winners anyway. And that's what our aim here is—for this country to emerge with a large victory. The largest, in fact, since 1948."

Wellsberg took a compact radio transmitter out of his pocket and started to switch it on.

"What are you doing?"

"I'm going to notify the blocker cars and have them cut those reporters off our trail."

"No," Harel commanded.

Wellsberg looked at him.

"Ben," Harel said softly, "those reporters are some of the best friends we have right now. Don't alienate them."

"I'm trying to protect you. That's my job."

"And winning their favor and confidence is mine."

"Surely they would understand the necessity."

"Yes. But it could also make them suspicious. Reporters are naturally an inquisitive lot. I've also found that their trust index is somewhat on the same level as espionage agents. Their position on everything is to believe they are being lied to on some level. A large portion of their job is to figure out the division between truth and falsehood."

Reluctantly Wellsberg put the radio away.

Harel sipped more wine. "Risky as you believe things were back there, the film footage of the assassination attempt—especially in light of how destructive it was—is pure platinum. We could not have manufactured something that would have so quickly focused the attention of the world on what we're trying to say here. Believe me, that attack represents a major coup for us."

"Perhaps. But you didn't have to enjoy it so much."

Harel laughed, and the noise was loud and vibrant. Wellsberg smiled in spite of himself. "We each have to test the brevity of life in our own way. Your days as a covert op in Iraq and Iran were probably fraught with more peril than you've seen me face."

"I was only a small cog in a big wheel. I could easily be replaced. I myself replaced a number of others."

"You're starting to believe the press we're putting out regarding my involvement."

"We would not be as far into this thing as we are without you."

"True. You also don't have the contacts I have in the rest of the Middle East and Germany. But that could have been arranged in time even without me."

Wellsberg curled his fingers into a fist. "We're so close to achieving what we want."

Harel nodded.

"It's maddening to think that although we are so close, we're also at the same time so close to losing everything."

"That's why this is a necessary gamble. For the moment things appear to be breaking in our favor. To start acting hesitant now would push the scales back the other way."

"Maybe."

"It would. Only truly desperate men ever really live up to their potential or live life to its fullest."

"So you've so often told me."

"It's true." Harel drained the wineglass and set it aside. "Has Canary reported in?"

"Yes. The attack on the American covert force in Bolivia was negated before they took any damage."

"And we still don't know who these people are?"

"No."

"You've worked with American Intelligence before. Haven't you got some idea of who they might be?"

"They're not DEA or CIA. Both of those agencies are scrambling themselves trying to find out who's behind the action in the Americas and Europe."

"What about the National Security Agency?"

Wellsberg's surprise showed in his face.

Harel was pleased.

"Not many people remember the NSA," Wellsberg said.

"Some of the companies I invested in over the years were funded by DARPA contracts." DARPA was a major mover and shaker buying into the cutting edge of technology, though usually buried behind layers of red tape. DARPA was also under NSA's bureaucratic thumb, so Harel had put effort into learning about them, as well. Money had been ventured in a number of investments, and the returns were still coming in from some of them.

"It's hard to say with NSA," Wellsberg said. "I doubt if any one person in that agency truly knows everything that goes on under their umbrella."

"Wasn't Canary affiliated with them for a time?"

"Yes. But only as a double agent for us. Not much information actually trickled out into our hands, but we knew about the Japanese manufacturing submarine screws for the Americans and the Russians before the news became widespread in the United States."

"Can't Canary check into NSA?"

"Unfortunately that avenue is no longer open to us."

"Where are the American forces headed now?"

"Switzerland."

"They're still tracking the Arabs and Germans?"

"Yes."

"With no hint of what is really at stake here?"

"Not as far as we can tell."

"And what does Canary say?"

"We're in agreement."

Harel considered that. "How much can you trust this person?"

"Canary is very expensive, and the information is vital."

"Yet we haven't been able to intercept the covert force either in Europe or the Americas."

"You know how shoddy the work that these Germans and Arabs perform is." A frown darkened Wellsberg's face. "You're living proof of that yourself."

Harel smiled. "True. Perhaps it's time we took a more active stance against them."

"You're talking about a bigger risk of exposure."

"We're so close now it may not matter. I'd rather get those people out of our way once and for all. Can you get one of your specialty teams on them?"

"Not without alerting Meyer Levin. He's still searching for Canary himself."

The limousine slowed, then made the left turn into the private drive staked out by armed security guards on the other side of the iron gates that wouldn't buckle under anything less than a full assault by an Abrams tank.

"Levin is becoming more trouble than he's worth," Harel said. "I know you have personal feelings of attachment to the old man, but he can't be allowed to become any more of a liability."

"I know."

"What about the covert agent he had staked out in my organization?"

"She's being kept in the basement of the house."

Harel nodded. He'd felt for some time that Levin had been working another angle than the obvious attempts at seeking Israeli connections to the action between the Jordanians, Iraqis and neo-Nazis. The old Israeli Mossad agent was as deadly and dangerous as a scum-covered pond. Still waters ran deep and were filled with treacherous snares that would take out the unwary with hardly a ripple. "You didn't mention her name when you contacted me earlier."

"There was no need. It would only have upset you at a time when you had to be at your best."

Harel realized the Mossad agent had penetrated more deeply into his inner circle than he'd at first believed. "Who is she?"

"Hannah Leor."

Harel looked deeply into Wellsberg's eyes. "You're sure?"

"Yes."

"She has been with me almost a year." Harel made it a point to get to know his brighter employees. Hannah Leor had possessed several qualities he'd cherished. She was clever, quiet and creative, never complaining about the heavy workloads that had been shifted onto her. It was a damned shame.

"It means that Levin has been suspicious longer than we'd previously believed."

"He moves slowly."

"That's one of his traits."

The driver pulled the limo into the attached garage, and the bulletproof door dropped into place behind it.

Harel took the lead and walked past the pair of guards watching the basement stairs. The light was on inside, revealing a stark room. Shelves built into the opposite wall bowed under the weight of jars of canned fruits and vegetables.

The woman was seated in a straight-backed chair, bound by her ankles and just below her breasts with rope. She was pretty, long blond hair streaked with dark auburn, framing a heart-shaped face that wasn't so much an exercise in perfection as it was in character. Her eyes flashed with anger, and the emotion was reflected in the set of her jaw.

There was an animal magnetism about her, and Harel had felt it. Although she was almost young enough to have been his daughter, she was the kind of woman he could have spent time with if he'd been so inclined. But women were a deterrent to concentration and focus, no more than a diversion from what he wanted out of his life.

"You work for Meyer Levin," he stated.

Hannah Leor didn't reply, but her eyes followed him as he paced in front of her.

"What have you learned since you've been with my organization?"

"Not to trust men with easy smiles and promises for a brighter future for Israel."

"What has Levin told you of me?"

She didn't answer.

"What have you told him about me?"

Silence was her only reply.

Harel stopped pacing and looked down at her. "You've told him nothing. If you knew anything, Levin would have leveraged some kind of response from his superiors. I still control them. You failed, Hannah."

"I may have failed, Dr. Harel, but never can it be said that I betrayed my country."

"Only because you weren't able to betray me. I *am* this nation's future. Levin has just blinded you to that fact."

"You're insane. You'll bury Israel in a bloodbath that you've triggered."

"Wrong. I'll cause it to rise like a phoenix from the ashes that the rest of the world would grudgingly give us." Harel leaned down to stare into her eyes. "How did it feel to be around me every day, knowing that at any moment you could be found out and killed?"

She tried to look away. Restrained fear made her lower lip tremble before she could stop it.

"Were you afraid? Did you wake in the middle of the night paralyzed with fear? Could you feel your heart beating after nightmares, your breath so tight in your lungs that it hurt to exhale or inhale?"

"You won't get away with this." Her voice sounded tight with forced control.

"God, I can only imagine what it must have been like." Harel's mind played with the concept, and he found his imagination becoming captivated by the inherent thrills in such a subterfuge. His pulse quickened till it thrummed in his temples. Before Wellsberg could move away, he reached inside the man's jacket and slipped the SIG-Sauer from the hip holster. The gun came away bright and hard in his hand. Harel's size was deceptive. He could move very quickly when he wanted to.

"Hey," Wellsberg protested.

"No," Harel said softly.

The ex-Mossad agent lowered his outstretched hand and took a step back.

"Did you ever think about dying?" Harel asked.

The woman closed her eyes and shuddered but said nothing.

Harel ignored the woman's obvious fright, lost in the pendulum swing of his own emotions. He pushed the muzzle of the pistol against her forehead.

Instead of trying to pull away, Leor leaned against the pistol but kept her eyes closed.

Taking the weight of her head against his arm, Harel said, "Did you ever think it would be like this? Alone and helpless? Did you think of having your throat slit or simply getting shot? Those thoughts had to be part of your everyday process. You couldn't have escaped them and, although you're young, you've seen enough to know that you really had no hope of escaping death forever. Could you feel how close you were on those days, or did you lie to yourself and say it could never happen?''

Leor's eyes snapped open, and she glared at Harel. "Do it, you vindictive bastard."

"Not vindictive," Harel admonished. "Merely curious and perhaps a bit envious. Yours was an insight to life that I've never experienced."

"Maybe you'll get the chance soon."

"Not likely. Even though you don't believe it, I am guiding Israel toward a brighter future. It's just a pity that you won't be around to share in it." Harel pulled the trigger and watched the woman's head jerk away from him as his arm bounced with the recoil. Blood spattered his face, and the sensation exhilarated him. Almost immediately the emotion seemed to drain from him, leaving him more empty than before. He returned the gun to Wellsberg.

Although Wellsberg didn't appear shocked, Harel knew the man well enough to understand that the ex-Mossad agent was disturbed by the events. "Have someone take care of this," he instructed, "and let's see about taking Levin out of the equation before he becomes a further annoyance."

HAROLD BROGNOLA had begun his law-enforcement career as a beat cop. He'd learned some lessons, had had others beaten into him by circumstances or other individuals who had been good, as well as bad, and had developed the instincts of a good manhunter over the years.

Gut feelings, a lot of cops called them. He was having one now, but he wasn't recognizing what he was seeing.

He stood in front of the TV-VCR system in the Oval Office with the Man at his side. He worked the remote control in his big hands, punching the buttons with a blunt forefinger. The cassette tape in the VCR was of the assassination attempt against Dr. Enoch Harel almost an hour ago. Kurtzman and his team had assembled it at Stony Man Farm, then passed a copy on to the head Fed by satellite relay.

He replayed the scene again, watching the yellow Volkswagen roll up to the flatbed truck then explode. His cop sense twitched again, but he still couldn't see what had triggered the response. Kurtzman had accessed the three major networks, CNN, BBC and a few other foreign stations, all of which provided a variety of different viewing angles.

"What are you looking for?" the President asked.

"I won't know until I find it." Brognola played another segment through with the broadcast function switched to slow motion. The explosion resembled something that would have been in a Sam Peckinpah movie. His gut called out to him again, then eased off as Harel's limousine glided through the wall of flames across the street. He'd missed it again.

The phone rang and the President answered it.

Brognola took a couple steps to his right, then ran through the next sequence. Again the yellow car slammed into the truck and blew up. The slow-motion feature let him see the roof of the car peel back like a sardine can. Figures moved around the flatbed. He concentrated on them, feeling his eyes burn from the strain of staring at the flickering pixels challenged by the slo-mo feature. The men obviously belonged to Harel's security entourage, and they were carrying fire extinguishers, as well as hexagon-shaped bomb shields. He finally had the subconscious pinging tracked down. Brognola took out a fresh cigar and unwrapped it.

"Something?" the Man asked.

"An incongruity," Brognola replied.

The President looked at the screen. "Want to tell me what I'm looking at?"

The limousine rolled through the flames again.

Brognola let the tape spin through the next sequence, then slowed it when the events reached their fiery climax again. For a brief handful of seconds Harel's security team surged forward. The clouds of fire retardant jetted out in slow motion as the men using the extinguishers laid into the sudden blaze. A trio of guards using the blast shields took Harel from the stage behind the protective barrier they put up.

"I don't understand."

"Watch this time." Brognola let the next scene roll. "See the fire extinguishers and bomb shields?"

"Yes."

"They had them ready."

"Obviously."

"How many fire extinguishers do you count?"

"At least eight."

Brognola froze a frame that showed one of the guards holding the extinguisher at his side. It ran the length from the man's waist to below his knee. "See the size of the extinguishers? Those aren't the little emergency units the Secret Service or a bodyguard unit would normally carry. Those are industrial-strength extinguishers."

"They knew about the car."

"Yeah."

"Harel knew about the car, too."

"I'd say so. The people he's got protecting him aren't known for sloppiness. In the last five years there have been seven attempts at either kidnapping or killing Harel by groups ranging from Arab terrorists to suspected business rivals. During the last two tries, his security people took no prisoners."

The President crossed his arms over his chest. "So you're saying Harel deliberately staged the attack."

"No. I'm saying Harel knew it was coming, and he allowed it to take place."

"And risked all those people?"

"Yeah." Brognola rolled the cigar over to the corner of his mouth. "It was a pretty cold-blooded decision. His audience didn't have the benefit of an armed security force waving blast shields around them."

Stepping back to the desk, the President lifted the phone and asked his secretary to get the CIA director on the phone. In less than two minutes, he was talking to the director.

Brognola let the tape keep running through. His stomach turned sour at the thought of the possible carnage that had been risked. He chewed two antacid tablets and washed them down with a fresh cup of coffee.

The President finished his phone call and turned back to the head Fed. "Two people in the crowd were killed by the bomb blast. Sixteen others were injured."

Brognola knew the CIA had been monitoring the speech through one of their covert agents. Kurtzman had been tapped into the CIA data base even before Striker and Phoenix kicked open the door against the Nazis and the Bolivian cartel. "That raises the stakes in Israel."

The Man nodded. "Sharon told me I've already got a call waiting from the State Department regarding the assassination attempt. The Israelis want to know what we're going to do about it.''

"They're not going to sit on their hands forever."

"No."

Brognola excused himself, went to the phone and punched in one of the shielded numbers he had for Stony Man Farm. Carmen Delahunt fielded the call, then shunted him over to Price's office. He put it on intercom so the President could listen in, as well. "I got the tape," he said without preamble, "and I noticed something."

"The fire extinguishers."

"Yes."

"We're already working it. Akira accessed the building-code files on the structures close to the Yad Vashem Memorial. There were only six fire extinguishers, and they were all type ABC models, strictly for conventional fires. The Volkswagen was carrying sodium-based alloys to make the fire burn hotter and longer. The fire engines that arrived on the scene would have been useless against that kind of blaze because water would only have made it worse."

"How do you know there were sodium-based alloys?" the President asked.

"Hunt turned it up on a spectographic analysis of the video footage. Give me access to your monitor, and I'll show you what we turned up."

Brognola made the adjustment on the set.

A picture coalesced on the screen. Pixels flashed and shifted, then became a fixed image centering on one of the guards carrying a fire extinguisher. The focus changed again, blowing up the image of the extinguisher.

"Notice anything out of the ordinary?" Price asked.

The extinguisher was a long red cylinder, the variety that Brognola was familiar with. He started to say no, then he saw it. Instead of the triangle, square and circle symbols usually on the extinguishers, this one carried a yellow star. "The star."

"Right. That star means the fire extinguisher was a type-D suppressor. Used only for fires involving flammable metals."

"And not something you could pick up at the local hardware store."

"No."

"How did Harel's people get them?"

"He owns a majority share in an aero-components machine shop that manufactures parts for the military. I can't track it for sure yet, but I'm betting that's the source."

"They not only knew when and where the attack was coming," Brognola said, "but they knew what to expect."

"I think so. Another facet of this thing is that having the type-D extinguishers on hand may allow them to identify the assassins."

"There's no doubt where that trail will lead."

"No. But now Harel and his people may be able to make an ironclad case of it. If so, they'll be able to put even more pressure on the current political situation."

"Stay with it and let me know what you turn up."

Price said she would, then hung up.

"Can't we prove that Harel knew about the bomb?" the President asked as he continued to stare at the frozen picture on the monitor.

"No. The fire extinguishers aren't damning evidence. They point us in definite directions because we were looking for this, but we can't go anywhere with it. If anyone accuses Harel, all he has to do is deny it. Right now we bear the burden of proof. And getting into a mud-slinging match with him wouldn't be a positive move at this time.''

''So we wait.''

Brognola nodded. ''Yeah. And that's the hardest part of operations as complex as this.''

CHAPTER SIX

A chill settled into Meyer Levin's bones. The Mossad field-agent control knew it didn't come from the sedan's air conditioner or the fact that the policeman driving the car woke him from a tired near coma induced by too many days of little or no sleep. He was dressed in one of his usual gray suits already marked by the burned pinholes from cigarette embers. The weave made most of them blend in.

"How much farther?" he asked.

Sergeant Zamir Givon negotiated a left turn, made possible on such short notice by the whirling cherry on top of the sedan. "Only a little way."

"You haven't moved the body?"

"No. My superiors told me to touch nothing till after you'd visited the crime scene."

"Your men are sure of the identity?"

"We ran her prints. There's not much left of her face."

Levin closed his eyes for a moment.

"Sorry," Givon apologized. "She was close to you?"

"Not by blood, but we shared several hard times together."

"I understand."

"How did you get my name?"

"When we ran her prints, we tripped some confidential alarms at your agency. My superiors told me to get you myself and keep this as quiet as possible."

Levin looked at the crowd already gathered at the crime site and the uniformed policemen waving traffic through the narrow street. "Somehow I don't think this is going to be very quiet."

"No. But then it wasn't supposed to be, or whoever killed her wouldn't have dumped her body in such a public place."

"How was she killed?"

"A pistol. Very close range."

Levin lit a fresh cigarette from the butt of his last. He felt himself grow colder inside. "Was she tortured?"

"As far as we can tell, there are no physical injuries other than the gunshot wound. We'll know more after the medical examiner has a turn at her."

The police sergeant's words rang hollowly in Levin's ears. After all the years of sanitary language in his own bloody profession, he shouldn't have given the callousness in Givon's words another thought. But he did. Hannah Leor had been a very special operative. She'd trusted him to be able to get her back out of the situation before things got too hot. He'd failed.

Givon pulled the sedan through the gap provided by his men working the street. He parked the car at the curb behind an ambulance that had both rear doors open and two white-suited orderlies in surgical gloves and masks standing outside.

Levin took his battered hat from his knee and got out. He slipped the hat on at once to avoid the sun beating down and the photographers. They might take his picture, but there were few who could tell them who he was, and even fewer who would be willing.

The police sergeant fell into step at his side.

"You've got men covering this area?" Levin asked as they headed into the alley between a jewelry store and a spice shop.

"Yes. I was told there could be some trouble with you actually on the scene yourself. After the attempt on Dr. Harel this morning, no one wants to take any chances."

Levin nodded. His superiors, at least the ones he still trusted, had advised him not to go. In a way it made sense, but in another he'd had to present himself to see what would happen. The Kevlar vest he wore under his jacket was hot and uncomfortable now that he was out in the heat. The wind was coming in from the desert instead of the coast. He glanced up and saw a policeman with a sniper rifle on top of the two-story spice shop. A concerned housewife was watching from inside one of the second-story rooms.

At the end of the alley, up against the rickety wooden fence closing it off, a tan blanket had been draped over a prone figure that looked shrunken and childlike in death. Two uniformed officers stood nearby.

Levin dropped his cigarette and crushed it underfoot as he walked. Hannah had always complained that he smoked too much.

Grass grew along the fence line where the asphalt ended, leaving almost a yard of open ground. Wildflowers grew among the twisted papers and empty containers and cans that were collected up against the faded planks. It was no place for the type of woman Hannah had been.

"Let me see her," Levin said, his voice tight with emotion. All the years of seeing the brave die so young, and he still hadn't grown calluses on his soul to protect him from the guilt involved with his job. He hadn't taken up drinking, as many of his colleagues had, but every time he looked in the mirror he knew how much the jobs had faded him over those years. Some days he felt as if he would never die, just get up one morning and fade completely away because there was nothing left of the flesh-and-blood man.

One of the officers knelt and carefully lifted away the blanket.

Levin automatically reached for another cigarette, then checked the movement. He said a silent prayer as he stepped forward, then carefully lowered himself to one knee by her head.

To further degrade the body, the murderers had stripped her naked and left her vulnerable. Blood flecked her upper torso, but none of it was stuck to her skin. She'd been clothed when they killed her. Her face was in ruins, bone showing through the torn flesh. Powder burns created unorganized tattoos across her features.

Quietly Levin took one of the woman's hands in his. The skin was cool but not too cool. Hannah hadn't been killed long ago. He turned the hand over and studied the thin scars crossing the middle finger, ring finger and pinkie. Hannah had acquired those three years ago from a terrorist's knife while on a covert mission in Beirut. The scars from the past made the present more intense. He replaced the hand at her side and pushed himself to his feet. "Cover her."

The officer carefully pulled the blanket over the body.

"Can I ask you what she was working on?" Givon asked.

"No." Levin walked away and lit a fresh cigarette. "Did anyone in the neighborhood see who left her here?"

"We've got a couple of descriptions and a possible make on the car, but they're ambiguous at best."

"I'll need copies of both."

Givon seemed hesitant. "This is awkward. This should be my case, given that it's a murder, yet I find myself restrained because she is one of yours."

Levin gave him a level gaze. "You have your job to do, Sergeant. I won't keep you from that. But if you find the animals who did this, your orders are to turn them over to me."

"What kind of working relationship will we have after that?"

"We'll have to wait and see. These are sensitive matters."

Givon nodded. After working a beat in Jerusalem for a number of years, the man would be experienced at being confidential about state dealings.

A falling object attracted Levin's attention. He glanced up, squinting as the sun lanced under the brim of his hat. For a frozen second he recognized the flailing man's uniform for what it was, then the man thumped flatly against the asphalt.

Givon clawed for the walkie-talkie attached to his belt.

Moving quickly, feeling the eyes on him, Levin tracked up the side of the building till he found the man standing where the police officer had been seconds ago. Since he was silhouetted against the sun, not many details about him were revealed. The Mossad control reached under his suit jacket for the pistol he carried in a paddle holster at his back. His fingers closed around the butt of the weapon when he heard the first boom of the big sniper rifle. Brick disintegrated beside his head, sending stinging chips ripping across his face.

The sniper was obviously having a hard time adjusting to the downrange shooting.

On the move, Levin ducked in beside a Dumpster only a few feet away. His foot slipped on a pile of cabbage, and the dull stink of foodstuffs and chemicals flooded his nostrils.

Two more rounds from the sniper rifle spanged into the metal walls of the Dumpster. Givon was shouting orders to his men as he squeezed off rounds from his own pistol.

Crouched behind the Dumpster, Levin peered at the rooftop of the spice shop. The sniper's head and shoulders were barely outlined above the ledge. He fired anyway, not really hoping to hit anything. His bullets tore into the ledge and made a ragged line about two yards across. The gunner hesitated for only a moment, then resumed firing.

Three uniformed policemen were sprinting down the side of the spice shop, heading for the fire escape mounted on the side of the building.

Levin shoved a fresh clip into his weapon and remained where he was. So far, the bullets weren't penetrating.

Abruptly the sniper jerked up from his position and went stumbling backward. Then the hollow boom of a high-powered rifle drifted over the street. The gunner jerked again, losing his hold on the sniper weapon, and two more booms echoed in the alley. The sniper peered at his bloody chest in disbelief. A heartbeat later he dropped to his knees and slumped forward.

Tracing the sounds of the rifle, Levin had to stare hard to make out the figure standing atop a building across the street.

It was a woman, straight and tall and lean, dressed in black jeans and a light-colored blouse. Her red hair was pulled back and hung in wings along the sides of her face. She didn't look as if she'd seen thirty yet, but her features held no emotion at all as she coolly dropped the powerful rifle she'd been holding. She touched a black-gloved hand to her forehead in a small salute that Levin felt was intended for him. Then she stepped back from the edge of the building and disappeared.

"Get that woman!" Givon roared. "Shut down the perimeters of this area and find her!"

Levin kept his pistol in his hand as he stepped out from behind the Dumpster. His heart beat rapidly under the weight of the Kevlar vest. The police sergeant's efforts would be wasted. They'd already allowed too many gawkers into the area to be able to close in on the woman. She was a professional, unhurried and unworried. All the searchers would find would be the rifle.

He crossed the alley and went up the fire escape to the rooftop. Flickering thoughts that there might be other snipers waiting to make a try for him sparked through his mind, but he ignored them. For now he was alive and moving, and the best defense was a good offense.

The three policemen who'd been ordered to make the assault up the fire escape were already surrounding the body when he got there. Sirens shrilled out on the street.

Levin glanced at the dead man. He'd been shot three times. The first round had caught him low in the shoulder, expertly placed so the expended force would shatter the bone and throw his body around, leaving him unprotected for the two bullets that had smashed into his heart. Despite the speed with which the shots had been fired, the two wounds in the corpse's chest could have been covered by a drink coaster.

It took a moment for the Mossad man's mind to flip through the mug shots in his memories and realize he'd known the man. There had never been a physical meeting, but he recognized the man as an operative some of the Mossad handlers used for long-distance terminations. His throat suddenly turned dry as the knowledge of how close he'd been to death fully came home.

He turned away from the dead man as the police officers started going through the pockets of the clothing. With the breeze at his back, he cupped his palms and lit a fresh cigarette. Sergeant Givon clambered over the ledge and moved toward him.

"Did you know this man?" Givon asked.

"No." The lie came easily to Levin's lips. He'd had a lifetime of experience.

"He wasn't Arabic."

"No."

"So it wouldn't seem to tie in with the attack on Harel as I was told to expect."

"No." Except that it did, and Levin knew it because he'd been the one who had assigned Hannah to investigate the businessman. He also knew that the woman who had taken out the assassin signified that Canary was making a move on the chessboard that had been shaped by the Arabs, neo-Nazis and those Levin was stalking in his own country. He had to wonder if the double agent knew any more now than he did, and if his trust had been misplaced. After all, he still did not know who Canary really was.

TURNING HIS JACKET collar up against the chill wind blowing through the streets of Zurich, Yakov Katzenelenbogen made his way through the marketplace taking up most of the space between a tropical-fish store and a tobacco shop. A building squatted over the area like a concrete Atlas, keeping the sky and most of the inclement weather at bay. The voices of the hustlers barked and echoed across the market in at least four different languages.

Katz strolled through the tables and walked to the line of public phones in the alcove behind the marketplace. The building above housed a number of businesses. During lunch hours the phone center was full. Now only a handful of people were spread out among them.

He chose one that gave him a partial view of the marketplace yet provided some security. His pockets were heavy with the P-226, a small radio transmitter and rolls of Swiss coin. Working one-handed, he cradled the receiver on his shoulder and broke open a roll, dropped in a coin and asked the operator for a number in Tel Aviv. He'd tried earlier, hadn't gotten the man he was trying for, but had arranged a message drop through a third party. He dropped in coins as the operator put the call through.

He glanced at the street as the phone rang.

Rafael Encizo had remained with the car as backup. The rest of the team was at the motel checking equipment and taking a breather while Katz found a new focus for their operations.

"Hello?" a male voice answered in Hebrew.

"We knew each other for a long time a few years ago," Katz said in English, not wanting to stand out in case anyone was eavesdropping, "and enjoyed a good friendship until our paths took us in separate directions. Do you know me?"

"I know the voice. I sometimes still think about you."

"As do I you."

"How have you been?"

"Well. Busy. These days it seems people in our profession are overworked."

"And confused. These are perplexing times."

"Is that a personal observation, or are you speaking of your own agenda?" Katz asked.

"Purely personal."

"We are free to speak?"

"About most things, yes."

Herb Marmelstein had been a brother in arms while Katz had been with the Mossad before moving on to Phoenix Force. A number of his colleagues had been concerned about his breaking ties, and he hadn't been free with where he was going next, though none of them expected him to quietly retire from his chosen field. Older than Katz, and having started in the espionage business as a teenager, Marmelstein had a long history and access to an even larger network of information.

"There are some things I need to ask," Katz said.

"If I can answer, I will."

"I need to know about an agent code-named Canary, supposed to be doubling for Iraqi and Jordanian interests these days."

Static crackled during the brief pause, and Katz had to feed more coins into the phone.

"That one," Marmelstein said, "is a ghost. A real, as the Americans say, will-o'-the-wisp."

"There is no one else I can ask. My own sources are unable to give me anything, and it appears this agent figures into some things I'm working on."

"You and your group have been busy hunting Hitler babies from what I have been told."

Katz said nothing. It was awkward, asking for a favor, yet being unable to be courteous at the same time.

"You have no need to confirm that, my friend. Meyer Levin contacted me after he conferred with young Uri Dan. I told him he could work with you, but not to expect too much cooperation in return because you played things close to the vest."

"I see," Katz said.

"How is the boy? I'd heard you lost a GSG-9 agent who was working with you."

"Uri Dan is fine. A compliment to his teachers. You stay very well informed for someone who's supposed to be retired."

"No one truly retires from this business, Yakov. You know that."

"Can you give me something on Canary?"

"A little. Meyer Levin has been inquiring about her, as well. I've never seen Canary myself, but I've had dealings through others. She's supposed to have been trained by the Brits, but walked away from them to turn freelance."

"Why?"

"The way I heard it, the money."

"She has no national convictions?"

"None that have been discovered. The Brits had her for three years as a deep throat on operations involving the IRA. After she walked away from that business, she began working with the Mossad."

"For the money?"

"Yes. She was paid by contract," Marmelstein confirmed.

"What kind of work did she do?"

"Information brokering."

"Nothing physical?"

"No. As far as I know, no one's ever seen her."

"How did she make contact inside the Mossad?" Katz asked.

"She approached one of the handlers through another agent she'd uncovered in England. Apparently she extended some properties to prove her reliability."

"They were valuable?"

"They were paid for, and she was added to the payroll."

"While she was still working for British Intelligence?"

Marmelstein sighed. "Yakov, I know there are people in our agency who don't approve of us spying on countries that are supposed to be our allies, but I—like several others—believe that watching ourselves with them is a necessity. No one safeguards Israeli interests as much as the Jewish people themselves."

Katz didn't argue, though he believed the Mossad had become too paranoid in passing years. That was one of the reasons he had joined Phoenix Force when Brognola had contacted him. "What happened with Canary after she began working for the Mossad?"

"The first few years, everything went well. Her information was always good, and she was able to cover much of Europe and America."

"Is she British?"

"I don't know. There was some rumor that she was American, but I don't think that was ever proven."

"You don't have a description of her?" Katz pressed.

"No."

"What about her language skills?"

"Very high. She was proficient in at least six languages, though most of them were the Romance languages, which share a common root."

"She was educated?"

"Yes. But whether an American education or a British one was never confirmed."

"She could have been the child of an American military career officer," Katz said. "That would explain the languages, and perhaps her interest in things of a political nature."

"I believe that was investigated at one time, but nothing solid ever turned up. For a time the Mossad had a contract out on her. The bounty was around a quarter-million dollars."

"That's surprising. Usually Mossad keeps everything on the qt."

"Yes, but in this instance they had no choice," Marmelstein explained. "Our agents couldn't trace her. The contract was offered to select few outsiders it was felt they could trust."

"But no one found her?"

"No. It was like she never existed."

"Why was the contract put out?" Katz asked.

"It was learned that she was doubling for someone else."

"The Iraqis and Jordanians?"

"No. The British."

Katz considered that. "So Canary doesn't stay bought?"

"No."

"Obviously the Iraqis and Jordanians don't know that."

Marmelstein grunted in agreement.

"How long has she been unavailable to the Mossad?"

"Five or six years. I forget. Another interesting facet is that the Mossad bounty has been quietly withdrawn."

"Leaving her an open door to return?"

"Maybe. Then again, maybe she never left."

"What are you saying?" Katz asked.

"When Levin first came to me about Canary, it wasn't known that she was working with the Arabs. He'd found out the contract had been cleared from the table. He was curious about that."

"Why?"

"I didn't ask."

"Did he have dealings with her?"

"Perhaps." Marmelstein chuckled. "Even one as old and wizened as myself doesn't know everything."

Katz smiled, then dropped more money into the phone at the operator's insistence. "Can you talk to the handlers who worked with Canary?"

"As you know, old friend, there has been a schism in our organization. There are those who are hawks. They see Israel capable of growing very rapidly these days with the influx of immigration from the Soviet countries adding to our population. Besides the additional skilled artisans and surplus of common laborers, a number of our new citizens possess surprising economic resources and see a way to edge Israel into a position of power in the European economy through investments into developing Eastern European countries. Then there are those who would prefer to take care of our problems here at home before embarking on new ventures which are sure to create more problems."

"And which camp do you fit in?"

"Yakov, I've lived with war enough to long for the day when our children's education doesn't include a familiarity with military weapons. But I feel that will never happen in our lifetimes, and maybe not ever if some very forceful steps are not taken."

Katz didn't comment. The marketplace was filling up as shoppers started their morning. "If something else comes up, can I contact you?"

"Surely. Perhaps we can help each other."

Katz thanked Marmelstein for his time and rang off. He got the operator again, then placed a call to Stony Man Farm through one of the cutout numbers he had memorized, and used a phone card this time that couldn't be traced. By using cash on the call to Tel Aviv, he'd ensured that people at the Farm didn't know about his talk with Marmelstein. It wasn't subterfuge. He protected people who worked with him. And one of the reasons Brognola had recruited him was for his contacts in the espionage field that they didn't already have.

Kurtzman answered.

Briefly Katz brought the computer expert up-to-date on what he'd uncovered about Canary. Kurtzman was strangely unresponsive and didn't ask many questions, but he did say that the Stony Man efforts had been fruitless. Katz didn't investigate the behavior. A lot of hours had been logged by everybody concerned. And the phone connection, disrupted by static as it was, might explain some of it. Conversations on international long-distance lines weren't often as informative or as satisfying as might be wished.

"I've got some information for you, too," Kurtzman said. "Those accounts you turned up belong to the Iraqis. The monies and valuables being transported out of the country with the help of the Jordanians are being converted into Swiss currency and left in banks in Zurich."

Katz thought that over, and the stirrings of a plan took shape in his mind. He glanced at his watch and saw that it was a little before 10:00 a.m. local time. "When did you say Rivera's flight was supposed to touch down?"

"Your time, a little after eleven."

"How far behind is Striker?"

"Maybe thirty minutes. Barbara cut things pretty close."

"You can reach him?"

"Yes."

"Good. Can you also access those Iraqi accounts in the time we have left before Rivera lands?"

"It'll be tricky. But I think we can do it."

"Fine. I believe I have a way to smoke the terrorists here into the open. Here's what I need you to do...."

COLONEL HECTOR RIVERA was a party of one from the Swissair flight from London. For a moment, unconsciously thinking he was still in uniform, he stood at the top of the debarkation ladder and looked around. His hands pulled at the bottom of the expensive suit jacket he now wore.

The pretty stewardess batted her eyes at him in perplexity.

Realizing he was holding up the other passengers, Rivera took a pair of Foster Grants from his jacket pocket and slipped them on as he took a fresh grip on his carryon and headed down the gantry.

A few limousines were parked in the waiting area. One of the liveried chauffeurs held up a small placard with Montoya printed on it. That was the name Rivera was currently traveling under, having made another identity switch in London. He grinned to himself as he walked toward the luxury car. He was a fugitive from his own country and would doubtless have been executed for his part in the drug trafficking if he'd stayed. But he was a fugitive with money, and that made all the difference in the world.

The driver opened the door, and Rivera climbed inside.

"The wine is in the cooler, sir," the driver said, "and the cellular phone you requested is in the hip case on the seat."

The phone was a compact flip model that looked like something out of the old "Star Trek" episodes Rivera had seen as a young man. He opened it briefly and said, "Beam me up, Scotty, I'm a rich man," grinning to himself as he clipped it onto his belt. He put his carryon between his feet, then opened the wine and poured himself a glass.

He gave the driver directions to his bank. He already had a suite reserved at one of the finer hotels, but first he wanted to check on his ill-gotten wealth. Once he verified that everything was okay there, he could get on with enjoying his forced retirement.

It took almost thirty minutes to reach the bank from the airport despite the driver's compliance with his request to hurry. He told the man to wait after they arrived, then went inside. Twenty minutes later, after being introduced to an affable assistant bank manager whose pleasure it was to finally meet a depositor of Mr. Eric Montoya's caliber, Rivera was in a small office setting up lines of credit and banking accounts that he could use while he was in Zurich. Now that his retirement had begun earlier than he'd imagined, he wasn't sure exactly what he wanted to do. Even though he'd had the hours to examine his options during the connecting flights, he'd thought of little besides the foreign women he wished to bed. In the end he'd had to admit that he was going to miss his old job. There was a certain lure to being in a position with so much power. Now he would be reduced to merely being a wealthy citizen. He sighed.

He was completing the final forms at a small, shielded table when he first saw the man walk by. His stomach churned immediately.

All of the Bolivian cartel members had been given pictures of the phantom covert team that had been blasting their way through the ranks of the Nazis in Germany. Though the pictures had been few and of poor quality, he was sure this was one of the men.

From the reports, he assumed this was also the leader.

The man was in his early fifties, barrel-chested and wore a black glove over his right hand. The suit wasn't off the rack, but it wasn't hand-fitted like the one Rivera wore. The ex-colonel's practiced eyes noticed the paddle rig for something at least the size of a full-scale 9 mm pistol at the man's left hip. The man in the pictures had had a metal hook for a right hand, but it was easy to assume that the prosthesis was interchangeable with others.

He finished the paperwork and remained seated in his chair. Despite the air-conditioning, perspiration beaded on his forehead. He found himself wishing he had a gun, but that had been impossible on the airline. He resolved to make getting one a priority.

The man went into one of the small cubicles with another of the assistant bank managers.

Straining his ears, Rivera heard snatches of the conversation next door. Evidently there was a big withdrawal being negotiated, and the need for security was being advised, as well as the bank's willingness to rectify whatever impropriety that had caused the depositor to decide changing banks was necessary. The depositor assured the assistant manager that no, everything was fine with the banking practices, but it was now time to move on. A few names were mentioned in context with the accounts. They sounded Arabic. Using a corner of an extra form, Rivera wrote the names down.

By the time the manager he was doing business with returned with his checks and bank cards, Rivera had reached a decision. He was aware of Tarim Sudair and

Shiraz al Najaf and their connections to the Nazis and the Bolivian cartels. He also had a number to reach them in Zurich, borrowed quietly during one of Bernardo Gomez's moments of preoccupation. Rivera had always tried to avail himself of interesting angles to be played at later times. It was easy to see that the man in the other room might be worth something to the Arabs. His mind was already hard at work trying to guess what that amount might be. He had put away a substantial amount over the years he'd been associated with the cartel, but he'd also learned to be greedy enough to realize that more was even better.

He hardly paid attention to the bank manager's explanation of the check-cashing policies and regulations about early withdrawals.

The man in the other room finished his business. As he passed through the corridor again, he placed an unfiltered Camel between his lips and lit it.

Rivera shoved his new passbook, checkbook and sheaf of Swiss francs into his jacket pocket and took off in pursuit of the man. There was no reason to believe the man would know him.

The man halted near one of the waiting areas close to a vault.

Moving carefully, working on the timing, Rivera stepped to the man's side as a couple of secretaries came down the hallway side by side. He bumped into the man, his hand going to the man's chest as if he was off-balance. His practiced fingers slid inside the jacket and lifted the wallet from the inside pocket. "Sorry," he said in English.

"It's nothing," the man replied, reaching out to help Rivera steady himself. "Are you okay?"

"I'm fine. Thank you." The wallet effortlessly slid up Rivera's coat sleeve. He'd learned several useful skills during his law-enforcement career. He excused himself and went on his way.

In the back of the limousine after ordering the driver to stay put for a few minutes, he opened the wallet and perused the contents. There was no driver's license, no credit cards, nothing that would identify the owner in any way. Yet the man had to have produced some kind of identification for the bank.

Rivera was about to put the wallet away in disgust when he noticed the credit-card receipt behind the pad of checks. He took it out and studied it. According to the information contained there, Mr. Lavi Potak had paid for a suite of rooms at an expensive downtown motel on his Visa card that morning.

Opening the cellular phone, Rivera dialed information and got the number for the Visa credit representative in Zurich. Within only a few moments, he discovered that yes, Mr. Potak was a valuable customer with a credit limit quite able to cover the three-thousand-dollar antique clock Rivera said the man was trying to purchase. And, the rep went on, please remind Mr. Potak that the purchase would be covered by insurance provided by the credit company till he was once more home.

Potak came out of the bank carrying a large attaché case. Two of the uniformed bank guards escorted him to his waiting Jaguar, their hands never far from their holstered guns. The man behind the steering wheel was lean and dark.

Rivera glanced at the attaché case as Potak got into his vehicle, wondering how much money it could possibly hold. He wasn't above armed robbery. He had experience in that field, as well. If the money was in Swiss bills, he guessed at maybe two hundred thousand dollars if it was in large bills. However, if it was in bearer bonds, the amount could be astronomical.

The Jaguar pulled away from the curb and into the morning traffic already thick with cabs and tourist rentals.

Rivera thumbed the intercom that linked him to the driver. "Follow the dark green Jaguar."

"Yes, sir."

"At a discreet distance, but don't lose them."

"Yes, sir."

Rivera felt anticipation thrilling through him as his mind juggled the pieces of the puzzle before him. His predatory instincts took over. If the man was the leader of the covert force, his presence at the bank hadn't been by chance, especially since that bank was one used by the neo-Nazis and the Bolivian cartel. It was no leap of faith to imagine the Arabs used the bank, as well, since some of their monies came from the same sources. But he wanted more information before he went anywhere with his discovery.

He used the cellular phone again and called Interpol. The connection to Paris took a couple of moments. He'd used the agency before, back in the early days when he'd blackmailed his way into the cartel and put his services as protector up for sale. There had been a few times since, when he'd broken up competition for Gomez and his cohorts. The agent he was connected with put him on hold, then verified that Colonel Hector Rivera was indeed on their list of contacts. Once he was cleared, Rivera gave them Lavi Potak's name and Visa account number, then stated that he believed Potak was in his country regarding drug trafficking.

The agent said it would take a few moments to track the information down.

Rivera said he would call back in fifteen minutes and thanked him for his time.

The Jaguar eased through the traffic at a sedate pace. The two men inside talked very little with each other and never turned around.

Rivera perspired nervously inside his new suit. If these men were part of the covert force that had put the neo-Nazis in Germany out of business, they were very deadly men. He didn't intend to put himself in jeopardy.

Ten minutes later the Jaguar pulled to the curb outside an office building that was something less than twenty stories tall.

Potak left his car, again carrying the attaché case.

After a moment's hesitation, Rivera told his driver to stay put, then got out, as well. He walked through the crowded sidewalk easily, glancing around in sweeps that imitated a number of other tourists.

Inside the building, he kept Potak in sight. For a moment he was bewildered about what to do if the man took the elevator. He wasn't going to board it with him, and if he lost Potak at that point, that was fine.

Instead, Potak stayed on the ground floor and took the left corridor leading into the recesses of the building. Never glancing around, Potak walked like a man with a purpose. Small offices filled that part of the building. The door Potak entered was marked with gilt lettering that proclaimed Hendersen Securities, Bonded by Lloyds of London, Appointments Only. A sticker in one corner advertised the presence of an alarm system. Thick steel bars were on the other side of the glass, and a guard—not a secretary—sat behind a small desk at the back of the first room. Potak was guided through another door to the side.

Not wanting to press his luck, Rivera left the building and returned to the limo.

"Sir?" the driver inquired.

"We wait," Rivera answered. He used the cellular phone again to call Interpol.

The agent had information on Lavi Potak this time. The man was an Israeli by birth but had lived in New York for the past twelve years. He was a businessman, specializing in efficiency training for the manufacturing industry. He'd killed a man in 1983 while in Beirut, but the charges had been dropped because no one could prove it wasn't self-defense. A number of European police agencies had paperwork but no charges against Potak regarding visa violations and questions concerning terrorist action within their borders. Nothing had turned up on Potak during the past five years.

Rivera broke the connection. Obviously Potak was more acquainted with those kinds of troubles than he appeared to be. Rivera poured himself another glass of wine and waited till Potak emerged from the building.

The attaché case the man carried this time wasn't the same one he'd carried in. He climbed into the Jaguar, and it slid smoothly away.

"Sir?" the driver said.

"Follow him."

"Yes, sir."

Rivera checked the number he had for Tarim Sudair's people in Zurich, then placed the call.

The man who answered spoke in Arabic.

"I need to speak with Tarim Sudair or Shiraz al Najaf," Rivera said in English.

"I know of no one by those names." The reply came in heavily accented English.

"Tell them I think I've found one of the men who've been hunting them."

"How did you get this number?"

"From Bernardo Gomez."

"He's dead."

"I was there when he died."

"Wait."

There was a pause, the distant drone of voices talking, then a new voice spoke. "This is Tarim Sudair."

"You don't know me," Rivera said, "but perhaps you know of me. My name is Hector Rivera."

"Yes. The Bolivian colonel. It was thought that you were dead."

"It was a close thing. Many others died."

"But not you."

Rivera barely kept himself from responding to the naked accusation in the other man's words. "No. I don't fight losing battles. Discretion is the better part of valor. I have some information for you. If I'm wasting my time, tell me."

"What is it?"

Quickly Rivera outlined the chance meeting inside the bank, then went into brief detail regarding his quiet pursuit of Lavi Potak.

"Where is he now?" Sudair asked.

"I'm following him by car. I can only assume he's returning to his hotel."

"Stay with him. Someone will be there soon. How will they find you?"

Rivera told him. When the connection broke, he knew the Jordanian was highly motivated to investigate the lead. From the sound of the man's voice, it wasn't just the possibility that Potak was the leader of the covert force that had reduced the neo-Nazi threat to cinders. Something new had happened. He scratched his chin and wondered what it was. It was hard to calculate what his services would be worth if he didn't know everything he'd done. But he'd already started pushing his expectations upward.

TARIM SUDAIR GLARED at the unblinking computer monitor set on the ornate mahogany desk. He was dressed in a dark business suit, as the rest of his people were, the clothing tailored to conceal the weapons underneath. "How much is gone?" he asked the computer operator.

"All of it," the man answered.

"How much was in those accounts?"

"Sixty-five million dollars."

Steeling himself, Sudair let his breath out through his nose, marshaling his remaining self-control. The hotel suite was large, roomy enough for his men and the German representatives still interested in working out a joint effort against the Israelis. The German neo-Nazis were dressed in street clothes that reminded him that they really were blue-collar terrorists in their mind-set. Their members would not willingly die for their cause, and the seeds of racial prejudice they carried within them were as dangerous as those planted so fiercely by the hated Jews. But, as Sudair had learned in his long career, politics did make strange bedfellows. Still, it had been assumed that the German terrorists would have been able to contribute more than they had. Instead, their forces were bent, broken and scattered in Europe and the Americas as if they'd been hit by a sudden sand storm that carried only cutting death.

"How was the money taken?" Sudair asked.

The man tapped the computer keys.

Unschooled in the computer technology, Sudair could only watch as frame after frame scrolled across the monitor.

"From what I can see here, someone must have interfered with the bank records by computer. They accessed our accounts, withdrew the money, then put it over into another account."

"And who owns this other account?"

"It was under the name Lavi Potak. He's an Israeli citizen—"

"Living in America."

The computer operator appeared surprised.

"Can't you break back into the bank and simply transfer the monies back into our accounts?" Sixty-five million dollars put a significant dent in the monies that had been ferreted from Iraqi citizens by caravan through Jordan. Once Sudair's superiors in Amman discovered the loss, things would go hard on him, even though Shiraz al Najaf was there to share the blame. The accounts were the ones handled by the cell operating outside of Zurich. Minutes after finding out about the theft of the money, he'd discovered only dead men still remained at the big house. It would take some time before they were able to ascertain how much information their enemies might be privy to.

"No." The man tapped more keys. "I've already broken in past the bank's safeguards, but the money has been removed from Potak's account."

"He withdrew it?"

"Yes."

It confirmed what Rivera had reported. Though Sudair didn't like the Bolivian because he'd cut and run from the situation in his own country and the Jordanian was averse to depending on those he considered cowards, he knew he was going to have to work with the man.

"Problems?" Derrik Raimund asked in English.

Sudair had been communicating in his native language. He glanced at the young German terrorist and said, "We have some new Intelligence regarding the men who destroyed your group in Germany."

Raimund's pale blue eyes narrowed. "I insist that you let my men and I help you go after them."

Sudair figured the National Vanguard must have taken Raimund straightaway from classes in university. The young man was filled with the flame of retribution and hadn't seen enough of the carnage left by the men pursuing them to know to be afraid.

Raimund was clean shaven, possessed an unlined face bearing no scars and those incredibly pale blue eyes that looked like something from a taxidermist's shop. His glasses were round lensed and further softened his features. Under the mop of blond hair parted down the middle and shaved ridiculously short on the sides, he seemed innocent. The rest of his men appeared to be pretty much the same. Still, there were thirty of them, and Sudair knew the value of cannon fodder.

"Of course," the Jordanian replied. "If you wish, I will let you lead the way."

Raimund smiled. "I'd like that."

He returned the younger man's grin, knowing Raimund wasn't practiced enough to see it for how false it was. He began issuing orders in Arabic, getting his troops ready to move out. Weapons were quickly checked, then replaced in the secret compartments built inside clothes

and suitcases. In minutes they had vacated their rooms
and made their way below to the waiting vehicles. Only
heartbeats after that, death rolled out onto the streets.

CHAPTER SEVEN

"Look alive, mate." David McCarter reached across the seat and nudged Calvin James into wakefulness.

The ex-Seal was instantly alert.

"The vultures have started to flock about." McCarter stared through the mud-filmed window of the rented car they were stationed in outside the hotel where Katz and Encizo waited like clay pigeons in their room.

The Arabs and neo-Nazis weren't the least bit guarded about their arrival. Three cars double-parked at the sidewalk beside the hotel and disgorged twelve men. Most of them looked European, but there were a few scattered Arabs. They divided without words, some of them heading for the main entrance, while the others covered the two side entrances and the parking garage built under the building.

"Doesn't look like they're pulling any punches, does it?" James asked.

"Not bloody likely at this point," McCarter said softly. He freed the Galil assault rifle with the attached M-203 grenade launcher from under his seat, then unsnapped the restraining strap over the Browning Hi-Power in its shoulder holster. A second Browning was beside the seat on his left.

James saw to his own equipment, including the M-249 SAW covered by a blanket on the rear seat.

McCarter tapped the transmit button on his headset as he checked the key to make sure a quick start was only a flick away. He hadn't liked leaving Katz and Encizo inside the building basically on their own, but there hadn't been any other way around it if they were going to make the play they'd staged. "Hey, Yakov."

"Go," Katz replied.

"You've got company, mate. A bloody lot of it, too."

"Understood. We'll handle things from here. See you below."

Fervently hoping so, realizing how chancy the play really was, McCarter hit the transmit button on the headset again. "Gary?"

"I copied." Gary Manning, the big Canadian, sounded tense, too.

McCarter pulled his driving gloves more tightly onto his hands and keyed the ignition. The engine started smoothly. With everything else going on and their focus so intent on their prey, he felt certain Phoenix's enemies wouldn't notice him. He waited, knowing that everything they had planned could fall apart like a house of cards. Except that Encizo and Katz would be buried beneath them if it fell.

"MOVE OUT," Katz ordered.

Encizo nodded and shouldered the duffel bag that had been lying on one of the beds. He screwed a silencer onto the barrel of the Beretta 92-F 9 mm in his hand as he strode toward the door.

Making a final adjustment on the Whip-it sling holding the silenced MAC-10 under his jacket, Katz followed the Cuban. The duffel carried the diamonds the bearer bonds had been traded for at the securities office. Gary Manning had maintained surveillance over the business and had radioed in reports about the terrorist assault on the office within a half-hour of his departure. According to Manning's reports, there had been a brief gunbattle that had left two of the Arabs dead and most of the men inside the securities exchange. Katz didn't regret the loss. The people who ran the securities office were as far outside the law as the terrorists. By now Tarim Sudair knew the sixty-five million had been converted into a liquid wealth that could be easily funneled out of the country and lost forever. Of course, there had been a twenty-percent shrinkage immediately that had gone to the securities exchange. It had given the Jordanian no alternative other than to try for an immediate recovery of the assets.

Katz kept the subgun out of sight under his blazer as they walked down the corridor to the bank of elevators. With their location on the eighteenth floor, it would take the terrorists time to reach them even after they broke through the desk personnel below.

A half-dozen people were impatiently waiting in front of the elevators.

Encizo crossed to the last elevator on the right and unclipped a radio transmitter from his belt. The Beretta was tucked away in one of the deep pockets of his trench coat. "Excuse me," he said in English.

The older couple who had been standing in front of the cage watching the slow crawl of the level indicators swinging upward gave ground reluctantly.

"Please," Encizo said. "Hotel security staff." Before joining Phoenix Force, he'd spent years as a Marine insurance investigator. He knew how to quietly turn on authority.

Katz stepped forward and edged the couple out of the way a little farther.

The man grumbled invective in German, but the woman saw the hook at the end of Katz's right arm and firmly dragged her companion back.

Working quickly, Encizo used his Leatherman Pocket Tool to pry the stainless-steel cover from the elevator's controls. Using the screwdriver attachment, he pulled two previously cut wires held together by black electrical tape from the inside of the mechanism and screwed them into the output and input circuitry of the remote-control device. He and Manning had rigged the transmitter and elevator controls hours ago while putting the plan together. It was designed to slave the cage to their commands. Satisfied with the connections, Encizo pressed the button.

The level indicator changed speeds immediately. There were no more stops as it went from the fifth floor to the eighteenth.

The crowd waiting for the elevators began to shift to that end of the floor.

Encizo stepped to the side and held up a hand. "Please stand back."

The people froze uncertainly.

Katz watched the level indicator light up number 18.

The bell dinged loudly and the doors parted.

Inside the cage two men glanced at Katz's metal prosthesis, then reached under their jackets as they shoved the three women in front of them out of the way. The women screamed shrilly, automatically struggling against their aggressors. Guns swept up in the hands of the two men.

Raking the MAC-10 into the open, Katz fired two 3-round bursts in quick succession. The .45-caliber bullets chopped through the faces of the two men and the thin wooden veneer behind them. The muffled thumping of the rounds cycling through the Ingram scattered the people behind Katz.

The two corpses twisted and fell against the back wall, sliding down to the floor.

His Beretta also bared now, Encizo moved forward and helped the women from the cage. He held the doors open as Katz entered. Across the foyer, the fire-escape doors burst open and two more gunners came forward, locking on to the fleeing Phoenix Force members instantly.

Encizo pulled the radio transmitter from the wire connection as he tapped the button for the seventeenth floor. The doors closed as bullets slammed into them and ripped through the sheet metal. The thunderous roars shook the cage.

The Kevlar vest Katz was wearing stopped one of the rounds but promised an awful bruise in the hours to come.

Pocketing the Beretta, Encizo quickly went to work on the control panel inside the elevator and attached the remote control device. "They came at us faster than we thought," he said as he finished.

"It was the receipt in the wallet I allowed Rivera to pick from my pocket at the bank," Katz said. "It had the room number on it."

Encizo nodded. "Ready?"

"Ready."

The Cuban punched the electronic control, and the cage seemed to drop away beneath them, leaving the impression of zero gravity. The jury-rigged remote control also overrode the safety features that kept the cage moving at a sedate pace.

Katz slipped his headset on and tapped the transmit button. "David?"

"Go."

"We've already had our first engagement."

"We can still pull the plug on this thing and fade away. Maybe Manning and I can work out something to take out Sudair."

"No. We're in good shape. We'll play it out."

McCarter cleared the frequency.

The cage stopped at basement level with enough force to require Katz and Encizo to lean against the walls to stay on their feet. The Cuban took the lead with his Beretta in his fist.

No one was waiting on the other side of the door, though three Arabs were streaking for the elevator, letting Katz know they must have been equipped with communications gear of their own. He pulled up short behind a concrete support pillar as bullets smacked into the concrete floor near him. Encizo took cover behind a banged-up Land Rover with a British flag hanging from the radio antenna. Spinning around the pillar, Katz took out one of the gunners with a clipped figure-eight that smashed the man backward into an open Italian convertible sports car.

The remaining two terrorists broke for cover.

Panicked shouts and women's screams echoed inside the enclosed space as a dozen or so civilians realized they were on a battlefield.

Encizo picked one of the terrorists off with a pair of 9 mm parabellums that took the man in the head, then broke immediately to flank the other man who was taking a defensive position behind a minivan.

The terrorist rose to intercept Encizo and fired hurriedly.

As the man came up with the Ingram in his fist, Katz had a brief impression of the Cuban being blown away. Bracing the machine pistol across his prosthesis, he hammered a fusillade through the windows of the mini-van that caught the gunner chest high and put him down. He changed magazines and moved out.

In the middle of the open space between the lines of parked cars, Encizo was struggling to get up.

"Rafael," Katz called.

"I'm okay. Body armor stopped penetration, but it knocked the wind out of me." Already on his feet, Encizo managed to break into a jog.

Katz reached their Jaguar first and caught the duffel when the Cuban threw it to him, storing it in the rear seat as Encizo slid under the vehicle. Despite the fact that the Arabs would want to take them alive or at the very least get their property back intact, they weren't going to take any chances with explosives. Rivera had already seen the car, although the ex-colonel thought it was only a rental. Instead, the plates had been borrowed from a rental car, and Price had arranged for the Jaguar after hearing Katz's plans.

"We're clear here," Encizo said.

At the near end of the basement-level entrance from the street, a midsize German economy car slewed into the parking garage on shrieking tires.

Reacting to the threat, Katz lifted the MAC-10 and sprayed the entire magazine across the front of the attack vehicle.

The windshield came apart in chunks as long scars ripped across the finish of the hood. White smoke hissed from the punctured radiator. Out of control, the car twisted and slammed into a line of parked cars. Little more than twenty feet away, a pair of men helped a young woman up from the floor and hustled her toward safety. A uniformed security officer dashed from his glass-encased cubicle near the street entrance.

Seeing movement still inside the car, Katz palmed a Thunderflash grenade from the small arsenal in his jacket pockets and heaved it at the car. The spherical grenade bounced hollowly and came to a rest against one of the front tires. It went off with a roar that hurt the ears and a blinding flash that left spots in the vision of the unwary.

Katz slid into the passenger seat as Encizo keyed the ignition.

The Cuban tromped on the accelerator and released the clutch. The powerful car responded immediately. Its tires spun briefly, then it backed out of the parking slot. He hit the brakes and it came to a halt, rocking restlessly like a big cat.

The security guard had his gun out and was taking a two-handed stance in front of them, shouting at them to stop.

Instead, Encizo shifted into second gear, sending the rear of the Jaguar wobbling with the increased power.

Three of the security guard's shots hit the windshield and left spiderweb cracks, but the bulletproof glass held.

Katz tapped his transmit button. "David, we're on our way out."

"Southbound lane's good to go, mate, but you're blocked on the northbound. You'll have to work it out."

"Understood." Katz repeated what McCarter had said and watched as the security guard threw himself into a dive and went rolling away.

Encizo nodded grimly and powered up the ramp leading out into the street. The undercarriage dropped onto the concrete surface, and abused metal screamed in protest. Outside he cut the wheels hard to the right and whipped into the line of traffic.

Katz swept the street with his practiced gaze, picking up the vehicles of the terrorists immediately, then spotted McCarter and James in their own car. The normal traffic gave way immediately, not wanting to be anywhere near the speeding Jaguar. He hit the transmit button again. "What about the police?"

"No sign of them," McCarter responded. "We make it out of here in the next little while, we should be in the clear."

"You're clear on this side of the building, too," Manning advised. "I'm moving into position. McCarter, you're my flanker."

"Roger."

Encizo drove with both hands, barreling through a red light in an opening between a soft-drink truck and a Federal Express delivery van.

Glancing over his shoulders, Katz saw the first of the terrorist vehicles pick up the pursuit, quickly followed by the others. He counted six. "Okay, we've got our tail," he said to the Cuban. "Get us back the way we need to go."

"Hang on," Encizo said. He clutched, pulled the Jaguar into the inside lane of traffic on the four-lane street in front of a German sports car, downshifted and let out the clutch and the brake at the same time. The nose was pulled down by the reduced transmission gear ratio and brakes, and the Jaguar willingly went into the skid Encizo created. Rubber whining, the car came around in smoking roils, making a full 180-degree turn. He pressed down on the accelerator as traffic behind him came to a standstill, then let out the clutch and went screaming back the way he'd come.

The first three terrorist vehicles were too surprised to do anything. The gunners in the fourth car had unlimbered their weapons and fired off several bursts that bounced harmlessly from the bulletproof glass and armor, and never fazed the run-flat tires. The fifth vehicle was in the process of reversing direction on a side street.

In front of them, the sixth car turned sideways across the two inside lanes of traffic and tried to block them.

Encizo waited till the last minute, tapped the brake, downshifted again and presented the passenger side to the lighter Honda Accord. The heavily armored Jaguar smashed into the side of the smaller car and knocked it aside. The metal crunched together and held as they skidded back up the street.

For a moment Katz found himself face-to-face with one of the German terrorists across two sheets of glass. He thumbed the power window down a few inches, stuck the barrel of the P-226 through the opening and fired.

The bullet cored through the window and knocked the man backward onto the driver as blood sprayed over the interior.

Then Encizo yanked the wheel again and freed them from the other car with a wobbling wrench. He wasted no time in gaining speed again, heading for the on-ramp of the highway that would take them west out of town toward Baden.

Katz glanced over his shoulder, watching as the terrorist vehicles regrouped and picked up the pursuit again. McCarter was still at the curb, waiting to fall into place. "Careful," Katz said. "We don't want to lose them."

"DON'T LOSE THEM!" Tarim Sudair shouted to his driver.

Reaching into the glove compartment, Sudair took out the courtesy copy of the Zurich street map. He traced the street on which they were presently traveling and quickly deduced his foes' probable destination. There was an on ramp not far from their present location. After that their quarry could flee the city, perhaps pick up aerial transport along the way between Baden and Zurich.

Glancing over his shoulder, Sudair looked at Rivera, who was gripping the seat belt around his waist. Two of his men sat beside the ex-colonel.

"I'm only going to be in the way," Rivera said. "I'm not even armed."

"And it's not going to change," Sudair said. The situation with the Israelis didn't feel right, and he couldn't dismiss the notion that Rivera might be setting them up. Still, with the money involved, he had no choice but to pursue.

Rivera swallowed hard as the car swung out wide around stalled traffic, then cut back to the right. The on ramp was only a few blocks ahead, and the Jaguar was already rolling up it.

The police-band radio mounted under the dash of the car relayed confused reports coming from the hotel. It would take time before the police force figured out what was really going on.

He switched frequencies and made sure the rest of the convoy that was still operable were following. Some of the team that had invaded the hotel had made it back out to the street, bringing the total number of vehicles up to seven.

The driver zigzagged through traffic and bottomed out going up the on ramp.

According to the map the highway followed the river north to Baden. It could be seen in the distance, a twisting blue-brown snake threading through the pines and snow-covered countryside.

Twelve miles whipped by before Sudair found what he was looking for. Quickly he alerted the rest of his team to continue the pursuit.

"The next turnoff," he told his driver. "Take it."

The man nodded, then cut the wheels sharply, sliding across the bow of a pickup truck. The wheels lost traction for a moment, and the driver tapped the brakes to regain control.

"Don't stop," Sudair commanded. "The highway goes out around a small town here. By cutting through, we can save something close to fifteen miles and maybe find ourselves in the lead." He braced a hand on the dash as he dropped the map to the floorboard, then drew his Glock-17 from his shoulder holster.

The car shot through a small intersection, throwing a wave of dirty brown melted snow across the nose of a station wagon that had just eased out from the four-way stop. The driver slammed on the brakes and came around in a one-eighty turn that almost clipped the sedan.

Once clear of the intersection, the road turned into a two-way street that held only straggling traffic. Sudair's driver negotiated them easily. Ten minutes later the highway came into view again. The land was noticeably elevated, coming out of a valley.

"Faster," Sudair urged.

The car shot up the on ramp and onto the acceleration lane.

Sudair stared hard through the back glass and made out the Jaguar in the distance and closing fast. "We are ahead of them." Looking in front of them again, he saw an eighteen wheeler parked at the roadside. "The truck."

Nodding, the driver slid in to a stop beside the big truck.

"Let's go," Sudair said. He glanced at the driver and spoke in Arabic. "You stay with this man. Kill him if he tries to escape."

Sudair kicked open his door, the Glock-17 in his fist, then raced toward the truck driver's door.

"What's going on?" the driver demanded in German as he stuck his head out the cab.

Showing him the barrel of the Glock, Sudair said, "Down! Out of the truck now!"

Sudair reached up and seized the front of the man's shirt, yanking him from the truck. His men piled in, and he pulled himself up behind the wheel and keyed the ignition. The engine protested for just a moment, then caught. He shoved the gearshift into first and pulled across the two lanes of traffic on his side of the divided highway.

Horns blared, and a compact car sideswiped the front bumper with a rending of metal.

In control of the truck, Sudair didn't pay any attention to the impact. The eighteen wheeler shrugged it off like a lethargic dinosaur as the diesel powered around in a turn that took it back down the highway in the wrong direction. Oncoming traffic scattered like insects. Holding on to the big steering wheel, moving through the transmission as he stepped down hard on the accelerator and gained speed, Sudair stared through the dirty windshield at the Jaguar less than two miles away.

He felt finally in control for the first time since he and the neo-Nazis had embarked on their forced retaliatory strikes. Here was an enemy that had tried to flee his wrath. He enjoyed the feeling for a brief few seconds as the speedometer climbed to ninety miles per hour, then he noticed the helicopter to the southwest.

"HEY, KATZ, you got some rolling thunder heading your way." Jack Grimaldi piloted the UH-1D Huey skillfully only a hundred feet over the Swiss terrain, sweeping down toward the eighteen wheeler. The helicopter had begun life as a transport ship, but that had changed early that morning as the NATO base in Germany received coded orders minutes before Grimaldi's and Bolan's arrival. Normally weaponless in civilian areas, the Huey now carried a McDonnell-Douglas M230 30 mm multibarrel cannon mounted under the belly, and a complement of 2.75-inch folding-fin aerial rockets bolted above the portside landing skid. The weapons system was jury-rigged above Grimaldi's head, and targeting was going to be by Kentucky windage, but the ace pilot had operated enough such arrangements in his career that it was second nature.

"Copied, G-Force," Katzenelenbogen's calm voice called back. "Are you prepared to assist?"

"Ready, willing and able, buddy." Grimaldi moved the yoke and swooped from the sky like a hunting falcon. "I'm on my way."

Civilian traffic along both sides of the divided highway had come to a halt as the drivers watched the events unfold. Only the terrorist vehicles and the Phoenix Force units were in motion. It left the battlefield more open for the punitive strike the Stony Man warriors had initiated.

Grimaldi dropped into the open space in front of the charging truck and kicked the rotor around to bring the port side slightly forward. Less than a mile separated the eighteen wheeler from the Jaguar.

One of the terrorists leaned out the passenger window of the truck and cut loose with an assault rifle.

Bullets chewed holes in the Plexiglas nose, and the rushing chill wind whipped in after it. Controlling an instinctive reflex to dodge and grab for the open sky, Grimaldi kept the Huey on track. With less than four hundred yards between them, he reached up and touched the toggle controlling the 2.75-inch rockets. A half dozen of them took flight. Grimaldi's sensitive touch felt the recoil shudder through the whirlybird.

Almost instantly a line of explosions ripped down the side of the truck. The cab took two direct hits just below the windshield on the passenger side, and the remaining four rockets slammed into the steel-sided tractor. The eighteen wheeler was staggered, and flames wreathed the cab. The trailer was a twisted hunk of burning wreckage reluctantly following the tractor rig as it drifted for the side of the highway.

Grimaldi pulled up, missing his fiery target only by yards. He heeled around in the sky and readied himself for his second pass. Reaching overhead again, he flicked the circuitry controlling the 30 mm cannon to life.

NESTLED BEHIND the winding brown winter grasses on a hill overlooking the kill zone, Mack Bolan lay prone with the butt of the Barrett .50-caliber sniping rifle snugly fitted to his shoulder. He was dressed for the play, wearing a thermal-lined blacksuit with web gear holding his secondary weapons. The Desert Eagle was sheathed in a counterterrorist drop holster on his right thigh, while the Beretta 93-R rode in shoulder leather. After he was finished with the Barrett, his primary weapon was going to be a Sage International modified Remington Model 1100 shotgun with a 10-shot Choate magazine extension and telescoping stock that had been used by the U.S. Navy Seals.

Keeping both eyes open as he sighted in on his first target, he saw Grimaldi's chopper narrowly avoid a col-

lision with the burning eighteen wheeler as it rumbled
awkwardly into the ditch along the highway and tipped
over. Encizo brought the specially modified Jaguar into
a tire-eating turn just over a ninety-degree arc that left it
partially facing the oncoming terrorist vehicles. The
passenger door opened and Katz got out, taking advantage of the armored bulk of the car.

The terrorist vehicles slowed uncertainly. McCarter and
Manning closed the gap from behind.

The cross hairs settled on the right front tire of the
second terrorist vehicle. Bolan's finger tightened on the
trigger, and he rode out the recoil. The .50-caliber round
flew true and tore a fist-sized hole out of the tire. It de-
flated immediately and jerked the car hard to the right,
bringing it into contact with the vehicle in front of it.
Both drivers fought to control the cars.

Moving on, the Executioner targeted three more tires,
making all the vehicles pull to the side of the highway
without endangering the civilian cars on the other side of
the thoroughfare.

He scrambled to his feet and sprinted for the Jeep
Cherokee parked on the downgrade behind him. Shoving the Barrett into the back seat, he slid in behind the
wheel. As he keyed the ignition, he tapped the transmit
button on his headset. "McCarter. Manning."

"Go," the Brit answered.

"Here," Manning said.

"Close it in and let's ring down the curtain." Bolan let
out the clutch, and the four-wheel drive scampered up the
side of the hill, going nose down on the other side as he
steered through the brush for the hell zone. He reached
to his side and freed the Remington 1100 from the dashboard clips.

MCCARTER SWERVED and brought the car around in a ninety-degree turn, presenting it broadside to the terrorist vehicles. "Okay, mate," he said to Calvin James, "step lively now." He pushed open the door and slithered out with the Galil assault rifle in his fist. He slung the belt containing the grenade-launcher rounds over his shoulder as he took cover. The aviator sunglasses cut down on the glare hovering over the highway.

James shoved himself out of the car as the first few rounds poked holes in the sheet metal and knocked chunks of safety glass from the windows.

Moving to the rear of the car, McCarter readied the M-203 and slid his finger into the trigger guard. He leaned around the bumper and squeezed off the round. The 40 mm warhead left the barrel with a *whomph* of impact, then slammed into the outside car in the middle of the confusion.

The explosion rocked the car and wrapped it in flames. Two terrorists were knocked down by the concussion. Working the Galil on semiautomatic, McCarter put them down to stay.

James was at the front of the car positioning the SAW on its bipod. A heartbeat later the weapon was rattling off long bursts of 5.56 mm hardball rounds that penetrated the terrorist cars.

McCarter reloaded the grenade launcher and saw Manning taking up a position behind his own car. The Canadian's CAR-15 punctuated the din of battle, and his first few rounds bracketed a blond-haired young German and threw him back into his car.

McCarter tapped his headset. "Any sign of Sudair, Najaf or Rivera?"

"Sudair was in the truck," Katz replied.

The eighteen wheeler, on its side in the ditch, was blazing even brighter.

"Oops," Grimaldi said. The Huey was hovering in the air as the 30 mm cannon scored hits on the car that had been trailing the big truck. The driver had reversed and tried to break away. At least four of the 30 mm rounds hit the car in the front end. The car swerved and bucked. Black smoke poured from under the burned and scarred hood.

"Sudair's toast," Encizo called out as he crawled from the wreckage of the truck.

"That leaves two," Bolan said. The warrior was en route in the Cherokee, plowing down bushes and small trees ahead of him.

McCarter squinted through the gun smoke drifting over the battle zone. Finding the two men was going to be like hunting for a needle in a bloody haystack, and until they did, they were going to have to be careful placing their shots.

BOLAN STEPPED HARD on the brake and brought the Cherokee to a halt outside the circumference of death the Stony Man warriors were laying down. Katz had his MAC-10 and was quietly picking his shots while creating general confusion with the rest of the clip. Although the Stony Man teams were only looking for specific prisoners, the Arab–neo-Nazi threat in Zurich was coming to an end today. Until they dug the roots out, though, it could grow another head just like the mythical Hydra. But it would take time. Bolan was determined that reestablishing that head in Zurich would be a costly investment.

Two Arabs broke from cover and raced for the Cherokee as Bolan climbed out of the vehicle. They fired wildly at him as they ran.

Seeing that neither man was one of the pair he was searching for, the Executioner swung the combat shotgun up and cut them down. The double-aught buckshot knocked both men backward, bloody rags of their shirts clinging to their chests.

Bolan stayed low as he sprinted to the blocked cars. Another round from the Remington sent a neo-Nazi scurrying for cover. Too anxious in his flight, the man tripped over a corpse. Before the terrorist could bring his weapon to bear, the Executioner fired again, subtracting another opponent from the field.

A car tried to break away, streaking for the median between the divided highways. Calvin James wheeled in pursuit, hauling the heavy SAW to his shoulder and cutting loose. The squad automatic weapon carried a 200-round clip, and Bolan judged from the sound of it that the rifle had been nearly full when the ex-Seal opened up.

The hardball rounds chipped paint, knocked the hubcaps loose, shredded the tires and ripped the lower body molding away. None of the bullets penetrated the passenger compartment because James had purposely kept his firing pattern low. Out of control, the car hit the rough terrain and rolled over on its side.

"I've got Rivera at this end," Grimaldi transmitted.

Bolan glanced in the chopper's direction and saw the Bolivian breaking away from the cannoned vehicle. An Arab got out behind him and dropped a pistol into target acquisition on Rivera. The Executioner knew the distance was something less than three hundred yards. He didn't have a weapon with that kind of range. He reached for the transmit button on his headset. "Jack."

"I see him."

The Huey swung around on an invisible axis and dipped its nose. Smoke belched from the 30 mm multi-barrel cannon, digging holes in the highway as the rounds tracked onto the terrorist. At least two of the rounds hit the Arab and disintegrated the human figure in an eye blink.

"Rafael," Katz called out.

"I have him," Encizo replied, peeling away instantly.

"One down, mates," McCarter called out grimly, "but we're burning up the clock here."

Bolan was aware of the doomsday numbers flickering out of existence. Even if they got away from the battle unscathed and in possession of the prisoners they'd come for, too much time spent here would leave the Swiss police hot on their trail. The first patrol units were only minutes away and closing fast.

He pounded along the concrete surface and carried the Remington in both hands before him, knowing Mc-Carter and Manning had already tracked him moving forcefully into the play. He leapt and slid across the back of a sedan with his feet forward, taking out the surprised gunner who had just noticed him.

Off-balance, Bolan tumbled to the ground, seeing a German terrorist tracking autofire toward him. The warrior touched off two eliminating rounds in quick succession. Then the Executioner ripped a grenade from his web gear and tossed it toward the open window of a parked car.

McCarter was moving in, as well, abandoning his Galil in favor of the Browning Hi-Power. The 9 mm pistol cracked with deadly authority, and terrorists went down like shooting-gallery targets from the grim efficiency of his marksmanship.

The thrown grenade erupted in the car, blowing out the windows and filling the interior with swirling white smoke. Fire crawled over the seats and splashed against the inside of the windshield fragments remaining in the frame. A flaming figure stumbled out.

Drawing his side arm, Calvin James dropped the human torch with a single mercy round through the head.

Bolan called out the action as the Stony Man warriors moved through the trapped vehicles and mowed down their opponents in a grimly proficient manner. They found Shiraz al Najaf in the third car they searched. The Arab struggled briefly and tried to bring a weapon into play. Manning smashed the glass out with his rifle stock, reached in and grabbed the smaller man's shirt. He slammed Najaf against the doorframe three times and jarred the Arab's pistol loose. Then he dragged Najaf out, tossed him to the ground and dropped a knee across the man's back, stunning him.

Bolan fired from the point as another Arab tried to draw a bead on Manning's back. The charge of buckshot caught the man and slapped him away as if he'd run into an invisible wall.

"Thanks," Manning said as he cuffed the Iraqi liaison's hands behind his back.

The warrior nodded and moved on, holding the empty shotgun in his left hand while he drew the Desert Eagle from the terrorist drop rig.

"I've got Rivera," Encizo radioed.

Bolan gazed at the clouds of black smoke that funneled upward to become one dark column drawing profanely across the blue of the sky. The whoosh of the flames was an audible undercurrent to the occasional gunfire. He peered through the billowing smoke and saw Katz less than fifteen feet away. Nothing moved or appeared to be alive behind the Israeli. The Executioner knew he'd left no one living on his own trek. He glanced at the Phoenix Force leader. "Time to go."

"Yes." Katz barked sharp commands to his troops.

Bolan tapped the headset transmitter. "Jack, dump the bird and let's get clear."

"Roger." Grimaldi quickly put the Huey down not far from the burning eighteen wheeler.

Encizo and Manning herded their charges toward the waiting Cherokee at a trot while James, McCarter, Katz and Bolan stamped out the final resistance offered by the handful of surviving terrorists.

As the rest of the team loaded into the 4WD and onto the running boards, Bolan took a can of yellow spray paint from his gear and walked to one of the terrorist vans. In block letters, he printed out "scorched earth" in English.

"A message?" Katz asked as he dropped into the passenger seat of the Cherokee.

Bolan keyed the ignition and waited on Grimaldi. "Yeah. They've been getting this one for a while."

After making a final adjustment inside the grounded helicopter, Grimaldi ran away from it at full speed. Before he reached the 4WD, an explosion rocked the countryside, echoed by smaller blasts as the unexpended rounds in the armament went up. Only fiery debris remained of the Huey, and the serial numbers on the parts had been removed with acid earlier. Since the Huey was a NATO and corporate model, the trail would turn cold for police investigators immediately.

Bolan knew the wet ground and snow drifts would keep any potential fires from spreading, and emergency rescue vehicles would be on the scene in moments.

Pulling himself up on the passenger running board beside James, Grimaldi said, "Ready, Sarge."

Shoving the gearshift into first, Bolan put his foot on the accelerator and swung the Cherokee around in a tight circle, heading back up the incline he'd come racing down less than three minutes ago. The 4WD shook and shivered as it powered over the rough terrain.

At the top, two more off-road vehicles were waiting under cover of a copse of short pines.

When the Cherokee rolled to a stop, Katz deployed from it, moving his men into two prearranged groups. Rivera went into one of the vehicles while Najaf accompanied McCarter and James in the other one.

Grimaldi dropped into the passenger seat beside Bolan and started shifting the ordnance from the vehicle they would no longer need.

The Executioner put the Cherokee in motion while the pilot finished up. The plan was to get away clean, but it was possible they'd have to pass a police roadblock along the way before they could get to the safehouse Price had arranged. The Desert Eagle and other personal weapons could be stashed in hiding places located within the vehicle. The glimpse the civilian motorists had of the Cherokee wouldn't be enough to identify it. Either way, the vehicle didn't figure into any long-term plans.

The next stop was going to be deep into the Middle East. Bolan was convinced of that, but he was only partially sure of what would be waiting there for them. And time was running out for any feints or soft probes. If they couldn't get the Intel they needed, they were going to have to force their opponents' hands. In a land of ancestral enemies, though, it was hard to figure out whom they were ultimately after.

There was no margin for error, and the perpetual storm clouds of war that hovered over the Middle East were already darkening with threat.

CHAPTER EIGHT

"We have common goals," Dr. Enoch Harel said in a soft voice. "We need land for the population that continues to flock to us, and Palestine needs a country for her people. We also need peace so that we can take our places as our heritages demand. For that to happen, we needed a common enemy." He pointed to the map on the wall of his den. "Jordan, and King Hussein." He paused, looking meaningfully at Zahid Faysal. "They are our enemies. Let's not forget that because we are feeling the pressure of the moment."

"Our task is great," Faysal said. "I'm well aware your people need to be goaded into this fight, and the Palestinian Liberation Organization is not the whole it once was, either." Then he lifted his glass of distilled water and said, "A toast to the new countries, and to the future they promise."

"Yes," Harel replied as he reached for his own glass of wine.

Wellsberg, too, joined in.

"Jordan poses a threat to Israel," Harel said. "Ever since her alliance with Saddam Hussein during the Gulf War, King Hussein's motives have been suspect. Now he continues to help out the Iraqis as they rebuild for war by ferrying their wealth across Jordan so they can purchase new war machines and supplies against the edicts laid down by the United Nations. In time we will be attacked again, and none of the Western powers are willing to help us. And as we have seen, their bombs are indiscriminate. They fall in this nation and kill Jews, Christians and Muslims alike. It's our responsibility to see that no more lives are claimed by Jordan or Iraq. And there are the promises Jordan has made to the Palestinians to create a nation for them within their own borders since 1974. It is time they honored that agreement."

A line bisected Jordan on the wall map, running horizontally.

Harel traced it with his forefinger. "We have managed a fair division, I think. Everything north of the Mojib River will go to create the new Palestine. Everything south will become Israeli holdings. As we have agreed, the West Bank will remain in contention, open to Israelis and Palestinians alike. Your organization's tentative accord with my government doesn't solve much, and who knows if it will stand. We men of daring and vision have to act, steer fate in the right direction."

"How soon?" Faysal asked.

Harel turned from the map. The timetable alterations had been the reason for today's meeting. "There are problems we had not really foreseen."

The Arab's wiry body tightened, and his face hardened into resolute lines. "What problems?"

"I received notification only a few moments ago that both Tarim Sudair and Shiraz al Najaf, the Jordanian and Iraqi representatives of the caravan proceeds being shipped from Iraq, were neutralized."

"Dead?"

"Sudair for certain. It is believed that Najaf may still be alive."

Faysal shrugged. "Neither of those men have information that will hurt us."

"No, but it will slow the Iraqi and Jordanian response to attack Israel. The word the Jordanian Intelligence has received is that they were taken down by an American counterterrorist force."

"Still, the Jordanians are paranoid enough to believe that Israel was ultimately behind that."

"Perhaps. But we need to speed things back up. If we lose momentum, we might lose international support, as well." Harel crossed the room to his desk and flipped through the notes he'd assembled.

"Israel must not come across as the aggressor in this," Wellsberg said. "Otherwise, we have gained nothing. Almost every time we have tried to expand our borders, the Western powers have made us give back our land acquisitions."

"Once the exodus has begun," Faysal said, "there can be no turning back. My people will not be patient much longer."

"I know. That's why I thought it best we speak of these things today. If events continue as they are, the Nazis and the Jordanians may come to realize they'd been played for fools since the beginning. Putting those two groups together took years of planning and counterplanning. I won't see it taken apart in mere days."

"Those groups have suffered drastically of late," Faysal said. "They should be even more willing to attack Israel now."

"They're confused by the presence of the American force."

"That could be explained away by American sympathy for Israel," Faysal suggested.

"Perhaps, but they're not accepting that at face value. They're starting to investigate."

"How much can they find out?"

Harel spread his hands. "At this point I'm not sure. We've kept a low profile. The Americans, Soviets and British don't know we've interceded in these affairs. All of them had staked out the various caravans coming from Iraq, but our paths never crossed."

"So what do you propose?"

Handing the Arab a paper, Harel said, "In only a few hours a group of Jordanian covert militia will launch a preemptive strike against Jewish politicians based here in Jerusalem. I don't know if they'll succeed on their own. However, with the help of some of your people, I'm sure they will."

"I understand."

"In fact, it would be well if they weren't as successful as they could be. A few bodies that could be identified later by investigators would be ideal."

Faysal merely nodded in agreement. "What about the agent you've been using? Canary? Isn't that her code name?"

Harel didn't let his surprise show, but Wellsberg's eyes narrowed. "Yes, it is."

"She's become known to us."

"I see."

"Can't you use her inside the Jordanian military Intelligence to leverage a Jordanian retaliation?"

"We're working along those lines now."

"It would be a good thing if she could let you know about the covert force stalking the Nazis and Jordanians. I'd heard she was once affiliated with the Americans."

"That's true. And that's also an angle we're seeking to use."

"Keep me apprised of the developments."

"Of course."

With a short nod, Faysal got to his feet and left the room in a swirl of his djellaba. Two of his personal guards fell into step with him as he passed through the door, and Harel's valet quietly closed it after the Arab entourage.

"I don't trust that man," Wellsberg said in the silence that followed.

"He doesn't trust us, either," Harel replied. "This is a relationship based on need, not mutual admiration. Once we have the situation well in hand, then we can deal with the Palestinian problem once and for all. They will never become a threat. After they are given their lands in Jordan, they will fight among themselves for who is to lead their new nation."

"And you, Enoch?" Wellsberg asked softly. "Will you attempt to step into the forefront of the new Israel?"

Harel chuckled and turned to face the Mossad agent. "Who told you to ask me that?"

"No one."

"Come now, Benjamin, who are you protecting? Chaim or Oren? Both of them have tried to second-guess my motivations from the start."

Wellsberg remained silent.

"At any rate, tell your friends to rest their worries. I have no political aspirations."

"After today you could become a hero to the Jewish people."

"I already am," Harel stated. "And in the future, I expect to be more of one. They'll write about me in history books. In the time before I die, I'll increase my wealth and get a chance to direct part of Israel's emerging new economy. That's all I want."

"Is it really?"

"Yes. Oh, come on, this nation has been raised on detailed histories of prophets and heroes. Any boy's dream would be to get the chance to be ranked among them."

Harel kept the smile from his face with difficulty, then thought about the potential problems the American covert force posed. "We need to take the counterterrorist squad off the board before they complicate things any further."

"Agreed. But how do you propose to do this?"

"With Sudair and Najaf out of the way, they have only one possible avenue to pursue. They'll come to the Middle East, to Jordan. Your people are still there?"

"Of course."

The handpicked Mossad crew had been attacking the caravans at different points before the American group had stepped in. Part of the wealth Harel had amassed for the Israeli efforts had come from the successful strikes the Mossad agents had pulled off. "Notify them. Give them orders to take the American agents down as soon as they're able, and dispose of the bodies. We want no proof of Western involvement in these matters."

Wellsberg nodded. "The United States may decide to take a more active role if their agents suddenly disappear."

"Then I think Israel could take that as a sign that retaliation is inevitable and go ahead with punitive action toward Jordan. Either way, we'll be freed up to do the things we want to do."

"I think so, too."

"But I also believe the Americans will try negotiation first rather than rely on military intervention in spite of their willingness to flex their muscle as they did in Somalia."

"They still maintain good relations with Saudi Arabia and have use of those bases. It's possible they could try to intercede from there."

"Let them." Harel smiled as he considered the map. "That way when the attack comes from Jordan, as it inevitably will, they can be on hand to offer assistance. Though it won't be needed, the Americans could help us turn this situation around much more quickly."

"It would be better if we could keep them out of it."

"Yes. But if we can't, it's better to manipulate them to our side. Meyer Levin is also becoming more of a problem. Your man missed him earlier today."

"That's being taken care of. In a couple of hours Levin's association with the Mossad will be terminated. I've placed enough information in his superior's hands to allow him to place Levin on investigatory leave. Given the man's temperament, he won't be able to leave the situation alone. He'll continue prodding at it blindly. And he'll die doing that."

"What about the woman who saved him? Have you found out who she was?"

"No."

"I wish we knew who she was."

"Has Canary been able to turn up anything on the assassination?"

"Nothing. She seemed surprised that we were behind the attempt."

"She knew that Levin has been investigating her?"

"Yes. She felt there would be no problem from that corner."

"This woman has quite an ego, doesn't she?"

Harel nodded. He was aware of Wellsberg's feelings toward women in general despite the conditions in Israel. The Mossad agent still felt espionage was a skill best practiced by men. "She has an ego, and deservedly so. I couldn't have put everything together in this amount of time without her."

"I don't like going to an outside source."

"If there had been another way, it would have been done."

"There was another way."

"And it would have taken more time." Harel shook his head and walked toward his desk. "We needed to strike while the iron was hot, while the Iraqis and Jordanians are drawing the combined wrath of the United Nations. We'll never be able to make this move again. Too many factors had to come together to enable us to make this one."

"You're right."

Harel didn't push the admission any further than Wellsberg was willing to offer it. "Then let's have one more drink to the health of the reborn Israel and get on with our agendas." He smiled.

Wellsberg returned a smile, but it didn't quite reach his eyes.

Deep within the other's gaze, Harel could see the same suspicion that had become rooted in Wellsberg when he'd killed the woman in the basement. It hadn't really been done out of any personal need for vengeance. It had been meant as a warning, and the Mossad man hadn't missed it.

"RIGHT INTO the lion's mouth."

"There just isn't any other way to do it, guy." Carl Lyons turned the collar of his windbreaker up against the chill breeze that raced across night-shrouded Los Angeles.

Hermann "Gadgets" Schwarz and Rosario "Politician" Blancanales flanked him as they crossed the paved parking area of the White Knight Bar & Grill. The tavern was located in a fringe area within the Sunset Strip district, within blocks of the cowboy and gay bars. Traffic moved steadily despite the late hour, and the city in the distance looked as if it was lit up with pseudosunlight.

Lyons ignored their cheerful bantering as he closed on the main entrance to the bar. He was dressed in a black turtleneck under the loud windbreaker, jeans and combat boots. His Government Model Colt .45 was in a jackass rig under his left arm. A Semmerling Derringer .45 ACP was a solid weight in his boot.

"And to look at the bright side," Schwarz said, "we've got Cowboy for company."

Cowboy John Kissinger, Stony Man Farm's chief weapons smith, had opted in on the play with Price's consent. The machinations at the California end of things were going to be risky at best. The mission controller had figured the extra firepower would be helpful.

Schwarz wore slacks, shirt and tie, covered by a gray sport coat with leather patches on the elbows. A Beretta 92-F rode his right hip, concealed by the jacket. His manner of dress would draw attention immediately inside the club, as Lyons had planned.

The White Knight Bar & Grill was a known hang-out for members of the Aryan Resistance Movement, Striker's first targets after being handed the assignment at Stony Man Farm.

During the flight to LAX, Lyons and the other members of Able Team had read the reports Price and Kurtzman had generated. Justin Pratt, the leader of the ARM, had fallen before the Executioner's guns, but a number of the movement's believers remained. Even Price felt they would be no more trouble for a while, but it was possible to use them to leverage events in the Middle East.

Lyons tapped the packet of photos inside the windbreaker. "Okay, we're going solo."

"Roger," Kissinger said over the radio comlink. "If you have any trouble, just holler and we'll come a-running."

Palming the ear-throat headset, Lyons shoved it into his pocket. His thumb slid the concealed transmit button into the locked-on position so Kissinger and Blancanales could listen in.

The interior of the bar was dark and gloomy, choked with stale, recycled air and cigarette smoke. Most of the clientele looked working-class, many of them wearing shirts or jackets that identified the companies they worked for. Others went in for the black-leather look or military trappings. Buck knives in belt sheaths seemed to be the rule rather than the exception. A quartet of uniformed security guards held down a booth in one corner, and their eyes drifted toward the front door instinctively.

Lyons filed them away in his mind. Even if they weren't licensed to carry in their present jobs, chances were they kept weapons of some kind tucked away. He swept the room with a level glance as four skinheads piled in behind him.

"There," Schwarz called in a soft voice. "At two o'clock in a booth. Wearing a red blazer. He is the new number-one man in the Aryan Resistance Movement since Striker whittled the top dogs down."

Lyons casually started across the room, heading for his man.

Luther Nix had served time for manslaughter in Sacramento in past years, and caught a couple of other brief vacations on state time for assault charges. Seven years ago he'd tied up with Justin Pratt's group and gained the benefit of better legal counsel.

Two men, big and burly, shared the table with Nix. They stood up as Lyons approached.

"You Luther Nix?" Lyons asked.

Nix glared up at him, then patiently dropped the butt of his cigarette into the closest of the dozen beer bottles scattered across the tabletop. "Who're you?"

"Cord Lakehurst. I'm with the Justice Department." Lyons flashed the ID. The growl of rage from the giant to his right caught him off guard. He'd figured neither of the bodyguards would have made a move without it being cleared by Nix.

Before he could set himself properly, a big fist smashed into his head. Stars spun in Lyons's vision as he fell backward, but he could dimly see the giant coming for him.

CHAPTER NINE

Hermann Schwarz sidestepped the flailing tangle of arms and legs as Lyons was bowled over by the bigger man.

"Oh, shit," the bodyguard with the beer gut said as he surged forward. "Moose done opened the ball now. You know how he feels about G-men." He telegraphed a haymaker at Schwarz's face.

Reaching into his jacket pocket, Schwarz dodged the blow and fisted his stun gun. He blocked the next swing, then rammed it into his attacker's groin and touched the button.

The sudden burst of stored electricity surged into the man's system with a white flash against denim as the discharge hissed and popped. The bodyguard jerked as his synapses temporarily disconnected. His eyes turned upward in his head, leaving only the whites showing.

Once he was satisfied the stun gun had completed its two-second discharge, Schwarz put his hand on the man's face and pushed him away.

The bodyguard took out a table as he fell, sending a pitcher of beer and mugs crashing to the floor. The table's occupants shoved away from their seats and swore vehemently.

Schwarz let the stun gun recharge as he checked on Lyons.

The Ironman wasn't quite holding his own. Moose's larger size and greater weight was an immediate advantage close in. The Nazi threw a hammer-fist that came up and over, smashing into Lyons's back as he tried to set himself. The Able Team warrior went to his knees on the floor, but pushed himself back up. A sweeping backhand collided with Lyons's face and sent the younger man backward.

"Shoot him," Schwarz advised as he drew his own Beretta 92-F and covered Luther Nix.

Moose looked perplexed for a moment.

Blood bubbled across Lyons's crooked grin as he got to his feet. "No way." He crooked a finger at Moose. "C'mon, big man, let's see what you've got."

"What the hell are you doing here?" Luther Nix asked.

Two more members of the brotherhood came at Schwarz from behind. He swiveled the Beretta out to meet them and thumbed the hammer back. They raised their hands and retreated.

"Actually," Schwarz said as he dropped into the booth across from Nix, "we're here to do you a favor." He kept the Beretta loose, ready to swing it in any direction.

Nix was heavyset, fortyish and sporting an Elvis-styled hairdo in spite of the receding hairline. A dangling cross earring hung from his left ear, and a tracery of fine scarring showed where it or others like it had been ripped free in the past. "Can't say that I remember the last time a Fed did me a favor."

"Maybe you've never seen a time when you needed it so bad," Schwarz said.

"You've got me intrigued."

"Good. What say you call off your guy?"

Nix laughed harshly. "Afraid your buddy will get hurt?"

Moose had picked up a wooden straight-backed chair and was swinging it at Lyons.

"No," Schwarz answered. "But it might be an idea if the local law didn't get involved in this."

"It's not my problem. I didn't do anything."

"Right. But if my partner gets pissed, I can't guarantee how cooperative he's going to feel afterward."

"Once Moose gets started, you can't stop him. You're going to be lucky if Moose doesn't hand him his head."

Lyons stepped into the swinging chair and blocked it with his forearm. The chair came apart like kindling and clattered across the floor.

Schwarz took a bill from his shirt pocket and flattened it on the tabletop in front of Nix. "I got twenty bucks that says my guy kicks your guy's ass."

"All right." Nix stacked two ten-dollar bills on the twenty and placed his back against the wall while he watched the fight. "Are you really from the Justice Department?"

"Yeah. Want to see my badge?"

"Later."

Before Moose could drop the broken ends of the chair, Lyons stepped in with two left jabs that set up a right cross and snapped back his head.

Roaring with rage, the bald giant rushed at Lyons with widespread arms. The big ex-cop ducked and grabbed a thick wrist as Moose's momentum carried him forward. Bringing the arm up behind the neo-Nazi's back, Lyons put a shoulder to his opponent's back and added more speed and power to the man's momentum.

Moose slammed into the wall with a violent crash, then collapsed onto the scattered debris that used to be a table and chairs.

Against the wall, Moose screamed obscenities and pushed himself to a wavering stance. Lyons reached into his jacket and brought out his .45.

Moose froze.

Without saying anything, the Able Team warrior stripped out of the windbreaker and the jackass rig. He tossed them onto a chair near Nix, then put the Colt Government Model on safety and threw it to Schwarz in an underhand toss.

Schwarz caught it easily without moving from his position. It was a gutsy play on Lyons's part, and he knew it. Even with the cover they had in place for this part of the operation, the neo-Nazi crowd at the White Knight would take some selling to buy the story they'd brought in with them. But the Ironman's apparent sense of fair play might buy them a few converts.

Moose came in more slowly this time, his big arms moving deliberately, pawing the air to draw some kind of reaction from Lyons.

Lyons didn't bite.

"Has your buddy got some kind of death wish?" Nix asked.

"No." As Schwarz watched the action, he realized another layer of Lyons's unplanned strategy. With his blond hair cropped neatly, not much longer than LAPD regulation standards, and his blue eyes, the Ironman represented the ideal Aryan warrior most of the men in the room wished they were.

The bald giant reached in and suddenly fisted Lyons's turtleneck.

Lyons fired a wicked series of jabs to his opponent's midsection, and the dulled impacts drifted over the interior of the club like a woodman's ax biting deep into a mighty oak. Moose appeared jarred for a moment, then shrugged the blows off like a dog shaking off bathwater. They struggled on, Lyons delivering overhand roundhouses and right crosses, his own face streaming blood from a cut above his left eye. Panting and heaving, Lyons continued the punishing blows until the bald giant sank to the floor with a shudder. A handful of men came forward and checked the big man. "He's alive," one of them said.

Lyons stood back, breathing hard.

"Look after him," Nix ordered. "If he needs to go to the hospital, somebody take him there."

The men picked Moose up from the floor bodily and carried him to a side room.

Schwarz took a handkerchief from his pocket and handed it to Lyons, then passed over the .45 and shoved the money into his wallet.

White teeth gleamed in the Ironman's smile, but the emotion in his blue eyes wasn't friendly. "You're a hard man to do a favor for, Luther."

"I'll see your IDs now," Nix said, "then I'll decide whether I want to call my lawyer before we continue this discussion."

Lyons shrugged into his windbreaker and offered his wallet for inspection.

Schwarz did the same.

"Lakehurst and Schwann," Nix said when he finished reading the information. "What do two federal marshals want with me?"

Schwarz made the Beretta disappear under his jacket but didn't put it away. Once a weapon was drawn because there was just cause, it was better never to let it get too far from hand. "We're here to try to save you from the bad deal Pratt started between the ARM and the Arabs."

Nix lit up a fresh cigarette. "Don't know what you're talking about."

"Pratt got himself iced down in Bolivia," Lyons said. He took the manila packet from the windbreaker and opened it with a thumb.

"I heard that a covert team of FBI or DEA agents were responsible for that."

"Not according to our sources." Lyons dropped two photographs from the packet onto the tabletop. "Recognize either of those guys?"

Schwarz scanned the pictures quickly, recognizing Sudair and Najaf.

Nix shifted the pictures around with his fingers. "No. Who's your source?"

"The CIA. This is Tarim Sudair. He was the Jordanian representative for the terrorist group ARM was doing business with. This is Shiraz Najaf. He was the Iraqi connection. Pratt knew about both of them."

"Why would the CIA be keeping tabs on Pratt?"

"Because of the Bolivian connection. You know the Company has used narco-dollars themselves. ARM and the Arabs weren't the first to think of it."

Nix's eyes narrowed. "And people in the CIA would just hand over information like this to a couple of Justice marshals."

Schwarz played the question calmly, setting the foundation for the fabrication they were about to sell to the new head of the Aryan Resistance Movement. "No. We asked for it."

"Why?"

Schwarz returned the suspicious level gaze full measure. "Because, like you, not everybody working in Justice is happy with the amount of political clout the hebes have in this nation's capital. Hell, they've had spies going through our files over the years. With the Commies gone, this country's not so damned dependent on

Israel as a military base. Maybe now's the time to be rid of them and their problems once and for all.''

Nix exhaled a thick lungful of smoke. ''You got any kind of evidence to back this up?''

Moving his hands deftly, Lyons shuffled out the remaining photographs.

Schwarz knew the work was good. He'd seen it. Kurtzman and Price had put it together from the L.A. Sheriff's Department files regarding the investigation of the Executioner's blistering blitzkrieg of the ARM training camp. Using the cybernetic systems' digitization equipment and artist's software, the Bear had created scenes of a swarthy-skinned attack force moving through the ruins of the training camp in forest camouflage. Some of the pictures had been dummied well enough from existing configurations to show parts of a firefight that had never happened.

''Who are these people?'' Nix asked.

''Arabs,'' Lyons answered. He pointed to each face in turn. ''Rasheed al Kabeer. Talil Amba. Fahad Wahhab. Jamal Hegailan. Every one of these people has been confirmed through CIA files as members of the Jordanian and Iraqi terrorist groups. You see the black armbands they're wearing?''

''Yeah,'' Nix said. ''That's an old French foreign legion strategy to identify members of their forces in an combat zone.''

''That's right. And it goes to show a lot of thought went into this strike before it happened.''

''The CIA took these pictures?''

''Yeah. They had an agent practically camping on top of that training area for weeks.''

''And he didn't try to interfere with these executions?''

"That wasn't why he was there. And it would have been suicide for him to try. You know what kind of casualties they took there."

"Who else knows about this?" Nix dragged a picture down to sit directly in front of him.

Schwarz looked at the photograph. It was of an Arab-looking man bayoneting a young man in uniform. He thought Kurtzman had gone a little far in the gore factor, but it definitely carried the necessary emotional impact.

"Nobody in the States," Schwarz said. "Officially we're out here on a follow-up investigation regarding the strikes against the ARM. We're supposed to turn in whatever names we uncover of other possible subversives."

Nix glanced up at him. "And unofficially?"

"There's someone with some stroke at the Justice Department who'd like to see you guys get the pound of flesh that's due you."

"They want us to take on the Arabs?"

"You figure on waiting around till they take the rest of you out?" Lyons asked.

"They haven't made a move toward us."

"So far. Christ, guy, are you sure you took a good look at those pictures?"

"I saw them."

Lyons snorted in derision. "Maybe if I wait a week, I can show the next ARM leader your picture. If there are any of you left."

"Back off, man. We take care of our own rat-killing around here."

"From the look of things, Pratt had you running with them."

"Pratt had an idea. We hate the Jews, and the Arabs hate the Jews. Financially it made sense to link up. Made sense militarily, too. Why the hell would they start attacking us?"

"You were raking in a lot of money from the cocaine circuit. Maybe they were tired of splitting the profits."

"Then they'd be stupid. They didn't have the connections locally that we did, and they didn't have the people in place down in South America. That'd be like cutting off their noses to spite their faces."

"They're Arabs," Lyons said. "I don't think they run too strong on brains even if they do hate the Jews."

"And they were already setting up an underground network to take over the distribution," Schwarz said.

"Is that a fact?"

Schwarz nodded. It was actually Price's supposition based on information Phoenix Force had uncovered in Switzerland. Whether it was true or not hadn't been ascertained. Sudair's forces had been ferrying information concerning the other group through their dispatches to the Jordanian office. Uncovering what the other group was really doing in California was another part of Able Team's assignment.

"What do you want from me?" Nix asked.

"We need to know the banking accounts and procedures used to move the money out of the U.S.," Lyons said. "We're going to shut the Arabs down."

"If I do that, they're going to know I sold them out."

"Yeah," Schwarz said.

Nix pushed the photographs back across the table. "Pictures or no pictures, I need more proof before I make a move like that." He pushed himself up from the table and started to walk away.

"Don't make a mistake here," Schwarz said softly.

Nix halted and turned to look at him. "We can take care of ourselves."

"Don't kid yourself. You are working on borrowed time."

"Think so?"

"Yeah," Schwarz said. "I can practically guarantee it."

Nix broke the eye contact and walked away.

Without a word between them, Lyons and Schwarz got up and made their way out of the tavern. Curious glances followed them all the way out the door.

"We kicked his ass," Schwarz said, "so we know we have his attention."

"We're going to keep kicking it, too," Lyons promised. "Wait till he gets to see phase two." He slipped his ear/throat headset from his pocket and hailed Blancanales and Kissinger.

Schwarz was aware of the sentinels Nix had sent outside the White Knight Bar & Grill to watch them leave. The ARM leader would deal. Able Team was going to keep the pressure on, and the man wouldn't have a choice. His gut told him the trail they were attempting to pick up was going to be a twisting and surprising one.

MACK BOLAN poured a cup of coffee from the stainless-steel thermos among the stores assembled for them from the galley of the USS *Cagney*. The liquid was dark and hot and fresh despite being lugged most of the length of the ship to the berths Price had arranged for the Stony Man teams.

The aircraft carrier was located in the Red Sea, a scant thirty miles from the Israeli coast. F-14 Tomcats and F/A-18E Hornets scrambled from the decks on regular recon missions high above the borders of Israel, Jordan and Iraq. Admiral MacEvey's standing orders were to keep an eye on things in Iraq according to guidelines handed down from the United Nations. The missive regarding the arrival of the Stony Man warriors via connecting flights from Zurich was eyes-only direct from the Pentagon. There hadn't been any explanations as to who they were or what they were doing there, but whatever they needed, they were to get.

Bolan sipped the coffee as Calvin James finished hooking up the satellite relay that would connect them to the Farm. He was dressed in jeans and a turtleneck and wore a pair of deck shoes. The steel flooring under his feet vibrated with the power of the engines as the carrier barely held steerageway in the sea. He worked his shoulders, feeling the hours piling up on him now that he was more or less at rest for the time being.

The rest of Phoenix Force and Grimaldi sat at the rectangular table occupying the center of the large berth. Trays of sandwiches, soups and bowls of fresh fruit were within easy reach, along with the dozen thermoses. All of the Stony Man warriors were dressed in civilian clothes while maintaining their personal side arms. They drew attention from the staff and personnel of the aircraft carrier immediately, but their time on deck had been limited. A Marine force had escorted them in quick double-time below-decks and made sure none of the off-duty sailors rubbernecking the clandestine arrival had taken pictures of the Stony teams.

Zurich and the interrogations of Najaf and Rivera had been hours ago. The Iraqi had maintained his silence and hadn't had much information to pass on even after James had administered truth serum. Rivera had willingly talked and had confirmed Price's questions about another Arab group working within the U.S. and on the periphery of the Bolivian leg of the cocaine operation, though he couldn't explain who they were or what they were doing there.

"Got it," James said as he stepped back from the computer monitor bolted to a swing-arm attached to the ceiling. He pocketed a small screwdriver and reached for the wide-bottomed coffee cup on the floor at his feet. A camcorder and a microphone were hooked into the feed system and mounted on top of the monitor.

Bolan pulled the radio handset from the unit at his side, pushed the transmit button and said, "Stony One to Stony Base. Over."

"Go, Stony One. You have Stony Base. Over." Kurtzman's voice sounded strong and healthy.

"Be advised that we're standing by for sat-com relay. Over."

"Roger, Stony Base is advised. We're making the relay connection now. Over."

A line of rainbow static rippled across the monitor screen, chasing silver-and-gray ghosts away, then it cleared, revealing a twin projection of Barbara Price and Aaron Kurtzman at the Bear's horseshoe-shaped workstation.

Bolan took his seat at the side of the table. His war book and the maps he'd requested from the ship's library were spread out within easy reach. Two mechanical pencils and a fine-tipped ink pen sat in a plastic case. He took up one of the pencils and got ready to add to the notes he'd already made regarding tentative hot zones in the three countries. The last communication they'd had from Price hadn't been specific as to what their missions were going to be.

He and Katz had agreed that they'd probably be split up, one group to Israel while the other went to Jordan, but beyond that neither could venture a guess for sure in what direction they were supposed to move. Most of the mission still seemed to be purely recon.

He glanced at Price's image on the clear screen. The mission controller was dressed casually, but her shoulders seemed slumped a little more than usual, and shadows pooled like pale bruises under her eyes.

David McCarter reached into the ice chest against the wall, extracted a can of Coke and cracked the seal with an audible hiss.

After a brief check on the visual and sound systems, Price said, "We've decoded a little more from the files Phoenix recovered and we've had some new Intel from the various Intelligence communities we're hard wired into. But we're still operating in the dark with no one target in our sights. Able Team is engaged stateside, working to broaden our understanding of the events that have brought us this far. When I know it, you'll get it."

"What about Canary?" Encizo asked. "The double agent that was named in those files?"

Price shook her head. "We've been unable to either confirm or dismiss her presence."

"What about information on the woman?" Manning asked.

"So far," Price said, "we haven't been able to find out anything about her."

Beside the mission controller, Kurtzman momentarily glanced down at his keyboard.

Bolan caught the movement, then looked at Katz. The Israeli commando locked eyes with him for a heartbeat, then looked away.

"She's got to have left a trail somewhere," McCarter said. "That bloody bitch seems to have us in her sights and appears to have the wherewithal to do that, which is pretty damned hard to do.''

"I know." Price's mouth was a thin, hard line. "We're working on it. Again, when I have it, you'll have it. Yakov."

"Yes."

"Phoenix's mission will be in Jordan. Aaron was able to pinpoint the location of the outpost that's been organizing the convoys from Baghdad. Your objective will be to take that outpost down and retrieve any information you can from it. The files have also confirmed that Phoenix was not the first successful strike against the convoys.''

"Others took them down?" James asked.

"Yes. According to Sudair's files, three other convoys were taken before Phoenix destroyed the one they were assigned to.''

"You said 'taken,'" Katz said.

"Right. The convoys were stolen away at different vulnerable points along the route.''

"What happened to them?"

"We don't know," Price said. "Maybe you can find out.''

"Any working hypotheses?" McCarter asked.

"At this point, no.''

"Bandits?" Encizo suggested. "The bedouin sometimes act in their own interests in those areas.''

"Maybe. But they'd have had to have extensive knowledge of where and when to hit those cargo trucks. The lesser-protected areas are seldom and far between, and security on those convoys wasn't lax. You people are aware of that from your own insertion.''

"Do you know what was in those convoys?" Bolan asked.

"No. There could be records at the outpost."

"If so," Katz said, "and they contained artwork, as did the one that we took down, it's possible that we could trace back the cargo if it's hit the markets."

"That's a possibility we're hoping will pay off. If you can get us some kind of manifests, we'll try to make the connections."

Bolan considered that, then filed it away, returning to thinking about why the convoys were targeted. "If those had been hit-and-git missions, the attackers would have simply destroyed everything, and they wouldn't have been prepared to take the cargo away."

Price nodded.

"There were no other exploratory strikes against the caravans?"

"Not from what we've been able to tell from Sudair's records."

"Meaning those attack groups already knew what was in those trucks before they hit them," Katz said.

"That's the scenario I've got in mind."

"We knew what was in those trucks, too," Encizo pointed out.

"So whoever it was," Manning said, "has Intel resources approximating our own."

"I think we can rule out amateurs," Price said. "Yakov, when you and your people hit the field near Amman, you need to keep in mind that those opposing forces may still be there. A fourth convoy was taken only a few days ago."

"Since we took ours," Katz said.

"Yes."

"Were the circumstances the same?"

Price nodded. "Everything was taken, and the convoy personnel were left for dead."

"The only real motive we're looking at here," Bolan said, "is profit. And the only Intelligence community near enough to reach successfully into Jordan is the Mossad."

"Or Israeli mercenaries looking to increase their coffers. The influx of Soviet Jews has weakened the national economy. But there still remains the fact that the Arab terrorists and the Nazi groups weren't ready to make the move against Israel. They were goaded into it. Until we find out who had the stick, we're still just whistling in the dark."

"How will we be going in?" Katz asked.

"I've got a HALO jump scheduled shortly after nightfall. The coordinates Aaron and I have turned up should put you within a few miles of the Jordanian outpost. Once we get you in place, we can triangulate you in to your target."

"Fine."

"Striker, you'll be going into Jerusalem. I'm working on arranging some local help on your leg of the mission, but a few more pieces have to fall into place. In the meantime Aaron has ferreted out a Jordanian strike force inside the city. We're uncertain what their goal is at this point, but we need to excise the terrorist cell. Jack, you'll be pulling the backup detail, on the ground and in the air."

Grimaldi nodded.

"Arrangements have been made regarding transportation and equipment. Yakov, Phoenix will have to procure their own wheels, and you need to keep a low profile while you're roving. I can get you into Jordan, but getting you out again could be some time in the doing. You'll all be receiving hard copy on the pertinent facts we've assembled here. Are there any further questions?''

There weren't. As always, Price's evaluation and summation of the various pieces of the mission were on target and divided into easily digestible components.

But Bolan noticed a difference about her that he couldn't put his finger on. They were lovers, taking time as it became available, in a relationship that had no future. But it had enabled him to see sides of her personality that few others were privy to. While his mind followed her logical progression and found no flaws with her suggested tactics, a subliminal query was definitely present.

Price signed off and the monitor screen blanked, leaving the warrior with his puzzling thoughts.

CHAPTER TEN

"Meyer."

Levin glanced up from the papers covering his office desk. His eyes ached from the strain of reading for so many hours, and his reading glasses, he noticed for the first time, had fingerprint smudges on them. A half-eaten cheese sandwich shared a saucer with a cup of coffee that had grown cold long ago and now only served as a paperweight. "Yes."

His superior, Eizer Knafy, stood ramrod stiff in the open doorway. Clad in a dark blue business suit, his beefy face freshly shaven beneath short-cropped cottony hair, Knafy looked every inch the commanding officer. "There is no easy way to say this, my friend."

Levin leaned back in his creaky swivel chair and rediscovered the aches and strains that he'd thought had disappeared long ago. He flicked ashes from the cigarette butt he'd been nursing onto the small gray mountain that overflowed his ashtray. Sparing a glance, knowing Knafy would wait because of the years they'd served together, he studied the office objectively. There wasn't, he had to admit, much of the man who had worked there that colored the walls. His children were grown and gone, two of them dead in battles that Israel seemed to be constantly waging, and his wife had passed away almost a dozen years ago. In reflection he decided maybe there was nothing of the man on the walls because there hadn't been much of the man left for a number of years.

Returning his gaze to Knafy, he said, "It's come to this, then."

Knafy couldn't meet his gaze. "Yes."

"When?"

"Now."

"By whose order?"

"I can't say."

"The hell you can't." Levin tried to fan the spark of anger that ignited within him, but it eluded him. He felt drained almost immediately.

"Meyer, please. Do not make this any more difficult than it already is."

"After all these years, after all these sacrifices, I should just go quietly?"

"Yes. Be the man that you are."

"My things?"

"Only personal items. Also, I need your Seven Star."

Levin shoved his cigarette into the cemetery of dead tobacco, then reached under his jacket and took out the Seven Star from the inside pocket. For a moment he weighed the creased and battered leather-bound daybook containing the phone numbers and contacts in code of the people he'd met during his career. He placed it at the edge of the desk.

Leaning forward, Knafy took the daybook and dropped it into his pocket. "Let's go."

There were no personal effects that Levin had to pack. He took his spare carton of cigarettes from the bottom desk drawer, allowed Knafy to search them quickly, then joined the man in the hallway. He looked once more into the room, surprised at the accumulated smoke still drifting in the still air and the tar embedded in the ceiling tiles.

"So what happens now?" Levin asked. He fell into step beside Knafy.

Two young men came in behind them, their coats left open so they could easily reach the holstered pistols at their sides.

"Now you walk away," Knafy said.

"Just like that?"

"I hope so."

"No one sees me as a threat?"

"No."

"And the reason my employment here is being terminated?"

"You've stepped on toes, Meyer. You knew you were doing that. Surely this can't be a surprise."

Levin thrust his hands deep into his pockets as they rounded a corner. He could feel the eyes of the other Mossad case officers on him as he passed offices and small public places within the building. He also felt their embarrassment. In a place that harvested international secrets, there was no way to keep his dismissal quiet—except from himself, and he'd been expecting it after the woman agent had turned up dead.

"Someone here wants me out of the way permanently," Levin said. "The attempt on my life yesterday was by an assassin regularly employed by the Mossad."

"I know nothing of that."

Levin believed him. "There is something rotten at the heart of us these days."

"Now you're talking treason." Knafy's eyes flashed.

"I'm talking truth. The reason I'm being forced out is because I started seeing through their smoke screens."

Knafy sighed. "Meyer, I know you truly believe what you're saying, but you're wrong. You're imagining demons. Don't let this be known. I'd rather think of you enjoying a well-earned retirement than lying in some unmarked grave."

Levin gave up. He'd been fighting against the current since the beginning of his private operation.

At the door Knafy paused. "There is something I'd ask of you."

"Yes?"

"Uri Dan. He's young and filled with a love for his people. Perhaps it's not too late to salvage his career."

Levin tore a corner from the cigarette carton, took a pen from his pocket and quickly jotted down a phone number. He passed it to Knafy. "That's the motel where he's staying in Bern."

"Bern. What was he doing there?"

"Destroying the enemies of this country. Maybe he'll tell you about it."

"What does he know of your suspicions?"

"He knows about Canary and he knows that Canary is working for us, as well as the Arabs."

"She's a figment of your imagination," Knafy said. "Canary died years ago."

"It was never proved."

"And if she didn't, the woman would never show her face in Israel again."

"As I recall," Levin said, "she never showed her face before. Why should she start now?"

Knafy had no answer.

Levin left him at the door, his shoulder blades tight against the expectation of a bullet plowing through the glass doors at any moment and ripping through his heart. He forced himself to breathe.

Traffic continued as normal out on the street. Hot-dog vendors called out their wares for people who were eating late lunches. No one seemed aware that Meyer Levin's personal world had just crumbled to pieces around him, or that he believed he was walking a tightrope above impending death even now.

He paused to light a cigarette, sucked in the smoke, then released it, catching sight of the beige sedan parked across the street. His stomach tightened as a mirthless grin plastered itself across his face. It appeared that waiting death was no longer patient. He reached into his pocket and fisted the Beretta Model 85 .380 he kept there. The pistol wasn't much use for more than close-up work, but it was comforting.

He struck out to the west, following the setting sun along the street, avoiding a pushcart filled with flowering buds and the plump woman operating it who hawked her wares so enthusiastically. His heart thumped solidly in his chest. It wasn't that he minded dying so much, but there still remained a number of things he hadn't finished—things that needed to be done.

The sedan rolled along at the side of the street. Obviously the two men inside didn't care if they were seen or not. Levin had no place to run. The remaining moments of his life had already been measured.

At the corner he paused, wondering if they would try to simply run him down in the street. He waited, hating risking a civilian but wanting to tilt the odds in his favor as much as possible. Two teenagers in cadet uniforms crossed the street in the same direction he was going, and he fell into step within arm's reach of them.

The sedan seemed to hesitate.

Levin didn't know his next move. In the next block there were opportunities where he could lose himself, but he doubted he could outrun his pursuers on foot.

When he heard rubber shriek on concrete, he fisted the compact Beretta and pulled it from his jacket, expecting the sedan to come hurtling down on him.

Instead, a faded blue Sirocco pulled away from the curb to his left, roared out onto the street and came to a stop beside him.

Levin whirled to face the new threat, extending the gun.

Before he could fire, the redheaded woman sitting behind the steering wheel of the old sports car reached out and neatly plucked the automatic from his grip. The two cadets stood frozen and perplexed.

The woman's hair was smoothed back from her face, and Foster Grants shielded her eyes. Her features strong and lean and hard; surely she was no more than in her early thirties. He recognized her as the woman who had saved him the previous day.

"Get in if you want to live," she said in Hebrew.

The beige sedan moved forward uncertainly.

Wasting no time, Levin ran around behind the sports car, using it for cover as the passenger in the sedan leaned out with a silenced pistol in his hands. He thumbed the Sirocco's passenger door open and threw himself inside, aware that the woman had extended her arm out her window with his pistol in her fist. The .380 barked rapidly, emptying the 7-round clip.

A triangle of white chips suddenly sprouted on the sedan's windshield. The gunner sagged inside the sedan.

Before Levin could properly seat himself, the woman dropped the empty Beretta in his lap, shifted into first, punched the accelerator down and released the clutch.

They powered around the corner, narrowly avoiding the sedan's driver, who'd maintained enough presence of mind to lunge the car out at them. The right-side tires went up and over the curb. Then they were straightened out, flying down the street toward the Israeli business section in the New City.

The woman shifted gears expertly, getting the most out of the racing engine disguised under the scarred hood.

"You're Canary?" Levin asked.

She shook her head. "No. I'm Catherine Hawkes. Canary assigned me to you."

"Catherine Hawkes?"

"Yes."

"I don't know you."

"No reason you should. We've never met." She glanced in the mirror and pulled into the right lane, gliding around the corner, obviously at ease with the city's topography.

"And what is your assignment?"

"To take care of you, make sure you stay alive till the end of this mission." She turned to him and gave him a small, warm smile. "After that, you're on your own."

"Yes. Of course. You're American?"

"I'm your guardian angel for the time being, Meyer. Let's leave it at that, shall we?"

"And Hawkes probably isn't your name. Canary and Hawkes, eh? Birds of a feather?"

Hawkes made another turn, the steering wheel held firmly in her leather driving gloves. "If you like puzzles so much, the next vending machine I see for newspapers, I'll pick you one up and you can do the crossword."

Levin fell silent for a moment. "I assume you have a plan."

"We seem to be making good on our getaway. Once I know we're clear, we'll talk to Canary."

"What does she want from me?"

"Your help. Appearances can be deceiving, Meyer, but Canary's trying to find out what's at the base of this the same way you were. Together we might just be able to pull that off."

"I have reason to be suspicious of her."

Hawkes looked at him, her emotions hidden behind the black lenses of the sunglasses. "Frankly I don't blame you, given the previous circumstances. But without her, you're a dead man."

"She knows I was terminated from the Mossad?"

"How else do you think I knew to be there?"

"I see. And how does she think I will be able to aid her, provided that I am persuaded to do that?"

"You've got contacts within Israel."

"I turned in my records before I left."

"You wouldn't be worth your salt if you didn't have a duplicate Seven Star tucked away somewhere in this city."

Levin had to agree.

CHAPTER ELEVEN

Maybe the town had once had a name. Yakov Katzenelenbogen wasn't sure. In the hard copy transmitted from Stony Man Farm, it was simply designated as K-41.

He'd had a chance to study it for an hour before Phoenix moved down into the shadowed night streets. It was laid out in a confused warren of avenues that reminded him of every Old World city he'd visited around the globe. The streets were narrow and twisting, not built with cars in mind. The buildings seldom rose higher than two or three stories, and were crowded together like a collection of children's blocks. Most of them were alabaster colored, either originally that hue or bleached by the hot and unforgiving sun for decades. Except for the occasional car, the sound of electric motors thumping and a scattering of electric lights in government buildings, it was easy to imagine that it was a scene from another century and that the oasis it had been constructed around still attracted bedouin in from the desert astride their camels.

Phoenix Force had crept into the town silently, leaving their abandoned parachutes miles back, buried under the desert sand.

McCarter and James had gone into town first and ransacked a clothesline for the robes they wore over their purple-and-green-checked desert camouflage. The flowing garments served to cover their weapons and combat gear, and also to blend them against the backdrop of buildings.

According to the information Kurtzman had processed, the building that was their target was located at the end of the alley they were presently traveling.

McCarter had the point position. James and Encizo carried the wings, and Katz and Manning followed along in their wake.

The smells of close-quarters living lay thick and heavy over the city, cloistering in the alleys. Third-world seaports were worse in Katz's opinion, but not by much.

"Okay, mates," McCarter announced over the headset channel, "we've arrived."

"We take this one by the numbers," Katz said. He drew the silenced SIG-Sauer P-226 from the shoulder holster under his right arm and flicked the safety off. "Calvin, you have the sniping position facing the north and east walls of the building. Rafael, you cover the south and west."

Both men confirmed the assignments and moved out.

Katz watched.

A scruffy dog rummaged the trash barrels less than three yards from his position against the wall of the apartment building just down from the target structure. It never knew he was there as it whined and struggled to get at whatever prize it was seeking.

Moments later James and Encizo radioed that they were in position.

"David," Katz said, "you've got the back."

"Roger." McCarter's wiry form melted into the darkness.

Looking over his shoulder, Katz glanced at Manning. "Ready?"

The Canadian thumped the small canvas pack strapped across his chest. "Oh, yeah."

"Set," McCarter transmitted back.

"On our way," Katz said. He struck out away from the wall, keeping the 9 mm pistol shielded beside his leg.

The dog saw them at once, jerked into a defensive posture, woofed twice, then tucked its tail between its legs and scampered away.

Katz took the wooden stairs snaking up the side of the building. The steps groaned under his weight.

The Jordanian outpost housed a skeleton crew of Intelligence agents managing the transport lines weaving across the harsh land from Iraq through Jordan. With the United Nations watching everything Baghdad did these days, neither country could afford to have the records tracked on anything to do with the caravans. Once the outpost was blitzed out of existence, it would take weeks if not months to reconstruct another nerve center to handle the trafficking.

At the top of the stairs, Katz pulled his AN/PVS-7A night-vision goggles from his web gear and fitted them over his head. His sight became instantly clear as he gazed back down the alley. At his side, Manning pulled on his own goggles. Though capable of turning night into day, the goggles would have been immediately apparent to anyone they'd accidentally run into. They'd always made Katz think of men with mosquito faces.

He tried the door and found it locked. Waving toward the lock with his metal hook, he stepped back out of the way and let Manning in.

Working quickly, the demolitions expert squashed a wad of plastic explosive over the lock and added a plug-in-type timer.

Katz fell in beside the door, watching Manning take the opposite wall. Holding up his empty hand, the other one filled with a Beretta 92-F, Manning ticked off fingers, counting down from four.

When there were no fingers remaining, the C-4 detonated with a loud bang.

"On my way," McCarter called over the headset frequency.

Katz wheeled around and kicked the shivering door. It gave instantly. Following it inside, he went low, allowing Manning to heave the chest pack into the center of the next room.

A weak bulb from an overhead light splashed green fuzz against Katz's goggles. Tracking movement easily, he fired two rounds into each target's head in calm synchronization. Both corpses went stumbling backward. One fell over the small, round dining table and brought it crashing to the floor. The other man knocked a dishpan of plates, cups and silverware from the cabinet, and soapy water cascaded across the wall.

"Lights out," McCarter said.

A muffled *bamf* came from across the room. The lights inside the apartment-office extinguished at once as the Brit's charge cut the power lines on his side of the building. A heartbeat later the pack Manning had thrown into the room went off in a chain reaction of detonations that flared briefly through the deep darkness filling the room. Already disoriented, the Jordanian shock troops completely lost whatever edge they might have had in sheer numbers.

Startled yells echoed off the plaster walls.

Although the night-vision goggles weren't able to fully penetrate the smoke given off by Manning's explosive concoction, they allowed the Phoenix Force warriors to see better than their adversaries, and the goggles also picked up the infrared dye marking their clothes so they wouldn't engage each other.

Moving through the kitchen, Katz bracketed a Jordanian in his sights as he was swinging an end table toward a window. The 9 mm round took the guy in the shoulder and spun him around, but it was too late to stop the table.

Glass smashed as the piece of furniture went sailing through the window. Fragments caught the moonlight before succumbing to the pull of gravity.

Katz's next two rounds put the Jordanian down for good, the muzzle-flashes blinking like a lighthouse strobe flash in the dark.

Manning cut loose with a silenced H&K MP-5. The muffled thunder spit angrily and knocked three Arabs back and down as they started firing. The big Canadian grunted with impact.

"Gary," Katz called, knowing he'd heard the slap of a bullet striking home.

"I'm all right. Body armor stopped the bullet."

Katz continued on. A man lunged at him out of the darkness. Using his elbow, he jarred the man with a sweeping blow that left him dazed, then slit his throat with the wickedly curved hook on his prosthesis.

An odd-shaped glow manifested itself in the doorway between rooms. "Secure here?" McCarter asked.

"Yes," Katz replied. He thrust a fresh magazine into the SIG-Sauer and saved the partially empty one for reloading later. "Did you find the computer systems?"

"In here."

Katz's nose and throat burned from the acrid smoke given off by Manning's dazzler package. He thumbed the transmit button on the headset. "We're going inside."

Encizo and James radioed confirmation of the message received.

"You're not going to have much time," James said. "The locals are already beating a path to your door."

"Understood. Buy us whatever time you can."

The flat cracks of the Beretta M-21 sniper rifles used by the two outside members of Phoenix Force filled the night air and rolled in through the smashed window. None of the civilians would be hurt by James's or Encizo's marksmanship, but it would keep them at bay.

The adjoining room held the computer system the Jordanians had been using. An elongated rectangle of moonlight fell onto the floor where McCarter had burst through. The Brit retreated to that side of the room for a moment and retrieved the LST-5C satellite radio he'd stashed there before invading the room.

A quick scan showed Katz the computer was equipped with a modem. He shoved the corpse out of the chair in front of the unit while Manning used a penlight to connect the power cords of the battery pack for the computer. Seconds later the monitor flickered to life.

Working with practiced skill, McCarter linked the satellite radio to the computer modem.

Activating the radio, Katz accessed the Stony Man frequency. "Phoenix One to Stony Base. Over."

"Go, Phoenix One, you have Stony Base," Barbara Price answered. "Over."

"We're ready for uplink now. Over."

"Affirmative. Stony Base is operational. Stand by."

The computer monitor suddenly filled with numbers, letters and symbols that scrolled across the screen with lightning speed.

"Phoenix One," Aaron Kurtzman said, "uplink is complete. However, there's a new wrinkle. The virus checks I ran on the incoming data reveal that the system you're in possession of was tapped by another source. I'm backtracking along those systems now. From the look of things, the spy system may belong to the Israelis. A lot of the archiving that's been done in the files has their earmarks. Over."

Katz swapped glances with McCarter. Since both of them were more familiar with Mossad espionage methods, they knew more about what to expect than Manning.

"Explains how the Israelis knew about the other caravan shipments," McCarter said.

Katz nodded, then checked his weapon. "But it doesn't explain why the Mossad unit didn't expose the trafficking to the United Nations investigators and shut the Jordanians and Iraqis down."

"Unless they were profiting from it. Literally."

Dismissing the question for the moment, Katz hit the transmit button. "Calvin. Rafael. Did you copy the transmission from Stony Base?"

Both men had.

The reports of the sniper rifles continued to roll across the area.

"Pull back," Katz ordered, heading for the front door. "We'll sort this out when we have more time."

Manning hung back only a moment, long enough to slap a chunk of plastic explosive onto the computer mainframe and add a remote detonator, then he was on McCarter's heels.

Katz didn't pause at the broken doorway but charged through it instantly. Rifle fire greeted him, ripping splinters from the wooden steps. He threw himself over the railing and dropped the two yards to the ground.

Abandoning the landing at the second floor, Manning and McCarter flung themselves into the alley. The Brit fell into a classic SAS parachute roll and came to his feet with his MAC-10 canted across his chest in the shadows hugging the alley wall. Manning seemed stunned for a moment. Linking his forearm through the Canadian's arm, Katz pulled Manning to safety under the shelter of the stairs as a burst of autofire tore turf from the spot where he'd been lying.

A whining engine sounded at the opposite end of the alley.

Gazing back that way, Katz saw bright headlights flare to life and rip away the protective night. Bullets spanged off the walls, searching for flesh-and-blood targets.

Katz aimed the SIG-Sauer from the point and triggered a half-dozen rounds, holding a low pattern. In back of the lights, the bullets sparked off metal, but the vehicle didn't stop coming. He tapped the transmit button. "Rafael."

"They're wild cards," the Cuban answered. "Not Jordanian police or military."

The general outlines of the approaching vehicle were those of a Land Rover. It was less than fifty yards away.

"Mossad," McCarter put in grimly.

Katz didn't disagree. There was simply no time, and the Brit was probably right. He stepped away from the building and lifted a boot to the locked door to his left. Running back down the alley was no option because the Land Rover would easily overtake them. The lock shattered when he kicked the door. Shuddering, the wooden barrier gave way. He hooked Manning by the sleeve and pulled him into the apartment. The night-vision goggles lit up a small room that was obviously being used as storage space. Books spilled from boxes stacked from floor to ceiling, and a pervasive musty smell clouded Katz's nostrils. Another door was at the rear of the room.

"Gary."

"Yeah."

"Are you all right?"

"Yeah. Just had the wind knocked out of me."

Katz twisted the knob with his prosthesis and stepped into another room filled with storage boxes. Rats, caught out in the open by the short-range infrared illuminator when it switched on automatically, scuttled immediately for hiding places. "Blow the computer."

"Right." Manning fumbled for the remote-control detonator while Katz searched for another way out.

The explosion overhead thundered dully and threw lightning out over the alley that was visible even through the apartment doors. It was fierce enough to destroy the LST-5C satellite radio, as well.

Brakes squeaked outside as the Land Rover rolled to a stop. Voices shouted to each other in Hebrew, and the troops fanned out in pursuit.

"Katz," McCarter called.

"Go." Katz found a window behind a stack of boxes containing clothing. He raked the boxes out of the way with Manning's help, then rammed his hook between the boards that had been nailed over it. The Canadian drew his Ka-bar knife and shoved it between the boards on his end of the window. Nails shrilled as they pulled free.

"You've got a couple blokes on your tail, mate."

"Affirmative. What about yourself?"

McCarter's breathing sounded ragged. "As the man said, the game's afoot."

The boards were cleared of the window, leaving the dirt-streaked panes beneath naked.

"What kind of covering fire do you want me to lay down?" James asked.

Katz answered immediately. There was no doubt in his mind that the Mossad commandos pursuing them were there without the full sanction of their country. The Israeli government these days would have played out the hand the way they'd found it and beaten both Jordan and Iraq up in international eyes. By keeping the caravan operation clandestine, the Mossad unit assigned to the Jordanians was working toward some other goal.

"Bring them down if they pose a threat to the team," Katz said. He smashed his prosthesis against the window, and glass went flying. Manning knocked a bigger passage through with one of the planks they'd ripped away. "Go, Gary."

Manning shoved his way through, his clothing ripping on the jagged shards left behind. He cursed with genuine feeling.

"They've got another vehicle at the opposite end of the alley," Encizo radioed.

Before Katz could pull himself through the window, his peripheral vision picked up a shadow closing in on him. He whirled instinctively a heartbeat ahead of an autofire burst that reduced a nearby box to cardboard pulp and shredded cloth.

Bringing the P-226 up, he fired three rounds point-blank into his attacker's chest as the man rushed him. The Mossad agent was knocked off stride but managed to stumble ahead. The Uzi in his hands tried to track on target.

Realizing that the man was protected by body armor, Katz stepped forward and uncoiled a wicked savage kick that rattled his teeth but succeeded in stopping his attacker's wild charge. The Mossad agent stood through what appeared to be sheer strength of will. Spinning on his toes, Katz powered through a side kick that came into bone-shattering contact with his opponent's jaw.

The man dropped as if he'd been poleaxed.

Katz spotted the second man as he settled back onto his feet. The SIG-Sauer came up into target acquisition as the Phoenix warrior sighted down his enemy's barrel. His finger tightened on the trigger, and he felt the pistol's recoil a heartbeat ahead of the muzzle-flash.

An incredible force smacked into Katz's chest and drove him backward. Letting his reflexes take over, he brought his arm around for a follow-up shot that proved to be unnecessary.

The second gunner was sprawled out on the ground.

The Phoenix Force leader operated quickly, ignoring the bruising ache in his chest under the Kevlar vest. He took the glove from the first man's right hand, slipped the metal case containing his cigarettes out of his pack and wiped the sides clean on his robes. Holding the container by its sides, he pressed it against the dead man's fingers, getting a good print off each digit. Moving back to the other corpse, aware of the activity going on outside the door, he made impressions of that man's fingers, as well.

"Sherf! Ami!" a man's voice called from the doorway.

Katz dropped the metal case into a plastic envelope that would protect the prints, then slid it into a slitted thigh pocket.

A shadow started to move into the room, led by a matte black rifle barrel.

Plucking an HE grenade from his web gear, Katz pulled the pin and lobbed it gently into the other room. He was halfway out the wrecked window when the gre-

nade went off, and the concussion slammed him off-
balance. The high-intensity light splashed over the
building facing the window.

Manning was crouched just outside, holding a defensive posture.

Katz waved the Canadian to his feet and set off at a jog
toward the escape route they'd chosen. Somewhere in the
distance a Klaxon howled like a mechanical beast. Operating inside Jordan without any kind of sanction would
result in the team being executed as spies, probably on the
spot. But that was only if the covert Mossad force didn't
get them first.

Thumbing the headset's transmit button, Katz said,
"Break off the engagement and fall back." He glanced
at the second story of the building and saw orange-and-
yellow flames spiraling up the walls. "Report when
you're clear."

Military vehicles sped through the streets on the other
side of the line of buildings fronting the main street. Foot
soldiers were already spreading out.

Twenty-three minutes later all of the Stony Man warriors were safely outside the search pattern moving
through the town, hidden by the desert sand dunes un-
dulating from the small pocket of civilization. Katz
spared a few more moments watching the surrounding
countryside through infrared binoculars. Judging from
the furtive movements by the people he observed, a
number of the Mossad unit had made good their escape,
as well.

James took the point and they skirted the area, making sure they didn't intercept any of the Mossad commandos by mistake. As they moved out, Katz's mind
stayed active with the possibilities the Mossad agents
represented. Any way it was sliced, there was a lot of

damage the covert team could still do if they had the clearance. But he didn't think Price would let the threat remain. He put more force into his steps and allowed his mind to toy with the variables of tracking the Mossad team in a hostile country with a nation's soldiers looking for them. All of the possibilities were grim.

"I NEVER THOUGHT I'd live to see the day I'd be wearing one of these things." Luther Nix shrugged inside the black windbreaker that had white block letters declaring Los Angeles Sheriff's Department across the back.

Seated behind the steering wheel of the unmarked Ford Taurus, Sheriff Orrin Conagher glanced at Carl Lyons and refrained from commenting with obvious difficulty.

The Aryan Resistance Movement leader didn't seem to notice the byplay.

Conagher hadn't been happy with the call to include Nix, but there'd been no choice in the end. Nix's information and cooperation were necessary to the case the sheriff's office was building. Conagher was a lean man who looked as if he'd spent his youth twenty years ago topping out broncs at rodeos instead of being a lawman. The mirror lenses of his sunglasses seemed cold and impersonal. Besides the black windbreaker, he wore a denim work shirt, jeans that were faded almost bone white in the contact areas and boots. A Smith & Wesson .44 Magnum rode on his hip in a worn Sam Browne holster.

Across the street, through the dirt-streaked windshield of the Taurus, Lyons watched the apartment building they'd had under surveillance for the past hour and a quarter. It was seven stories tall, thin and angular against the wide-set business structures on either side of it. A half-dozen television aerials poked out from the top, and someone had erected a greenhouse with plastic sheeting for sides. The room rates were weekly or monthly, and rarely were contracts of any kind involved.

The sentries were easy to spot. Three Arabs lounged at a table in the window of a donut shop across the sidewalk on Lyons's right. A cellular phone sat next to the salt and pepper shakers. Another pair of Jordanians worked the sidewalk in front of the building with shirts loose enough to conceal the mini-Uzis they carried. Lyons had had to use his binoculars to spot the guns.

"Gonna keep dragging on like this," Conagher said in his characteristic drawl, "and we're gonna have problems with the local traffic."

Glancing at his watch, Lyons saw the time was 4:19 p.m. He looked over the seat at the ARM leader. "What about it, Luther?"

"Like I said, these people usually take delivery between four and four-thirty. Give it time."

"How do you know that?" Conagher asked.

"Pratt had them staked out."

"Figuring on a little side action by taking out one of the delivery vans if the chance presented itself?"

Nix looked into the rearview mirror to meet the sheriff's eyes. "You got a suspicious mind, lawman."

Conagher scratched his beard stubble with a fingernail and didn't say anything. The mirrored lenses never wavered.

Lyons changed the position of the CAR-15 nestled between his knees, hoping to restore his circulation.

After a beat Nix went on. "Pratt didn't trust them. With good reason, it turns out."

"Of course, Justin Pratt was a shining example of a model citizen," Conagher said.

"I don't have to talk to you. My deal's with Lakehurst."

"He ain't always going to be around."

Lyons shifted in his seat uneasily. He wasn't too happy about the way the situation was going, either. Nix had been guaranteed immunity from the bust in return for his providing witnesses to come forward against the Jordanians helping move the Bolivian Nazi cocaine through stateside routes. He had been convinced that the Arabs were double-dealing his organization by the strike against his headquarters. Luckily he hadn't been there at the time, a fact that Lyons and his men took into consideration before the devastating raid along with the Stony Man blacksuits, all of them disguised as Arabs.

Swiveling his head slowly to scan the street again, Conagher lifted the radio handset and checked in with the units hidden away in the surrounding blocks. The sheriff's department had the area quietly contained and were ready to swing into action.

"There," Nix said, pulling himself forward.

Lyons slipped his hand down the barrel of the CAR-15 and released the safety as he gazed in the direction the ARM leader was indicating.

A sleek Dodge Caravan rolled down the four-lane street, coming out of the glare of the descending sun. It was painted a metallic electric blue and had a mural of a long-eared pink rabbit standing on its hind legs on a surfboard cresting a high wave. Twin radio whips shot up from the front of the vehicle, arced over the van and were tied down to the rear bumper and resembled a giant grasshopper's quivering antennae.

"That's them?" Conagher asked.

"Yeah," Nix answered.

"They don't go in much for the way of subtlety, do they?" Lyons asked as he dropped his hand into his windbreaker pocket, then clamped the ear-throat headset into place. The tiny speaker growled in his ear when he flicked the set to life. He quickly apprised Blancanales and Schwarz of the situation.

The sheriff reached for the handset again and alerted his teams.

Nix leaned forward excitedly, eyes narrowed and focused on the suspect vehicle. "Still don't see why I can't have a gun to defend myself," he grumbled. "I'm not going out there to get my ass shot off for you guys."

"No," Lyons and Conagher said together. It was the one issue they'd agreed on fully from the beginning. Nix had constantly been promising revenge for all the dead men discovered at the ARM mansion outside the city.

"No," Lyons repeated, palming a set of handcuffs from his belt, "you're not." Conagher glanced at Lyons and noticed the gleam of steel in the big Able Team warrior's fist. He gave a small nod of approval.

The van cruised to a stop in front of the apartment building, and the driver got out. Movement stirred on the passenger side, and the interior lightened, signaling that the side door had been opened.

The sheriff fisted a sturdy walkie-talkie and reached for the door-release lever. Before Nix knew what was happening, Lyons slapped one of the cuffs around his beefy wrists. It clicked metallically as it snapped closed.

"What the hell is this?" Nix asked, jerking at his captured arm.

Levering his body across the seat, Lyons used his weight and position to maneuver the ARM leader's wrist close enough to the restraining bar mounted above the door to lock the other end securely. "For your own good."

"We made a deal!" Nix bellowed.

Conagher looked back over his shoulder, his weathered face impassive and his gaze mirrored and merciless. "You keep making noise like that, Luther, you might just tip off those boys over yonder. They decide to shoot up this car, you just lean on down and kiss your ass goodbye, 'cause you ain't going nowhere."

"Damn you," Nix whispered vehemently.

"We still have a deal," Lyons said. "I just want you out of the way so we can take care of business here." He opened his own door, but didn't shove it out.

A small group of men had emerged from the apartment building and started carrying out cardboard boxes.

Two unmarked sheriff's cruisers sped in from the east, whipping in behind the van at a discreet distance to block a retreat, while another pair swooped in from the west, blocking forward progress. The heads of the Jordanians jerked around to take in the threats. More sheriff's cars, these marked with insignia, flaring lights and screaming sirens, rounded the corners at both ends of the block. Pedestrian traffic came to a standstill along the sidewalks, except for the fringe elements that quickly had something to fear and quickly melted into the alleys.

One of the Jordanians assumed control and began shouting orders. Automatic weapons ranging from the previously viewed mini-Uzis to 9 mm Viking Vixens and at least two Steyr AUGs that Lyons could see quickly appeared and were put to use.

"Hit it!" Conagher ordered, then dropped the handset into the floorboard as he hoisted his Winchester Model 1200 combat shotgun into a ready position.

Pushing himself out of the passenger seat, Lyons took the field, pulling the CAR-15 to his shoulder and targeting a man ripping a burst of autofire that skated from the concrete surface of the street in front of Conagher. The Ironman's finger took up the slack and ripped off two 3-round bursts that slammed into the Jordanian's chest, spinning him against another man running toward the interior of the apartment building with a box. They went down in a tangle of arms and legs, and the cardboard box erupted in a scattering of plastic pillow packs that slid across the sidewalk.

The sheriff fired a round from the 12-gauge that caught the pillow packs with a full load of double-aught buck. The bags turned inside out as the pellets took them, and the powder contained inside turned into a swirling white cloud.

Lyons continued charging, using sweeping motions with the assault rifle to clear the way. The snipers posted along the nearby rooftops had been augmented by Cowboy John Kissinger and some of the specialists among the blacksuit shock troops. The booming reports of the single-round shots fired from the heavier sniping rifles were audible even in the din created by the sudden firefight. The 7.62 mm rounds cut a swath through the ranks of the terrorists.

"Ironman," Blancanales called out over the headset.

"Go."

"We've got the back door."

"Kick it in and go."

"On our way."

Closing on the sidewalk, most of the Jordanians cleared from the apartment entrance, Lyons leapt a corpse and fired the last of the CAR-15's magazine into a face peering at him over an Uzi. He stripped the empty clip from the assault rifle and shoved in a fresh magazine.

Conagher made it to the door and crouched, thumbing more shells into the shotgun. Lyons wanted to move forward, but Conagher seemed eager to take the point. "Let me," he said.

Lyons nodded. "Okay, I'll cover you, then."

Without hesitation, Conagher moved into the building in a defensive crouch. A shotgun blast took out a potted plastic palm and a terrorist gunner lying in wait.

Before the Jordanian's body hit the tiled floor of the foyer, a deputy had taken Conagher's place at the door and Lyons was already in motion behind the sheriff.

The headset buzzed in Lyons's ear. "Go."

"We've got the back secure," Blancanales reported. "We're on our way in, so be on the lookout for friendlies in the field of fire."

"Roger." Lyons began the hump up the stairway following Conagher, amazed at the older man's speed and agility.

At the top of the stairs, a terrorist moved into a holding position and sprayed a burst of 9 mm parabellums downward. The sheriff dodged to the side, slamming hard into the wall, while Lyons dived for cover as a whizzing round tugged at his borrowed windbreaker.

The shotgun *ba-loomed* with grim authority, and the Jordanian went down in a bloody flurry.

Gathering his feet under him, Lyons pressed on. According to the Intel they'd gathered from Luther Nix and his ARM associates, the Jordanians were housed primarily in the third and fourth floors. A lengthy communications with Price and Kurtzman at Stony Man Farm had given Lyons and his team the backgrounds and faces of some of the major players Nix had revealed in the Jordanian conduit.

They didn't slow at the second-floor landing but powered on, their breaths ragged and dry in their throat. Lyons hit the transmit button on the headset. "John."

"Go," Kissinger responded.

"The outside?"

"We're in good shape here. Confirming targets on the third and fourth floors. We'll take them at your go."

"Affirmative. Gadgets?"

A pair of Jordanians attempted to block access to the third-floor landing, but two deputies firing over Conagher's and Lyons's heads convinced them that they were fighting a losing battle.

"Go," Schwarz radioed back.

Lyons made the turn at the third-floor landing and set himself up in position across the hall from Conagher as they prepared to push through the emergency exit door. "The top?"

"Secure. But somebody's going to be pissed about the shape their greenhouse is in."

"Come on down. Pol?"

"Go."

"In position?"

"And ready."

"Close it in. John, your people have your clearance."

On the other side of the door, shots thundered along the third floor and the next one up.

"Clear," Kissinger reported a few seconds later.

Rushing through the exit door, Lyons rattled a burst of 5.56 mm tumblers that chewed fist-sized holes in the acoustic ceiling tiles over the fleeing men. White powder drifted down along with irregular chunks that fell over the men's heads and shoulders. "Get down on the floor!" Lyons yelled.

The Jordanians halted, dropped their weapons and turned around with their hands in the air.

"Get down on the floor!" Lyons repeated.

They obeyed slowly.

"Fan out," Conagher commanded the seven deputies who followed them, "and get those men into custody."

"Yes, sir," a husky young brute replied as he fished handcuffs from his belt.

"Watch them," Lyons said. "They're not like your average street hood. They don't mind sacrificing themselves for their cause."

Blancanales came into view at the opposite end of the corridor, and the deputies with him fanned out and started taking the rooms one by one. Lyons and Conagher did the same. Most of them were empty on the ends, and many of them had corpses draped across the furniture and carpeted floors, proof of the marksmanship camped around them. Bullet holes had cored through the windows, scattering glass and ripping gouges in the cheap paneled walls.

Resistance was brief and futile in most cases. After taking a prisoner himself, Lyons went to the next room where a pair of deputies moved in to cuff a prisoner lying in the middle of the room. When they moved the Jordanian, the guy looked up at them and smiled a huge white grin. A live grenade was cupped in his palms near his abdomen.

"Get back!" Lyons yelled from the doorway.

The concussion of the explosion washed over him, followed almost immediately by the flying bodies of the deputies.

Struggling free of the human debris, Lyons checked the terrorist and saw that his body had been husked out by the explosion. A glance at the first deputy showed that a significant portion of the man's face had been torn away, leaving his frightened blue eyes staring out in horror from a mask of blood. A heartbeat later the light in those eyes winked out.

The other deputy was dazed and bleeding from several superficial cuts, but his body armor had taken the brunt of the blast.

"Christ!" Conagher said as he strode into the room.

Lyons pushed himself to his feet and watched as the sheriff knelt by the dead man and pressed his fingers to the deputy's throat. "He's gone," the Able Team warrior said softly.

"Dammit," the sheriff whispered hoarsely. "He was a good man. Had two kids."

Outside in the hallway, a smoke alarm suddenly shrilled to bleating life.

Lyons moved through the doorway and saw thick clouds of white haze streaming from a room two doors down. He jogged over to it, holding the Colt Government Model at the ready, then shoved his way through the huddle of deputies clogging the entrance.

At the far end of the room, manning a fire extinguisher with Spartan efficiency, Blancanales fought a blaze on top of a small desk near the room's television set. Two deputies were piled atop a Jordanian on the broken-down bed. On closer inspection, Lyons realized the fire Blancanales was fighting was licking at a pile of papers, account books and floppy disks. A laptop computer had been smashed on the floor near the desk, and the recognizable remnants of a modem lay near it. The phone had been fragmented, as well.

With a final hissing burst from the fire extinguisher, Blancanales put the flames out. Black smoke drifted from the charred objects.

Taking a pen from his pocket, Lyons sifted through the burned mess. "Good job, buddy. Looks like you saved some of it."

"If the foam doesn't go ahead and destroy it."

"Leap of faith, guy. It had to be done."

"Hey, cop," the prisoner on the bed called.

Lyons turned to the man, crossed the distance to the bed and looked down at him. He recognized the Jordanian from the Stony Man briefs. "Rafi bin Baz."

"You know me." A crooked and bloody smile twisted the Arab's lips. He was sinewy and thin, with scars woven into the mosaic of age lines crinkling his face. His gray face still showed strands of the coal black it had once been.

"No. I know of you."

"Do you have a warrant?"

"Yeah."

Baz licked his bleeding lips. "You can never hold us. There is the matter of diplomatic immunity."

"You think so?"

"Yes. We will be deported as undesirables. It has happened before."

"Not this time," Lyons promised. "You're busted here on charges of conspiracy in drug trafficking. Under the recent revisions in international laws upheld by the United States, you're facing a trial. And from the look of things, a conviction won't be far behind." He looked up at the deputies. "Get him out of here."

Outside in the hallway, Conagher was attending to final instructions to his deputies, then dismissed the men, turning to Lyons. "Something?"

"Yeah. Rafi bin Baz." The big Able Team warrior nodded toward the departing deputies escorting Baz.

"He was one of the top brass on this whole little shooting match, wasn't he?"

"Yeah."

Conagher scratched at his jawline with a thumbnail. "Wonder how he'd feel if he found out who ratted him out."

"Figured it might help us later when we interrogate him. Let's catch up." Lyons set off with long strides, followed by the sheriff, and they reached the street together just as the two deputies were about to load Baz into the rear seat of a cruiser.

"Hold on," Conagher called out. "We'll take that one."

Baz's eyes widened with speculation as the sheriff and Lyons took him by the elbows and directed him away from the marked cruiser, but he didn't say anything.

A handful of uniformed deputies had blocked the street off with red-and-white sawhorses unloaded from the four-wheel-drive units. Media vehicles had already started to gather, and parted reluctantly to allow passage for the arriving ambulances.

"Somebody we wanted you to see," Conagher said as he guided the Jordanian to the parked cruiser.

Luther Nix glared out from behind the rear window, then used his free hand to give Baz the finger.

Without saying a word, the Jordanian spit onto the glass.

As he watched the strands of blood and spittle track down the window, Lyons figured the act pretty much symbolized the whole atmosphere that had really existed between the Aryan Resistance Movement and the Jordanian terrorist group.

CHAPTER TWELVE

Aaron Kurtzman glanced up as Barbara Price finished the latest in a long string of calls on the scrambled cellular phone. He wouldn't have thought it possible the day before, but the mission controller was looking even more pale and drawn, but there was no way he was going to suggest she slow down. The lives of too many people were riding on every stage of her planning. Although he had told her that he knew she had blocked computer access to information regarding Canary, and that he expected an answer to explain her actions when it would no longer endanger the mission, he still felt more on the fringe of things with this mission than he had ever been. He didn't like the situation and hoped once it was cleared up it would not occur again.

She shut the phone off, then secured it in the holster belted at her waist. "What have you got?"

"A brand-new mystery," the Bear replied. He played a riff on the keyboard in front of him, and the images on the monitors arrayed across the horseshoe-shaped desk flickered and changed.

"What are you working on?"

"Here are the bank statements, accounts and computerized records Able Team turned up in L.A. after their action regarding the drug trafficking the Jordanians and the Aryan Resistance Movement were doing with their Bolivian connection." He correlated the lines of figures, dates and names in his mind, mentally prepping his presentation to keep it as succinct as possible. Price had made everyone aware of the time crunch they were on since Phoenix had tumbled to the covert Mossad group in Jordan. "I've got some stuff ready on the prints Yakov sent to us, as well."

"You found something." It was a statement, not a question.

"More than I'd thought. Look." He flipped through the disk files. "This is a list of the transactions the Jordanians and ARM were doing regarding the cocaine shipments."

"Who kept the records?"

"Rafi bin Baz."

"And he knew what the ARM was doing with their share?"

"No. But he did keep himself abreast of how much they were pulling down in net profits."

The center screen shifted, revealing the accounts Kurtzman had turned up from his investigation.

"What's this?" Price asked.

"Those are the accounts Baz was regularly depositing their share of the profits into. I took what Pol was able to salvage after the fire closing their wrap-up of the stateside connection, then Akira and I built on our little foundation of knowledge, threading each new piece into the overall mosaic we knew we were searching for. I'm sure these are most of the accounts of the businesses they were using to ship money out of the United States."

"Where was it going?"

"Switzerland."

"The same accounts the Iraqi caravan sales were hitting?"

"No. A lot of the same banks, though."

"What about the ARM money?"

Kurtzman shrugged. "Beats me. Maybe they were buying jackboots and swastikas. Either way, those funds faded from sight."

"But you know where the Jordanian money is?"

"Wrong. I knew." Kurtzman tapped more keys. "Watch. These are the domestic accounts as of the time Lyons and the sheriff's office made their bust." He gazed down the line of figures, no longer awed by the amount of money involved. Several other operations he'd been privy to had had more in the way of income slopping through different accounts and false corporate fronts. "However, this is what those same accounts are going to show when the banks open at nine o'clock in the morning."

Without fail, the balance in each account had been reduced, no more than a couple of thousand showing in any of them.

"Someone siphoned the money off," Price said.

"Yeah."

"Who?"

"This is where it gets even more interesting." Kurtzman leaned into his keyboard and worked quickly. "It took Akira and I both some fancy footwork to get to the bottom of this." Names, times, accounts and amounts shifted with eye-blurring speed on the monitors, then froze.

"These accounts are in L.A., too," Price said.

"Uh-huh."

"Who are they registered to?"

Kurtzman pressed another button, and the list of accounts resolved itself into five names.

Price's eyes narrowed as she studied the list. "Who are these people?"

"Foreign investors who were given a clean bill of health and invited to start their own companies inside the continental U.S. You get three guesses about their nationality, and the first two don't count."

"Israeli."

Kurtzman showed her a mirthless smile. "Bingo."

"We've got our connection to Harel." A wan grin was reflected on Price's face.

"Almost. Still requires a leap of faith to get there from here. None of these people tie directly to anything Harel has interests in—"

"But they do travel in the same economic circles."

"You bet."

Price took a trip back to the ice bin for a can of iced tea. It was saying something about the fatigue factor building up in the beautiful mission controller that she wasn't staying with juice and was going for the caffeine content. When she returned, she asked, "How long will that money stay stateside?"

"At least four or five more hours. After that they may be able to electronically transfer it to Switzerland."

"Where it'll be out of our reach. I don't want that."

"So what do you want to do?"

Price appeared distracted, pulling at her lower lip. "Leave it. I'll take care of it. What else do you have?"

Kurtzman turned back to the computer. "When Akira and I were fumbling our way through the banking systems, we turned up some other interesting items. Behind each of those accounts the Jordanians and Iraqis have set up regarding the cash flow coming out of Baghdad is a set of computer commands designed to shift the monies from those accounts to others. Same way we worked the deal for Yakov."

"What accounts?"

Pressing more keys, Kurtzman revealed the accounts. "And these lead more directly back Dr. Enoch Harel. They're spread over a number of businesses Harel either owns outright or has a controlling interest in."

"And Harel would be a national hero for such a coup."

"Probably. But what would he need the money for?"

"That's part of what we have to find out."

Kurtzman gazed at the screens. "And once he puts that programming into play and absorbs the cash, he stands every chance of starting a war that could envelop the whole Middle East."

"That part of what he's after is pretty clear. War is inevitable in any of Harel's machinations. We just need to know the rest of it. Keep me informed on this. The instant Harel makes those shifts, I need to know."

"You got it."

"What about the fingerprints Yakov sent to us?"

Kurtzman moved on. The screen cleared, then split and depicted two faces. Both men seemed young and hard-edged. "Aharon Gil and Moshe Year."

"Mossad?"

"Very. They're part of the Metsada, the—"

"Secret Mossad within the Mossad."

Kurtzman looked at her in surprise, then checked it. Highly speculated knowledge of the different Intelligence communities was her forte. His was stretching cybernetic eyes, ears and hands over the world to work magic.

"Who was handling them?" Price asked.

"A guy named Rimon Jacobsen."

"I'm familiar with him, but get me a dossier prepped just the same."

"Right."

"Anything else?"

"Just the detail work if you want to see it."

"Later. Right now I want to start acting on some of this information."

Kurtzman nodded.

"You did good, Aaron," Price said. "We're about to get a handle on this thing." She plucked the telephone from her hip as she walked toward her office.

"Maybe," Kurtzman said in a voice that barely reached his own ears. But Canary was still out there, and Canary knew every move they made almost before they made it. A cold chill shivered down his spine as he realized how exposed Striker and Phoenix Force were in enemy territory. Then he pushed the dark thoughts out of his head and turned his mind to the task at hand.

"Hello."

"Hal, it's me."

"Hold on." Brognola reached down and switched the connection to the speakerphone on the President's desk. The television across the room was still playing newsreels, but there was no voice. Instead, an undertone of blues with a focus on saxophone flowed through the Oval Office.

The Man glanced up from the chair behind the desk.

"Price," said Brognola.

"Go ahead, Ms. Price," the President said as he turned off the music.

"Able Team turned up an unexpected plus out in California," Price said, then launched into a quick explanation of the money disappearing from the established Jordanian accounts.

"I understand that these monies once belonged to the terrorists," the President said, "but I fail to see what you're getting at."

"Harel has something in mind for those profits," Price replied. "Otherwise, he wouldn't have set up safeguards in California and Switzerland to get his hands on them."

"But we don't know why he wants them."

"No."

"Then I don't understand what you're asking."

Brognola felt a grin slide into place and a certain lightening of his spirits. He slipped a fresh cigar from his pocket, stripped the plastic from it, paused to smell it, then jammed it into the corner of his mouth. He rarely smoked these days, but he still enjoyed the taste of the rough-cut tobacco. "What she's getting at is those funds in California are accessible to us. They're profits from drug-related business, and we can prove it. Under federal law we can seize them, as well as the companies that are being used to transport the funds."

The President leaned back in his chair and steepled his fingers together. "I see."

"There's every chance we might be able to smoke more of Harel's overall plan into the open by seizing those assets," Brognola said. "At the very least, we can put increased pressure on him."

"Fine. Let's do it."

"What about Able Team?" the head Fed asked.

"They're out of the loop for now," Price replied. "They're working on adding another kink to the false trail we're laying down in Jordan."

"Okay. I'll call in some favors from a few guys I know in the DEA and the Federal Marshal's Office. Actually, if they make those busts, they'll be adding to their own coffers. And it sounds like it won't be pocket change, either."

Brognola paused and looked at the President. "And the sooner the better. Things are rolling in Jerusalem now, and I'll let you know how things go here."

Brognola was finished. He listened to the dead air for only a moment, then reached for the phone to make the first call to set things into motion. It felt good to be part of the effort to go on the offensive. Now if there was just time for everything to come together.

THE SCOWL on Dr. Enoch Harel's face deepened as he watched the news footage filling the television. On-screen, men wearing jackets marked DEA and Federal Marshal deployed in front of different businesses and broke down doors. Employees were rushed out onto the sidewalks and made to lie down in uniform rows. Other footage showed the managerial staff of a glass factory herded into a paddy wagon in handcuffs.

Routinely every federal officer in charge of each scene offered only a no-comment in response to questions from reporters. The news anchors went on to say that although the investigations seemed to be extensive and well coordinated, no one had learned yet why those businesses were being targeted.

Anger simmered inside Harel. As he reclined on one of the big sofas in front of the television, he snapped off the sound with the remote control. Without thinking, he removed his pince-nez and began cleaning them with his handkerchief. When he realized what he was doing, he stopped and felt even more anger. The process of cleaning was a sign of his inner nervousness. While exploring a brief flirtation with gambling in his younger days, he'd paid dearly to learn of the habit. The cardsharks called it "a tell."

"They know about us now," Benjamin Wellsberg said as he continued to stare at the screen.

"And what of it?" Harel snapped.

"This complicates things."

Harel shoved himself up from the sofa and settled his pince-nez back onto his nose. "Come now, surely you didn't think this was going to remain uncomplicated. You've been in Mossad operations for nearly all of your adult life."

"Yes. And experience tells me that we should be preparing a statement of denial about any of this."

"So prepare it."

"I can't. You know that." Wellsberg turned to eye him fiercely. "Those economic ties between the cocaine monies and our involvement are unbreakable."

"Again, what of it?" Harel walked to the wall holding the map of the new Israeli nation he was hoping to create from the ashes of Jordan.

"They can present their case to the United Nations."

"What will that do? Prove that prominent citizens of Israel are involved in stealing from Jordanian terrorists who are guilty of bringing cocaine into the United States? What punishment would you suggest in that light?"

Wellsberg's face hardened. "You and the others have gotten too greedy, Enoch."

"Too greedy?" Harel whirled on the man. "You are Mossad, and as such, you are in charge of the military aspects of this operation. Even in covert Intelligence, you had budgets to contend with. Can you even guess how much money might be needed to settle these new lands and hold them against everyone who would try to take them from us?"

"The people who move into those lands could take what they needed from what God has provided."

"That's not what I'm talking about. God doesn't rain down tanks and warplanes like manna from heaven. We'll need those to hold that land. And without protection, how many Jewish citizens do you see willingly moving into an undeveloped war zone?"

Wellsberg didn't reply.

"None of them," Harel said. He touched the part of Jordan that he was intent on absorbing into Israeli borders. "We'll have to provide jobs, as well as protection. The American suspicions, even if they pass them on to the United Nations, will do nothing to stop us. We still have the situation under our control."

"You're forgetting the covert forces that are arrayed against us. Our involvement in Jordan has been exposed, as well," Wellsberg argued.

"It doesn't matter. In the end Jordan will still be compelled to make what will be assumed to be an unprovoked attack against Israel. An attack that we'll use as an excuse to invade that country. When we do, our allies in the PLO will join us."

"I think you're trusting them too much."

"And I think you're borrowing trouble. You can't begin every phase of a mission with the belief that it is doomed to failure," Harel asserted.

"There are so many things that have to be right."

"They will be. Remember our fail safes planted within the Israeli Defense Department and the Metsada team we have planted in Jordan. Whether King Hussein willingly wants to or not, his military *will* attack Israel." Harel smiled, anticipating success in spite of the news footage continuing to roll across the television. "Or at least it'll certainly look like that."

SQUARING HIS SHOULDERS and taking a final deep breath as he watched Schwarz fire a forefinger pistol at him in silent support, Rosario Blancanales put his hand against the metal door of the interrogation room and pushed his way inside.

He was dressed in a dark blue business suit that was tailored but left without the frills. His tie hung loosely under the plain tie tack, and the temporary sheriff's-office ID hung at the end of a short black cord and an alligator clip.

Rafi bin Baz, his wounds tended and dressed so that patches of gauze and adhesive tape mirrored his features, sat in a chair at the end of the rectangular table in the center of the room. One side of his jaw was decidedly swollen and purplish. He wore an orange jumpsuit provided by the county penal supplies.

At Baz's side was a plump, swarthy man, dark eyes evasive behind his thick-lensed glasses. His name was Azim Quraishi, and he was a lawyer based in the L.A. area specializing in legal problems between the local community and Middle Eastern businesses. He was also qualified in criminal matters.

Blancanales's specialty was communications between people. He'd earned his nickname back in Vietnam while working with the Executioner, operating as a liaison and interpreter. Up against the Arabs, he had a language deficiency, but Price had already worked that out. Behind the one-way glass lining the wall over Blancanales's shoulder where Carl Lyons and Sheriff Conagher were lounging over a coffeepot, there was also a Stony Man blacksuit Price had ordered flown in from the Farm. The guy had an extensive background in the Middle Eastern theater.

The hearing aid Blancanales openly wore in his left ear was actually a shortwave radio connecting him to the blacksuit.

"Gentlemen," the Politician said as he laid his pad and tape recorder on the tabletop. He pulled the chair back and seated himself, then examined the notes he'd scribbled in the margins beside the questions he'd written on the legal pad.

"You can't use the recorder without our permission," Quraishi said.

"Of course not. Sorry." Blancanales reached out and clicked the recorder off. It was a small concession, and one he'd deliberately set up to set the tone for the meeting. His main thrust was to deliver information, not obtain it.

Quraishi opened a compact daily planner and flipped to a note section, then he retrieved a pen from under his jacket. "Your name?"

"Costa. Rudolpho Costa."

Baz leaned over for a quick conference in Arabic.

The hearing aid hummed in Blancanales's ear. "He's telling the lawyer that he saw you during the raid, that he doesn't think you're connected with the sheriff's office."

Quraishi's eyes didn't move from the Able Team warrior's face. Once Baz leaned back, the lawyer asked, "What is your position in this case?"

"I'm part of the federal task force sent down to investigate your client and his associates."

"He recalls seeing you."

"I remember him, too."

"How long have you been assigned to this case?" Quraishi asked.

"Only days."

"Days."

"Yes."

"Yet you were able to obtain search warrants on such short notice."

"My office has a good working relationship with several judiciary bodies."

"Obviously."

Blancanales touched the legal pad in front of him. "There are questions I must attend to."

"Of course." Quraishi waved magnanimously.

Fixing his eyes on Baz, the Politician asked, "Have you been advised of your rights?"

"Yes."

"And you've had them explained to you."

"Yes."

Quraishi cleared his throat theatrically. "My client is an intelligent man, Agent Costa, and he knows his rights."

"I was there, Counsellor. I happen to know Mr. Baz thought he was going to be protected by diplomatic immunity. I want the truth laid bare here so there are no further misunderstandings."

"Let him talk," Baz said.

The lawyer acted offended, but quieted.

"There'll be no extradition," Blancanales said. "You're going to be charged for drug trafficking, and here in the United States that's a serious offense." He reached into his pocket and took out a pack of Egyptian cigarettes that a blacksuit had obtained from a tobacco shop earlier. "Do you smoke?"

Baz nodded.

With a flick of his wrist, Blancanales sent the pack spinning across the long tabletop. A package of safety matches was tucked into the cellophane.

Lifting the pack in his manacled hands, Baz nodded his approval. "Egyptian. Not bad. Your American cigarettes barely whet the appetite for someone used to real tobacco."

"So I'd heard." Blancanales leaned back in his chair till his shoulders were in firm contact with the seat back. He dragged the legal pad on top of his crossed knees and settled into the questioning while the Jordanian cupped his hands and lit a cigarette. The interrogation was standard operational procedure, questions that had already been asked by the sheriff's team of investigators.

Baz categorically denied being involved in drug trafficking, saying that his people had evidently gotten the wrong packages from the delivery pickup station. He didn't try to excuse the guns or the excessive force used by the Jordanians, pointing out instead what a dangerous place the United States was.

Blancanales kept the questions coming, listening to the voices, as well as the words. Nothing rang off center, but neither did he get anything he could use. Finally he broke off the interview, excused himself and headed for the door.

The blacksuit interpreter translated Baz's request.

"Just a moment," Quraishi said.

The Politician turned to face the man.

"Mr. Baz would like to know how you obtained the federal warrants for search and seizure."

"Someone within the organization turned them in."

"Who?"

Blancanales put on a show of hesitation.

Quraishi snapped his fingers impatiently. "Come on, now, Mr. Costa. This is all information that will be allowed me during discovery."

"Yeah." Blancanales put a hand on the door and acted like a bureaucrat trapped in the system. "Luther Nix sold you out in exchange for immunity."

Baz's response was immediate and explosive, accompanied by several hand gestures.

The interpretation issuing from the hearing-aid receiver was totally superfluous. Baz explained that he'd seen Nix in the sheriff's car, but thought that they were being set up by the sheriff. Quraishi quietly told him that there was no way they were being lied to now, because everything they were being told in the interrogation room had to be the truth. Baz took up a couple of minutes swearing eternal vengeance against the neo-Nazis, and Luther Nix in particular.

Marshaling his acting ability and voice control, getting ready for the main pitch, Blancanales looked at Baz and said, "You're not the only one upset here. The sheriff's department was counting on getting a lot of bucks out of this deal from the permitted seizures. But when they searched those accounts, all the money had been removed."

Quraishi's quick hands betrayed him, the fingers straying to where the empty cellular-phone holster hung at his waist. He rolled over a Rolex-wrapped wrist to check the time.

Leaving the room and pulling the door closed behind him, Blancanales met Conagher, the blacksuit and Lyons coming out of the observation booth.

"He was surprised," the Ironman said.

Blancanales smiled as they walked down the hall, intent on clearing the area before the terrorist lawyer left the room. "Very surprised."

"The money is gone?" Conagher asked as they turned the corner.

Lyons nodded. "Yeah. Long story and—as yet—unreleased. But don't worry, I managed to cut you guys in for sixty-five percent of the take. Figured you'd want something to give that deputy's family. As soon as it can be cut loose, it's yours."

"Thanks."

They paused in the hallway, and a deputy with a concerned expression bolted out of the elevator and headed toward Conagher. "Sheriff, we're having a hell of a time in the cell blocks where we're keeping those baby Hitlers and those A-rabs. Three men have already been taken to the infirmary."

Part of the ARM had been rounded up during investigatory sweeps around the mansion where Able Team had hit them. They'd still been in possession of illegal weapons and amounts of cocaine. Conagher and Lyons had decided to hold them for the twenty-four hours permitted before booking to provide a welcoming committee for the arriving Jordanians.

"I'd better take care of that," Conagher said with a dark scowl. "Now that our point has been made between the two groups, I'll kick the ARM guys back onto the streets after their lawyers process them through the court and post bail." He glanced at Lyons. "I suppose you people will still be underfoot for a while longer."

Lyons nodded.

"Let me know if I can do anything for you," Conagher said. "As long as it remains fairly legal."

Blancanales grinned at the exchange. After the two lawmen had gone, he asked, "Did you talk to Barb and Aaron?"

"Yeah."

They fell into step together and headed for the second floor where Schwarz was getting a debrief on everything

Stony Man Farm had turned up in the past couple of hours.

"And?" Blancanales prompted.

"Now we're out of it," Lyons said, "but things as far as Phoenix and Striker get dicey. They're down to the splitting-hairs stage."

MACK BOLAN eased out of the rented Ford under the cover of night, drifting easily into the narrow, twisting streets of the Old City in Jerusalem. A cool, dry breeze whispered in from the desert and stirred the shadows stretched out beneath the moon.

He was dressed in dark colors, and a baseball cap shadowed his features. The Beretta 93-R was slung in shoulder leather, and a collapsible H&K PSG-1 High Precision Marksman's rifle rode in a cloth duffel over his shoulder.

As he turned into the alley he'd chosen three blocks from his car, his mind restructured the battle zone, playing with all the variables he'd established for the skirmish. Things were going to happen very quickly, and there wasn't much margin for error.

When he made the corner, he could see the first lights of the Eliahu Hotel across the street at the end of the alley. They were hard and white against the edged darkness framing the mouth of the alley.

Moving up to a trot now, knowing the second hand of his watch was sweeping inexorably toward the time of the attack, he used his hands and vaulted to the top of a Dumpster halfway down the alley. After sitting and watching the Jordanian terrorist cell for the past two hours, then trailing them to their destination, the activity felt good. The increased circulation warmed him and loosened his muscles.

His fingers dug into the irregular cinder-block surface of the textile retail building, and he pulled himself up. The toes of his work boots found purchase, and the going got easier. By the time he reached the third floor, his cardiovascular system was working at full tilt.

Although he hadn't been able to make a move against the safehouse the Jordanians had set up in the Old City, he had figured out what their target for tonight was. The news station he'd listened to while on recon had provided additional details about the political gathering between representatives of Jewish and Palestinian lobbying groups on the West Bank. As during the Gulf War, the two factions had decided that the enemy without was more dangerous than the enemy within.

The meeting between the two groups had started over an hour ago, and instant media coverage had descended on them. Although the time in Israel was 4:00 a.m., back in the States where many Jewish supporters were watching live telecasts of the meeting with interest, it was 9:00 p.m. on the East Coast and 6:00 p.m. on the West Coast—prime viewing time for a lot of people who would take quick interest in the form of financial support.

The Jordanians planned to make a student attack on the assembly and peel off before retaliation could be effected. Their targets were such that it would be open season on anyone who was there, including the Palestinians, who had caused problems in Jordan over the years.

Bolan had been unable to effectively intercept the six-man team that had been assigned to the strike when they'd left the safehouse. He was gambling on his skills to prevent major bloodshed at the hotel.

Opening the duffel, the Executioner quickly assembled the sniper rifle. Chambered with .308 Winchester rounds, the PSG-1 was outfitted with a 20-round box magazine and a Hensoldt 6 × 42 telescopic sight that had been reconfigured for StarTron night-sight capabilities. The short stock slid into place, and he locked it down with wing nuts. Two extra clips were mounted in a leather holder that locked on to the rear of the stock like saddlebags. He'd detached the folding bipod before packing the weapon. All of his shots would be on the fly, not allowing the bipod to be of practical use.

Crouched by the eaves, he worked the action and fed the first round into the breach, then canted it against the low wall. On his knees, he took the small night glasses from his jacket pocket and scanned the hotel.

The hotel was huge and ornate, a stone spear thrust up out of the belly of the city. Moonlight turned the surface of the building into a pale gray iridescence, pockmarked by the scattered lights that were still on.

At the foot of the building facing the textile plant where Bolan had set himself up, a banquet area had been arranged. Long tables were covered with finger foods and dozens of different drinks. White-coated waiters and cocktail waitresses in elegant evening dress circulated among the guests. Part of the festivities were shielded by the overhanging eaves of the building. Electric lanterns hung from the hotel and from poles strategically placed throughout the entertainment area.

The distance across the four-lane street to the hotel from the textile plant was something less than one hundred yards. Bolan had already sighted the rifle in at that yardage.

He scanned the surroundings again, looking for the faces he'd memorized from his recon on the safehouse, wishing it had been possible to remove the threat then. According to the Intel Price had access to, warnings had already been phoned in to the Jewish and Palestinian politicians, but both groups had refused to be cowed by threats. Price had ventured the thought that several of them were looking for the kind of media glamour Dr. Enoch Harel had garnered earlier.

More than a hundred people had gathered in the tree-lined confines of the banquet area. A stone fence ran around the outside perimeter. Most of the security people overseeing the festivities blended in with the well-groomed men and the elegant women accompanying them, but Bolan's sharp eyes caught the miniradios plugged in to their ears and the thumb mikes as they relayed messages. Beyond the stone fence Israeli military police made a more obvious bulwark against violence, and some of them were pulling the valet work at the front of the hotel.

Reaching into his mind, Bolan switched off the emotional part of the man and became a waiting gunsight. Sometimes targets in the jungles of Vietnam had taken days of waiting in one spot to take a single shot designed to change an entire front of the NVA's communications ability.

The ice sculpture of three dolphins breaking the surface of an ice blue sea on the center table gleamed wetly. A woman tugged on her male companion's arm and made him look as she ran her fingers along the frozen skin of the sculpture.

Over her shoulder the Executioner found the first of his targets taking the field.

He raked the battle zone in quadrants, finding four of the six in less than a minute. He figured the remaining two had taken up stations at the outer perimeter of the banquet area.

A speaker climbed to the podium set a little apart from the food-laden tables, and a crowd started to gather. The man tapped the microphone experimentally. Television cameramen moved in closer, and electric arcs of light combatted the light streaming from the lanterns.

Knowing the time was winding down to zero, Bolan fisted the PSG-1's pistol grip and pulled the buttstock into his shoulder. The metal and matte black, high-impact-resistant plastic stock was cool against his cheek.

He kept both eyes open, focusing on the whole field of view and switching to the targets through the scope only when he needed to.

The Jordanian terrorists moved through the crowd, and the warrior could see the predatory stalking instinct come alive in them. Their hands were beneath their jackets.

The fifth man came into view as Bolan put the chain of events together in his head. The Executioner took up slack on the trigger and fired the first round, pulling through easily and riding out the recoil, aiming at the back of the man's head where the head joined the spine. The recoil took the terrorist out of his view, then he was locking on to the second man as reaction to the initial shot settled into the crowd. He punched the next round through the man's cheek as the guy's head snapped around.

The third target was an impossibility. If Bolan had taken the shot, the bullet would have passed through the man's head and struck a civilian standing beside him. Using an economy of skill, the Executioner dropped the fourth man with a bullet through one eye. The fifth man went down with a bullet striking home just under his chin that drove him down and backward.

Moving back to the missing target, Bolan registered the hits. Every Jordanian he'd shot had fallen and stayed down.

In the parking lot, explosions ripped through the stationary cars in a staccato booming that lifted the vehicles several feet into the air and reduced them to flaming chunks of debris. Evidently the terrorist team had been busy delivering party favors before crashing the banquet.

The third terrorist was scrambling for cover, firing the automatic pistol he carried with impunity.

Fixing him in his sights, Bolan put two .308 rounds through the man's back and smashed him to the ground. He sent a third shot coring through the target's head in case he was wearing body armor.

A cluster of security men collapsed on a man in one corner of the banquet area. When Bolan checked the activity through his scope, he found the missing sixth man and disregarded him because it was obvious that one was no longer going to be a threat.

Alarms screamed out in the streets, and vehicles mounted with official whirling cherries sped out of hiding to block traffic.

Bolan knew he was only minutes away from being discovered atop the building. As he started to move, new action caught his eye.

A small phalanx of men carrying short, blunt automatic weapons broke cover across the street and ran for the stone wall of the hotel adjoining the thoroughfare. Muzzle-flashes sprayed out at once. The leading police cars broke in different directions to avoid the wall of bullets that leapt out to meet them. Two separate crashes tangled up what had been planned as a well-rehearsed rescue attempt, wrapping five cars around each other. Civilian traffic froze.

In the banquet area the security teams were regrouping to meet the new threat. Some of them herded the banquet attendees from the open areas back into the hotel. Shouted orders, garbled and confused when interspersed with the gunfire, rattled across the street. Someone thought to extinguish the lanterns, and full night descended over the area.

Shouldering the sniper rifle again, Bolan stood up and began firing methodically into the group bearing down on the hotel grounds. He estimated the new attackers to be at least twenty men strong. Some of their number were already strewn across the street.

Explosions boomed erratically before and in back of the stone wall. A moment later another wave of grenades were thrown, but they were fewer in number.

Bolan changed magazines. The attackers were turned back at the wall like a wave breaking against a high shore. He fired at them, putting two down before the police vehicles finally surged forward and surrounded the survivors.

Abandoning the sniper rifle, ignoring the questions that came to his mind, Bolan concentrated on his own escape. He took a grappling hook from an inside pocket of the bomber jacket, shook the flukes from their recessed positions and hooked it at the building eaves. He paid out the nylon cord, then clambered down hand over hand, reaching the alley floor as a car wheeled around the corner from the street and slammed into the side of the building. Metal grated and sparks flew as the driver attempted to free his vehicle from the cinder blocks.

Sparing a brief glance over his shoulder, Bolan sprinted for the opposite end of the alley. At first he thought one of the police units had tracked him. That belief was removed when a passenger stepped out of the stalled car with an RPG-7 over one shoulder and fired on an approaching police car.

The warhead sped true, slamming into the target with a deafening detonation. The hood peeled back and flew away like a square Frisbee, and flames washed over the windshield.

A voice screamed something from inside the car. The guy wielding the rocket launcher dropped the depleted weapon and threw himself back into the car. The bumper fell from the front of the vehicle, and the engine growled as it powered up to propel the car over the metal bar.

Bolan hadn't understood the words, but he had recognized them as Arabic. As he ran, he pulled the Dumpster into the middle of the alley, hoping to slow the car rushing up behind him. He freed the Beretta and raced for the mouth of the alley.

A bonging impact sounded just behind him. He elbowed his way around the corner of the building as bullets spit and darted from the cinder-block surface.

The car skidded out onto the next street, fishtailing wide as the driver tried to bring it around to follow Bolan.

The warrior dropped to one knee, took advantage of a car parked in front of him and slid his empty hand under his gunhand. The Beretta's open sights dropped over the passenger window as the gunner reemerged. Squeezing the trigger evenly, Bolan placed three shots into the man's chest, knocking him back into the vehicle.

The taillights flared as the driver hit the brakes and brought the car around in a one-eighty. Then it came roaring forward.

Coming to his feet, the Executioner presented his gun side to the car, ignoring the wash of bright headlights glaring at him. He concentrated on the dim shadow behind the steering wheel on the other side of the cracked windshield. The 93-R bucked in his fist repeatedly.

He waited till the last second to make his move, knowing by the canny weave of the front end that the driver was still alert. The sedan hit the edge of the curb, jerked up and roared over.

Bolan threw himself to the right, not bothering to stay on his feet but going immediately into a shoulder roll that took him away from the rampaging bulk of the car. The rough pavement abraded his exposed wrist and palm, and he came up on his knees, the Beretta tracking back onto the car.

Metal was rent as it smacked into the building where he'd been standing. A plate-glass window exploded inward, and floor-length drapes wrapped around mannequins and sent them tumbling. Escaping vapor from the ruptured radiator hissed and threw white clouds of steam into the air. The rear door screeched as it was forced open, then a man tumbled uncertainly to his feet. The machine pistol in his hand wavered wildly.

On his feet now and in motion, the Executioner kicked the weapon out of his attacker's hands, then followed up with a forearm that smashed the man back against the wrecked car.

A groan escaped the man's lips as he started to slither to the sidewalk.

Grabbing the man's clothes, Bolan pulled him from the car, catching sight of another man inside trying to bring his gun into play. He lifted the Beretta and fired point-blank, putting two parabellum rounds into the gunner's face, breaking the window behind him.

The sounds of pursuit neared, streaming from the alley.

Taking most of the semiconscious man's weight as his own, Bolan stepped back with his prisoner, trying to decide if his own escape could include making off with a prisoner for later interrogation. Grimly he dragged the gunner behind him. Too many people had either died or been injured at the political meeting in the banquet area. He had to know why and he had to know who had been responsible.

A speeding midsize Volvo fishtailed around the corner two blocks from the alley, passing Bolan's waiting rental. For the first time the big hellfire warrior noticed that his own car had been blocked in by other cars. Getting out of the maze would take some time. He kept the Beretta at his side and ready as he pulled his captive toward the rental vehicle.

Voices were echoing the length of the alley now, letting him know the Israeli military and police units had started a foot pursuit.

Abruptly the Volvo braked near him, as if the driver had suddenly spotted him.

Bolan froze, waiting to see what would happen. In the crawling confusion of the tightening security web, telling friend from foe was next to impossible. While it hampered him, he was intent on using it against everyone looking for him, as well.

A brunette stuck her head out the window. "Get in!"

A shadow moved in the rear seat, hands busy holding something to its face. A man's voice said, "Desiree, what the hell do you think—"

"Getting a goddamned exclusive, Marshak, so shut the hell up." The woman reached over the seat and popped the rear door open. "C'mon, guy. I'm an American TV reporter. My name's Desiree St. Cyr. Maybe you've heard of me."

"No," Bolan replied.

Sirens screamed as units obviously raced around the opposite ends of the blocked street in front of the hotel.

"Fine," St. Cyr said in a hard voice. "I've got a car and you don't, and if the Israelis catch you here with that guy, I get to cover your execution. How's that sound?"

Bolan holstered the Beretta and used both hands to haul the prisoner across the street to the waiting car.

The man in the backseat rolled into the front, and moonlight gleamed on the camera in his hands.

Shoving the Arab against the far side of the seat, Bolan reached up and tagged the lock, then ripped the button off so it couldn't be released. Before he could scramble completely inside, the woman had the Volvo in motion. As he leaned over to slam the door, he saw the first of the whirling red cherries color the street behind them.

CHAPTER THIRTEEN

Meyer Levin didn't attempt stealth as he approached the house because he was no longer young and spry. He just walked quietly. If seen by neighbors while skulking, they might be prompted to call the police to investigate. The odds were that if any saw him now at this early-morning hour, no alarm would be raised because he walked so confidently.

But inside, his nerves restlessly coiled and uncoiled like snakes parching on hot desert sand. He kept his hands jammed deep into the pockets of his long coat, his right one curled tightly around the Beretta .380.

The yard was carefully landscaped, and the cloying smell of the rose garden filled his nostrils. He craved a cigarette.

The garage was a two-car unit, but he knew Gozal Dinure no longer kept two cars. His wife had died almost twenty years ago at the hands of Palestinian assassins. They had been friends during those times, each helping the other through times of grief.

However, times had changed. Events had thrown them in different directions, though both had remained in the Mossad. He'd visited Dinure a few times since his wife's passing, spent hours drinking beer and talking while Dinure worked in the wood shop set up in the second bay of the garage.

As he stepped into the shadows fronting the garage, Catherine Hawkes emerged from the recess.

The tall woman was dressed all in black, her red hair hidden under a black watch cap, her face smudged beyond recognition with greasepaint. "Two men inside besides Dinure," she said in a low voice that didn't carry. "The alarm system on the grounds was complicated but I finessed it. The one on the house wasn't nearly so hard to spoof."

"The men?" Levin asked.

"Guards."

"Dinure?"

"He appears well. Sleeping."

"In his bedroom?"

"Yes."

"And the guards?"

"One's sacked out on the couch. The other's working his way through a pot of coffee."

Levin looked at the woman. She'd been impeccable in the execution of her mission. And she'd been close-mouthed, only giving him the information she thought he needed, then selling whatever else he demanded at a dear price. When it was something she was convinced he didn't need to know, it wasn't for sale at all. In many ways she reminded him of Canary when he'd worked with the woman the first time ten years ago and believed he'd been betrayed by her. Hawkes never admitted personal knowledge of Canary or even hinted at the parameters of her present assignment. Blind trust was something Canary had often been in the position of enforcing during their relationship in those days. He'd admired—and feared—her for it.

She knelt by the lock of his side door of the garage, and a set of matte black picks appeared. Although her hands were covered by thin black gloves with the palms cut out, her movements were deft.

The lock clicked open.

Mixed scents of pine, machine oil, varnish, stripper and paint crowded out the odor of the roses when the door opened.

Hawkes drew an oversize air pistol from a holster hung low on her right thigh and went inside.

Taking the .380 from his jacket pocket, Levin followed. The slick surface of the poured concrete whispered beneath his soles.

"You know the way?" Hawkes asked.

"Yes." He felt her hand slip inside his.

"Then lead."

He went by touch, making his way carefully. He found the car and the workbench by feel. It helped to remember that Dinure had always been a neat individual. He pictured the large tool wall in his mind, recalling that every piece of equipment had been carefully placed on it and the shape of that tool outlined in yellow paint for easy recognition.

He felt sawdust under his shoes and stopped.

"Problem?" Hawkes whispered into his ear. Her breath was warm.

"Sawdust on the floor. Gozal was always meticulous about his work areas, both here and in the Mossad."

"There was a bottle of whiskey and a tall glass on the dining table. Dinure was snoring heavily when I reconned his room."

"Perhaps, but he never used to work while drinking."

"Maybe he's been stressed out lately."

"And people change." He moved ahead, skirting the circular saw and finding the door leading into the laundry room. He tried the knob and found it wasn't locked.

"What's next?" Hawkes asked.

"The laundry room, followed by the kitchen."

"Okay. I've got it after that. Get behind me."

Levin did.

Hawkes opened the door, extending the air pistol ahead of her. Only the silent bulks of the washer and dryer stood in front of them. Light gleamed from the top and bottom of the door after that.

"Lucky," Hawkes said. "The door opens toward us."

Tightening his grip on the Beretta, Levin closed on her, at her shoulder as she went through the door.

A big, blocky man wearing a dark suit with the jacket hanging over the back of a chair in the breakfast nook stood at the patio glass doors holding a mug of coffee. Levin surmised a gust of cooler air had drifted in over the room and caught the man's attention because he started to turn around.

Without hesitation, Hawkes lifted the air pistol and fired twice. Both darts sank deeply into the man's throat, their dark blue feathers prominent against the flesh tones.

The man struggled against the effects of the drug invading his system. He flailed wildly, trying to pull the pistol from his shoulder holster, not realizing the strap was holding it in place. As he sank to his knees, his eyes rolling up in his head till only the whites showed, the guard slumped unconscious to the floor.

Kneeling, Levin laid his fingers against the man's throat. The pulse was weak and thready. "How long?"

"Hours," Hawkes promised. "He'll have a hell of a headache when he wakes up."

But at least the man would still be alive. Levin was satisfied with that. With everything that was going on, he had trouble being sure who his enemies were these days. Enough innocents had died so far.

They walked into the living room, and Hawkes fired two more darts into the sleeping man's abdomen while he reclined on the couch. He came to for just a moment, then went quickly back under.

In the bedroom Levin flipped on a small lamp by the bed and looked down at Dinure.

The man had aged and seemed to have gotten smaller in the years that had passed. Though nearly twenty years younger than Levin, Dinure appeared almost the same age. The hair was gray now, framing a bald spot at the back of his head, and the ragged knife scar across the back of his left shoulder had paled from pink to antique white. Dinure slept on his back, snoring unmercifully, with his arm thrown across his eyes.

Levin put his hand on his friend's shoulder and gently shook him awake.

Dinure came to slowly. His rheumy eyes blinked and looked glazed under the soft light. "Meyer."

"Yes."

Dinure worked hard to push himself into a sitting position.

The woman kept him covered, the air pistol never wavering.

"Who's she?" Dinure ran a hand across his face, then through his hair. His days-old beard sounded raspy.

"Someone who has an interest in the things we must discuss."

"Who let her in?"

"I did."

Dinure was more focused now. "And the gun?"

"She doesn't know you."

"I see."

Levin took his cigarettes from his pocket and lit one.

"May I?" Dinure said.

"I didn't know you smoked." Levin extended the pack.

"There are a lot of things you don't know, Meyer."
Dinure took a cigarette, then leaned in close for a light.

At his side, Levin saw the muzzle of the air pistol move
imperceptibly. He had no doubt that Hawkes would fire
if a threatening move was made. For the first time he realized that she probably didn't trust him, either. "Those
are the things we must talk about, my friend."

"I don't know if my head is in such good shape for
this. I think I drank too much. At the time it didn't seem
like enough."

"Give me your arm. I'll help you." Levin took his
hand, pulled him to his feet, then draped Dinure's arm
over his shoulder. The woman followed at a discreet distance. Gamely he made his way into the kitchen past the
fallen guards.

"Are they dead?"

"No."

Dinure sighed. "That's good. I don't think they're bad
boys. Just misdirected."

"The problem is," Hawkes said in an icy voice,
"there's a lot more *misdirected* boys out there ready to
kill people."

The smile that fitted itself to Dinure's face looked more
like a death's-head grin, and about as pleasurable.
Looking at him, Levin suddenly missed the old friendship he'd had with the man, back when they could talk
about the craftsmanship of birdhouses rather than covert operations that led only to shallow graves.

"I've come to the conclusion, dear lady, that the world
is like a snake devouring itself. Though it struggles in the
attempt and seems capable of doing the task, it will die
before it sees the completion. But as long as it keeps
feeding, it seems to be happy because it's too stupid to
recognize any other way."

Levin seated the Mossad case officer at the small dinette and removed the whiskey and glass. "Coffee?"

"No."

"That wasn't a question concerning your preferences. Where is it?"

"The pantry."

Levin looked, found a nearly empty bag, then rinsed the pot and put a fresh one on. Within seconds the fresh-brewed smell started filling the kitchen.

"What brings you here, Meyer?"

"Rimon Jacobsen."

Dinure studied Levin as he sat. Hawkes made the air pistol disappear, but stood near the pantry door, taking an observational stance that deliberately wouldn't intimidate Dinure. "How much do you know?"

"Enough to make educated guesses, but not enough to work with. Jacobsen has a team working deep in Jordan, stationed near El Zerqa. I also know that Jacobsen was your protégé, just as you were mine. I think that he would talk to you about things he wasn't supposed to."

"The same way I talked to you about things I wasn't supposed to." Dinure nodded. "They were right to get rid of you, Meyer. You never did know when to leave well enough alone."

"This situation," Levin said with quiet authority, "does not classify as 'well enough.'"

The other man's gaze shifted away from Levin's. The older Mossad agent got up from the table, found cups in the cabinets and poured out for the three of them.

After sipping his coffee, Dinure said, "They made a deal with the PLO."

Levin knew how much that must have hurt Dinure. His wife had been killed by a PLO attack. After giving so much of his life in defense of his country, then his wife's life, as well, he must have been cut to the bone by such a negotiation. "Who? The Mossad?"

"Some of them were involved. Wellsberg, for one. There are others. The man mostly responsible for the agreement was Harel."

"Dr. Enoch Harel?"

"Yes."

Levin glanced at Hawkes. The woman didn't appear to be surprised by the name. He'd been working on that angle himself, and it had resulted in Hannah Leor's death.

"They knew you suspected Harel," Dinure said. "That's why the woman you placed inside his organization was terminated, and that's why they decided to kill you."

"You knew?"

"That part I learned this morning. But there was nothing I could do about it. After Rimon confided in me, I started a quiet investigation of my own. I was intercepted and placed under house arrest a week ago."

"I didn't know."

"They've got this thing organized to the decimal point, Meyer. I don't think anyone can stop them."

"What are their aims?"

"There's a large faction of the PLO already in place inside Jordan waiting for the signal. Once war begins between Jordan and Israel, they're going to help pull Amman down and kill King Hussein."

"War may not be inevitable." Levin freshened his friend's coffee.

"It will be," Dinure said with real conviction. "Harel and Wellsberg and Canary have labored hard to make sure there could be no turning back from this thing."

"Canary?"

"Yes. Surely you remember her."

Settling back in his chair, his backbone suddenly feeling as if an ice spider had spun a frosty web over it, Levin nodded. "I remember her."

Hawkes's face was impassive.

"Tell me about it," Levin said.

As DESIREE ST. CYR made a right turn with the police sirens howling clearly behind them, the terrorist lunged at Mack Bolan without any kind of warning. The tight turn added extra momentum to the man's weight and strength, and the warrior had his hands full for a moment.

"Oh, shit," Marshak said from the front seat.

A knife appeared from the Arab's robes and slit the plastic covering the back seat only inches from the Executioner's face.

Bolan captured the knife wrist and leaned in with a wicked elbow that slammed his attacker's jaws together. Teeth broke and blood and saliva exploded from his torn lips. To stop another move, the warrior twisted the wrist and popped the knife free. He rammed his open hand forward, catching the terrorist in the throat with the Y between his forefinger and thumb.

The man choked immediately, then became paralyzed as Bolan continued the pressure.

"God, Des, he's killing him!"

Bolan saw St. Cyr's eyes flash in the rearview mirror as she watched him. He wondered if she was having second thoughts about the exclusive she wanted.

Abruptly the terrorist sank back against the seat cushions and remained immobile.

"He's dead," Marshak whispered.

"He's unconscious," Bolan corrected as he checked the carotid artery for a pulse. He extracted a roll of ordnance tape from his pocket and tore off strips as St. Cyr continued jockeying through the late-night traffic. Quickly he bound his prisoner. A brief check through the back glass still showed no signs of pursuit.

"You're American, aren't you?" St. Cyr asked.

"Yeah," Bolan replied as he produced the Beretta and fed a fresh clip into it before putting it away again. He reached into his jacket and took out his war book. A penlight from another pocket lit up the street maps of Jerusalem he had inside.

"What're you doing?"

"Finding the fastest route out of here."

"I already know it," St. Cyr said. "Relax."

Bolan watched the progression of turns the woman made and became convinced she really knew the route as well as she professed. "Pull over to the curb."

Suspicion dawned in the reporter's eyes. "Why?"

"To change drivers."

"No. I can drive as well as you can, and even if you could drive better at high speeds, there's no pursuit to escape."

Drawing the Beretta out from under the jacket again, Bolan said, "Pull over."

"No way, Jack. No way am I cutting loose this story. When I realized you were sniping from the top of that textile plant and figured your escape route, then got lucky enough that my car wasn't blown up and I didn't get caught in that confusion of traffic, I busted my ass to get there first."

"For Christ's sake, Des," Marshak said. "Give him the goddamned car before he kills us both."

St. Cyr narrowly avoided a stalled taxi in her lane and got lucky that the adjacent one was empty. Her eyes flicked back to the rearview mirror, and she returned the warrior's gaze full measure. "He won't kill us."

"Shit! And maybe he can't let us live, either. Have you given that any thought?"

"Yes. If that was true he'd have already shot us both."

"Now, there's a cheery thought," the photographer complained.

Without saying anything, Bolan reached into the reporter's lap and took the camera away. The Beretta went back into shoulder leather. His fingers found the releases, then popped the camera open. Stripping the film out, he fed it through the open window and watched it disappear along the street.

"Hey!" St. Cyr exclaimed angrily.

"I need a phone," Bolan told her. "Public, but in a place where we can leave this guy without being noticed."

"If you try to ditch us . . ."

"It'll be done," Bolan replied.

Her gaze was stony.

Ignoring her unspoken wrath, he searched the Arab's pockets. Aside from extra magazines for the machine pistol, Israeli paper money and coins and Israeli ID, undoubtedly falsified, the man had nothing on him.

As St. Cyr pulled into the dark parking lot of a closed diner and rolled slowly up to the pay phone outside the building, Bolan took an additional strip of ordnance tape from the roll and bound the man's feet together. The eyelids flickered, showing signs of impending consciousness. Another strip sealed the mouth after the Executioner made sure his prisoner could breathe through his nose.

He got out.

St. Cyr started to follow.

"Stay in the car."

He crossed to the phone, used a credit card that would lead investigators nowhere and had to wait five minutes for the connection to be made.

Carmen Delahunt switched him over to Barbara Price's office.

"Are you still operative?" Price asked when she picked up the phone.

"Yeah. You caught the news releases?"

"Yes. Things are still confused at that end. Intel is slow getting back to us."

"There's a new player in the game," Bolan stated.

"Or an old one finally surfacing. I'll know within the hour and get back to you."

Bolan shifted, his eyes constantly roving over the darkened streets. A couple of helicopters had taken to the air, the sound of their rotors throbbing and distant. They swirled like dragonflies over the hotel, its top stories visible among the cluster of buildings. Their searchlights stabbed down like flaring daggers spreading from a thin hilt. "I'll have to get back to you. I'm going to be mobile for a while. Not all of the Jordanians were taken down during that raid."

"I've got a meet for you set up with someone else. Can ya make it?"

"In Jerusalem?"

"Yes."

Bolan turned that over in his head. Usually if there were resources to be had in a country on a mission this tight, Price made the Stony Man warriors aware of it. And the mission controller sounded as though the meeting was important. "I've got a prisoner."

"Jordanian?"

"No. That's what I need to find out."

"The people you'll be meeting can probably help you with that."

"Fine, then. I've also got an added wrinkle at this end."

"What?"

"A reporter tagged me at the banquet. She only knows I was connected to the takedown of the Jordanians. She wants an exclusive."

Price paused.

Bolan could see the set of her features in concentration in his mind's eye even though thousands of miles separated them. He'd found over the years that their mental efforts coincided more often than not.

"Who is she?" Price asked.

In the car the reporter was looking restless. Marshak was gazing at the captured terrorist in the back seat like a man who'd just found a rattler in his sleeping bag and hadn't made up his mind whether it was going to strike. "Desiree St. Cyr. I'm not familiar with her."

"CNN. She's been covering the Israeli end of things from the beginning. She's a good reporter. Hal noticed her pretty early and had a dossier worked up on her. How's the relationship?"

"I feel like the target of a starving chicken hawk."

"No trust?"

"None. We met maybe twenty minutes ago."

"We can use her. Don't break contact."

"Okay."

"I need to set some things in motion. Can you be at this number ten minutes from now?"

When Bolan glanced at the street, everything was still quiet. "If not, I'll get back in touch with you as soon as possible."

Price acknowledged and broke the connection.

The warrior cradled the receiver, knowing from the tone in the beautiful mission controller's voice that the final cards in the play were about to be dealt. He wondered vaguely how many of them she'd been keeping hidden, then walked back to the Volvo to break the news to St. Cyr.

GALVANIZED into action, her mind whirling with all the new Intel the past hour had seen come into the Stony Man computers, Barbara Price walked out of her office toward Kurtzman's desk.

"What's up?" the cybernetics expert asked.

"Have you IDed any of the dead terrorists in Jerusalem yet?"

"A few. Carmen ran them through international channels. We're feeding the news reports into the programming as soon as we can lock on to it, but the Israelis are closing down the area and shutting the media out."

The wall screen at the far end of the room was divided into quadrants and was alive with four different broadcasts detailing the attack at the hotel. The lower left seemed to be shot from an aerial viewpoint. Another showed the police and military efforts at containment from a distance. A third depicted only a gloved hand over the camera lens. The last one panned over the crowd, then broke to replay the action when it had been the hottest.

"Who were they?"

"They belonged to one of the larger splinter groups in the PLO."

Price glanced at the five faces scattered across Kurtzman's personal monitor. "And that group is headed up by Zahid Faysal."

Kurtzman's eyes locked on her in silent contemplation. "I won't ask you how you knew that, because you'd have to tell me a Tarot reading, and I know there's not a deck in there."

"Get me a CIA and Mossad jacket on Faysal as soon as you can."

"Hunt's already working on it."

"You've been in contact with Phoenix?"

"McCarter called in—" Kurtzman consulted a legal pad hanging from a desk drawer, then checked his watch "—fifteen minutes ago. They're still lying low."

"When's their next communication due?"

"Forty-five minutes. We've got them on hourlies unless something breaks."

"Something's broke. When they get back in touch, I need them."

Kurtzman nodded.

"Are those dubbed film clips I asked for coming along?"

"Done. Two hours ago. We've been waiting on you."

"Any word on the Mossad force in Jordan?"

"No."

Price retreated momentarily for a can of iced tea, more to organize her rushed thoughts than for any real desire for the drink. Anger at herself rushed through her when she remembered how she'd asked Striker if he was still operative. She hadn't even bothered to ask him how he was, but had just come across like someone out kicking the tires before a long-distance trip.

She curled her shaking hand around the tea and walled the emotions away. She'd deal with them later. Dammit, she was professional enough to do that.

Kurtzman's eyes showed that he wanted to ask her if she was okay.

She locked her gaze with his and put the question out of his mind. "Has the Jordan military Intelligence found out who the dead Israelis were?"

"No. They're making accusations, but there's been no response from Israel. I've monitored some of the Intel going into Amman. They seem pretty confused there."

Price nodded. "I've downloaded and read your reports on my computer. It looks like Pol's disclosure in L.A. is having the desired effect."

"For a time." Kurtzman rolled his shoulders. "It was a good plan, Barb, and I'm not taking anything away from it, but it may not buy us enough time."

"It already has," she said confidently. "Let me know when you get everything ready. And I need that report on Enoch Harel's personal property assets. We're going to do a final debrief when Phoenix checks in the next time."

"We're that close?" Kurtzman acted surprised.

"Yeah." Price turned away, pulling the cellular phone from her hip holster as she walked back toward her office, punching in the White House number she had for Brognola and the President. "In fact, we're going to have to hurry like hell to catch up."

"THIS WAY, Ms. St. Cyr."

The reporter looked at the stoic young man who opened her car door in the underground garage of the office building she'd thought locked and guarded. The businesses housed above were predominantly American or American influenced.

The man was tan and handsome under a shock of thick, ash blond hair. But the assault rifle slung over his shoulder was cold and deadly, especially in light of the violence she had witnessed not even an hour ago. He stood waiting patiently beside the door, making no move to force her to go.

St. Cyr returned her gaze to the big warrior she'd picked up after the attack. "What the hell is this?"

"Your story," he said. He opened his door, got out, then opened the rear door and took the bound Arab out, draping the man over one broad shoulder.

"My story is with you, mister."

"Not anymore." With the unconscious man's weight distributed over his shoulder, he walked away.

"Wait." St. Cyr leapt out of the Volvo, wishing she'd brought Marshak with her instead of agreeing to leave him at an all-night restaurant.

"Can't."

For the first time she saw that another man was standing beside an idling Ford LTD only a short distance away. The shadows draping the garage almost faded the waiting car from view. Without pause, the big man stowed his captive in the trunk, then walked around to the front of the car.

St. Cyr started to walk around her own car, and the young man blocked her way without trying to restrain her.

When she turned to go the other way, she bumped into a third man she hadn't even realized was standing there. "You son of a bitch!" she shouted. "We had a deal! I saved your goddamned life back there! At the very least I kept you out of an Israeli jail!"

He paused, and a light smile touched his lips. "Yeah, you did. Maybe I can return the favor some day." Then he was behind the wheel and accelerating away a heart-beat later.

St. Cyr glared at the man who'd opened her door. "This had damned well better be good, buddy, or I'm going to start screaming conspiracy at the top of my lungs as soon as I hit the streets."

"Yes, ma'am."

Provided, she thought with sudden, icy realization, she ever saw those streets again.

The man took the lead, heading to the right where a dim set of lights advertised the location of the elevator. The second man flanked her after she got in.

"How did you people get the right to use these offices?" she asked to break the tense silence as the doors closed and the cage streaked upward.

"Even if we knew," the first man said, "I doubt we'd be at liberty to say."

"Cross your heart and hope to die, huh?"

"This line of work," the other one said, "Somebody always crosses it for you."

Her throat turned dry. She shoved her hand inside her pocket and found the tiny 35 mm camera Marshak had given her before she'd left him. The photographer hadn't been happy about the chance she was taking, but it had obviously been a relief to him that he hadn't had to come along. Satisfied that the camera was still at the ready, she took out the roll of hard candy she kept there and popped one into her mouth. She offered the pack to the two men. "Candy?"

"No, ma'am."

The other man declined also.

The elevator came to a gentle, bouncing halt on the fourteenth floor.

The blond guard held her back with a palm while he checked the dark corridor outside. A light flashed from the left. Unclipping a small flashlight from his belt, the guard returned the signal, then they proceeded out into the hallway.

"This way," he said.

St. Cyr followed. "Am I meeting someone?"

"Audio and video uplink. No person to person."

"Am I giving the interview or am I the subject of one?"

"As I understand it, you're being debriefed on some aspects of this mission."

"Why?"

"I don't know."

"And if you did?" St. Cyr pressed.

"I'm sure I wouldn't be allowed to tell, ma'am."

"Of course not." St. Cyr framed questions in her mind, using the mental agility her chosen field had required and honed over those years. A good reporter could get information from a rock even though it couldn't talk as long as the right approach was taken. A news audience was just as receptive to unanswered questions as it was to ones that had answers.

The guard paused at a door, produced a key and let them inside.

"Isn't that risky?" St. Cyr asked.

"What's that, ma'am?"

"The uplink." She hurried on, tagging the more important question as the end of one that could only have a single response. "I mean coming that far through Israeli defenses."

"We were told you were clever."

St. Cyr shrugged.

He waved her into the suite of offices, moving her along to one of the rear cubicles. The fluorescent lights were muted, soft even after the gloom lining the halls. The windows had been covered with thick black cloth that had been tacked into place with thin spikes. She was sure that no one could see in, nor would they ever know they were there. Palming the pocket camera, she waited for an opportunity to use it.

A metal desk sat in front of the back wall. If there'd been any pictures or personal items in the room, they'd been removed. She wasn't sure if she'd recognize the office again if she saw it.

The guard walked over to the television-camcorder arrangement on the desktop and switched it on. He gestured to the chair in front of the desk. "If you'll sit, I'll adjust the camera."

"They'll see me, too?"

"Yes."

St. Cyr kept a smile from her face. Point scored, whether the guy wanted to admit it or not. Now she knew she would be able to see them, as well. Moving slowly, she positioned the palm-sized camera between her hands and aimed it at the television. Marshak had told her distance wouldn't be a problem, that he could develop almost anything within a ten-foot radius. The television couldn't be more than eight feet away.

The guard, satisfied with the camcorder, flicked another switch and said, "Base, this is Press. Over."

"Go, Press," a woman's voice said. "You have Base. Over."

"Ready to achieve uplink. Over."

"Roger, Press. Uplink going . . . now."

Eyes focused totally on the television screen as it cleared, St. Cyr was only gradually aware of the guard leaving the room.

The view of the woman was from midchest up. She wore a kelly green blouse without any special identifying marks, and had honey blond hair and features any camera would have loved.

St. Cyr gave Marshak's little hideaway two quick chances to capture that face. It took some careful maneuvering with her thumb to keep from revealing the presence of the camera. "They told me I couldn't bring a tape recorder or take notes."

"No. You'll be given hard copy and film for everything you need."

Surprise must have shown on St. Cyr's face.

The woman smiled briefly, then moved on. "How much do you know about the attack at the Eliahu Hotel?"

"I know that the Jordanians precipitated it, that members of the PLO followed up on it and that at least one American agent tried to either prevent it or escalate it by sniping the Jordanians in the crowd."

"How do you know about the PLO?"

"I listened to the reports from the Israeli police and read between the lines."

The woman nodded. "But you don't know about the American agent."

"Not for sure, but I know enough to make an educated guess."

"News isn't a series of educated guesses."

"It can be if a reporter presents them to a party that refuses to refute them. Ask the people on '60 Minutes.'" St. Cyr kept the threat veiled but pushed it into the pot all the same.

"Who would you present them to?"

"The United States government."

"Even if you could narrow the field down to that one nation, there are a lot of branches to be covered."

"I'm willing."

The woman shook her head. "No. You want short-cuts, trust me. That's how someone in your business gets those all-important exclusives. If you start beating on doors, you're going to be there awhile. By the time you get squared away and realize you're wasting your time, the story will have already been broken by someone else."

"You're sure of that?"

The woman's gaze was uncompromising. "You can bet the Pulitzer on it. If I can't work with you, I'll find someone else."

St. Cyr thought that over, studying the other woman's face, knowing that she wasn't bluffing. At least, not completely bluffing. "Why me?"

"Because you've already got high visibility in that country, and because you're known for developing—and protecting—your own resources. I've had you researched. I like what I saw."

"Blue smoke and mirrors," St. Cyr said in mild rebuke. "I was also the one who tumbled to your guy on top of that textile plant. This could be your way of keeping me quiet till you can get that covered."

"If I hadn't asked him to bring you along this far, you wouldn't be here now. Don't flatter yourself."

"Bullshit. Who's kidding who here? You're looking for shortcuts, too, and that's another reason I'm here now," St. Cyr declared.

"Yes."

The admission was freely given, and the reporter had trouble trying to figure out exactly how she was expected to deal with it.

"There are things here that have to be kept quiet. At least for a time. Events are reaching a critical point in this portion of the Middle East."

"And what's your part in this?" St. Cyr pressed.

"I'm trying to stop the undercurrent of violence short of war."

"How?"

"I can't give you all of that. Yet."

"But you will?" St. Cyr let her disbelief show and took time to snap off another frame of film.

"You're going to do something for me first."

The reporter didn't hesitate. Her business was filled with back scratching, and it had sometimes come from as high up as the White House. News wasn't always simply the truth. It was too often only what a reporter could find out and verify, or what was passed out like pablum from government agencies, including the CIA. "What do I have to do?"

"You're aware of the terrorist–neo-Nazi links that have been exposed in Germany, the United States and South America?"

"Yes."

"There's been a major falling out between those two groups stateside. Only hours ago a federal task force operating on information provided by the Aryan Resistance Movement shut down a Jordanian terrorist cell in L.A. that was trafficking in cocaine. The Jordanian military Intelligence is already aware of this."

"You're saying King Hussein was aware of the terrorist activity in the United States."

"I can't say for sure if that's true, but I do know a lawyer acting on behalf of the arrested terrorists placed a call to Amman shortly after finding that out. Also during that time, an Intelligence outpost in Jordan was hit by what will be believed to be a neo-Nazi strike force."

"You say it *will* be believed."

"After we present our case," the woman said, "I'm sure the Jordanians will have cause to believe that."

"Why?"

"Because I have footage of the attack on film." A window opened on the screen to the woman's right.

Images formed there, already in motion. The setting was clearly an alley between low buildings. Gunfire threw sparks in a number of directions, but soundlessly because there was no audio gain on the video track. Shadows took shape and fought and died.

"What was this Intelligence outpost?" St. Cyr asked.

"You're aware of the caravans of wealth being ferried from Baghdad through Jordan in spite of the trade embargoes against Saddam Hussein?"

"I'd heard of them, but they had never been confirmed."

"This outpost was the one used by the caravans to decide on shipping routes to use."

"And the neo-Nazis attacked it? Why?"

"To embarrass Jordan. Once this comes to light, the United Nations will want to investigate further."

"They'll only get a slap on the wrist," St. Cyr pointed out. "Unless you can prove that outpost was used to direct those caravans."

"I can. But we're going to wait on that. For now I want the Jordanians to believe they were attacked by the neo-Nazi groups they were trying to work with."

"Who really attacked that outpost?"

"That doesn't matter."

St. Cyr vented her anger in a calculated attempt to leverage information. "The hell it doesn't! You're wanting me to get onto public television and lie to a news audience."

"Trust me when I say that it's been done before."

"Not by me," St. Cyr argued.

"Maybe not. But you get to tell them the truth later, and I guarantee you an exclusive on what's really been going on between Israel and Jordan. You'll come out of this just fine."

"Say that I agree to do this. What will these false reports do?"

"Buy time. Allow some things to happen that have already been put into motion. And if we're lucky, maybe save a lot of lives."

"In return, I get an exclusive."

"To what may be the biggest story of your life."

"You make it sound enticing."

The woman on the television screen smiled and folded her arms across her chest. "Let's not play coy anymore. I'm offering you the best deal you're going to get in Israel. You'd be a fool not to take it, and if I thought you were a fool, I wouldn't be talking to you."

"I don't know that I especially care for your view of the news, either," St. Cyr said.

"The news is a tool. You use it to get bigger raises and more perks every year. Remember, I've reviewed your file. I know the deals you've already made in the past. Mostly you've cut ones that I can't fault you for, and none that I could hold against you. The news is your job. For me, it's a tool, and I'm going to get as much use from it as I can to push those countries away from war. Do we have a deal?"

"Yes."

The woman smiled. "Good. Call the guard back into the room."

St. Cyr crossed the room and asked the guard back into the room.

He came to parade rest in front of the television. "Yes, ma'am."

"She has a camera. Confiscate it and lose the film."

"Yes, ma'am." The guard turned to face St. Cyr.

The reporter's hand tightened around the tiny 35 mm camera, then reluctantly she dropped it into the guard's upturned palm. After removing the film from the camera, he held the film up, using a matte black Zippo to light it, waited to see that it was burning well, then tossed it into the empty wastebasket beside the desk. Smoke curled up, trailing insubstantial fingers against the ceiling.

"You don't miss much," St. Cyr said with only a trace of resentment.

The woman looked at her. "I can't afford to." Then the image shattered with an inaudible pop and shrank into a tiny pinprick of white light that extinguished a second later.

St. Cyr took a deep breath and let it out, impressed as hell in spite of herself. Whoever the woman was, she was pure hell on wheels when it came to getting what she wanted. Glancing up at the guard as he stirred the ashes of the film, she said, "I was told you had some materials for me."

"Yes, ma'am."

"Well, let's get a move on. If I'm going to lie to millions of people, I may need a little more preparation than usual."

CHAPTER FOURTEEN

Dawn was stabbing insistent purple-and-rose daggers into the eastern skies over Jerusalem when Mack Bolan found the two people Barbara Price had sent him to meet.

The woman was tall and redheaded, dressed in casual wear that marked her as a European tourist but didn't call attention to her. She sat at a small table in a Greek café near the Jaffa Gate. The long-stemmed yellow rose in crinkled green paper on the tabletop was the confirmation of their identities. The woman's hair was in a French braid, carefully pulled back out of the way. The small black handbag at her side looked feminine but was roomy enough to carry a full-size .45.

The man sat across the table from her, looking worn and weathered inside a long jacket. His eyes under his hat brim caught Bolan's momentarily, then slid on past. He leaned his head back and expelled a long streamer of gray cigarette smoke.

Bolan was now in worn jeans, hiking boots and sweatshirt, fading him into the background among the manual laborers and tradesmen, and the loose flannel shirt worn with the tail out and the sleeves rolled up covered the Desert Eagle .44 in a paddle holster at his back.

Moving into the line working its way along the counter, the warrior scanned the dozen people scattered around the café. None of them appeared interested either in him or the people he was meeting. He paid for a large coffee and two baklava, picked up his tray and made his way to the table. Ignoring the empty seat beside the woman, he sat down next to the man.

The woman appraised him coolly, as if intrigued by his decision of seating.

Bolan returned her frank gaze full measure, blew on his coffee and sipped. It was strong and dark and faintly bitter. Women, he'd found over the years, could still be surprisingly creative when turning their hands to violence. And proximity was always a distraction. If the man made a move on him, the Executioner knew he could expect a more traditional approach.

"Striker," she said with a disarming smile that didn't completely touch her eyes.

"Yes," he said.

"I've heard a lot of good things about you."

"Then you're one up on me, because until today I'd never heard of you."

"You can trust me."

Bolan nodded. "I was told that." Price had been very forthright in speaking of Catherine Hawkes, of her character and of her abilities. It didn't surprise the warrior that the mission controller had a number of associates. Anyone who regularly worked in the dark undercurrent of society developed relationships with people either like themselves, acquaintances that could be used to an extent or mortal enemies.

"And this is Meyer Levin."

The Executioner looked at the older man and swapped nods, nothing like shaking hands, which would have indicated to any observers that this was a meeting of strangers. He'd been briefed on the Mossad case officer's career earlier in the mission when Phoenix had partnered for a time with Uri Dan. Using the plastic knife and fork he'd gotten at the counter when ordering, the warrior made short work of the Greek pastries. The hollow feeling in his stomach went away, and the coffee washed away the clinging fatigue that the few hours of sleep aboard the aircraft carrier had staved off for a time.

"Do you still have your package?" Hawkes asked.

"Yeah." Bolan knew she was referring to the captured Arab he had in the trunk of his car.

"Have you opened it?"

"No. There hasn't been time."

"I don't think there'll be much gained there, but we have to make the effort."

"I agree."

She finished her coffee, blotted her lips on a napkin and said, "Are you ready?"

"Yes." Bolan made a final pass for a refill and a plastic cap for the cup before leaving with the pair. As they passed through the door ahead of him, he scanned the sidewalks in front of the café and across the street. No one appeared to be watching them.

He pointed them in the direction of his car.

Hawkes moved confidently, pausing at a small Fiat long enough to remove a duffel bag from the trunk before taking her place at the passenger seat of Bolan's vehicle. Levin took the rear seat on the same side.

After keying the ignition, Bolan put the car in gear and rolled out of the parking area toward the street.

Hawkes pointed him to the east.

Levin scooted forward and leaned on the seat, filling the warrior's rearview mirror. "You've been debriefed over the situation?"

Bolan exchanged glances with the Mossad man. "I know you and Hawkes broke into a line to Enoch Harel."

"And Harel's scheme to take over Jordan with the help of the PLO, then divide it between the Palestinians and the Israelis."

"How does he figure on doing that?"

"My resource knew nothing more than the loosest of parameters. Discovering the mechanics of Harel's treachery to this nation still lies before us."

"I read the file on Ruben Weizman," Bolan said as he took the left turn Hawkes indicated. "The information indicated that he's in the upper echelon of economic developers working on deals inside and outside Israel. There was no mention of his involvement with Intelligence circles."

"He's not." Hawkes slid on a pair of dark sunglasses, then unlimbered a SIG-Sauer P-226 from her handbag and kept it under her thigh. "Weizman's as close to a number-two spot in Harel's organization as Harel allows. He's keeping everything very tight, yet he's moving surprisingly fast now that the chips are down."

"Benjamin Wellsberg is the head of the covert faction of supporters Harel has inside the Mossad."

"How widespread is that faction in the Mossad?" Bolan asked. He tailed a produce truck closely, keeping an eye on the traffic behind them. Despite Hawkes's directions, he took a right-hand turn.

She glanced at him from behind the dark lenses but didn't say anything.

Levin showed no kind of reaction at all. "There is a core group that knows what's going on. Harel's made good connections. A lot of the moves that have been made inside the Mossad appear political on the surface, with no underpinnings of subterfuge."

"Like your dismissal?" Bolan asked.

"Shit," Hawkes said with a wry grin, "you don't believe in pulling punches, do you?"

The Mossad field control revealed no expression.

Bolan flicked a hard gaze in the woman's direction. "If they'd wanted punches pulled on this thing, they wouldn't have dealt me in."

"Exactly like my dismissal," Levin said, breaking the brief, tense silence that followed. "I stepped on toes long before now. And I wouldn't take the hint to back off this operation."

"So it was easier to get you out of the way."

"Yes. And it was also a decision to make that removal a permanent one. She prevented that."

"You guessed?" Bolan asked as he made a series of turns that took them back onto the route Hawkes was navigating. There were still no signs of a tail, but it was possible that trouble was simply waiting at the other end of the journey.

"Women's intuition," Hawkes replied.

"Actually," Levin said, "her contact had tapped into Mossad covert Intelligence and found the TOS orders."

"What happens to the core group?" Bolan asked.

"If we can take Harel, Wellsberg and a few of the others down, we might be able to nip this thing in the bud. That's the best we're hoping for. With the leaders out of the way, maybe the war hawks will subside and let reason take over again."

"For a while," Hawkes said quietly.

Levin shrugged. "I think we would all settle for that."

"How much does Weizman know?"

"We're not certain."

"Then it would make more sense to take Wellsberg down."

"If possible," Levin said, "we'd make the attempt. Wellsberg has been underground for some time, and is usually very heavily guarded even if we could find him."

"So we take the chance on Weizman," Bolan said.

"The schedule on this thing is moving up," Hawkes said. "The Metsada unit in Jordan got hit last night. The Jordanians aren't going to play the fools forever. They'll attack, thinking to earn themselves some breathing room from the Israelis, as well as from the UN investigators that will be pulled in regarding the caravans from Iraq. If Harel's scenario is closed quickly, the pent-up pressure may leak away without spilling over across the Middle East." She looked at the warrior. "Weizman's our only shot. If he doesn't know anything, we get even bloodier on this."

Bolan nodded. "Then we'll work on stacking the odds in our favor."

BAUSCH & LOMB field glasses at his eyes, Bolan scanned the thin ribbon of highway heading west back to Jerusalem. Traffic was sparse, with nothing headed their way. He lay atop a hill partially covered by the branches of a scraggly and twisted acacia. Withered yellow grasses that were brittle and hard poked the exposed skin of his neck and forearms. At his side was a Parker-Hale Model 2100 Midland bolt-action rifle chambered in .243 Winchester and equipped with a Bushnell Banner 4 × scope. It had come from Hawkes's store of munitions and would be better suited for the work ahead than the heavier rifle the Executioner had.

In the valley before the hill, parked at the side of the highway, the woman sat inside the car made available by Price's arrangements. The plates were clean, and registered to a married couple who correlated with some of the ID Bolan had shared with Hawkes.

The plan was simple, and all of them had agreed on it after a brief discussion. If it didn't get them inside the estate where Weizman was hiding out, more-drastic measures would have to be taken. They wanted events to progress as smoothly and quietly as possible. Hours still remained before they could strike against the forces Harel had arrayed in his quest for expansion.

A car topped the hill in the distance. The image wavered uncertainly in the heat.

Bolan used the field glasses to bring it into proper focus. The vehicle was a dark blue limousine with a boomerang-shaped aerial on the back hood. When he scanned the front plates, the numbers and letters were the ones he'd been given. The car was still three hundred yards from Hawkes's position.

The warrior tapped the ear-throat headset and said, "Now." He exchanged the Bausch & Lomb for the Parker-Hale, snugging the rifle into his shoulder.

Twenty feet away Meyer Levin drew himself up from the cover of a eucalyptus tree and took a fresh grip on his pistol.

Without hurrying, Hawkes popped the hood on the car from inside, then got out and walked around front. She raised the hood all the way and set off a small smoke bomb under the engine that spewed white vapor in a slow cloud. Her figure was definitely female, but the loose folds of her overshirt hid the angular lines of the small pistol at her back.

Bolan flicked the rifle's safety off.

As the limousine passed the warrior's position, the brakelights flared, bright red against the glaring sun reflected from the desert sand and the highway surface. The signal came on, and the luxury car eased behind the stranded vehicle.

Hawkes had turned up the Intel on Weizman, discovering that the manufacturer routinely had his personal limousine fully serviced before using it for extended trips. She'd checked around and found that Weizman had left the car at his usual garage in Jerusalem overnight. It had been due out at eight-thirty. It was nine-twenty now, so the pit crew must have been close to being on time. The two guards inside the car obviously felt they had a few minutes to spare to rescue an attractive redhead.

The guards got out of the limousine, their hands automatically smoothing the tailored clothing over the concealed weapons.

Letting his breath out slowly, the Executioner dropped the cross hairs over the driver's cheekbone as he'd discussed with Hawkes. The passenger would have a harder time bringing his gun into play.

Hawkes met the men with a pleasant smile, teeth white under the black sunglasses. But they were made uncomfortable by something, perhaps an intuitive sixth sense, and after a quick look at each other, reached hesitantly for their weapons, as if for reassurance.

Tightening his finger, taking out the slack, Bolan squeezed the trigger. The buttstock thumped into his shoulder. He worked the bolt and rammed another cartridge home, focusing on the second man as the first tumbled to the ground. Hawkes rolled back to the parked vehicle, taking cover as she reached for her weapon.

The remaining guard tugged a MAC-10 from under his arm and tried for a two-handed grip.

Bolan fired as the man was ducking toward the armored limousine. The .243 Winchester round carried a 100-grain soft-point. The bullet punched through the guard's right shoulder with enough force to throw him off-balance. The Executioner worked the bolt again, tracking up the guy's arm to his forehead. When he squeezed the trigger the third time, the round snapped the band of his target's amber-colored sunglasses and sent the pieces flying while the explosive force of the bullet snapped his head back. The harsh crack echoed over the highway, fading in the distance.

Hawkes popped up over the rear of the sedan with her pistol held neatly in two hands. Her face was impassive as she trotted out and checked both downed men. Her brief nod let Bolan know both of them were out of the play. She holstered her weapon and grabbed the shirt collar of the man nearest the highway and began dragging him away.

Taking up the Parker-Hale, Bolan jogged down the hillside, followed by Levin. By the time he reached the car, Hawkes was working on the second body.

The warrior lifted the trunk lid and reached in past the wide-eyed Arab for the round-bladed shovel they'd bought at a hardware store on the way out of Jerusalem. Once Hawkes deposited the second corpse in the runoff ditch beside the road, Bolan covered them with a light dusting of sand that would camouflage them for a time.

"Nice shooting," Hawkes said.

"You set them up."

"Let's hope everything else turns out as easy."

Levin had taken a bar towel from the rear of the luxury car and was wiping the last of the blood spattering the windshield and fenders. When he was finished, he dropped the cloth to the ground and kicked sand over it.

Pushing her hair up on top of her head, Hawkes reached inside the limo and pulled on the chauffeur's cap, then took a dark jacket from the sedan and shrugged into it. The jacket and hat weren't a perfect disguise, but behind the smoked windows they would pass.

"Let's go," Bolan said, storing the shovel in the trunk and closing it, then sliding the rifle into the rear seat of the sedan.

Hawkes clambered behind the wheel of the limousine and shoved her pistol under her thigh. Levin took over the sedan.

Taking a cut-down Ithaca Model 37 12-gauge shotgun and a prepacked canvas bag from the sedan, Bolan jogged back to the limo and slid into the rear seat. He keyed the intercom between the driver and the back section. "Roll it."

Hawkes waited for a Volkswagen minibus to go skating by, then tromped the accelerator, pulling smoothly onto the highway. Weizman's estate was less than two miles away.

Bolan checked his watch. Only four minutes had passed since the limousine first pulled over to the edge of the highway. The numbers on the probe clicked over softly in his mind. The Desert Eagle .44 was loose in shoulder leather under his arm.

The surrounding land was featureless except for low hills, sand and scrub brush that defiantly held on in spite of the desert sun.

"Coming up," Hawkes said.

The soldier glanced to the left, looking north, and saw the white stone wall that ran around Weizman's estate. It was eight feet tall, topped with embedded glass and sharp pieces of metal to dissuade intruders. The security equipment surrounding the home was top-of-the-line. Bolan was counting on the human factor in the equation to be the downfall.

Hawkes made the turn onto the access road and drove for the guardhouse a hundred yards off the highway. Bolan laid the Ithaca across his knees and placed his empty hand on the door release. Rolling the window down, Hawkes slowed the limo to a stop, then honked the horn impatiently.

The guard stood up inside the structure. "Weizman's been waiting on you. Called me and wanted to know where the hell you were like I was supposed to know." He reached up beside the door.

Then electric motors chugged into life, and the massive iron gates slid in opposite directions.

Hawkes nosed forward, driving at a moderate speed. The landscaping on either side was like something from a fairy tale, and gave the estate the appearance of being an oasis in the middle of the desert. Trees and flowering bushes and plants flowed over carefully tiered areas that broke up the otherwise flat land.

The access road led to a circular drive in front of the three-story house. Hawkes pulled up in front and stopped.

"Well?" she asked.

"Wait," Bolan answered.

"Won't he be suspicious when we don't get out of the car?"

"He won't have to be suspicious at all if we do get out." The warrior watched the main entrance. The numbers whispered silently by, approaching the time of a critical decision. Then the door opened, and Weizman walked out with two men following him.

The industrialist was short in stature, but well built, with developed shoulders that showed signs of workouts, and a narrow waist. His hair and eyes were dark, and his skin was ruddy. Gold glinted at his wrist, fingers and midchest.

One of the men reached for the door.

When it started to open, Bolan rammed his foot into it, propelling the door into the man. With a muffled grunt of pain, he went down. The Executioner fired from inside the limousine as the guy went for his gun. The 12-gauge pattern cut a bloody swath across the man's chest and knocked him flat.

At the front of the vehicle, Hawkes erupted from her side of the car and whipped her pistol across the top. She fired three times, all of them taking her target in the upper chest.

Weizman swiveled around to break into a run. Alarms suddenly screamed out across the immaculate grounds.

Stepping from the limousine, Bolan grabbed the back of the industrialist's jacket and yanked with enough force to pull the man from his feet.

Weizman tried to jerk his body around, scrabbling hard to take a swing at Bolan.

The warrior delivered a butt stroke with the Ithaca, then shoved him into the luxury car while he was still dazed.

Gunfire spit from areas around the house, thunking solidly into the armor plating of the limo. He racked the slide and returned fire, cutting a man down from beside a eucalyptus tree less than forty feet away. He slapped the top of the car with his palm. "Go!"

Hawkes swung back into the car and gunned it, leaving twin tattoos of rubber staining the unblemished pavement of the circular drive.

Standing inside the car and hanging on to the open door with his free hand, Bolan targeted a security guard running through the trees with a machine pistol beating a staccato across the side of the limo. The warrior fired off the point, cutting the man's legs out from under him and dumping him down a stretch of terraced flower beds.

The gate was back in place. On the other side of the bulletproof glass, the security guard was scrambling to get set.

Slinging the shotgun, Bolan reached into the limo and grabbed the canvas bag. He threw it by the strap, landing the bag only a few feet from the guardhouse, then ducked back inside the vehicle as Hawkes bore down on the gate. Before he could shut the door, a harsh impact rocked the big vehicle and a ringing clang echoed through the interior. The gate slammed the open door shut and dug metal fangs deeply. The rear bumper was torn off and left lying in the access road.

Bolan reached into his pocket and came up with the remote control. Glancing through the rear window, he saw the gatehouse guard rush outside and fire after at them.

"You waiting for a drumroll or something here?" Hawkes demanded from the front. "They've got other vehicles back there, you know."

"I packed that bag tight," Bolan replied. "We can't be too close when it goes up." A heartbeat later his thumb dropped over the detonator, closing the circuit.

The resulting series of explosions destroyed the guardhouse and ripped the gates from their moorings. One of them went spinning high into the air, then came arcing back down at an angle with enough speed and force to shear two tree trunks in half. Flames from the incendiaries kicked in and dropped a lake of fire over the nearby surroundings. Waves of concussive force shivered through the length of the limousine.

Bolan settled back into the seat, checking on his newest prisoner.

Weizman huddled defensively in the center of the wide floor, his arms crossed over his chest. He was bleeding from the corner of his mouth.

"Are we clear?" Hawkes asked.

After a quick survey over their backtrail, Bolan said, "Yeah."

The limousine hurtled down the highway toward the point where they would leave it behind and link up with Levin once more. By the time the security guards got organized again, they'd be long gone.

"Who are you?" Ruben Weizman demanded, struggling to get up.

Dropping the shotgun in line to cover the man, Bolan said, "Believe it or not, but I'm the guy you're going to tell your deepest and darkest secrets to. And damned quick, because I don't think we have much time."

"THE LATEST outbreak of violence has left several people confused in the Middle East. What was beginning to shape up as a border dispute between Israel and Jordan based on the religious differences that have kept the holy war alive for two thousand years is now starting to look like a falling out among terrorist groups."

Dr. Enoch Harel stared hard at the big-screen television, the anger like a flailing mace inside his chest. "Who is this woman?"

"Desiree St. Cyr," Wellsberg answered. "She's American, with CNN. Her résumé includes a number of assignments in the Middle East."

"Where did she get her information?"

"I don't know."

Harel whirled on the Mossad agent, unable to keep his frustration at bay even though he knew he wasn't setting a good example for the other five men in the room. They were already nervous without thinking he was out of control. "Then why the hell haven't you found out?"

Wellsberg faced him, his eyes holding no hint of embarrassment. "I've got people who are trying. When they find something out, they'll let us know. She appears to be very well protected."

"Dammit!" Harel said. "You're supposed to be in charge of finding these things out!"

"I am in charge," Wellsberg said. "And I'm getting it done as fast as I can. Your greed concerning those monies made by the Jordanians and Nazis from their drug trafficking could well be what tipped our hand today."

"Gentlemen." Saul Nahum was a reed-thin man in his early seventies. Nahum had fought the Nazis during World War II, then pursued them vigorously to the ends of the earth after Nuremberg. He'd gone on to do quite well for himself in business, but still funded Nazi-hunts as a matter of course. Once the old man had taken an enemy on, that enemy was there for a lifetime. Also when he spoke these days, most people listened.

Harel turned his attention to the man.

"I'd like to suggest that our arguing now is moot and possibly detrimental to everything that we have worked for this far," Nahum began.

Wellsberg nodded.

The other four men in the room represented industrial interests and had only limited regular military experience. Only Wellsberg and Nahum had worked in covert Intelligence. At his age, Harel was one of the youngest men in the room, and he knew it had been his energy and sense of vision that had brought them this far. On their own they would never have achieved all that he had pushed them to do. Even Wellsberg had been reluctant to take the chances he'd persuaded him to take.

"We have a potentially bad situation," Nahum said. "But it's nothing that we can't take control of."

"I don't know," David Admony said. "It might be better to cut our losses and simply forget this before the United Nations or the Americans get any more involved. We should still be able to disappear without any repercussions. They can't hunt us in our own country."

"No." Harel's voice thundered throughout the spacious room.

They all looked at him.

"If we back away now, we will never be this close to achieving it again." Desperation flared within him, causing some of the frustration, anger and resentment to fade. He wouldn't let those feelings jeopardize or stand in the way of his goals and his glory.

"Time has always been on the side of people with the Jewish faith," Nahum said. "For almost two thousand years we endured global persecution and living without a homeland. We've made progress and we've learned now to be patient with our advances."

"We only have a toehold on what should have been our birthright." Harel let out a shaky breath. "We are in the process of midwifing the dreams this nation has had since 1948, of bringing our children's futures within their grasp."

He read the hunger in their gazes, even Nahum's rheumy eyes.

"We have the means to bring this confrontation about with or without the Jordanians' willing participation. They are our enemy. The whole world knows that. And the whole world is sick of Saddam Hussein and all his posturing and posing. At this juncture they see King Hussein as betraying the rest of the world. Even the United Nations is preparing to make sanctions against Jordan. *Now* is the time. We can't let it pass us by."

"I agree with Enoch," Ovadia Kauly said. He was the youngest of the lot and had much to gain with his wealth coming from the structural manufacturing business. "We must seize the opportunity and do with it what we will."

"Even if we are discovered," Harel pointed out, "all it can cost us is a public rebuke. Our allies are already deserting us in the middle of a conflagration that is lapping at our borders. If we stay our hand, we risk growing progressively weaker as we start to struggle under the weight of our own numbers—increased by the continued immigration from the Eastern European countries—until the Muslims think all they have to do is feed off a fatted corpse."

"There've already been lies unleashed in this thing," Wellsberg said in the silence that followed Harel's words. "Ours won't be the first, even if they are discovered."

The news reporter was doing a voice-over while a film clip was being broadcast. According to her monologue, the film footage was of a Jordanian outpost being attacked by members of either the Aryan Resistance Movement or the National Vanguard. Both groups of Nazi terrorists—the reporter went on to say—had sustained severe damage while working with their Arab counterparts. St. Cyr hinted broadly that the coalition between terrorist groups was initially born of an effort to unite against their common enemy—Israel—but that the Jordanians had secretly kept an agenda of their own, hoping to use the Nazis to take the blame for strikes they were unwilling to initiate.

"You have proof of those lies right there," Harel said, nodding toward the television. "That outpost was attacked by an American covert force, which was in turn attacked by a group of Mossad elite that was stationed in Jordan. Yet there is no mention of either the Americans or Israelis. As yet, we haven't been discovered. If we're to make a move, it must be now."

"Is there any sign that the Jordanians are prepared to make the first move against us?" Nahum asked.

"They've massed their armies along the border," Harel replied. "But they won't take that first step soon."

"So we'll take it for them?"

"Yes. We have two options open to us. We'll use them both if necessary."

"When?"

"At sundown. Our military is far superior to theirs, and the night can be just another weapon in our arsenal. The Americans proved that during their nocturnal attack on Iraq in the Gulf War. Our people are just as well equipped and just as well trained."

"And the PLO will join us?"

"Yes."

Nahum looked at his companions, who nodded in turn, then at Wellsberg. "Benjamin?"

The Mossad man's face tightened. "We could have used more time, but there may not be another moment like this."

"Then we're in agreement."

"Yes."

Harel dropped the broken wineglass into a trash container, took another one from the rack above the bar and lifted the bottle of imported wine in one big fist. "A drink to success, then. Overnight Jordan shall fall, and a new Israel shall see the dawn."

CHAPTER FIFTEEN

Barbara Price adjusted the headset, tweaking the microphone into position at the corner of her mouth and watching the wall screen at the far end of the computer lab as images flickered across the pool of rainbow-tinted gray.

At his desk Aaron Kurtzman was orchestrating the downloading of information in preparation for the debrief. His fingers clacked their way across the keyboard rapidly.

"Ms. Price."

The mission controller glanced up at Carmen Delahunt. "Yes."

"I have Phoenix and Striker routed into the comnet. I'll plug you in when you're ready."

"I'm ready." Price took a deep breath and let it out. The legal pad with her notes carefully organized on the top sheet felt hard and sharp in her hand. An electric click sounded in her ear. All the lies were about to be stripped away, but she had to wonder what effect the truth was going to have in their place.

"We're go," Kurtzman said.

Price keyed the headset's transmit button. "This is Stony Base. Phoenix One, Stony One, do you copy? This is Stony Base. Over."

"Phoenix One copies," Yakov Katzenelenbogen's deep voice rumbled. "Over."

"Stony One copies," Striker replied. "Over."

"Be advised that this line is secured and scrambled. We can talk freely here, gentlemen."

The wall screen suddenly split into two frames as the visual reception from Jordan and Israel was bled into the feed. On the left were Striker, Hawkes, Levin, Grimaldi and Paul MacDonald, the blacksuit strike force leader Price had infiltrated into Jerusalem to run backup for the Executioner. They were dressed in desert camos, the purple-and-green squares blurring in the camera's focus. They were still in the safe house she'd arranged in Jerusalem.

On the right Phoenix Force was arrayed in a semicircle, squatted down on the sand and rock of their location in northern Jordan.

"The man we're after," Price said, "is Enoch Harel."

The wall screen flickered and changed, showing what was being broadcast to both reception units.

"Harel is the spearhead for an Israeli movement designed to bring Jordan to its knees, followed by a swift invasion of that country by Israeli and PLO troops. At my guess, with the amount of pressure that has been applied through the media and Intelligence circles, I think the strikes will come shortly after sundown."

"Why would the PLO join with the Israelis?" Rafael Encizo asked.

"Striker discovered that while interviewing one of the Israeli business magnates allied with Harel. According to the deal Harel made with Zahid Faysal, the splinter group of the PLO under Faysal is supposed to get the other half of Jordan to create a new Palestine."

"That's very generous," Katz said. Light reflected from the metal hook at the end of his arm. "On the surface."

A wry grin twisted Price's lips. "I think we can all agree that it wasn't Harel's intention to let the PLO keep those lands."

"But it was a good bargaining chip to get the PLO involved," Meyer Levin said. "They have a number of believers who would willingly die to see their cause advanced."

"Plus, having the PLO in your pocket has the advantage of having an army already inserted behind the lines," David McCarter added. "You put those people into play, they could do a lot of damage to transport facilities, communications and Intelligence-gathering units in a very short amount of time."

"Right," Price said. "And that's exactly what their part in this scenario is. Harel helped coordinate the union of the Jordanian terrorists and the neo-Nazis behind the scenes through the help of an agent code-named Canary. Deals were made between the groups, and things looked very lucrative. In reality, Harel had bought people within all of those organizations to push for joining forces. Canary helped bring those investments to fruition."

"To provide a larger aggressor to threaten Israel?" James asked.

"Exactly." Price placed her legal pad on Kurtzman's desk. "It was an easy bet that Jordan and King Hussein wouldn't initiate a confrontation with Israel. However, a terrorist force that was global might not be so hampered."

"And if a strong enough move was made against Israel," Bolan said, "Jordan could still be held accountable."

"Yes," Price said. "There were plans that if the attacks by the terrorist groups continued against Israel, covert military units would slip into Jordan to ferret them out. Israel would defend itself by pointing out all the deaths that had resulted because Jordan had allowed the terrorists to hide within their borders.''

''An action like that would have precipitated an attack by Jordan at some time, too,'' Levin said.

''It had to build slowly,'' Price said. ''Events were carefully planned to create schisms within Jordan till there was nothing left to do but attack.''

''But on the surface it wouldn't be known that Harel and his organization were secretly goading the Jordanians into the war,'' Manning stated.

''It was simplicity,'' Price said, ''even though the steps necessary in getting there were precarious. Either way, even if Israel was found out without the threat being negated, Jordan would have had no choice but to attack.''

''Which still would have played into Harel's plans,'' Hawkes said.

''Yes. And if we blow this, it could still go the way Harel and his supporters want it to. At the moment we've maneuvered King Hussein and his cabinet into believing the neo-Nazis may be responsible for the attacks on the caravans and for the violence inside Jordanian borders. But that won't last. Harel knows that. However, he can't afford to wait until we're able to come forward with the truth. Once King Hussein finds out the United States military is willing to intervene on their behalf to stop an all-out war in the Middle East, he may check any hostile action he wants to take against the Israelis.''

''Leaving Israel as the aggressor,'' Katz said.

Price nodded. ''If that happens, the other nations of the Middle East who would normally be fence sitters— such as Saudia Arabia, Egypt and perhaps Libya—would take up arms to force the Israelis back inside their borders."

"If they didn't decide to try to destroy them once and for all," MacDonald said. His youthful face was grim and hard.

"The United States couldn't allow that to happen," Bolan said. "We might not be willing to intercede as often or as far as we have in the past, but we still couldn't let Israel be removed from the map with possible continued terrorist attacks against America coming from those areas."

"So either way," Grimaldi said, "Harel has negotiated himself into a win-win situation."

"At first glance," Price said, "it may look like that. But the bastard didn't count on us. We can go in and neutralize him and his whole organization and place the blame squarely where it belongs." She glanced at Kurtzman and nodded.

The big cybernetics specialist stroked his keyboard and erased the video links. A map of northern Jordan quickly appeared on the wall screen.

"I'm assuming Harel is going to his backup plans now," Price said, "since we've blunted the possibility of a Jordanian-based attack and he knows an American covert team is breathing down the back of his neck. Striker extracted this information from Ruben Weizman, one of Harel's elite cabinet of financiers. Aaron, get me the coordinates."

A blip quickly flashed onto the screen, and latitude and longitude numbers printed out beside it.

"Phoenix, this is your assignment. The covert team of Mossad agents you encountered last night has possession of a dozen mobile Scuds stolen from Iraq the previous year during the confusion of the American air attacks into the no-fly zones. The units they're mounted on have fully amphibious transporter-erector-launcher capabilities. They intend to move to this location, set up, then launch those missiles into targets around Tel Aviv, deliberately missing the more populated areas of the city."

"What kind of warhead are they using?" Katz asked.

"Conventional two-thousand-pound bombs. No nukes, chemicals or bacterial agents."

"Giant firecrackers," Manning commented. "Except with the guidance systems those damned things have, they could accidentally drop them into the heart of Tel Aviv and kill a lot of innocent people."

"Right," Price said. "Weizman didn't know their precise location, but he did know the launch point. Now we do. I've researched the area through satellite and came up with a strategy you can improvise on, Yakov."

The wall screen changed, revealing a topside view of a rocky, windswept chasm spanned by a narrow bridge.

"Along the route Weizman outlined, those Scud transports have to cross this bridge."

"And what's the purpose?" Katz asked. "They could fire the missiles from anywhere."

"Harel wants the Scuds to be traced back to Jordan. From the chosen position, the aircraft carrier you people regrouped on will pick up the missiles as they streak across the border. That way the attack will be verified through an outside third party, giving Israel a blank check for an armed response."

"Understood."

"Can you get me the specs on the bridge?" Manning asked.

Price looked at Kurtzman, and the big man nodded, turning his attention to the keyboard. "Coming through now, Gary."

The wall screen changed again, becoming a three-dimensional representation of the bridge. Two massive arms supported it from either end, and five peaks of the upper chord railings ran its length. Numbers quickly spun like fruit on a slot machine to inscribe the length, height and breadth of the structure, freezing when they reached the proper measurements.

A moment later Manning said, "A cantilever truss with a suspended span. Piece of cake. Some of my best work has been bridges."

"Take the Scuds out there if you can," Price said. "If not, we may have to rely on the Patriots the aircraft carrier has on board."

"But that might trigger an attack from the Jordanians anyway," Katz said. "They'll think they've been fired upon and react to that."

"Right. I'd rather not take that chance if we don't have to. Either way, if those Scuds get by you, the situation has got a real good opportunity to go ballistic."

"They won't get by," Manning promised.

"Striker," Price said, "your part of the mission is to neutralize Harel and his secondary backup. Aaron and his team will attempt to circumvent the computer spoof that Harel has set up to interfere with Israeli intelligence radar systems. Have you debriefed your team?"

"No. I was awaiting confirmation."

"You've got it."

The wall screen rippled and went back to the video links. On-screen, Bolan opened a folder and spread it out before Grimaldi and MacDonald, the only two members of his group who hadn't learned of the secondary offensive set up by the Israeli war hawks. The blacksuit team would be debriefed again later as they took the field.

"Essentially," Bolan said, "the secondary fail safe is designed to work off Israeli paranoia rather than a physical attack. Cutouts have been hooked into Israeli computers to make it look like Tel Aviv is under a Scud attack in the event that the missiles weren't in place at the proper time. Around the city, again in places where civilian losses and property damage will be at a negligible amount, explosives have been planted by sympathetic Mossad forces that will simulate a Scud attack. Cosmetically, in the event of an investigation later, pieces of Scuds saved from the missile attack by Iraq during the Gulf War were buried with those charges so pieces of them will be found."

"Simple," James said.

"Yes," Price replied, "but with the mood that's over those countries, it could very well work."

"What kind of deadline are we looking at here?" James asked.

"As near as we can guess, sometime shortly after nightfall at your end. Any efforts Harel makes after that may not have the impact he needs to bring this off." Price scanned their faces. "It doesn't give you much time."

"Once this thing starts," McCarter said, "it won't last long, either. One way or the other."

"True. Striker, there's additional hard copy on the hardsite Harel has set up west of Jerusalem. We managed to cull a few favors here and there without setting off any alarms, and did some satellite recon of the area that will aid you in your insertion. I've cleared a Sea Stallion helicopter to land at Jerusalem, and it's waiting for you people. Keep in mind, though, that once you void your flight plan, you're fair game for the Israelis."

"We will."

"There's one other topic I'd like to address," McCarter said.

"What?"

"That bloody bitch Canary. She kept the neo-Nazis and Jordanians dogging our tracks at every step. What's going to happen to her at the end of this bonny little chase?"

Price was aware of Kurtzman's eyes on her. She retained her composure, having already dealt with this issue in her mind.

Before she could say anything, Katz said, "Canary's no longer a threat or a problem." A small smile lit his eyes.

"How do you know?" McCarter asked.

"Because," Bolan said, "you're looking at Canary."

A tense silence filled the uplinks. Price faced the men she'd lied to and she didn't let herself wonder even for an instant if they'd ever trust her again. They were professionals. They would understand. Only Hawkes wasn't surprised.

"Son of a bitch," Kurtzman said in a low voice that was filled with awe.

Price crossed her arms, but it was the gesture of one who was at ease with herself, nothing defensive or distancing about it at all. "Canary was an identity I had before coming here." She left out any reference to Stony Man Farm because Levin and Hawkes weren't privy to everything about the operation. "One of several. When I discovered the covert Israeli action mounted by Harel, I brought that alias back out and used it. As Canary, I was able to get further behind Harel's machinations without ever leaving here. He bought information. Canary was notorious for selling information for personal gain, and for being purely motivated by mercenary interests. By selling that information to Harel, and aiding him where I could, I could come closer to figuring out what he was going to do with it. Unfortunately some of the information I had to sell him concerned you."

"So you sold us out time and again," McCarter said.

"Yes, and I didn't like it, but my hand was forced in a way by the threat presented. All I can say now is that I never again want to deal in secret."

A faint smile twitched at the corners of the Brit's mouth. "Well, I hope you got top dollar for it."

"I did, each and every time." She met the gaze of every man in the uplink. "If there's anything I can do for you, let me know. If it can be done, it will be. Until then, Godspeed." She reached down without hesitation and broke the connection.

At the other end of the room, the wall screen blanked.

Price turned and locked eyes with Kurtzman, knowing the man was staring at her. "And?"

He shook his head. "I wouldn't have had the guts to stage a play like that and hope I could stack the deck enough to keep everybody from getting hurt."

"There were people who got hurt."

"Yeah, but you managed to contain it, and you know that."

"I hope I do."

"You do. In your heart you do, and so do they."

"How do you feel about it?"

"You're a class act, Barb, but I've always felt that way. I've never seen anyone cut a line so fine. You did the right thing."

She nodded, knowing only the events of the next few hours would tell the tale. "Call me if I'm needed. I've got to brief Hal and the President.'' She turned and walked away without another word.

FULL DARK had descended over the broken landscape in northern Jordan. Shadows surged over the moonlit terrain, pooling menacingly around scrub bushes and rocks. Myriad stars lay scattered across the black velvet sky like a dusting of sugar glaze.

Crouched in his own share of the shadows and night, Yakov Katzenelenbogen scoured the area east of the chasm at the foot of the series of hills he'd taken refuge in. The Zeiss binoculars he used were equipped with night lenses that amplified the available moonlight and starlight and rendered the countryside visible.

Nothing moved in the distance.

Taking a break from the lenses, he glanced down at the chasm and the bridge that was their initial objective. The hump to get to the crossing had been a seventeen-klick jog with full packs. They'd managed to shave almost twenty minutes off his estimated time of arrival.

There were no real roads leading up to the bridge, just patches of paths where the sand had been worn down to rock. The opposite side of the chasm was at a decline, dropping nearly ten yards from one end of the bridge to the other.

The bridge itself was ninety yards long and ten yards wide. At the peaks of the upper chords running like a series of Vs hooked together by railings, the distance to the floor of the bridge was seven yards. It was constructed of timber over a steel skeleton and gave the appearance of having been there for decades.

The team hadn't had enough explosives on hand to complete the assignment, but a raid on the munitions stores at the town where they'd leveled that communications outpost the previous night had settled that. According to the interplay between the Jordanian troops that Katz listened to on their radio, the Jordanians still weren't aware that their stores had been lightened.

Manning was a human pendulum beneath the bridge over the ninety-foot drop to the jagged stone floor below. The demolitions expert hung by a sling from the lip of the lower chords, working his explosives into the vulnerable spots of the structure. On the opposite side, Calvin James worked in sync with the Canadian, and their voices kept up a constant chatter over the headset frequency.

McCarter and Encizo worked topside, following the directions Manning had already given them. The Brit used a wheelbarrow they'd also appropriated to trundle the eighteen-kilo ammonium-nitrate block demolitions charges to the far end of the bridge where the Cuban was finishing digging the last of five pits to contain the breaching charges. In quick succession, they dropped the explosives into the holes, then began covering them up, running wires from the radio relays to the side of the bridge where the electronic receiver was left free to receive the detonation signal when the time came.

Tremors shook the ground beneath Katz, slowly escalating in intensity. He took up the binoculars again and scanned the landscape. Topping a crest at least two thousand yards distant, a Land Rover bounced up and over, the weak yellow lights sparking against the Zeiss's lenses. Behind the four-wheel-drive unit, the first of the Scud carriers jolted slowly into view.

Evidently the drivers were having some problems with the loose sand. The front tires seemed sluggish and had trouble biting into the sand, propelled more by the immense weight they were carrying rather by the power of the driving wheels. The missiles were thick sausages atop the carriers. The caravan started carefully down the last defile leading to the bridge.

Tapping the transmit button on the headset, Katz said, "Get clear."

"Two minutes," Manning transmitted back.

Katz leaned back into his cover and tripped the LST 5-C satellite radio to let Stony Base know they could send in Striker and his hard teams. The plan had been to engage both of the Israeli fail safes as simultaneously as possible, beginning with Phoenix's physical sightings of the Scud carriers.

At the side of the bridge, McCarter dumped the wheelbarrow over the chasm. It spun and flipped as it plummeted into the stone sides of the gorge, coming apart, the pieces whirling into the chasm at the bottom. Then the Brit joined Encizo and sprinted for the Phoenix-held side of the structure.

"You may not have it," Katz said. He reached back for the Galil Model 308 assault rifle, flipped the safety off and hunkered down behind the sniper scope. A moment more and he had a 40 mm grenade fitted into the M-203 launcher underneath.

Manning was still hanging from the side of the bridge, working as patiently as a spider spinning its web.

"Gary," Katz said.

"A minute, minute and a half tops," Manning said.

The sound of the carriers' engines rumbled into the cavity in the foothills.

"You may not have it," Katz said. He moved in a crouch, heading for the encounter area, his feet carefully avoiding any loose rock.

McCarter and Encizo had reached the safety of the sheltering darkness.

"Got to be done," Manning said. "Otherwise, we've all wasted our time here."

"Understood. Use your discretion."

"Calvin," Manning called. "Haul your ass out of here. There's nothing more you can do."

"On my way," James responded. The ex-Seal hauled himself up hand over hand, then sprinted down the length of the bridge.

Katz settled into position, drawing a bead on the driver of the Land Rover. When the time came, he was going to take the man out first and hopefully help create a logjam of confusion. The heavy 7.62 mm slug wouldn't be deflected by the windshield even at that distance.

Manning was in motion now, but the Phoenix Force leader didn't know if there was enough time left for the Canadian to get clear. The Land Rover was less than two hundred yards from the bridge, and the Scuds were right behind. His finger tightened on the trigger.

BOLAN HUNG halfway out the open bay of the American Navy transport helicopter as it swooped down out of a midnight sky toward the desert floor. He was outfitted in desert camo over a Kevlar vest. Web belts held extra magazines for his weapons and assorted combustibles. Sheathed in shoulder leather, the Beretta 93-R made a counterpoint to the heavier Desert Eagle .44 Magnum strapped into a counterterrorist drop holster on his right thigh. A Kevlar-lined helmet caught the wind as he turned his head, and the Plexiglas bubble goggles kept the whirling sand out of his eyes. His lead weapon was a Remington Model 1100 combat shotgun with a 10-shot Choate magazine extension filled with one-ounce slugs in the event the entrenched Israelis were wearing body armor. With the slugs the body armor didn't count for as much because the impact would still knock a man from his feet, making him vulnerable for a follow-up round.

Grimaldi was at the controls of the whirlybird, homing in on the LZ in spite of the wild thermals that covered the desert floor at night.

Blacksuit leader Paul MacDonald stood at the warrior's side, compact and ready. Catherine Hawkes was close behind, standing tall and emanating deadly professionalism. Meyer Levin would be remaining behind with Grimaldi, acting as navigator.

Nine blacksuits were tight and ready in the cargo area, hands filled with rappeling ropes if they needed them.

"Ready," Grimaldi called in a tense voice. "They've seen us, so we're coming in hot."

"Soften them up as much as you can," Bolan said. He glanced down, seeing the desert only twenty feet below, streaking past like a broad, sandy river.

The hardsite had once been a training post for the Israeli army. Located twenty-eight miles southwest of Jerusalem, just north of Gath, the base was constructed above and below ground, had been used for tactical maneuvers and communications gathering and had been left vacant for the past fifteen years. Dr. Enoch Harel had purchased it six years ago and had been secretly outfitting it during that time.

Blending into the landscape, rising up on a swell of the desert floor, the structure overlooked the depression leading up to it. Behind was a stand of rock that would have provided better cover but made access to the hardsite more difficult. The satellite dish on top of the upper floor suddenly started rotating, and lightning blisters of autofire illuminated the terrain in front of the hardsite.

Flipping the toggle on his headset, Bolan accessed the second channel open to him. This one connected him directly to Stony Man Farm as long as Grimaldi booted the frequency in through the helicopter's communications systems. "Stony One to Stony Base. Over."

"Go, Stony One, you have Stony Base," Barbara Price said. "Over."

"Firestarter's trying to access the domestic party favors. Over."

"Roger. We have the signal here. According to the Bear, we can give you a seven-minute window. Over."

"Affirmative." Bolan checked his watch and made a note of the time. The satellite dish had to be taken out before 11:53 p.m.

"Stay frosty out there, Stony One," Price said. "Stony Base will be standing by." She cleared the channel.

Grimaldi opened up the minigun mounted under the chopper's belly. The chopper shook and shivered in response.

Under the moonlit sky, craters opened up in the smooth sand swooping up out of the depression. Some of the autofire died away.

The aircraft swooped lower. Less than two hundred yards from the hardsite, aware that the helicopter was taking hits now, as well, Bolan threw himself out the open bay.

He flailed, regaining his balance in spite of the rotor wash, plunging feetfirst to the ground beneath him. When he landed, the powdery sand broke part of the impact, and he negated most of the rest of it by going into a parachutist's roll. His helmet picked up a lot of sand along the way, but it sifted out as he got to his feet. His goggles protected his eyes.

Ahead of him, Hawkes and MacDonald were hitting the ground, followed in quick succession by the rest of the blacksuits. The final three had to use the rappeling ropes to close part of the distance as Grimaldi heeled the helicopter into the sky. Sparks flared from the metal underbelly of the chopper, letting everyone know the gunners were definitely getting the range.

Bolan ran, putting everything he had into the effort. The second hand was sweeping away the seven minutes. At best, with a full pack and the powdery sand slipping away underfoot, it would take him nearly thirty seconds to make the hardsite. And that was only if one of the gunners didn't take him out on the way.

MANNING SLAMMED the final sheet of M118 Block Demolition Charge to the first three he'd applied to the wooden pier support fifteen feet below the bridge deck, bringing the thickness up to two inches. By the time he added the radio detonator, the sound of the approaching Scud carriers was a growling rumble in his ears.

He wished he'd had a chance to go over everything, but there'd been no time from the beginning. He'd known that, accepted it, but just hadn't been comfortable with it. Tumbling a bridge of these dimensions was a science, and something he didn't take lightly.

"Gary!" McCarter called over the headset. "Get your bloody arse out of there!"

Reluctantly Manning turned his thoughts away from the job and concentrated on fleeing. There was no way he could clamber to safety. Even if he made the bridge in time, the approaching Mossad team would be alerted. If by some miracle they didn't put a round between his shoulder blades, they definitely wouldn't continue to roll up onto the bridge with nothing but clear thoughts in their heads.

He unwrapped the grappling hook he'd carried as a backup over the line when clambering down below the bridge, and shook out the extra length. Whirling the hook over his head, he let it fly, aiming for a middle distance of the forty feet that separated him from the chasm's lip.

The hook flew true and caught in the lower truss work of the bridge.

Manning pulled it taut, wrapped it around his fist and studied the angle for a moment. Then he ripped his Kabar free of his combat harness and slashed the support rope. There was a sickening moment of free-fall, and almost immediately afterward a harsh flash of pain that sizzled the length of his arm as it seemed to try to come free of his shoulder.

He twirled like a dervish as he went spinning toward the end of the bridge. The structure blurred by overhead. He had a hard time getting his bearings, finally giving up and trusting his sense of momentum to be his guide.

The lights of the Land Rover in the lead of the deadly caravan played over the truss work, and the sound of the engine changed pitch as it rolled out onto the bridge and the chasm started echoing the whining growl.

He passed the center point of his swing, arcing toward the edge of the chasm, and his speed started to decline. He realized that the rope wasn't long enough to put him on safe ground. Knowing there was no way to get a second attempt, he released his one-hand hold on the rope at the apex of his swing. Forward momentum carried him a few more feet. He hoped it was enough.

Still off-balance, he twisted and tried to set himself, wondering if he'd made it or if he'd just started the long fall to the chasm floor. Without warning, he slammed into rock on his back. His breath gusted out of him, and for a moment he felt like a turtle that had been turned upside down. His arms and legs worked; he could feel them moving, but they were unable to turn him over. Warm blood trickled down his neck from a laceration below his ear.

Then the paralysis drained away from him, and his lungs sucked in another breath of air, pulling in dust that set off a coughing fit.

"Gary," Katz called.

The voice sounded tinny and faraway.

Manning realized it was because the ear receiver had been jarred loose from his ear. He plugged it back in as he rolled over to his knees, then hit the transmit button. "Here," he said in a choked voice. He glanced up, saw the Land Rover had already reached the opposite side of the chasm, counted back and found that the final Scud carrier was rolling onto the structure. "Blow the goddamned bridge."

For a moment he could feel the anticipatory silence that filled the radio frequency.

Then the bright flashes of the explosives going off in timed sequence imprinted on his eyes, followed almost instantly by the hollow, booming roars of the detonations. He looked on with the pride of a true craftsman.

Five of the carriers were on the bridge when it blew. The two pier supports went first, the closest one shearing away at fifteen feet below the bridge while the other one sheared just below the deck. The explosives had been staged so that a whiplash effect was created. Smaller charges snapped the truss supports in both the upper and lower chords, allowing the bridge to begin folding up.

Before the staggering bridge could even start to level out, the forty-pound breaching charges at either end of the structure went off, shoving the structure out into the chasm. It twisted like a dying snake and broke into sections, spilling to one side and dumping the big transport carriers into thin air. On the Phoenix-held side of the gorge, the breaching charges had been emplaced to shear away a large section of the rocky ground. Three of the Scud carriers got washed away in the ensuing rockslide. They clattered down the side of the chasm, rolling over and over like a child's toys until they came apart.

The final carrier that had started out onto the bridge hovered for just a moment, almost balanced at the edge of the gorge. Then it slowly tipped forward and went crashing down.

Manning stared down at the wreckage that littered the chasm floor, then gathered up his Galil assault rifle and started making his way down the chasm to finish the bloodletting, knowing Encizo was somewhere out there on his way to join him.

CHAPTER SIXTEEN

"Incoming!" Jack Grimaldi shouted in warning.

Mack Bolan continued his broken-field running, shoving off hard with each thrust of his legs, keeping the Remington combat shotgun up high across his chest. His lungs burned from the effort. Less than a hundred yards remained before he reached the hardsite. Now they could make out the sandbag walls of the gun emplacements. The unique sounds of Browning .50-caliber machine guns hammered into the sporadic confusion of autofire from assault rifles and the thump of 40 mm grenade launchers.

The big chopper came screaming down out of the heavens, the minigun chattering a deadly staccato rhythm that wouldn't be denied. Sandbags burst from the impact of the 20 mm rounds, spilling corpses over the low walls.

Then canisters tumbled free of the helicopter in front of the hardsite, already trailing white smoke. Once they were on the ground, they unleashed a cloud that filled the battle zone.

Using the cloud as cover, Bolan charged into the front lines of the Israeli offensive. Shadows flitted through the white smoke, looking ghostly against the cratered landscape.

One of the shadows turned on the warrior, seeing for the first time that he was an enemy.

The Executioner dropped the 12-gauge into target acquisition and touched off a round. The one-ounce slug caught the Israeli in the center of the chest and sent him flying backward. Without breaking his stride, Bolan changed directions and fired a follow-up round that almost decapitated the gunner. He dived behind the low wall of the gun emplacement as another .50-caliber operator opened up on him. Lying against the shielding sandbags, he could feel the bullets striking home, vibrating the sand.

Rolling over on his side, he freed a fragmentation grenade and lobbed it toward the other gun emplacement. It erupted a second later, and dirt and sand rained down on him, plinking against his helmet. He gripped the shotgun and pushed himself to his feet. It was seventy yards to the hardsite. Less than two minutes remained before Kurtzman's capability to contain the deadly signal Harel and the war hawks were attempting to send was exhausted. The gunners had managed to pin down the Stony Man forces for a while before they were able to move up.

Before he'd gone three steps, something smashed into the top of his left shoulder and leveled him. His mind spun for a moment, seizing on the fact that he'd lost the Remington. He rolled over on his stomach as two more rounds slammed into his body armor. Finding the shotgun in the sand, he closed his right fist around the plastic stock and crawled back toward the empty gun emplacement.

"Striker." It was Catherine Hawkes over the headset.

"Go." He glanced at the ruin of his left shoulder. Blood was already staining the desert camo dark. He stuck his finger into the hole, found the torn flesh that marked the entry wound over the deltoid muscle.

"Are you all right? I saw you get hit."

Searching for the woman through the whirling smoke given off by the canister, he saw her push herself up from her position and race toward him. Bullets smacked into the ground at her feet. This time he could see the snipers up on the roof of the hardsite.

Hawkes came sliding in beside him in a fair facsimile of a baseball player stealing a base. She had her M-16A-2 at the ready immediately.

"I caught a round," Bolan said as his questing finger found the larger exit wound lower down on his back. It didn't feel as if any lasting damage had been done to the muscle groups, but the numbness was spreading. He'd have to will the arm to function properly. "Lucky, though. Through and through."

"You're bleeding like a stuck pig."

"Yeah."

Hawkes canted her assault rifle against the sandbags, then reached down for one of the bandannas she'd tied around her left leg on the short flight from Jerusalem. Once she had it loose, she wrapped it around the Executioner's wounded arm.

Using that hand anyway in spite of her direction not to, Bolan tapped the transmit button on the headset. "MacDonald."

"Go."

"Hold your men in place. They have the high ground for the moment."

"Yes, sir. I've got two snipers of my own."

"Get them deployed."

"Yes, sir."

Pain almost swept the warrior's awareness away when Hawkes tightened the makeshift bandage. His combat senses saved them both, picking up an Israeli attacker as the man came leaping toward them. Bolan lifted the 12-gauge and fired from the hip. The recoil almost tore the shotgun from his grip even when it braced against his biceps.

But the attacker went spinning away, the one-ounce rifled slug tearing through soft throat tissue, dumping a corpse to the sand.

"Shit, that was close," Hawkes said softly as she finished with the bandage. "That should slow the bleeding. Can you use it?"

"Yeah." Bolan rolled over on his side and thumbed cartridges into the Remington till the magazine was full once again. The second hand of his watch had started on the last full sweep it had left. The satellite dish atop the hardsite was still operational even though it had taken some rifle fire. "Jack."

"Go, buddy."

"I've got snipers on the high ground."

"I see them."

Bolan's shoulder was throbbing unmercifully now. He blocked out the pain as much as he could. "Can you take them out?"

"On a suicide run, maybe."

"I need them gone."

"You give me the high sign," Grimaldi answered.

In the distance the helicopter lifted and circled around, preparing to begin the attack.

"I've got this," Hawkes said, pointing to the M-203 grenade launcher mounted under her assault rifle.

"Are you any good with it?"

"I can hit the broad side of a barn."

Bolan checked his watch. "You've got twenty seconds to score a direct hit on that satellite dish before I ask that pilot to attempt the impossible."

Without replying, Hawkes leaned into the sandbags and shouldered the M-16.

Crouching beside her, Bolan provided covering fire.

She squeezed the trigger unhurriedly, immediately reaching for another 40 mm grenade draped on a belt from her shoulder. She opened the breech of the grenade launcher and popped the fat cartridge inside, no expression betraying her emotions as the first round went wide of the target.

The Executioner cut down two Israelis who attempted to overrun their position. The autofire was punctuated by sniper fire now, and slow thunder filled the hell zone.

With seven seconds left, Hawkes's second round struck the dish and scattered it into hundreds of flaming pieces.

"Now," Bolan said, "put some CS up on that rooftop." He gathered his feet under him.

Hawkes reloaded smoothly and dropped three 40 mm grenades of CS gas on top of the structure in quick succession.

Bolan tapped the transmit button. "Jack."

"On my way, guy."

The helicopter streaked for the building, the minigun hammering out 20 mm carnage. On the rooftop, tear gas rolled over the snipers, rendering them helpless for a short time while the dry desert wind quickly snatched it away.

"MacDonald," Bolan called.

"Yes, sir."

"Your men are to move on my go."

"Yes, sir."

"Get your demolitions guy ready. We're going to take the inside just the way we planned it."

"Yes, sir."

Grimaldi operated with customary efficiency, hammering the top of the hardsite with minigun fire that left survivors in question. Before he could clear the area, an RPG-7 scored a direct hit on the chopper's rear rotor. It spun out of control, whirling around and around like a possessed eggbeater.

"You're on your own, Sarge!" Grimaldi yelled.

Silently wishing his friend good luck as the helicopter jerked out of sight over the range behind the hardsite, Bolan hit the transmit button and called for the charge. He took the point, the shotgun coming up, firing, cutting down the first man who tried to intercept them.

STANDING beside Kurtzman, Barbara Price watched the events on the split wall-screen at the far end of the computer lab. On the left the tiny figures of Phoenix Force swarmed over the hulks of the surviving Scud missile carriers. On the right Striker was leading his troops against the hardsite's final external defenses. Both views were from satellites high overhead, and were shown in infrared. It was eerie watching them with no audio link except for the occasional communication through Grimaldi's radio.

Then even that died suddenly.

On the wall screen the yellow figures continued moving in silence, spitting muzzle-flashes from their rifles that registered as heat patterns, as well.

"The Israeli military knows about the attack outside at the hardsite," Kurtzman said quietly. "They're scrambling a dozen fighter jets and deploying ground forces by helicopter."

Price made herself look at everything objectively. "The jets won't be able to do much besides recon. Things down there will be a confused mess to them. It'll take the ground forces at least ten or fifteen minutes to get there. By then it'll be over."

"That's going to leave Striker and his people to draw the heat."

"Not if we contain this at the LZ and exploit it across the media." Price raised her voice. "Carmen."

"Yes, ma'am."

"Get me Desiree St. Cyr and the President, and patch it through to my line."

"Which one do you want first?"

"The reporter. She can do me the most good."

Delahunt went to work.

Price turned to Kurtzman. "Get me a secure line that's capable of video uplink."

The Bear set to work at once. "What have you got in mind?"

"We're going to feed this footage directly to CNN and have St. Cyr break the real story. Oh, yeah, I'm going to need some software that can tie into a TelePrompTer in Jerusalem."

"A TelePrompTer?"

"Yep. I'm going to have to write St. Cyr's story for her as I go."

"Have you ever done any news stories?"

"I've been around them. Besides, I don't have to give her much more than the bare bones. She's good enough to improvise and keep the attention of her audience. She'll make it work." Price marked the time in her mind.

"I've got St. Cyr," Delahunt said.

Price lifted the cellular phone from the holster at her hip, quickly outlined the unfolding events and asked the reporter if she could arrange immediate airing on CNN. She held while St. Cyr made a call on another phone in her hotel room. She was back in less than forty-five seconds.

"We're shooting from the hotel lobby. Give me a minute to get the TelePrompTer tied into my cellular phone. Dammit, I look like shit."

"They can use a file photo," Price said.

"Screw that," St. Cyr said. "This may mean the Pulitzer. I'll brush my hair out on the way down in the elevator." She hung up.

"Ready," Kurtzman said, offering her his keyboard.

Price pulled up a chair and began typing, making spelling errors and grammatical mistakes but not caring. The gist of the story was what was needed, not the packaging. She let Delahunt put her through to the White House. In terse sentences she outlined what was going on in Israel.

"What can we do here?" the President asked.

Brognola chuckled. "Ms. Price, you can answer that."

"A call has been made to the Israeli president to have him tune in to CNN. The whole story is about to go live."

Checking her watch, Price found that three minutes had elapsed. The ground forces streaking from Jerusalem were probably only ten minutes away. "Striker and the Stony Man team are only infrared figures on the screen. There's no way they can be identified, which makes them easy targets if the Israeli military decides to eliminate them. But I don't think they can do it if public broadcasting is showing the rest of the world that an American covert unit is in there trying to prevent a war in the Middle East."

"Carry on," Brognola said, and Price broke the connection.

When she called St. Cyr back, the reporter was in place and waiting. Kurtzman made the necessary patches, and

Huntington Wethers verified that the reporter and the developing story were being carried live from CNN.

"You'd make a hell of a publicist," Kurtzman said with faint admiration, "if you decided to put your mind to it."

"Be quiet and don't bother me. Does aggressive have one *g* or two?"

Kurtzman started to answer.

"Never mind." Price typed in *hostile*.

"Hostile," Kurtzman said. "I like that more than aggressive. More zing."

"You can critique it later. Till then, shut up. Dammit, does the *E* key always stick like this?"

KATZ TIGHTENED his finger on the trigger, pulled it through. The Galil recoiled against his shoulder.

On the other side of the cored windshield, the Land Rover's driver jerked backward as his head came apart. Abruptly the four-wheel drive's engine raced and propelled it toward a treacherous part of the incline. For a moment it looked as if it might make the climb, then it flipped over.

"Gravity," McCarter cracked, "it's *not* just a good idea. It's the *law.*"

Moving the Galil slightly, Katz targeted the surviving Mossad agent emerging from the upside-down Land Rover. He stroked the trigger and punched a 7.62 mm round through the back of the man's neck, shoving his spine through his ruined throat. The man was dead before he hit the ground.

The surviving three Scud carriers didn't waste time considering their options. The lead transport powered up and tried crunching past the overturned Land Rover. The four-wheel-drive vehicle twirled at the impact, and the sound of rending metal screamed along the gorge.

"Fire in the hole!" Calvin James warned.

As he pushed himself to his feet, Katz had a brief impression of the ex-Seal's LAW sending its 94 mm warhead streaking into the front of the last Scud carrier. An orange-and-black fireball swirled up over the crushed cab, evidence that no one inside could have survived.

Running now, Katz made good time across the broken terrain, zeroing in on the passenger side of the transport carrier. He dropped the Galil and pulled the SIG-Sauer P-226 from its holster. Coming abreast of the door, hearing the winch motors as the driver attempted to raise the Scud into firing position even though he was steering the cumbersome vehicle, the Phoenix Force leader reached up for the door latch with his hook and pulled himself aboard.

The passenger was rolling the window down and starting to thrust the short snout of an Uzi through the space.

Katz fired through the door. Sparks flamed from the sheet metal and stung his face, but the passenger fell away. He yanked the door open, and the corpse tumbled out.

The driver turned to him in astonishment and reached for the holstered Beretta on the dashboard.

Without hesitation the Phoenix Force leader fired three rounds that struck his target in the face. With the carrier out of control and headed for a deep defile, Katz released his hold on the vehicle and landed on his feet.

The carrier trundled over the short precipice and disappeared from view. An instant later an explosion shook the earth and lit up the black skies with a sheet of ocher lightning. The concussive force knocked Katz from his feet. When he got back up, he tasted blood, then realized he'd split his lip in the fall.

He trotted back to the battle zone, finding McCarter and James finishing up with the remaining truck. Holstering his side arm, he snatched up the Galil in passing. At the edge of the chasm, he glanced down and saw Encizo and Manning moving through the twisted wreckage. He tapped the transmit button on the headset. "How are things down there?"

Manning answered. "Only us and the casualties. The fall did most of the work."

"Wrap it up," Katz instructed. "We're out of here in ten minutes. Someone might have noticed that Scud going off."

"If they didn't notice that one," Manning promised, "they'll damn sure notice when the rest of them go off."

"Calvin," Katz said, "use the radio and let Price know we've completed this part of the mission." Reaching into his web gear, he took out the plastic charges Manning had formed to trigger the explosive reaction in the missiles. With them safely out of the hands of the Mossad war hawks, there was no way they were going to leave them for the Jordanians in light of the present situation with Israel.

Nine minutes later the team had finished with the Scuds and stood reassembled at the top of the chasm.

"We may have finished first," James said with a grin, "but Striker and his group are getting all the attention." He quickly outlined Price's bid for safely extracting Bolan and his unit.

It bought a moment of levity, but Katz knew the mind of each man was occupied with how the other team would fare in the end. There were no guarantees in their profession, and every possibility walked hand in hand with death. The somber thoughts settled in as they headed south toward the pickup point and put the carnage behind them. Only minutes later they heard the first of the Jordanian fighter jets streak by.

Less than two minutes later the Scuds started exploding, rendering any infrared and thermal-imaging devices on board the planes useless. As Katz looked back at the chasm and saw the funnel of rolling smoke twisting over the battle zone, he couldn't help thinking that clouds like that might some day hang over the entire Middle East. He hated to think that that was the only kind of future that could be given to the children of those countries. But for now another chance had been given. As a soldier, he was professional enough to realize he'd done the best he could. But the thought only provided cold comfort at best.

"THE OUTER perimeter guards have fallen, Enoch."

Harel didn't reply to Wellsberg's statement. His attention was riveted on the newscast on the television mounted on brackets in the upper corner of the hardsite's nerve center. Lemon yellow ghosts flowed across the screen toward a dark structure that vaguely looked like the building they were in. He curled up a fist and smashed it into the communications console next to him.

Every man in the long room was staring at him, the technical operators, as well as the soldiers. There wasn't much room between the computer banks and planning tables. The fluorescent lighting filled the nerve center. "The satellite dish?" he asked.

"Gone," the communications operator said from his seat behind the tracking station.

The satellite necessary to relay the signal to the preprogrammed files lodged deep in military Intelligence's computers and to the waiting bombs scattered around Jerusalem was still within range. They just couldn't reach it.

"What about the group in Jordan?"

"Our communications with them ended abruptly. I can't raise them."

"And there's no sign that their Scuds were fired?"

The young communications officer rechecked his equipment. "We're booted into the Tel Aviv radar stations. The skies between here and there are clear except for identifiable aircraft."

"What are they?"

"MiG-21s, probably. They're scrambling toward the area where Vermillion Group was supposed to set up and fire."

"Damn." Harel stared at the television screen again, seeing a reporter he remembered from different telecasts he'd participated in. Her picture was in a small window down below the lemony ghosts. The words "live transmission" kept flowing across the bottom of the television.

In seconds, in a voice filled with quieted passion, the reporter quickly stripped away every facade Harel had carefully erected over the past years. Every word she spoke was a nail in the coffin housing his dreams. Only the worms would have them now. His mind flailed around like a striking scorpion's tail, looking for some kind of leverage.

The gunfire coming from up above echoed into the underground chambers in dulled and muffled cracks and thumps.

Wellsberg waved four men to the room's main access door.

"Sir."

Harel glanced over at the young soldier rushing up to Wellsberg carrying a squarish radio pack.

A stony grin covered the Mossad commander's face. He held the radio pack out to Harel. "Portable satellite-communications device, Enoch. We still have a chance at pulling this off in spite of the Americans and the television coverage. If Tel Aviv is apparently under attack, it won't matter what CNN is broadcasting."

"Then get it set up," Harel said, clearing a table of maps and sheets of paper covered with figures and coordinates.

"It won't work in here. We need to be outside. Can you send the program away from this room?"

Pushing aside the computer operator, Harel reached under the console and removed a 486 DX laptop equipped with a modem from the shelving. He flicked the power switch, and it came to life. It had been the backup system, in case they'd suffered a power outage during a critical moment. The satellite dish had been wired to its own generator.

"Now I can," Harel said, and he felt good because maybe the dreams were going to live after all.

"Let's go," Wellsberg said, "while we've still got the chance." He summoned four armed men from the group and assigned the rest of them to maintain a holding action for as long as they could. Tension mixed with resolve showed on the faces of the soldiers and technicians.

The lead soldier went through the door at the rear of the room. A tunnel opened up in the middle of the rocky range at the rear of the hardsite. They'd be able to send the signal from there.

Harel ran hard, following Wellsberg. "I figured you'd want to surrender as soon as those men breached the outer defenses."

The Mossad commander shook his head. "You and I have had our disagreements, Enoch, but they've been over styles of approach, never in what our goal was. Israel *must* grow."

Harel grinned in spite of the fear that clung to his back with lizard's talons. "You and I, Benjamin, we'll be heroes, lauded by our people for generations."

"I hope so. But save your breath for running. We still have a distance to go."

Clutching the laptop computer to his chest, Harel ran on, following the flashlight beams the Mossad agents played in front of them. He was certain it was too late for anybody to stop them.

PAUSING at the side of the hardsite, Mack Bolan blasted out the bulletproof window to his left with repeated shots from the Remington Model 1100. The one-ounce rifled shotgun slugs couldn't penetrate the glass, but the series of assaults pushed it out of its frame and left a gaping space.

Catherine Hawkes was at his side, recharging her M-16A-2.

"Gas," the Executioner said. "Hit it now."

The woman's only response was to step away from the wall and fire the M-203 grenade launcher in through the opening. The 40 mm warhead thumped inside the room as it went off.

Ignoring the pain of his wounded arm, Bolan finished reloading the shotgun with double-aught buck shells from the bandolier draping his chest. He shucked the Kevlar helmet and tossed it away because it would have restricted his vision. He tapped the headset transmit button. "MacDonald."

"Go," the blacksuit commander responded.

"Your demolitions man?"

"Here."

"Put him on me. We're going in."

A shadow separated from the small knot of men just down from the warrior's position. Small-arms fire tracked the blacksuit as he ran.

Locating the sniper, the Executioner leveled the shotgun and triggered a pair of rounds that shredded the top of the sandbags the Israeli gunner was using for cover. When the man tried to pop back up again, Hawkes picked him off with a single round through the head.

The corpse spun away from the sandbags.

Gripping the shotgun in both hands, the sling wrapped around his left forearm, Bolan looked at the munitions man. "You know the target?"

"Yes, sir."

"No hesitation, and you can't die until you've got the job done."

"Yes, sir."

"Ready?"

The blacksuit held up both hands, displaying the shaped charges in his fists. "Yes, sir."

"MacDonald," Bolan called. "We're go." He turned and sprinted down the side of the building, ducking in quickly through the oversize entrance door that had almost been torn away by a direct hit from a LAW. Cutting the corner too sharply, he bumped into the door and jarred his wounded shoulder. For a moment he thought the pain was going to pull him out of his head and throw him into a tunnel of ebony cotton. Through sheer force of will, he kept himself conscious.

The interior of the first floor opened into an entryway that was cluttered with debris from the 40 mm grenades that had wreaked damage inside. Tunnels at the extreme left and right led back farther into the hardsite, to the mess area and barracks. The left tunnel, the one leading to the galley, had a series of double-wide steps that led down to a checkpoint fronting the nerve center of the hardsite. Price's Intel on the structure had been infallible except for the fact that Harel and his associates had probably done a few cosmetic changes and updated the hardware.

Gunners flanked both tunnels and fired from the mouths.

Bolan put a booted foot on a nearby metal desk and shoved it out into the center of the floor. Bullets immediately chopped into it, sparking in the weak light given off by the emergency lights.

"Satchel charges!" MacDonald roared to his men.

"Yes, sir," two men called back.

An Israeli leaned around a corner, preparing to lob a grenade at the entrance.

Shouldering the 12-gauge, Bolan fired at the exposed hand.

The spread of double-aught buck took the Israeli in the hand and arm before he was able to release the grenade. There was a pained howl, a garbled warning, then a muffled explosion that tossed a corpse out onto the floor.

"Satchel charges," MacDonald ordered. "Left and right. Mark!"

The two blacksuits leaned forward like bowlers, pitching their deadly packages underhanded. An assault rifle chattered, and the man on the right came spinning back, shoved by the flying bullets.

Hawkes stood up in front of the man protectively, the M-16 at her shoulder. Her weapon barked once, and the gunner tumbled into a boneless heap.

Knotting his fist into the downed man's BDU, Bolan pulled the blacksuit clear of the field of fire.

The satchel charges blew, collapsing part of the reinforced concrete roof over both tunnels. Two blacksuits streaked for each tunnel to engage in a holding action. The exchange of gunfire was blistering and quick. Gray dust cycled around, turning their desert camo an off-white.

Using a penlight from his combat harness, Bolan flashed the beam into the wounded man's eyes. They were wide and staring, hovering on the edge of shock. A ragged tear ran the length of his forehead, exposing the skull under a jagged flap of flesh. A torrent of blood seeped into his uniform.

"Elevate his head," Hawkes ordered.

Bolan put his palm behind the blacksuit's head and lifted. They'd already lost one man out in the desert.

Working efficiently and quickly, Hawkes took another bandanna from her leg and knotted it around the scalp wound.

"Get those charges in place," Bolan commanded.

The munitions man sprang from cover and ran to the center of the floor. Shaped plastic explosives slapped onto the concrete floor.

"Morphine?" Bolan asked. He'd found two more wounds in the man's right arm and leg.

"No, sir," the blacksuit said. "I get this bleeding stopped, I'll be walking out of here on my own."

Bolan laid the man's head down gently on the folded camo jacket Hawkes had stripped out of. "You do that, soldier." He unholstered the man's side arm and pressed it into the guy's palm. "Keep our backs covered."

"Yes, sir."

"Fire in the hole!" the munitions man yelled as he dived away from the shaped charges.

Curling up protectively over the wounded man, Bolan forced up his left arm enough to cover his head.

The plastic explosive went off with enough force to jar the hardsite like a tooth in a loose socket.

Looking back up through the smoke filling the entryway, Bolan saw the yawning four-foot-wide pit that had opened up in the floor. He fisted the combat shotgun and pushed off at full steam. The confusion in the nerve center below could only last a precious few seconds, and there was no way to retrieve them once they were gone.

Hawkes was hot on his heels, MacDonald a half step behind her.

The Executioner stepped off into the pit, picking up visual information literally on the fly.

The hole had opened up in the center of the communications section as he'd planned, and the waves of concussive force and flying debris had blown the combatants in all directions. More debris in the form of large chunks of the ceiling littered the area at Bolan's feet. A number of the computer hardware cases were belching electrical smoke and sparks.

The warrior landed hard, unevenly on the odd-shaped lumps of rock scattered across the floor. For a moment he thought he'd sprained his ankle despite the bracing effect of the tightly laced combat boots. His left shoulder protested at the sudden stop, and he could feel fresh blood seeping out over his chest and back. Black comets spun dizzyingly in front of him, and a dull roaring sounded in his ears.

He brought the shotgun up as he fought to clear his mind. The targets were already marked in his peripheral vision, and he put them down by the numbers, wheeling to his left, away from Hawkes as she came plummeting through the hole. His Kevlar vest stopped at least three rounds that he counted.

MacDonald followed the woman, and their combined firepower convinced the people who were still alive to quickly surrender.

"Striker," a blacksuit's voice came over the headset.

Bolan recognized it as Raitt, one of the topside men. "Go."

"The Israeli military just arrived, sir. I've had contact with them over the hand unit. They're requesting permission to assist."

"Permission to assist," MacDonald whispered in wonderment. "Christ, I figured we'd all be political prisoners for a while if we were caught."

For the first time Bolan saw the satellite relay hooked into the overhead television. On-screen, the blurred outlines of a transport helicopter disgorged a dozen men framed in sickly yellow in front of a structure he recognized as the hardsite as seen from above. He had no doubt that Barbara Price had managed the save in some fashion. He tapped the transmit button. "Invite them in. We could use the help on the mop-up."

"Yes, sir."

A quick search proved that Harel and Wellsberg weren't among those present. A panicked guard volunteered the information that Harel, Wellsberg and an armed contingent of men had bolted from the nerve center through the exit door with a mobile satellite unit and a laptop computer.

Bolan went in pursuit at once, breaking into a full run once he was past the door. Perspiration covered his face, and the foul taste of the blackface leaked into his mouth. He sucked in the cooler air gratefully, running as hard as he could with the Remington canted across his chest in the ready position.

The exit tunnel was narrow and dark. His penlight chiseled through part of the clinging gloom. The stone walls were roughed out, still showing signs of the sharp picks that had gouged them into shape.

He reached the exit almost before he knew it.

Evidently he took the two Israelis waiting on him by surprise, as well. They opened fire late, swinging wildly to cover him from higher ground.

The Executioner dived as 5.56 mm tumblers chewed into the sand and rock in the area he'd just vacated. The landing was rough and jarred the breath out of him.

Anticipating an easy kill, one of the gunners broke cover and came to a full stand with his assault rifle to his shoulder.

Bolan rolled, dragging the shotgun into play. The range was fifty feet. He pulled the trigger three times as quickly as he could, absorbing the traumatic recoils like body blows.

The sheet of buckshot swept the gunner from sight as the piercing blasts rolled over the ridge.

The ruby dot of a laser sight burned into one of Bolan's eyes as he scanned for the second man. The warrior threw himself behind a boulder, having trouble making headway in the carpet of sand that covered the stone floor of the ridge. A bullet slammed into his body armor between his shoulder blades.

A flat crack split the echo of the first weapon.

"Go," Hawkes yelled from the mouth of the tunnel.

The body of the second man came tumbling down the incline.

Without pause Bolan gathered his feet under him and took up the pursuit again, heading for the high ground.

The ridge was large and spacious, giving Harel and Wellsberg plenty of room to run. He thumbed more cartridges into the shotgun, sticking with the double-aught shells.

To his left he saw the Israeli transport helicopter hovering over the battleground that had been in front of the hardsite. Bodies looked like fallen shadows against the sand, and flames still dotted the perimeter.

Fighter jets streaked across the starlit sky, the glow of their afterburners looking like skating comets on a field of black ice.

"Sarge." Grimaldi's voice came through the headset sharp and clear.

"Are you okay?" Bolan asked as he cut around a high stand of rock that suddenly opened onto a decline. His feet slipped as he made his way down, but he didn't slow, turning the headlong rush into a barely controlled slide that brought a cloud of sand spilling after him.

"Fine. Levin and I both got out of the chopper. We collected a few bumps and bruises that a few days' rest will see squared away. I take it you're looking for Harel."

"Yeah."

"I've got him spotted."

"Put him down," Bolan instructed. "He and Wellsberg have a secondary system that can set off the charges around Tel Aviv."

"No can do, buddy. Between Levin and myself, all we got are handguns, and we're out of range. I can navigate you to him."

"Do it." Bolan changed course as Grimaldi directed. His breath felt like molten lava in his lungs, and his shoulder was a flaming sheet of pain. He dodged boulders and leapt over broken ridges that would have tripped him, sometimes seeing them too late and having to push himself back up with his hands. After a couple of falls, blood streaked his palms and fingers.

"You're there," Grimaldi said. "Good luck, amigo."

The Executioner didn't break stride as he rounded the last bend of the narrow trail he'd found.

Wellsberg must have heard his boots drumming against the exposed stone and shuffling through the loose sand, because when the four men in the group came into view, the three soldiers among them had their weapons trained in his direction.

Breaking hard to the right, like a tight end powering into a buttonhook for a pass play, Bolan surged toward the edge of the ridge. Bullets kicked at his heels. Then he threw himself forward, sliding on his stomach, trusting the camo jacket and Kevlar vest to give him some protection against the abrasive rock. As he passed over the ridge, he saw that it dropped almost twenty feet.

He ditched the shotgun and scrambled for a handhold to stop his forward momentum. The fingers of his right hand found purchase. He closed them. His nails broke and tore, and pain flashed up his arm.

But he stopped.

Clinging over the drop one-handed, remembering that Harel was already working on the laptop's keyboard, he kicked his feet and made his other arm come up and find a hold, as well.

"Get him!" someone yelled.

The sound of running feet approached the ridge's edge.

Finding a toehold, Bolan drew the Desert Eagle from the drop holster and flicked the safety off. When the first face peered over the ridge, he punched a 240-grain boat-tail hollowpoint through the center of it. The corpse dropped without a sound over Bolan's head and bounced from the side of the incline, rolling like a rag doll.

A triburst of autofire sounded from the left, then the second Israeli soldier tumbled past Bolan as the Executioner leveraged himself to the top of the ridge with the .44 in his fist.

As he cleared the top, he saw Wellsberg taking aim at Catherine Hawkes as she tried to wheel to face the Mossad commander. Eyes blurring from sweat and blood and pain, the Executioner dropped the Desert Eagle into target acquisition. His finger tightened on the trigger.

A muzzle-flash leapt from Wellsberg's pistol.

Hawkes went spinning away.

Concentrating solely on his target, Bolan put three rounds into the Mossad commander, battering him to the ground with the heavy .44 slugs. He couldn't spare any time for Hawkes. Either the woman was alive or she wasn't.

Harel was taking cover behind a cluster of boulders. The Coaxial cable connecting the portable satellite's phone handset to the laptop was a skinny snake slithering through the sand.

Unable to target the financier and not knowing how much time was left, Bolan sighted in on the portable satellite as it reached out thousand-mile-long fingers into space. He fired the remaining four shots in the Desert Eagle, kicking the unit into the air with the first round, then making it jump with each successive bullet.

If Harel hadn't already triggered the explosives, the man wasn't going to be able to.

Tossing the empty .44 away, Bolan struggled to pull himself up on the ledge. His muscles were trembling with shock and fatigue, the adrenaline flow working against him now. He staggered into a standing position, arms feeling like leaden weights, and snapped the restraining strap from the Beretta 93-R.

With a ferocious yell, Harel came out of hiding and ran straight for Bolan, then launched himself into a flying tackle.

The Executioner tried to meet the man head-on and take the brunt of the charge, then control him. But Harel's greater size and weight proved too much for him to handle in his present state.

Bolan sprawled backward, landing hard on the ground, followed by a crushing impact as Harel came down on top of him. For a moment he lay there stunned, watching as Harel got to his feet like some mythical giant.

"You bastard," Harel said. Blood trickled from his nose and the corner of his mouth. "You just destroyed every dream I've ever considered worth having." His big hand plucked the Beretta from the shoulder holster and fumbled for the safety.

Summoning his remaining strength, firing it with the resolve he'd always had to see things through to the bitter end, Bolan shoved himself to his feet.

Harel retreated, grinning as the safety snicked off the pistol. More confident now because he was armed, he stepped forward and thrust the pistol into the warrior's face. "How does it feel, knowing you're about to stop dreaming?"

Moving with eye-blurring speed, concentrating on the necessary motions and ignoring the pain that filled him, Bolan palmed the Randall survival knife from his combat harness. His left hand flicked out, blocking the Beretta away as he stepped inside Harel's arm. The knife came around in a short, tight arc, glinting in the moonlight for just a moment before it was buried to the hilt in Harel's left eye. The sharp point broke through the back of the man's skull with an audible crunch.

"You're through," Bolan said in a chill voice, "and I'm still here standing."

He plucked the Beretta from the erect corpse's slack fingers, then put his hand against Harel's chest and pushed the dead man over the ridge.

The corpse bounded and spun as it slid to the bottom of the ridge.

Bolan stood swaying uncertainly.

"Striker." The voice came from behind him.

He glanced back and saw Hawkes weaving unsteadily on her feet. "You're alive," he said.

"Looks like we both are," she replied.

Unable to stand any longer, the Executioner sat down, leaning on his good arm. "I'm going to sit here for a minute and catch my breath."

"Me, too."

"You did good, Hawkes."

"So did you, soldier."

As they sat there in silence, listening to the headsets as the Israelis joined forces with MacDonald and the blacksuits to complete the rout of the hardsite, Bolan looked out over the night. Then he rested his forearms on his drawn-up knees, knowing that any length of time spent in that position was going to leave him stiff and sore but not caring.

A peaceful feeling came over him. When a soldier signed on to a war everlasting against the cannibals who would suck the life from the world, all a man could ask

for was a place to stand his ground. And until the final
numbers ran through on his personal mission, the Executioner would be standing that ground hard.

Join Mack Bolan's latest mission in

THE TERROR TRILOGY

Beginning in June 1994, Gold Eagle brings
you another action-packed three-book in-line
continuity, the Terror Trilogy. Featured are
THE EXECUTIONER, ABLE TEAM and
PHOENIX FORCE as they battle neo-Nazis
and Arab terrorists to prevent war in the
Middle East.

Be sure to catch all the action of this gripping
trilogy, starting in June and continuing through
to August.

Available at your favorite retail outlet, or order
your copy now:

Book I:	JUNE	FIRE BURST (THE EXECUTIONER #186)	$3.50 U.S. $3.99 CAN.	☐
Book II:	JULY	CLEANSING FLAME (THE EXECUTIONER #187)	$3.50 U.S. $3.99 CAN.	☐
Book III:	AUGUST	INFERNO (352-page MACK BOLAN)	$4.99 U.S. $5.50 CAN.	☐

Total amount	$_____
Plus 75¢ postage ($1.00 in Canada)	$_____
Canadian residents add applicable federal and provincial taxes	
Total payable	$_____

To order, please send this form, along with your name, address, zip or postal code,
and a check or money order for the total above, payable to Gold Eagle Books, to:

In the U.S.
Gold Eagle Books
3010 Walden Ave.
P. O. Box 9077
Buffalo, NY 14269-9077

In Canada
Gold Eagle Books
P. O. Box 636
Fort Erie, Ontario
L2A 5X3

TT94-2C

**Adventure and suspense in the midst
of the new reality...**

JAMES AXLER

DEATH LANDS ®

Rider, Reaper

A peaceful interlude for Ryan Cawdor in the mountains of
New Mexico becomes a blood-soaked game of survival as Ryan's
idyll becomes a mission of revenge. His quarry on a cross-desert
manhunt is the General, a man who grimly prepares to destroy
his pursuers.

Hope died in the Deathlands, but the will to live goes on.

Available in August at your favorite retail outlet, or order your copy now by sending
your name, address, zip or postal code, along with a check or money order (please do
not send cash) for $4.99 for each book ordered, plus 75¢ for postage and handling
($1.00 in Canada), payable to Gold Eagle Books, to:

In the U.S.	**In Canada**
Gold Eagle Books	Gold Eagle Books
3010 Walden Ave.	P. O. Box 636
P. O. Box 9077	Fort Erie, Ontario
Buffalo, NY 14269-9077	L2A 5X3

Please specify book title with order.
Canadian residents add applicable federal and provincial taxes.

DL22

**Sabotaged U.S. satellite defenses leave the
Mideast prey to a hungry predator...**

**STONY
MAN™ 12
BLIND EAGLE**

The strategic defense team of Stony Man™—the President's
ultimate secret weapon—faces a shadow enemy with
international branches and a fearsome technology: the
ability to blind the superpowers by jamming their spy
satellites. The enemy hits big, then hits bigger—with
strategically launched clashes in the Middle East that draw
the U.S. into the fire.

Available in September at your favorite retail outlet, or order your copy now by sending your name, address, zip or postal code, along with a check or money order (please
do not send cash) for $4.99 ($5.50 in Canada) for each book ordered, plus 75¢
postage and handling ($1.00 in Canada), payable to Gold Eagle Books, to:

In the U.S.	In Canada
Gold Eagle Books	Gold Eagle Books
3010 Walden Avenue	P. O. Box 636
P. O. Box 9077	Fort Erie, Ontario
Buffalo, NY 14269-9077	L2A 5X3

Please specify book title with your order.
Canadian residents add applicable federal and provincial taxes.

SM12

Don't miss out on the action in these titles featuring THE EXECUTIONER®, ABLE TEAM® and PHOENIX FORCE®!

The Terror Trilogy

Features Mack Bolan, along with ABLE TEAM and PHOENIX FORCE, as they battle neo-Nazis and Arab terrorists to prevent war in the Middle East.

The Executioner #61186	FIRE BURST	$3.50 U.S.	☐
		$3.99 Can.	☐
The Executioner #61187	CLEANSING FLAME	$3.50 U.S.	☐
		$3.99 Can.	☐
SuperBolan #61437	INFERNO	$4.99 U.S.	☐
		$5.50 Can.	☐

The Executioner®

With nonstop action, Mack Bolan represents ultimate justice, within or beyond the law.

#61182	LETHAL AGENT	$3.50	☐
#61183	CLEAN SWEEP	$3.50	☐

(limited quantities available on certain titles)

TOTAL AMOUNT	$
POSTAGE & HANDLING	$
($1.00 for one book, 50¢ for each additional)	
APPLICABLE TAXES*	$_____
TOTAL PAYABLE	$_____

(check or money order—please do not send cash)

To order, complete this form and send it, along with a check or money order for the total above, payable to Gold Eagle Books, to: **In the U.S.:** 3010 Walden Avenue, P.O. Box 9077, Buffalo, NY 14269-9077; **In Canada:** P.O. Box 636, Fort Erie, Ontario, L2A 5X3.

Name:_____

Address:_____ City:_____

State/Prov.:_____ Zip/Postal Code:_____

*New York residents remit applicable sales taxes.
Canadian residents remit applicable GST and provincial taxes.

GEBACK7

Don't miss the next installment of

THE Destroyer

Infernal Revenue
Created by
WARREN MURPHY
and RICHARD SAPIR

A fiendish artificial intelligence chip known as *Friend* boots up disaster for CURE....

Friend has covertly hijacked the new computer system at CURE and screws up the database so efficiently that both Remo and Chiun quit—just as *Friend* releases a stealth virus that will hold the world hostage to technoterrorism! Can a reluctant Remo and determined Chiun work to foil the greatest threat CURE has ever faced?

Look for it this September, wherever Gold Eagle books are sold.

Or order your copy now by sending your name, address, zip or postal code, along with a check or money order (please do not send cash) for $4.99 ($5.50 in Canada), plus 75¢ postage and handling ($1.00 in Canada), payable to Gold Eagle Books, to:

In the U.S.	In Canada
Gold Eagle Books	Gold Eagle Books
3010 Walden Ave.	P. O. Box 636
P. O. Box 9077	Fort Erie, Ontario
Buffalo, NY 14269-9077	L2A 5X3

Please specify book title with order.
Canadian residents add applicable federal and provincial taxes.

DEST96

**Don't miss out on the action in these titles featuring
THE EXECUTIONER®, ABLE TEAM® and PHOENIX FORCE®!**

SuperBolan

#61434   **TAKEDOWN** $4.99   ☐
War has come back to the Old World, carried out by a former Romanian
Securitate Chief and his army of professional killers.

#61435   **DEATH'S HEAD** $4.99   ☐
While in Berlin on a Mafia search-and-destroy, Bolan uncovers a covert
cadre of Soviets working with German neo-Nazis and other right-wing nation-
alists.

Stony Man™

#61892   **STONY MAN VIII** $4.99   ☐
A power-hungry industrialist fuels anarchy in South America.

#61893   **STONY MAN #9 STRIKEPOINT** $4.99   ☐
Free-lance talent from the crumbling Russian empire fuels Iraq's nuclear
power.

#61894   **STONY MAN #10 SECRET ARSENAL** $4.99   ☐
A biochemical weapons conspiracy puts America in the hot seat.

(limited quantities available on certain titles)

TOTAL AMOUNT	$
POSTAGE & HANDLING	$
($1.00 for one book, 50¢ for each additional)	
APPLICABLE TAXES*	$ _____
TOTAL PAYABLE	$ _____

(check or money order—please do not send cash)

To order, complete this form and send it, along with a check or money order for
the total above, payable to Gold Eagle Books, to: **in the U.S.:** 3010 Walden Avenue,
P.O. Box 9077, Buffalo, NY 14269-9077; **in Canada:** P.O. Box 636, Fort Erie, Ontario,
L2A 5X3.

Name:_____

Address:_____ City:_____

State/Prov.:_____ Zip/Postal Code:_____

*New York residents remit applicable sales taxes.
 Canadian residents remit applicable GST and provincial taxes.

GEBACK7A